"I have heard from the Sardar," Samos said to me. "They ask for the arrest and detention of one reputed to be an enemy of Priest-Kings."

"Who is he?" I inquired.

"His name," said Samos, "is Tarl Cabot."

"That is absurd!" I cried. "How can I have betrayed their cause? I have never pledged a sword to them, never sworn a fidelity oath in their behalf. I am my own man, a mercenary of sorts, one who has labored in their behalf."

"I think you should conveniently disappear from Port Kar, until I manage to resolve these confusions and ambiguities," said Samos.

Then I told him, "I think I have just killed an agent of Priest-Kings."

JOHN NORMAN

Books available from DAW:

HUNTERS OF GOR
MARAUDERS OF GOR
TRIBESMEN OF GOR
SLAVE GIRL OF GOR
BEASTS OF GOR
EXPLORERS OF GOR
FIGHTING SLAVE OF GOR
(Jason Marshall I)
ROGUE OF GOR
(Jason Marshall I)
ROGUE OF GOR
(Jason Marshall II)
GUARDSMAN OF GOR
(Jason Marshall III)
SAVAGES OF GOR
BLOOD BROTHERS OF GOR
KAJIRA OF GOR
MERCENARIES OF GOR
DANCER OF GOR
RENEGADES OF GOR

GHOST DANCE
TIME SLAVE
IMAGINATIVE SEX

CONTENTS

PLAYERS
OF
GOR

JOHN NORMAN

DAW BOOKS, INC.
DONALD A. WOLLHEIM, PUBLISHER

1633 Broadway, New York, NY 10019

Cover art by Ken W. Kelly.

First Printing, March 1984

5   6   7   8   9

PRINTED IN U.S.A.

1

SAMOS

I looked up from the board, idly, as the woman, struggling, in the grasp of two guards, was thrust into the vicinity of our table.

"It is your move," said Samos.

I regarded the board. I moved my Ubar's Tarnsman to Ubara's Tarnsman Five. It was a positioning move. The Tarnsman can move only one space on the positioning move. It attacks only on a flight move.

The woman struggled fiercely in the grasp of the two guards. She could not, of course, free herself.

Samos studied the board. He positioned his Home Stone. It was, looking at the tiny counter at the edge of the board, his tenth move. Most Kaissa boards do not have this counter. It consisted of ten small, cylindrical wooden beads strung on a wire. The Home Stone must be placed by the tenth move. He had placed it at his now-vacated Ubar's Initiate One. In this position, as at the Ubara's Initiate One, it is subject to only three lines of attack. Other legitimate placements subject to five lines of attack. He was also fond of placing the Home Stone late, usually on the ninth or tenth move. In this way, his decision could take into consideration his opponent's early play, his opening, or response to an opening, or development.

I myself, whose Home Stone was already placed, preferred a much earlier and more central placement of the Home Stone. I did not wish to be forced to sacrifice a move for Home-Stone placement in a situation that might, for all I knew, not turn out to be to my liking, a situation in which the obligatory placement might even cost me a tempo. Similarly, although a somewhat more central location of the Home Stone exposes it to more lines of attack, it also increases its mobility, and thereby its capacities to evade attack. These considerations are controversial in the theory of Kaissa. Much depends on the psychology of the individual player.

Incidentally, there are many versions of Kaissa played on Gor. In some of these versions, the names of the pieces differ, and, in some, even more alarmingly, their nature and power. The caste of Players, to its credit, has been attempting to standardize Kaissa for years.

A major victory in this matter was secured a few years ago when the caste of Merchants, which organizes and manages the Sardar Fairs, agreed to a standardized version, proposed by, and provisionally approved by, the high council of the caste of Players, for the Sardar tournaments, one of the attractions of the Sardar Fairs. This form of Kaissa, now utilized in the tournaments, is generally referred to, like the other variations, simply as Kaissa. Sometimes, however, to distinguish it from differing forms of the game, it is spoken of as Merchant Kaissa, from the role of the Merchants in making it the official form of Kaissa for the fairs, Player Kaissa, from the role of the Players in its codification, or the Kaissa of En'Kara, for it was officially promulgated for the first time at one of the fairs of En'Kara, that which occurred in 10,124 C.A., Contasta Ar, from the Founding of Ar, or in Year 5 of the Sovereignty of the Council of Captains, in Port Kar.

The fair of En'Kara occurs in the spring. It is the first fair in the annual cycle of the Sardar Fairs, gigantic fairs which take place on the plains lying below the western slopes of the Sardar Mountains. These fairs, and others like them, play an important role in the Gorean culture and economy. They are an important clearing house for ideas and goods, among them female slaves.

The woman stifled a cry and stamped her foot.

Samos, his Home Stone positioned, looked up.

It was now two days before the Twelfth Passage Hand, in the year 10,129 C.A. Soon it would be Year Eleven in the Sovereignty of the Council of Captains, in Port Kar. It seemed, somehow, only recently that the five Ubars, who had divided Port Kar between them, had been deposed. Squat, brilliant Chung and tall, long-haired Nigel, like a warlord from Torvaldsland, had fought with us against the fleets of Cos and Tyros, participating with us in the victory of the Twenty-Fifth of Se'Kara, in Year One of the Council of Captains; remained in Port Kar as

high captains, admirals in our fleet. Sullius Maximus was now a
despised and minor courtier at the court of Chenbar of Kasra,
Ubar of Tyros, the Sea Sleen. Henrius Sevarius, freed, now a
young man, had his own ship and holding in Port Kar. He owned
a luscious young slave, Vina, whom he well mastered. She, now
a love slave, had once been the ward of Chenbar, Ubar of Tyros,
and once had been intended to be the free companion of gross
Lurius of Jad, the Ubar of Cos, thence to be proclaimed Ubara of
Cos, which union would have even further strengthened the ties
between those two great island ubarates. She had been captured
at sea and had fallen slave. Once marked and collared, of course,
her political interest had vanished. A new life had then been hers,
that of the mere slave. I did not know the whereabouts of the
fifth ubar, Eteocles.

We were in the great hall in the holding of Samos, in Port
Kar. The room was lit by torches. Many of his men, sitting
cross-legged at low tables, as we were, were about. They were
eating and drinking, being served by slaves. We sat a bit apart
from them. Some musicians were present. They were not now
playing.

I heard a slave girl laughing, somewhere across the room.

Outside, in the canal traffic, I heard a drum, cymbals and
trumpets, and a man shouting. He was proclaiming the excellen-
cies of some theatrical troupe, such as the cleverness of its
clowns and the beauty of its actresses, probably slaves. They had
performed, it seems, in the high cities and before ubars. Such
itinerant troupes, theatrical troupes, carnival groupings, and such,
are not uncommon on Gor. They consist usually of rogues and
outcasts. With their wagons and tents, often little more than a
skip and a jump ahead of creditors and magistrates, they roam
from place to place, rigging their simple stages in piazzas and
squares, in yards and markets, wherever an audience may be
found, even at the dusty intersections of country crossroads.
With a few boards and masks, and a bit of audacity, they create
the mystery of performance, the magic of theater. They are
bizarre, incomparable vagabonds. They are denied the dignity of
the funeral pyre and other forms of honorable burial.

The group outside, doubtless on a rented barge, was not the
first to pass beneath the narrow windows of the house of Samos
this evening. There were now several such groups in the city.
Their hand-printed handbills and hand-painted posters, the latter
pasted on the sides of buildings and on the news boards, were
much in evidence. All this had to do with the approach of the
Twelfth Passage Hand, which precedes the Waiting Hand.

The Waiting Hand, the five-day period preceding the vernal equinox, the first day of spring, is a very solemn time for most Goreans. During this time few ventures are embarked upon, and little or no business is conducted. During this time most Goreans remain within their houses. It is in this time that the doors of many homes are sealed with pitch and have nailed to them branches of the brak bush, the leaves of which have a purgative effect. These precautions, and others like them, are intended to discourage the entry of ill luck into the houses.

In the houses there is little conversation and no song. It is a time, in general, of mourning, meditation and fasting. All this changes, of course, with the arrival of the vernal equinox, which, in most Gorean cities, marks the New Year.

At dawn on the day of the vernal equinox a ceremonial greeting of the sun takes place, conducted usually by the ubar or administrator of the city. This, in effect, welcomes the New Year to the city. In Port Kar this honor fell to Samos, first captain in the Council of Captains, and the council's executive officers. The completion of this greeting is signified by, and celebrated by, a ringing of the great bars suspended about the city. The people then, rejoicing, issue forth from their houses. The brak bushes are burned on the threshold and the pitch is washed away. There are processions and various events, such as contests and games. It is a time of festival. The day is one of celebration.

These festivities, of course, are in marked contrast to the solemnities and abstinences of the Waiting Hand. The Waiting Hand is a time, in general, of misery, silence and fasting. It is also, for many Goreans, particularly those of the lower castes, a time of uneasiness, a time of trepidation and apprehension. Who knows what things, visible or invisible, might be abroad during that terrible time? In many Gorean cities, accordingly, the Twelfth Passage Hand, the five days preceding the Waiting Hand, that time to which few Goreans look forward with eagerness, is carnival. The fact that it was now only two days to the Twelfth Passage Hand, explained the presence of the unusual number of theatrical and carnival troupes now in the city.

Such troupes, incidentally, must petition for the right to perform within a city. Usually a sample performance, or a part of a performance, is required, staged before the high council, or a committee delegated by such a council. Sometimes the actresses are expected to perform privately, being "tested," so to speak, for selected officials. If the troupe is approved it may, for a fee, be licensed.

No troupe is permitted to perform within a city unless it has a license. These licenses usually run for the five days of a Gorean week. Sometimes they are for a specific night or a specific performance. Licenses are commonly renewable, within a given season, for a nominal fee. In connection with the fees for such matters, it is not uncommon that bribes are also involved. This is particularly the case when small committees are involved in the approvals or given individuals, such as a city's Entertainment Master or Master of Revels. There is little secret, incidentally, about the briberies involved. There are even fairly well understood bribery scales, indexed to the type of troupe, its supposed treasury, the number of days requested for the license, and so on. These things are so open, and so well acknowledged, that perhaps one should think of them more as gratuities or service fees than as bribes. More than one Master of Revels regards them as an honest perquisite of his office.

The woman struggled in the grip of the guards. She stamped her foot again. "Tell these boorish ruffians to unhand me!" she demanded.

I, too, now, looked up.

Her eyes flashed at Samos, over her veil. Then they looked angrily at me, too. "Now!" she demanded.

Samos nodded to the guards, scarcely moving his head.

"That is better!" she said, jerking angrily away from the guards, as though she might have freed herself, had she chosen to do so. She angrily smoothed down her long, silken, capelike sleeves. I caught a glimpse of her sweetly rounded forearm and small wrist. She wore white gloves.

"This is an outrage!" she said. She wore tiny, golden slippers. Her robes of concealment, silken and flowing, shimmered in the torchlight. She adjusted the draping of the garment, an almost inadvertent, unconscious movement, a natural vanity.

"What is the meaning of this?" she demanded. "I demand my immediate freedom!"

One of the slave girls, one kneeling a few feet away, before us and to our right, at a table, one of those who was naked, save for her collar, laughed. Then she turned white with fear. She had laughed at a free woman. Samos turned to a guard and pointed at the offending slave. "Fifteen lashes," he said. The girl shook her head in misery. She whimpered with terror. These would be lashes, she knew, with a Gorean slave whip. It is an efficient instrument for disciplining women.

The blows were delivered with suitable force, with authority, but in an evenly spaced, measured fashion. There was nothing personal, or emotional, in the beating. It was almost like a natural force or a clockwork of nature. There was enough time between the strokes to allow her to feel each one individually and fully, and enhance, maximizing, the irradiations of its predecessors, enough time for her, in the fullness of her pain, imagination and terror, to prepare herself for, and anticipate, fearfully and acutely, the next blow. It was not much of a beating, of course. She had erred. She was being punished. Then she was lying on her belly, on the tiles, the beating over. She did not even dare to move her body, for the pain. Samos had been rather merciful with her, I thought. If he had been truly displeased with her, he might have had her fed to sleen.

We now returned our attention to the woman in the silken, shimmering robes of concealment, standing before our table. Her eyes were apprehensive, over her veil. I could see that the beating of the female slave had had its effect on her. She was breathing deeply. Her breasts, rising and falling, moved nicely under the silk.

"May I present," inquired Samos, "Lady Rowena, of Lydius?"

I inclined my head. "Lady," said I, acknowledging the introduction. To a free woman considerable deference is due, particularly to one such as the Lady Rowena, one obviously, at least hitherto, of high station.

She inclined her head to me, and then lifted it, acknowledging my greeting.

Lydius is a bustling, populous trade center located at the estuary of the Laurius River. Many cities maintain warehouses and small communities in Lydius. Many goods, in particular wood, wood products, and hide, make their way westward on the Laurius, eventually landing at Lydius, later to be embarked to the south on the ships of various cities, lines and associations. The population of Lydius, as one might expect, is a mixed one, consisting of individuals of various races and backgrounds.

The woman drew herself up to her full height. She looked at Samos, angrily. "What is the meaning of my presence here?" she demanded.

"Lady Rowena is of the merchants," said Samos to me. "The ship on which she had passage, enroute from Lydius to Cos, was detained by two of my rovers. Her captain kindly consented to a transfer of cargo."

"What is the meaning of my presence here?" repeated the woman, angrily.

"Surely you are aware of the time of year?" inquired Samos.

"I do not understand," she said. "Where are my maidens?"

"In the pens," said Samos.

"The pens?" she gasped.

"Yes," said Samos. "But do not fear for them. They are perfectly safe—in their chains."

Slavers remain active all year on Gor, but the peak seasons for slaving are the spring and early summer. This has to do with such matters as the weather, and the major markets associated with certain feasts and holidays, for example, the Love Feast in Ar, which occurs in the late summer, occupying the full five days of the Fifth Passage Hand. Also, during these seasons, of course, occur the great markets associated with the fairs of En'Kara and En'Var. These are the two major seasonal markets on Gor, exceeding all others in the volume of women processed.

"Chains?" she whispered. She shrank back, her hand at her breast.

"Yes," said Samos.

"I was hooded," she said. "I do not even know where I am."

"You are in Port Kar," he said.

She staggered. I feared she might faint.

"Who are you?" she whispered.

"Samos," said he, "first slaver of Port Kar."

She shuddered with misery. A tiny moan escaped her. I saw she had heard of Samos, of Port Kar. "What hope have I?" she asked.

"None," said Samos. "Remove your veil."

"Make my maidens slaves," she said. "They are good for little else. But I am a free woman!"

"Do you think you are better than they?" asked Samos.

"Yes," she said.

"You are no different from them," he said. "You, too, are only a female."

"No!" she cried.

"Remove your veil," he said.

"I am too beautiful to be a slave," she said.

"Your veil," said Samos, gently. She was, after all, a free woman.

Some of the slave girls, some naked, some scantily clad, looked at one another. Had they so dallied in their compliance, hesitating perhaps even an instant in their immediate and absolute obedience, serious punishments would doubtless have been theirs. They were, of course, only slaves.

"Please, no," said Lady Rowena.

"You are my prisoner," said Samos. "Doubtless you are

aware that you could be stripped absolutely naked at my slightest word."

She put her hands to the veil and, delicately, unpinned it, dropping it to the side.

"Brush back your hood," said Samos.

She did so and, putting back her head, drew forth and freed, with both hands, long, golden tresses, which she arranged before her. They were in two plaits, one before each shoulder; they hung almost to her knees.

"Unbind your hair," said Samos.

She unplaited her hair and, with her head down, shook it loose, and smoothed it. She then, again, lifted her head.

"Put your hair behind your back," said Samos.

She did so.

She then stood before us, regarded, as a woman.

"What is to be my fate?" she asked.

Samos and I regarded her admiringly. Several of the men did so as well. Several of them changed their position, to come about, near and behind our table, where they might see better. I heard soft cries from more than one of the slave girls. They, too, were impressed. The woman straightened her body. She could not help but bask in the warmth of our appraisal.

I turned about a bit.

I saw a blond-haired slave girl, in a brief, revealing tunic, sneak on her knees near to Samos. It was Linda, a former Earth girl, one of the preferred slaves of Samos. She was looking at the standing woman with fear and anger. She reached out to touch Samos' sleeve. He shook free, a small gesture, of her touch.

I then returned my attention to the standing woman.

"As you can see," she said to Samos, "I am too beautiful to be a slave."

I had seen thousands of slave girls who were more beautiful than she but, to be sure, there was no doubt about it; she was quite beautiful.

Samos did not speak.

"What is to be my fate?" she asked.

"You are too beautiful not to be a slave," said Samos.

"No!" she cried. "No!"

"Take her below," said Samos to one of the two guards flanking the woman. "Put the iron to her body, left thigh, common Kajira mark, and, I think, for the time, a common house collar will do for her." She looked at him, aghast. Then her two arms were seized by the guards. Samos looked down at the board. "It is your move," he said. I, too, returned my attention to the board. The guards made as though to conduct the woman from our presence. The business with her, we assumed, was done.

She struggled. "No!" she cried. "No!"

Samos looked up, and the guards held her where she was. "Do you protest?" he asked.

"Certainly!" she cried.

"On what grounds?" he asked, puzzled. She was his by legitimate capture, and he could do with her whatever he pleased. Any court on Gor would have upheld this.

"On the grounds that I am a free woman!" she said.

"Oh?" he asked.

"Yes!" she said.

I could see that Samos was annoyed. He wished to return to his game.

"I would rather die than be a slave!" she cried.

"Very well," said Samos. "Strip her."

In moments her clothing was half torn from her, and was down about her hips.

"Why are you taking away my clothes!" she wept.

"In order that the blood not stain them," he said.

"Blood!" she cried, in consternation. "I do not understand!"

Then she was naked and thrown on her knees, her right side facing us. Even her gloves and slippers had been removed. One of the guards held her on her knees, bent over. The other guard took her hair in both hands and, by it, pulled her head down, and forward. The back of her neck, with its tiny, fine, golden hair was bared.

"What are you going to do?" she cried.

Samos signaled to another of his men, who unsheathed his sword.

The fellow laid the edge of the blade gently on the back of her neck, and then he lifted the blade away and upward. He grasped the hilt with both hands, his left hand extending somewhat beyond the butt end of the hilt. In this way considerable leverage can be obtained. Several of the slave girls looked away.

"What are you going to do!" she screamed.

"Behead you," said Samos.

"Why!" she cried.

"There is no place in my holding for a free woman," he said.

"Enslave me!" she cried.

"I cannot believe my ears," he said, skeptically.

"Enslave me!" she cried. "Enslave me!"

The fellow with the blade lowered it a bit, and looked at
Samos.

"Is this the proud Lady Rowena of Lydius who speaks?"
inquired Samos.

"Yes," she wept, helpless in the grip of the guards, her body
bent forward, her head down.

"The proud free woman?" he asked.

"Yes," she wept.

"Let me understand this clearly," said Samos. "In spite of
the fact that I am willing to accord you the dignity of a swift and
honorable death, one fitting for a free woman, you would choose
instead, and prefer, the degradation of slavery?"

"Yes," she said.

"Speak clearly," he said.

"I beg slavery," she said.

"You understand, of course," he said, "that the slavery for
which you beg is one which is total and absolute?"

"Yes," she said.

I smiled to myself. It would be a Gorean slavery.

"You seemed to think earlier," said Samos, "that such a
slavery might be all right for your maidens, but not for yourself."

"I was wrong," she said. "I am no different from them. I,
too, am only a female."

The fellow with the blade lowered it. The Lady Rowena,
doubtless, saw it, near her neck.

"I am troubled," said Samos.

The Lady Rowena twisted her head to the right, wincing, from
the hold of the guard, with two hands, on her hair, to regard
Samos. Her face was agonized. Her lip trembled. "Grant my
petition, I beg you," she said.

"I hesitate," said Samos.

"Do you hesitate," she asked, "because of some lack of
certitude as to my nature, for fear of some impropriety or subtle
lack of fittingness in such an action?"

Samos shrugged.

"Dismiss such reservations from your mind," she said. Her
body suddenly shook with sobs. "My pretense to freedom was
always a sham. I am now ready to be a woman. Indeed, in this, I
sense a possible fulfillment greater than any I have hitherto
dreamed. How marvelous to cast aside the artificiality of roles
and become, at last, what one truly is, one's self!"

"Speak more clearly" said Samos.

"It is appropriate that I be enslaved," she said.

"Why?" he asked.

"Because," she said, "in the deepest heart and belly of me I am a slave."

"How do you know?" he asked.

"It has been made clear to me in my needs," she said. "It has been made clear to me in my feelings. For years it has been made manifest to me in hidden thoughts and secret desires, in countless recurrent dreams and fantasies."

"Interesting," said Samos.

"Enslave me," she said.

"No," he said.

She looked at him with horror. The fellow with the sword renewed his two-handed grip on its hilt.

"Pronounce yourself slave," said Samos. The fellow relaxed his grip on the hilt.

"Do not make me do this," she begged. "Pity me! Consider my sensibilities!"

His face was expressionless.

"I am a slave," she said, pronouncing herself slave. Several of the slave girls cried out. There was now a new slave on Gor.

At a gesture from Samos the fellow with the blade resheathed the weapon, and the two guards who had held the girl in position released her, standing up.

She was now on her hands and knees, naked on the tiles, before the table. She looked wildly at Samos. "See the slave!" laughed more than one of the slave girls, pointing at her. They were not reprimanded. The girl, frightened, looked from face to face. The words had been spoken. They could not now be unspoken. She was now rightless, only a nameless animal, incapable of doing anything whatsoever to qualify or alter her status.

"Slave! Slave!" laughed the slave girls.

At a gesture from Samos the two guards pulled the girl to her feet and held her before us.

"Take her away," said Samos, "and throw her to sleen."

"No, Master!" she screamed. "Please, no, Master! Mercy, Master!"

I could see that he was not too pleased with her who had formerly been the Lady Rowena of Lydius.

"Master!" she cried.

She was turned away from us. Her toes barely touched the tiles. She was utterly helpless in the grip of the guards. She looked wildly back, over her shoulder. "Why are you doing this?" she cried. She did not, of course, question his authority, or his right to do with her as he pleased.

The guards hesitated, holding her in place, her back to us, in case Samos might be pleased to respond to her. In a moment, if Samos did not speak, they would proceed on their way, she in helpless custody between them.

"It is one thing to be a slave," said Samos. "It is another to be permitted to live."

"Why would you do this to me?" she sobbed, over her shoulder. "Why would you have me thrown to sleen?"

"I think," said Samos, "there is still too much of the free woman in you."

"No!" she cried. "There is no more free woman left in me! The free woman is gone!"

"Is it true?" he asked.

"Yes," she cried, "yes, Master!"

"What, then, is left in you?" he asked.

"Only the slave!" she cried.

"What do you mean—in you?" he asked.

"I spoke loosely, Master," she wept. "Forgive me. That which I only and totally am is now a slave!"

"It is one thing to be a slave," said Samos. "It is another to be an adequate slave."

"Master?" she asked, in misery.

"Keeping you would be a waste of collar and gruel," he said.

"No, Master," she said. "I would strive to serve well. I would strive desperately to be found worthy of being kept in my collar, and to be pleasing within it!"

"You do not have what it takes to be a good slave," said Samos. "You are too stupid, cold and self-centered."

"No, Master!" she said.

"You lack the talent, the intelligence of the slave," he said.

"No, Master, no!" she cried.

"Release her," said Samos.

The girl, released, turned about and threw herself in supplication to her belly before the table. She lifted her head. There were tears in her eyes. "Let me prove to you that I can be acceptable as a slave!" she begged.

"Do you realize what you are asking?" he asked.

"Yes, Master!" she wept.

"What do you think?" Samos asked of me.

I shrugged. The decision, it seemed to me, was his.

"Please, Master," begged the girl, tears in her eyes.

"Do you think you can be pleasing?" Samos asked the slave.

"I will try desperately, Master," she said.

"Stand," he said.

She stood.

"Straighten your back," said Samos. "Suck in your stomach. Thrust out your breasts."

Tears ran from her eyes.

"Remember, my dear," said Samos, not unkindly, "you are no longer a free woman. You have now entered a new life altogether, in which rigidities and inhibitions are no longer permitted you, a form of life in which, in many ways, you are strictly and uncompromisingly controlled, but one in which, in other ways, your deepest desires and needs need no longer be restrained, but may be, and must be, fully liberated, a form of life in which you, though categorically subjected to the perfections of absolute discipline, that of the total slave, are, paradoxically, freed to be yourself."

She looked at Samos, wonderingly.

"These things may now seem hard to understand," said Samos, "but they, and their reality, if you are permitted to live, will soon become clear."

"Yes, Master," she said, gratefully. I saw that she, already, now a slave, deeply sensed the truth of his words.

Then his eyes were hard, and she trembled.

"Lift your hands to the level of your shoulders," he said, "and flex your knees, slightly.

She complied.

Samos then signaled to the musicians, who were seated to one side, that they should prepare to play.

"What is it that a man wants from a woman?" asked Samos.

"Everything, and more," she whispered.

"Precisely," he said.

She trembled.

"I suggest that you do well," said Samos.

"Yes, Master," she said.

"You dance, and perform, for your life," he said.

"Yes, Master," she said.

"Are you ready?" he asked.

"Yes, Master," she whispered.

Samos signaled again to the musicians, and they began to play a sensual, slow, adagio melody.

"I had placed my Home Stone," said Samos, turning his attention to the board. "It is your move." That was true. It was my eleventh move. I considered the board and the placement of his Home Stone. An attack, I thought, would be premature. I would continue my development. I would attempt to secure the center, garnering thereby the mobilities and options commonly attendant on the control of these customarily vital routes. He who controls the roads, some say, controls the cities. This, of course, is not strictly true, not in a world where most goods can be carried on the back of a man, not in a world where there are tarns.

"It is the sleen for her," I heard a man say.

Samos glanced at the dancer.

I, too, glanced at her. She was not trained. She did not know slave dance. Her movements were those of a virgin, a white-silk girl. She had not yet been taught slave helplessness. No man yet in his arms had taught her the exquisite, transforming degradations of the utilized slave, the wrenching surrender spasms, enforced upon her by his will, of the conquered bondwoman, experiences which, once she has had them, she is never willing to give up, experiences which she comes to need, experiences for which she will do anything, experiences which, whether she wished it or not, put her at and keep her at, the mercy of men.

"She is clumsy," said Samos. He was irritated. I saw he did not wish, really, to have her killed.

A man laughed at her, as she tried to dance before him. "Her throat will be cut within the Ahn," laughed another man. Another man turned away from her, when she approached him, to have his goblet of paga filled by a luscious, half-naked, collared slave.

"Clumsy, clumsy," said Samos. "I thought she might have the makings, somehow, of a pleasure slave."

"She is trying," I said.

"She does not have what it takes," said Samos.

"Her body is richly corved," I said. "That suggests an abundance of female hormones, and that, in turn, suggests the potentialities, the capacities for love, the sensibilities, the dispositions of the pleasure slave."

"She is not acceptable," said Samos. "She is inadequate."

"She is trying desperately to please," I said.

"But she is not succeeding," he said.

"She has a lovely body," I said. "Perhaps someone could buy her for a pittance, for a pot girl."

"She is not adequate," said Samos. "I will have to have her destroyed." He looked back to the board.

I saw several of the slave girls looking fearfully at one another. I do not think that they cared much for their new sister in bondage, the former Lady Rowena of Lydius, who perhaps in some subtle way, perhaps by virtue of her former background, held herself superior to them, but, too, I do not think they cared to have her thrown alive, screaming, to sleen. She was, after all,

now, like them, only a slave. "Dance, you stupid slave," hissed
one. "Do you not know you are a slave? Do you not know you
are owned?"

A wild look, one of sudden, fearful insight, came over the
face of the dancer. She had not thought, specifically, objectively,
it seemed, about this aspect of matters. But, of course, she was
owned. She was now property. She could now be bought and
sold, like a tarsk, at the pleasure of masters.

She belonged to Samos, of course. It had been within the
context of his capture rights that she had, as a free woman, of
her own free will, pronounced upon herself a formula of
enslavement. Automatically then, by virtue of the context, she
became his. The law is clear on this. The matter is more subtle
when the woman is not within a context of capture rights. Here
the matter differs from city to city. In some cities, a woman may
not, with legal recognition, submit herself to a specific man as a
slave, for in those cities that is interpreted as placing at least a
temporary qualification on the condition of slavery which condition,
once entered into, all cities agree, is absolute. In such cities,
then, the woman makes herself a slave, unconditionally. It is
then up to the man in question whether or not he will accept her
as his slave. In this matter he will do as he pleases. In any event,
she is by then a slave, and only that.

In other cities, and in most cities, on the other hand, a free
woman may, with legal tolerance, submit herself as a slave to a
specific man. If he refuses her, she is then still free. If he accepts
her, she is then, categorically, a slave, and he may do with her
as he pleases, even selling her or giving her away, or slaying
her, if he wishes. Here we might note a distinction between laws
and codes. In the codes of the warriors, if a warrior accepts a
woman as a slave, it is prescribed that, at least for time, an
amount of time up to his descretion, she be spared. If she should
be the least bit displeasing, of course, or should prove recalci-
trant in even a tiny way, she may be immediately disposed of.

It should be noted that this does not place a legal obligation on
the warrior. It has to do, rather, with the proprieties of the codes.
If a woman not within a clear context of rights, such as capture
rights, house rights, or camp rights, should pronounce herself
slave, *simpliciter*, then she is subject to claim. These claims may
be explicit, as in branding, binding and collaring, or as in the
uttering of a claimancy formula, such as "I own you," "You
are mine," or "You are my slave," or implicit, as in, for
example, permitting the slave to feed from your hand or follow
you.

"Dance, fool!" cried one of the slave girls to the former Lady Rowena of Lydius.

"See the free woman!" laughed one of the slaves. "It is the sleen for her," said another.

"Please men!" cried another. "What do you think you are for?"

"Like this!" cried a brunette, leaping away from the tables to the tiles, tearing away her silk.

"Do not interfere," warned a man. The brunette, terrified, seized up her silk, and shrank back behind the tables, into the shadows, where, huddled, knelt other slaves.

She who had been the Lady Rowena fell sobbing to her knees, helpless on the tiles, covering her face with her hands. The music stopped.

"You are cruel, all of you!" cried out Linda, the blond Earth-girl slave of Samos, springing to her feet. All eyes turned towards her. "You put us in collars! You take away our clothes! You make us serve you! You do with us as you please!" She looked beautiful, in her brief tunic, barefoot, her body filled with passion, her small fists clenched, in her collar.

"And you love it!" laughed a man.

"Yes!" she cried. "I love it! You cannot know how I love it! I come from a world where there are almost no true men, a world where manhood is almost educated and conditioned out of existence. I come from a world of love-starved women. I did not know what true men were until I came to Gor, and was put in a collar! Here I am disciplined and trained, here I am owned and fulfilled! Here I am happy! I pity even my free sisters of Gor, who are so far above me, for they cannot know the overwhelming joys and fulfillments which are mine, and I pity a thousand times more my miserable free sisters of Earth, so far away, longing for their collars and masters!"

There was then silence. She hurried to the side of the girl kneeling on the tiles. She crouched beside her, putting her arm about her shoulders. She then looked at us. "But this is only a poor slave," she said. "She is new to her condition. She is trying to please. It is just that she does not yet know how. Please be kind to her. Give her some time. Let her learn. Is she not beautiful? Do you not think she could learn to be pleasing? Show her mercy!"

It was then again silent.

Numbly, Linda rose to her feet and walked back about the tables. She knelt behind our table, her head down.

"With your permission," I said to Samos. I rose to my feet

and went to the girl, now prone, red-eyed, on the tiles. I
crouched down beside her.

"Oh!" she cried.

I turned her over, handling her with authority, as a slave is
handled.

She looked up at me.

Never before, doubtless, had she been handled like this. "Her
face is beautiful," I said, "her body is curvaceous, her limbs are
fair. It seems she should bring a good price."

She gasped, appraised as a female.

"But what is inside a woman is more important," said a man.

"That is true," I said. Some of the most succulent and
exciting slaves I had known were, I suppose, at least compared
with some of their sisters in bondage, comparatively plain in
appearance. Such women constitute marvelous bargains in a
slave market. They cost far less than many of their higher-priced
sisters and yet, in the long run, are worth far more. Many men,
upon returning home, thinking they have bought an average girl
within their means, discover instead, to their delight, that they
have purchased a dream. To be sure, the matter is complicated.
Slavery, for example, marvelously, subtly, tends to bring out the
beauty in a woman. Many women, after a year or two in
bondage, become so beautiful that they can double or triple their
price.

"Men desire women," I told her.

"Yes, Master," she said.

"And you belong to that sex," I said, "which is maddeningly,
exquisitely desirable."

"Yes, Master," she said.

"And you are," I said, "I think, objectively, a beautiful
member of that sex."

"Thank you, Master," she whispered.

"It therefore seems not inconceivable that men might find you
desirable."

"Yes, Master," she whispered.

"Does that please you?" I asked.

"It terrifies me," she said.

"Do you have normal feelings toward men?" I asked.

"I think so, Master," she said.

"Now that you are a slave," I said, "it is not only permissible
for you to yield to these feelings, but you must do so."

"Master!" she whispered.

"Yes," I said, "for you are now a slave."

"Yes, Master," she whispered, shuddering.

"That makes quite a difference, doesn't it?" I asked.

"Yes, Master," she said.

"She does not have slave reflexes," said a man.

I pulled her by the hair up to a sitting position, and then, by the hair, bent her head back.

"Oh!" she winced.

"Keep the palms of your hands on the tiles," I said. She did so. Her knees were slightly flexed.

"Oh! Oh!" she cried suddenly.

"Keep your palms on the tiles," I said.

"Yes, Master!" she said. "Yes, Master!"

"She does have slave reflexes," I reported.

"Yes," said the man.

"Yes," said another man.

"Are men now of greater interest to you?" I asked.

"Yes, Master!" she said.

"We are now going to put these things together," I said. "First, you are an exquisitely desirable woman. You are the sort of woman who could drive a man mad with passion. You are the sort of woman to possess whom men might kill. Furthermore, your beauty and desirability is increased a thousandfold because you are a property girl, a slave."

"Yes, Master," she whispered. "Oh, Master!"

"Men are now of even greater interest to you, are they not?" I asked.

"Yes, Master!" she wept.

"Keep the palms of your hands on the floor," I said.

"Yes, Master," she said.

"That handles things from the point of view of the man," I said.

"Yes, Master," she said.

"Now," I said, "second, let us consider things from the point of view of the woman, from your point of view."

"Master!" she cried.

"Keep the palms of your hands on the floor," I said.

"Yes, Master," she whimpered.

"As a slave," I said, "it is not only permissible for you to yield to your deepest, most stirring, most primitive, most over-whelmingly feminine urges but you must do so, shamelessly, unqualifiedly, completely."

"Yes, Master," she cried, and thrust herself suddenly, piteously, against my hand.

I then, by the hair, pulled her about and threw her lengthwise, prone, to the tiles.

She looked up at me, over her shoulder. I saw wildness in her eyes. I saw that she had begun to sense what it might be to be an aroused slave.

"Whip," I said, to a man, the fellow who had earlier disciplined the foolish slave who had permitted herself, without permission, to display merriment over the plight of a free woman.

The whip was placed in my hand.

"Master?" asked the girl, apprehensively.

"I do not believe you were given permission to stop dancing earlier," I said.

"No, Master," she said.

"As you are a stupid girl and new to your condition, your punishment, this time, will be light. Three lashes."

"Three!" she sobbed.

"Do not expect masters to be so lenient with your stupidity in the future," I said.

"No, Master," she wept.

Then, doubtless for the first time in her life, she who had been the proud free woman, the Lady Rowena of Lydius, naked, and on her belly on the tiles, felt, like the common girl she now was, the slave whip of Gor.

"Stand," I told her. "Back straight, belly in, breasts out. Lift your hands to your shoulders, flex your knees."

"I have been whipped," she said, disbelievingly.

"See the difference?" said a man to another at his table. "How she stands?"

"Yes," said the other.

I touched her here and there, with the whip, deftly, correcting a line, or the tension of a curve.

She shrank back from the touch of the whip. She now knew what it could to do to her. She had felt it. After a girl has once felt the whip the mere sight of it is usually enough to bring her immediately into line. "What hangs upon the wall?" a master might ask. "The slave whip, Master," she responds. "How may I be more pleasing?"

I handed the whip back to the fellow who had had it, and returned to my place at the table of Samos.

He signaled the musicians, and they began, again, to play.

I gave my attention to the board. It was my move. I did not bother, then, to glance at the former Lady Rowena of Lydius. She was a mere slave, dancing for masters. Doubtless, too, as the evening wore on, other girls, too, perhaps Tula, and Susan, and Linda, would be ordered to the floor, to dance before strong men, then perhaps, each in her turn, one by one, to be dragged to the tables.

I moved my Ubara's Rider of the High Tharlarion to Ubara's Scribe Three. This, supporting the center, would also open a file, developing the Ubara's Builder. The Gorean dancer is expected, usually, to satisfy the passions she arouses. "It is your move," I said to Samos. I gathered, from the cries of pleasure, from the clapping of hands, the striking of hands on shoulders, that the new slave might be proving not unacceptable. "How is she doing?" I asked. "I do not think it will be necessary, at least immediately, to throw her to sleen," said Samos. He was regarding the dancer. "It is your move," I said. Samos put his chin on his fists and examined the board. I lifted my head and looked across the room.

I saw that it was a slave who danced before the men. She gyrated but inches from a burly oarsman, then leaped back, eluding his drunken grasp. She moved between the tables, a slave, an owned woman. Then she was kneeling beside a man, kissing and caressing him, and then, as though it were involuntary, as though her hands were tied behind her and she was being pulled back, away from him, by a rope, she retreated from him. In a moment she was showering another man with her hair and kisses. Then she offered a man wine, holding the goblet, pressing it against her belly, swaying sensuously before him. She was then again in the center of the tiles, among the tables. She made as if to speak, and then, suddenly, stopped, as though startled. Then she took a wad of her long, golden hair and, swiftly balling it, thrust it, as though insolently, in her mouth. She then looked at the men reproachfully. It was as though a man, perhaps not desiring to hear her speak, had gagged her with her own hair. There was laughter. She drew the hair from her mouth, drawing some of it, in loosening it, deeply back between her teeth, with her head back, as though she might have been in the constraint of a gag strap, all this to the music, and then her hair was free, and, with a movement of her head and movements of her hands, beautifully, she draped and spread it about her. It seemed then she withdrew modestly, frightened, behind the hair, drawing it like a cloak or sheet about her, as though by means of this piteous device she might hope desperately to conceal at least some minimal particle of her beauty from the rude scrutiny of masters. But it was not to be permitted.

To a swirl of music, taking her hair to the sides, holding it, parting it, with clenched fists thrust behind her, twisting, her body thrust forward, her beauty was suddenly, it seemed as though by command, or by the action of another, brazenly bared. "Good!" said more than one man. There was a striking of shoulders in Gorean applause. Even some of the slave girls cried out with pleasure. The girl had done it well. Then she was again dancing among the tables. Her movements gave much pleasure. She entertained well. If Samos had known she would prove this good he might have put her in bells or a chain. I doubted that some of the things she had done, in all their abundance and richness, had been merely thought up on the spur of the moment. I suspected that many times in her dreams and fantasies she had danced thus before men, as a slave. Then, lo, one night in Port Kar she found herself truly a slave, and so dancing, and for her life.

As the music neared its climax she returned before our table, dancing desperately and pleadingly. It was there that was to be found her master.

She lowered herself to the floor and there, on her knees, and her sides, and her belly and back, continued her dance.

Men cried out with pleasure.

Floor movements are among the most stimulatory aspects of slave dance.

I regarded her. She was not bad. She was, of course, not trained. A connoisseur of slave dance, I suppose, might have pointed out errors in the pointing of a toe, the extension of a limb, the use of a hand, not well framing the body, not subtly inviting the viewer's eye inward, and so on, but, on the whole, she was definitely not bad. Given her lack of training, a lack which could, of course, be easily remedied, she was not bad, really. Much of what she did, I suppose, is instinctual in a woman. Too, of course, she was dancing for her life.

She writhed well, an utterly helpless, begging slave.

Then the music was finished and she was before us, kneeling, her head down, in submission to Samos. She lifted her head to regard Samos, her master. She searched his face fearfully, for the least sign of her fate. It was he who would decide whether she would live or die.

"It is my hope, Master," she said, "that in time I might not prove totally unacceptable as a slave."

"You may approach," said Samos.

She did not dare to rise to her feet. She crawled, head down, on her hands and knees, to the edge of the table. There, near the table, she put her head down and kissed the tiles. Then, rising up a little and approaching further, still on her hands and knees, she turned her head, delicately, and kissed the edge of the table, her lips touching partly the surface of the table, partly its side.

"Do you beg to live?" he asked.

"Yes, I beg to live, my Master," she said.

"On what terms?" he asked.

"Your terms, Master," she said, "only as a total slave."

"Kneel," said Samos.

She knelt, back on her heels.

Some of the men of Samos had now gathered about, near the table.

"For the moment, at least," said Samos, "you will not be thrown to sleen."

"Thank you, Master!" she cried. "Thank you, my Master!"

Samos then nodded to one of the men standing about, the burly oarsman from whom earlier, eluding him, she had danced away.

He took her wrists and tied them together, with her own hair, before her body, leaving a length of the hair for a leading tether.

She looked up at the oarsman.

"See that you continue to prove adequate," said Samos.

"Yes, Master!" she said.

She was then drawn to her feet by the hair tether and, bound, was led across the tiles to the oarsman's place.

"Tula!" called a man. "Let Tula dance!"

Several men shouted their agreement to this. A long-legged brunette was thrust to the center of the tiles. She had high cheekbones, a tannish skin and a golden collar. Her bit of silk was ripped from her.

"Tula!" cried men, and, sensuously, she lifted her arms, and, standing, excitingly posed, awaited the instruction of the music. She would show the men what true dancing could be.

Across the room I saw she who had been the Lady Rowena of Lydius, her arms, her wrists still bound with her own hair, about the neck of the oarsman. His hands were on her. Her lips were pressed fervently to his. He lowered her to the tiles beside his table.

The music began and Tula danced. I saw other girls moving closer to the tables, subtly taking more prominent positions, hoping perhaps thereby to be more visible to the men. Tula was Samos' finest dancer. There was much competition among his girls for the second position. My own finest dancer was a wench named Sandra. Some others, for example, Arlene, Janice, Evelyn, Mira and Vella, were also quite good.

She who had been the former Lady Rowena of Lydius suddenly cried out.

"It is your move," I told Samos.

"I know," he said.

He moved his Ubara's Rider of the High Tharlarion to Ubara's
Builder Three. This seemed a weak move. It did open the
Ubara's Initiate's Diagonal. My Ubar's Rider of the High
Tharlarion was amply protected. I utilized the initial three-space
option of the Ubar's Scribe's Spearman. I would then, later,
bring the Ubar's Builder to Ubar's Scribe One, to bring pressure
to bear on the Ubar's Scribe's file. Samos did not seem to be
playing his usual game. His opening, in particular, had been
erratic. He had prematurely advanced significant pieces, and
then had lost time in withdrawing them. It was as though he had
desired to take some significant action, or had felt that he
should, but had been unwilling to do so.

He moved a spearman, diffidently.

"That seems a weak move," I said.

He shrugged.

I brought the Ubar's Builder to Ubar's Scribe One. To be
sure, his opening had caused me to move certain pieces more
than once in my own opening.

Tula now swayed lasciviously, insistently, forwardly, before
the table. I saw Linda, kneeling somewhat behind Samos, regard
her with fury. Slave girls commonly compete shamelessly for the
favor of the master. Tula, with those long, tannish legs, the high
cheekbones, the wild, black hair, the golden collar, was very
beautiful. It is pleasant to own women. But Samos paid her
little, or no, attention. With a toss of her head she spun away.
She would spend the night in the arms of another.

Samos made another move and so, too, did I.

I heard soft gasps and cries from across the room, the fall of a
goblet, and squirming. The former Lady Rowena of Lydius's
hands were no longer bound but they were now held above and
behind her head, each wrist in the hands of a different man. She
was on her back, thrown across one of the low tables.

Tonight, Samos seemed off his game.

I wondered if anything might be wrong.

"Did you want to see me?" I asked. It was unusual for Samos
to invite me to his holding simply for a game of kaissa.

He did not respond. He continued to regard the board. Samos
played well, but he was not an enthusiast for the game. He had
told me once he preferred a different kaissa, one of politics and
men.

"I do not think you brought me here to play kaissa," I said.

He did not respond.

"Guard your Ubar," I said.

He withdrew the piece.

"Have you heard aught of Kurii?" I asked.

"Little or nothing," he said.

Our last major source of information on this matter, as far as I knew, had come from a blond slave named Sheila. I recalled her kneeling naked before us, the slave harness cinched on her in such a way as to enhance her beauty. She had spoken obediently, and volubly, but she had been able, all in all, to help us but little. Kurii, doubtless as a security measure, entrust little vital information to their human agents. She had once been the Tatrix of Corcyrus. She now belonged to Hassan of Kasra, often called Hassan, the Slave Hunter. I had once been in Kasra. It is a river port on the Lower Fayeen. It is important in the Tahari salt trade. When Samos had finished with her, she had, at the command of Hassan, still in the harness, served the pleasure of both of us. She was then hooded. The last time I saw her Hassan had put her in the bottom of a longboat at Samos' steps, descending to the canal. He had tied her ankles together and pulled them up behind her body, fastening them there with a strap passed through a ring at the back of the slave harness. I suspected she would not be freed from the hood, except for its lifting to feed and water her, for days, not until she was in Hassan's keep in Kasra. I had little doubt he would see to it that she served him well.

I nodded. From the testimony of Sheila, and other sources which seemed to corroborate it, we gathered that the Kurii might now be turning to the patient strategems of piecemeal subversion, the control of cities and their eventual linkages in networks of power, to win a world by means theoretically within the laws and decrees of Priest-Kings. Indeed, for such a strategy to eventually prove successful, it seemed not unlikely they would have at least the tolerance of the Sardar itself. I shuddered. It would not bode well for humans, I thought, if some form of liaison, or arrangement, were entered into between Priest-Kings and Kurii.

"Have you heard aught from the Sardar?" I asked.

Samos looked up from the board.

Outside I could hear the sounds of yet another troupe traversing the canal, with its raucous cries, its drums and trumpets. There had been several such troupes, theatrical troupes, carnival troupes, this evening. It was now only two days to carnival, to the Twelfth Passage Hand.

"Late in Se'Var," said Samos, "a Torvaldsland voyageur, Yngvar, the Far-Traveled, bought paga in the Four Chains."

I nodded. I knew the Four Chains. It was owned by Procopius Minor. It was near Pier Sixteen. Procopius Minor is not to be confused with Procopius Major, who is an important merchant in Port Kar, one with interests not only in taverns but in paper, hardware, wool and salt. I had never heard of Yngvar, the Far-Traveled, until recently. I did not know him. The time of which Samos spoke was about two months ago.

"In his drinking, this Yngvar told many stories. One frightens and puzzles me. Some fifty pasangs northeast of Scagnar he claims that he and his crew saw something turning and spinning in the sky, like webbed glass, the light spilling and refracting through it. They then saw a silverish disklike object near it. These two objects, both, seemed to descend, as though to the sea itself. Then a little later, the silverish object departed. Curious, frightened, they rowed to the place where the objects had seemed to descend. There was not even a skerry there. They were about to turn about when one of the men saw something. There, not more than twenty yards from the ship, half submerged, was a large, winged creature. They had never seen anything like this before. It was dead. They poked it with spears. Then, after a time, it slipped beneath the water and disappeared."

"I have heard the story," I said. To be sure, I had heard it only a few days ago. It, like other stories, seemed to circulate through the taverns. Yngvar, with some fellow Torvaldslanders, had signed articles and taken ship northward shortly thereafter. Neither Samos nor myself had been able to question them.

"The dating of this occurrence seems unclear," I said.

"It was apparently not recent," said Samos.

Presumably this had happened after the time I had gone to Torvaldsland, or, I suppose, I would have heard of it while there. Interesting stories move swiftly through the halls, conveyed by merchants and singers. Too, such a story would be widely told, one supposes, at a Thing-Fair. I went to Torvaldsland in the Rune-Year 1,006. Years, in the chronology of Torvaldsland, are counted from the time of Thor's gift of the stream of Torvald to Torvald, the legendary founder and hero of the northern fatherlands. The calendars are kept by Rune-Priests. That would have been 10,122 C.A., or Year 3 of the Sovereignty of the Council of Captains in Port Kar. I suspected, though I did not know, that the events recounted by Yngvar had occurred from four to five years ago.

"It was probably a few years ago," said Samos.

"Probably," I granted him.

"The ship was probably a ship of Priest-Kings," said Samos.

"I would suppose so," I said. It did not seem likely that a Kur ship would move openly in Gorean air space.

"It is an interesting story," said Samos.

"Yes," I said.

"Perhaps it has some significance," said Samos.

"Perhaps," I said.

I recalled, long ago, in the Nest, when I had seen the dying Mother. "I see him, I see him," she had said, "and his wings are like showers of gold." She had then lain quietly on the stone. "The Mother is dead," had said Misk. Her last memory, interestingly, it seemed, had been of her Nuptial Flight. There was now, doubtless, a new Mother in the Nest. Yngvar and his fellows, unwittingly, I was confident, had witnessed the inauguration of a new dynasty among Priest-Kings.

"Have you heard anything from the Sardar?" I asked, again.

Samos looked down at the board. I did not press him. His reticence to respond directly puzzled me. If he had heard something, of course, it was perhaps none of my business. I had no intention of prying into his affairs, or those of Priest-Kings. Also, of course, perhaps he had heard nothing.

We played four more moves.

"You are not playing your usual game," I told him.

"I am sorry," he said.

A new girl, Susan, was now dancing. She who had been the Lady Rowena of Lydius was on her belly on a table, clutching its sides, her teeth gritted. Tula was being handed from man to man. Some of the other girls, too, were now being used by masters. And others were licking and kissing at them, and whispering in their ears, begging for attention.

We played another pair of moves.

"What is bothering you?" I asked Samos.

"Nothing," he said.

"Is there much news?" I asked.

"Tarnsmen from Treve had raided the outskirts of Ar," said Samos.

"They grow bold," I said.

"Cos and Ar are still at odds," he said.

"Of course," I said.

"The building of ships in Tyros continues," he said.

"Chenbar has a long memory," I said. Much of the naval power of Tyros had been destroyed in the battle of the 25th of

Se'Kara. This had taken place in Year One of the Sovereignty of the Council of Captains, in 10,120 C.A.

"On Cos, as our spies have it," said Samos, "there is much training of men, and a recruitment of mercenaries."

"We could strike at the shipyards of Tyros," I said, "ten ramships, a thousand men, a picked force."

"The yards are well fortified," he said.

"Do you think Cos and Tyros will move?" I asked.

"Yes," he said.

"When?" I asked.

"I do not know," he said.

"It is interesting," I said. "I cannot see Port Kar as a great threat to them. The power of Ar in the Vosk Basin would seem a much greater threat to their influence, and their sphere of trade."

"One would think so," said Samos.

"Matters are complicated there now, of course," I said, "by the formation of the Vosk League."

"That is true," said Samos.

"What is the nature of the training being given the men on Cos?" I asked.

"Infantry training," he said.

"That is interesting," I said. It did not seem likely to me that infantry, at least in its normal deployments and tactics, would be successful in an assault on Port Kar. This had primarily to do with her situation, in the northwestern portion of the estuary of the Vosk, the waters of the Tamber Gulf and Thassa before her, the vast, trackless marshes of the Vosk's delta behind her.

"Can it be," I asked, "that Cos is planning to challenge Ar on the land?"

"That would be madness," said Samos.

I nodded. Ar is the major land force in known Gor. The Cosian infantry, meeting her on land in open battle, in force, would be crushed.

"It seems clear then," said Samos, "that they are planning on using the infantry against Port Kar."

I nodded. Cos would never challenge Ar on the land. That was unthinkable.

"That is what is bothering you?" I asked.

"What?" he asked.

"The possibility that Cos and Tyros may move against Port Kar," I said.

"No," he said.

"What is bothering you?" I asked.

"Nothing," he said.

"Are you disturbed by the proximity of the Waiting Hand?" I asked.

This is a frightening and difficult time for many Goreans.

"No," he said.

"Let us stop playing, and adjudicate the game as a draw," I suggested.

"No," he said. "It is all right."

I moved my Ubara's Builder to threaten his Ubar. This movement of the Builder produced a discovered attack on his Home Stone by my Ubara's Initiate. He interposed his own Ubar's Builder, which I then took with the Initiate, a less valued piece. The Initiate's attack, of course, continued the threat on the Home Stone. He then took the Initiate with his Ubara's Builder, and I, of course, removed his Ubar from the board with my Ubara's Builder.

Samos turned to Linda. "Dance," he said. She leaped to her feet and hurried to the center of the tiles. Susan, then, was pulled by the hair to the place of a keleustes, one who marks time, usually on a pounding block or a ship's drum, for oarsmen. In some navies, and on ships of some registry, the office of the keleustes is referred to as that of the hortator. He reports directly to the oar-master. The oar-master, like the helmsmen, of which two are generally on duty at any one time, most Gorean ships being double ruddered, reports to the captain.

We watched Linda dance. It seemed she had eyes only for Samos. Her fingers played teasingly with the disrobing loop at her left shoulder.

"Strip, slave," said Samos.

She drew at the disrobing loop. There was Gorean applause. She danced well. There was little left in her now of the Earth female. How happy and fulfilled she was on Gor. To be sure, she was only a slave.

I returned my attention to the board, as did Samos.

"It is capture of Home Stone in four," I said.

He nodded. He removed his Home Stone from the board, resigning.

He lifted his head, regarding Linda. "She is pretty," he said.

"Yes," I said.

"Do you believe that I am your friend?" he asked.

"Yes," I said.

"Do you trust me?" he asked.

"Yes," I said.

She writhed well, the Gorean slave.

"Why did you invite me this night to your holding?" I asked. "Surely not merely to play kaissa?"

He was now resetting the pieces. He would take Yellow this time.

"Ubar's Spearman to Ubar Five," he said.

This move attacks the center and opens a diagonal for the Ubara. It also makes possible a positioning move, if it be desired, for the Ubar's Tarnsman. I made the same move, matching him positionally in the center, stopping an advance on that file and securing the same advantages for the Ubara and Ubar's Tarnsman. This is one of the most common opening moves in kaissa.

We played twice more that night. I won both games easily, the first with a battering ram of Spearmen and Riders of the High Tharlarion on the Ubar's side, and the second with a middle-game combination of Ubara's Scribe, Ubara and Ubar's Tarnsman. It was now late. Linda lay curled on the tiles near Samos. She was naked, save for her collar. She was beautiful and curvaceous. She was his.

"Captain," said one of two guardsmen standing before our table. They were the fellows in whose custody the free woman, the Lady Rowena of Lydius, had earlier been drawn to our attention. The woman who had been the Lady Rowena of Lydius was now again in their custody. She was now on her knees between them, facing us, her arms held high and to either side of her, each of her wrists in the grasp of a guard. She was now a slave.

"Is it the sleen for her, Captain?" asked he who was first of the two guardsmen, he who had just spoken.

"Dorto, Krenbar," said Samos.

"Yes, Captain," said the men. Dorto was the oarsman who had opened the former Lady Rowena of Lydius for the uses of men. Krenbar was another oarsman. He had used her twice in the evening, after putting her through intricate slave paces each time.

"Does this slave," asked Samos, "give some indication that she might eventually prove to be at least somewhat adequate in a collar?"

"Yes, Captain," said Dorto. "Yes, Captain," said Krenbar.

"Tonight, as you know, my dear," said Samos, "you danced, and performed, for your life."

"I beg to have been found pleasing," she said.

"Based on the evidences submitted by Dorto and Krenbar,

and my own judgment in the matter, your performances, at least for a new slave, have been found acceptable.''

I thought she might almost faint with relief.

"Accordingly, at least for the moment, you will not be thrown to sleen.''

"Thank you, Master!" she said.

"You are Rowena," he said.

"Thank you, Master," she said, named. There is some security in a slave having a name. Most masters will not name a slave whom they are planning on having immediately destroyed. It would be a waste of name. To be sure, names may be put on slaves and taken off them on a master's whim.

"Though you have been spared, at least for now, do not grow complacent," said Samos.

"No, Master!" she said.

"You are now, like any other slave, you must understand, under standard, unconditional slave discipline.''

"Yes, Master!" she said. She was now a slave like any other, neither more nor less.

"Take her below," said Samos to he who was first of the two guardsmen. "Mark her, left thigh, common Kajira mark. Collar her, common house collar.''

"Yes, Captain," he said. In the case of the girl, Rowena, of course, as she was already a self-pronounced slave, the brand and collar were little more than identificatory formalities. Nonetheless she would wear them. They would be fixed visibly and clearly upon her. This is in accord with the prescriptions of merchant law. Too, for all practical purposes, they make escape impossible for the Gorean slave girl.

"Then bring her to my chambers," said Samos.

"Yes, Captain," said he who was first of the two guardsmen.

"Master!" protested Linda.

Samos looked at her, and she lowered her head. "Forgive me, Master," she said.

"I shall try to be pleasing, Master!" Rowena avowed, frightened.

Then the two guardsmen pulled her about and conducted her from our presence.

"She is fat," said Linda. I did not think this remark was fair on Linda's part. The slave, Rowena, was not fat. She was sweetly shapely. To be sure, by a strict regimen of diet and exercise, she would soon be brought, in a manner congenial to her basic structure, within indisputable latitudes of slave perfection.

The Gorean slave girl is not a free woman. Accordingly she must keep herself beautiful.

"Do you not like Linda any more?" she pouted.

"Yes, I like you," he said.

"Linda can please you more than Rowena," she said.

"Perhaps," said Samos.

"I can, I will!" she said.

"Who?" asked Samos.

"Linda can, Linda will!" she said.

"To your kennel," said Samos.

"Yes, Master," she said, taking up her tunic, rising to her feet, tears in her eyes.

She hurried softly, her bare feet on the tiles, toward the door.

"Slave," said Samos.

"Yes, Master?" she said, turning and, addressed, dropping to her knees.

"Do not fret," he said. "Tomorrow night it will be you who will be chained at my slave ring."

"Thank you, Master!" she said.

"And tonight, for you have not been fully pleasing," he said, "tell the kennel master to put you in close chains."

"Yes, Master!" she laughed and, happily, dismissed, clutching her tunic, rose to her feet and scurried away. She would not spend a comfortable night, locked in the steel of close chains, but she was radiantly happy. She had been reassured of the interest of her master.

"What are you going to do with the slave Rowena?" I asked.

"She is one of a lot of one hundred," said Samos. "They are to be sold at the fair of En'Kara."

"The slave, Linda," I said, "doubtless would have been pleased to hear that."

"She will doubtless learn of it, in one way or another, sooner or later," said Samos.

"Doubtless," I said.

I rose to my feet. I was stiff from having sat for so long. I suspected Samos cared for the Earth-girl slave, Linda. It was no secret in Port Kar that the shapely collar-slut was first on his chain.

Samos, too, with a grunt, rose to his feet. "Ah," he said.

We looked about. The men and slaves had left the room. We were alone.

Our eyes met. I saw in his eyes that he wanted to speak to me, but he did not do so.

"Your men and boat are waiting," he said.

He accompanied me from his holding to the small landing, with its steps, leading down to the water, outside.

I stepped down into the longboat and, shaking him by the shoulder, awakened Thurnock, the blond giant, he of the peasants. He awakened the rowers. I took my place at the tiller. One of Samos' men cast the line into the boat.

"I wish you well," said Samos.

"I wish you well," I said.

We then pushed off, thrusting against the steps with the port oars. In a moment, with unhurried strokes, we were making our way down the canal, back toward my holding. The canal was dark now. In two days, however, it would be lit with lanterns, thrust out on jutting poles from the bordering, clifflike houses, and strung with garlands and flags. It would then be the time of the Twelfth Passage Hand, the time of carnival.

I heard the ringing of the time bar from the arsenal. It was the Twentieth Ahn, the Gorean midnight.

I was very puzzled as to why Samos had invited me to his holding tonight. I was sure that he had wished to speak to me. But he had not, however, done so.

I dismissed these considerations from my mind. If he chose to keep his own counsel, it was not mine to inquire into his motivations.

I thought that I had played kaissa well tonight. To be sure, Samos was not an enthusiast for the game. He preferred, as I recalled, a different kaissa, one of politics and men.

2

CARNIVAL

"Master!" laughed she who seemed to be a naked, collared slave, flinging her arms about my neck, pressing her lips fervently, deliciously, to mine.

"Oh!" she cried, as my hands checked her thighs. She was truly a slave. The brand was on her left thigh, high, just under the hip. Sometimes free women, during the time of carnival, masquerading as slaves, run naked about the streets.

I slid my hands possessively up her body and then, between my thumbs and fingers, held her under the arms, half lifting her, half pressing her to me. I then returned her kiss. "Master!" she purred, delighted. I then turned her about and, with a good-natured, stinging slap, sped her on her way. She disappeared, laughing, among the crowds.

"Paga, mate?" inquired a mariner.

I took a swig of paga from his bota and he one from mine.

I stepped to one side, nearly trampled by a gigantic figure on stilts.

I was jostled by a fellow blowing on a horn.

There might easily have been fifteen thousand people in the great piazza, the largest in Port Kar, that before the hall of the Council of Captains. It was ringed with booths, and platforms, and stages and stalls, and booths, and platforms and stalls, too, with colorful canvas, with their eccentrically carved wood, with their fluttering flags, and signs, like standards, illuminated by lamps and torches, throngs gathered about them, and flowing between them, bedecked and studded the piazza's inner precincts.

39

Here it seemed there were a thousand things for sale and a hundred shows. Sweating men, stripped to the waist, with wands tipped with cylinders of oil-drenched, flaming wool, appeared to swallow fire. Jugglers performed awesome tricks with rings, balls and sticks. Clowns tumbled; acrobats spun and leapt, and climbed, one upon the other, until, abetted by the gravity of Gor, they swayed thirty feet above the crowd. One man somersaulted on a strand of tarn wire strung between posts. Another fellow had a dancing sleen.

The lovely assistant of a magician, dressed in the robes of a free woman, but unhooded and unveiled, so probably a slave, appeared to put him in manacles. She then helped him into a sack inside a trunk. When he crouched down, lying in the trunk, she seemed to tie shut the sack over his head. She then, with great show, thrusting bolts home, seemed to close and lock the trunk. As a last touch she flung three hasps over three staples and seemed to secure the whole system with three padlocks. A fellow from the audience was invited forward to test the locks. He tried them, stoutly, and then, grudgingly, attested to their placement and solidity. He was requested to retain the keys. The lovely young woman then stepped into a nearby vertical cabinet. The crowd looked at one another. Then a drum roll, furnished by a fellow to one side, suddenly commenced and, steadily, increased in volume and intensity. At its sudden climax, followed by an instant of startling silence, the door of the vertical cabinet burst open and the magician, smiling, to cries of surprise, of awe and wonder, stepped forth, waving, his hands free, greeting the crowd. He wasted not a moment but searched out the startled fellow with the keys and began swiftly, one by one, to unlock the padlocks. In a moment, thrusting back the externally mounted security bolts, the padlocks already removed, he had the trunk open. The crowd was breathless, sensing what might, but could not, be the case. He jerked the sack inside to an upright position. I noticed that it was now secured with a capture knot, a knot of a sort commonly used in securing captives and slaves. He undid the knot. Then, to another drum roll, he opened the mouth of the sack. At the climax of this drum roll, after its moment of startling silence, the figure of a beautiful, naked, hooded female, her wrists locked in slave bracelets, sprang up. The magician bowed to the crowd.

It seemed the act was done. But few coins were flung to the platform. "Wait!" cried a man. "Who is it?" asked another. "It is not the same one!" cried a fellow, triumphantly. The magician seemed distraught, in consternation. It seemed he could not wait to gracefully evacuate the stage. "Show her to us! Show her to us!" cried the crowd. Reluctantly, as though yielding most unwillingly, as responding only of necessity to such peremptory duress, he unbuckled the hood. Then he drew it off with a flourish. It was she! The same girl, of course! She smiled, and shook her head, throwing her lovely tresses behind her. Then, as the crowd cheered, and coins fell like rain on the platform, she, helped by the magician, stepped forth from the sack and trunk. She knelt on the platform, smiling. She wore a collar. This was easily detected now that she was neither hooded nor in the robes of a free woman. She still wore the slave bracelets, of course. I had little doubt that they were genuine, and confined her with snug and uncompromising perfection. That would be a typical Gorean touch.

I myself threw a golden tarn disk to the boards. The slave looked at it in wonder. Perhaps she had never seen one before. It would buy several women such as she. "Thank you, Kind Master!" she cried. "Thank you, Kind Sir!" called the magician, snatching it up.

"They are skillful," commented a man, standing near me.

"Yes," I granted him, and then turned away, back into the crowd.

The man who had spoken was not masked, nor was I. On the other hand, masks are common at carnival time. Many in the crowd wore them. Popular, too, at this time, it might be mentioned, are bizarre costumes. Such things, maskings, and disguisings, and dressing up, sometimes in incredible and wild fashions, are all part of the fun of carnival. Indeed, at this time, there are even parades of costumes, and prizes are awarded, in various categories, for most ingenious or best costume. Most of the dressing up, of course, is not done for the sake of winning prizes but just, so to speak, for carnival, just for the fun of it. It is something that is done at carnival time. To be sure, I suppose there are various psychological benefits, too, other than the simple fun and pleasure of it, attendant on the maskings and disguisings. They might, for example, give one an opportunity to try out new identities, to relieve boredom, to break up routines, to release tension, and so on. They also provide one with an opportunity for foolery, jokes, pranks and horseplay. Who was that fellow, for example, who poured paga on one's head? And who, the free woman might wonder, was that fellow who gave her so sudden, so unexpected, so fierce a pinch? Indeed, perhaps she is fortunate that her very veil was not lifted up and her lips pressed by those of a stranger, or was it a stranger? And who are those fellows in the robes of the caste of physicians, apparently administering medicines to one another, after which they leap and roll about, seemingly in great distress? Are they physicians? It seems more likely they are sawyers or sailmakers from the arsenal. Carnival, too, with its freedom and license, is often used by both men and women as a time for the initiation of affairs, and for arrangements and assignations, the partners often not even being known to one another. In such relationships another advantage of the mask is clearly demonstrated, its provision of anonymity to the wearer, should he or she desire it.

Masks, incidentally, at times other than carnival, are not entirely unknown on Gor. They are often used by individuals traveling incognito or who do not, for one reason or another, wish to be recognized in a certain place or at a certain time. Their use by brigands or highwaymen, of course, is a commonplace. They are also sometimes used by gangs of high-born youths prowling the streets, usually looking to catch a slave girl for an evening's sport. Lower-caste gangs, engaged in similar pursuits, seldom affect masks. They can afford, of course, to be relatively open about their interest, and its indulgence. They are comparatively invulnerable to the nuisances of scandal.

"Paga!" cried a fellow.

We exchanged swigs from our botas. He reeled away into the crowd.

Three fellows walked by supporting swirling carnival figures. These particular constructions had huge, stuffed, bulbous, painted heads, and great flowing robes. They were some nine feet tall. They are supported on a pole and the operator, holding the pole, supporting the figure, is concealed within the robes. He looks out through a narrow, gauze-backed, rectangular opening in the robes. The figures bobbed and nodded to the crowd.

Children fled by, playing tag.

I saw a woman stripped to the waist. She had a brief cloth tied about her hips. She was collared. She looked at me, over her shoulder, and turned away.

In at least a dozen places on the great piazza there must have been groups of musicians.

I saw Tab, a captain once associated with my holding, one with whom I still had occasional dealings. He was with his slave, Midice. She clung to his left arm. It was too crowded here even to heel him properly. I called out to him. But, in the press, and noise, he did not hear. His scabbard was empty. So, too, was mine. We had checked our weapons before entering the piazza.

"I shall have to trouble you for your sword, Sir," said one of the Arsenal Guards, on duty here tonight.

"No," had said another. "Do you not recognize him? That is Bosk, the Admiral, he of the Council of Captains."

"Forgive me, Captain," had said the man. "Enter as you are."

"No," I said. "It is perfectly all right." I surrendered my sword to him, and the knife, too, I commonly carried, a quiva, a Tuchuk saddle knife, balanced for throwing. I myself had voted in the council for the checking of weapons before entering the piazza during carnival. The least I could do, it seemed to me, was to comply with a ruling which I myself had publicly supported.

I remembered now where I had seen the man who had spoken to me near the platform of the magician. He had been waiting near one of the checking points opening onto the piazza, that point through which I had entered. It was there that I had seen him.

The checking of the weapons is accomplished as follows: One surrenders the weapons and the guard, in turn, tears a ticket in two, placing one half with the weapons and giving you the other half. This ticket is numbered on both ends. In reclaiming the weapons one matches the halves, both with respect to division and number. My half of the ticket was now in my wallet. The ticket is of rence paper, which is cheap in Port Kar, owing to its proximity to one of Gor's major habitats for the rence plant, the vast marshes of the Vosk's delta.

"Captain," said a voice.

I turned about. "Captain Henrius?" I asked. He, grinning, thrust up the mask. It was he. I thought I had recognized the voice. The young Captain Henrius was of the lineage of the Sevarii. Once he had been of my house but now held sway in his own house. With him was his lovely slave, Vina, who once had been intended to be the companion of gross Lurius of Jad, then, sharing his throne, to be proclaimed the Ubara of Cos. She was now a slave in Port Kar. I had not recognized her immediately for the gaudy paints which had been applied to her body. She knelt beside Henrius, holding to his thigh, that she not be forced away from him in the crowd.

"Someone is looking for you," said Henrius.

"Who?" I asked.

"I do not know," he said.

"He suggests that you meet him among the purple booths, in Booth Seventeen."

"Thank you," I said.

Henrius, then, with a grin, readjusted his mask, drew Vina to her feet and, with her in tow, by an elbow, vanished in the crowd.

I looked after them. I was fond of them both.

A free woman, in swirling robes of concealment, veiled, appeared before me. "Accept my favor, please!" she laughed. She held forth the scarf, teasingly, coquettishly. "Please, handsome fellow!" she wheedled. "Please, please!" she said. "Please!"

"Very well," I smiled.

She came quite close to me.

"Herewith," she said, "I, though a free woman, gladly and willingly, and of my own free will, dare to grant you my favor!"

She then thrust the light scarf through an eyelet on the collar of my robes and drew it halfway through. In this fashion it would not be likely to be dislodged.

"Thank you, kind sir, handsome sir!" she laughed. She then sped away, laughing.

She had had only two favors left at her belt, I had noted. Normally in this game the woman begins with ten. The first to dispense her ten favors and return to the starting point wins. I looked after her, grinning. It would have been churlish, I thought, to have refused the favor. Too, she had begged so prettily. This type of boldness, of course, is one that a woman would be likely to resort to only in the time of carnival. The granting of such favors probably has a complex history. Its origin may even trace back to Earth. This is suggested by the fact that, traditionally, the favor, or the symbolic token of the favor, is a handkerchief or scarf. Sometimes a lady's champion, as I understand it, might have borne such a favor, fastened perhaps to a helmet or thrust in a gauntlet.

It is not difficult, however, aside from such possible historical antecedents, and the popular, superficial interpretations of such a custom, in one time or another, to speculate on the depth meaning of such favors. One must understand, first, that they are given by free women and of their own free will. Secondly, one must think of favors in the sense that one might speak of a free woman granting, or selling, her favors to a male. To be sure, this understanding, as obvious and straightforward as it is, if brought to the clear light of consciousness, is likely to come as a revelatory and somewhat scandalous shock to the female. It is one of those cases in which a thing she has long striven to hide from herself is suddenly, perhaps to her consternation and dismay, made incontrovertibly clear to her. In support of the interpretation are such considerations as the fact that these favors, in these games, are bestowed by females on males, that, generally, at least, strong, handsome males seem to be the preferred recipients of such favors, that there is competition among the females in the distribution of these favors, and that she who first has her "favors" accepted therein accounts herself as somewhat superior to her less successful sisters, at least in this respect, and that the whole game, for these free women, is charged with an exciting, permissive aura of delicious naughtiness, this being indexed undoubtedly to the sexual stimulations involved, stimulations which, generally, are thought to be beneath the dignity of lofty free women.

In short, the game of favors permits free women, in a socially acceptable context, by symbolic transformation, to assuage their sexual needs to at least some small extent, and, in some cases, if they wish, to make advances to interesting males. There is no full satisfaction of female sexuality, of course, outside of the context of male dominance. I wondered what the free woman whose favor I wore would look like, stripped and in a collar. How would she look, how would she act, I wondered, if slave fires had been lit in her belly. I did not think she would then be distributing silken scarves to make known her needs to men. She must then do other things, such as putting a bondage knot in her hair, offering them wine or fruit, dancing naked before them, or kneeling before them, whimpering and whining for attention, licking and kissing at their feet and legs.

I saw again the woman in the collar, she who was stripped to the waist, she who had a brief bit of cloth tied about her hips. As our eyes met she looked away, quickly.

I took a step towards her and she turned hastily away, frightened, and began to make her way through the crowd. I followed her, indirectly, circling about. As I had expected, in a few moments she stopped and turned about, to see if I was following. She stood there, uncertainly, scanning the crowd, looking back the way she had come. Had she been pursued? She did not know. Then suddenly I stepped behind her and pulled her back against me. She could not move. She was as helpless, my hands upon her beauty, as one locked in one of the body cages of Tyros.

"Sir!" she said, frightened, stiffening.

"Sir?" I asked.

"Master!" she quickly said, correcting herself.

"You are a slave, aren't you?" I asked.

"Yes, of course!" she said.

"Of course, what?" I asked.

"Of course, Master!" she said.

"You have nice breasts," I said.

"Thank you, Master," she whispered.

I slid my hands down her body, to her waist, and hips, holding her all the while.

"You have a nice body," I said. "I think you would bring a good price on the slave block."

"Do you think so?" she asked, pleased.

"Yes," I said. "But what is this cloth at your hips?" I asked. "Its quality, incidentally, seems a bit too good to be accorded to a mere slave." My hands, reaching about her, fumbled at the strings on her left hip.

"Do not remove it," she begged, "please! Please!"

My hands paused.

"As you are a mere slave," I said, "what possible difference could it make?"

"Please," she begged.

"Very well," I said. I removed my hands from the string, but held her in place, facing away from me, by the waist.

"May I turn around?" she asked.

"No," I said.

She shuddered with pleasure, commanded, placed under the will of another.

"There are doubtless slavers in the piazza tonight," I said. "If you do not want the collar, you should not court it."

"As I am only a mere slave," she said, "I could not possibly begin to understand the words of Master."

She cried out as I, half spinning her about, tore the cloth from her hips.

"It seems your master forgot to brand you," I said.

She snatched back the cloth and, angrily, tearing it and pulling it, refastened it about her hips.

"Take me to a pleasure rack," she said.

"You are a free woman," I said. "Go yourself."

"Never! Never!" she said. "You know I cannot do that!"

"Master," said a voice. "I am a slave. Take me to a pleasure rack!"

I looked down. Kneeling on the tiles of the piazza at my feet was a naked slave.

"I have not forgotten your kiss," she said. "Take me to a pleasure rack, I beg you!"

I remembered her. She was the naked, collared slave who, a few moments ago, had seized me and kissed me. I had returned her kiss, in the fashion of a master.

"I have sought you in the crowds," she said.

The free woman cried out in fury.

I reached down and drew the slave to her feet and then, holding her by the arm, turned away from the free woman.

The free woman gasped, rejected, scorned, of less interest than a slave.

The slave now held my arm, I permitting it, closely, that she not be pulled away from me in the crowds.

"This is not the way to the pleasure racks," she said.

"You must be patient," I said.

"Yes, Master," she moaned, pressing more closely against me. She would be patient. She had no choice in the matter. She was a slave.

I looked back and saw the free woman, turned away, forlorn, her arms clutched about herself, half crouched over. Her body shook with sobs. She trembled with need. I saw that she had strong drives. I smiled. Such drives would bring her, sooner or later, to a man's feet, the only place they can be satisfied.

I paused to watch a portion of a farce. I would let the girl clinging to me increase in her heat.

The girl playing the part of the Golden Courtesan was not unlike Rowena, whom I remembered from three nights ago in the holding of Samos. She had something of the same beauty, the same figure, the same long, golden tresses. The role of the Golden Courtesan, incidentally, when it occurs in more sophisticated Gorean comedy is usually played, like the other roles in such comedies, and in most forms of serious drama, masked. One possible reason for this, though I think tradition probably has much more to do with it, is that such roles in more sophisticated comedy, like roles in more serious drama, are generally played by men. In the major dramatic forms Goreans generally, mistakenly, in my opinion, keep women off the stage. Some feel this practice is a result of the fact that women's voices carry less well than men's voices in the open-air theaters. Given the superb acoustics of many of these theaters, however, in which a coin dropped on the stage is clearly audible in the upper tiers, I feel the practice is more closely connected with tradition, or jealousy, than acoustics. Too, it might be noted that many dramatic masks have megaphonic devices built into them which tend to amplify the actors' voices. If women are generally precluded from participation in the major dramatic forms, they are, however, more than adequately represented in the great variety of minor forms which exist on Gor, such as low comedy, burlesque, mime, farce and story dance. To be sure, these women are usually slaves. Free women, on the whole, affect to find the professional stage, particularly in its manifestations in the minor forms, unspeakably disgusting and indecent; they feign horror at the very thought of themselves going on the stage; would it not be horrifying to be so scandalously exhibited; it would be much the same thing, surely, as being displayed publicly on a slave platform or a slave block. They usually attend performances incognito.

I have mentioned that masks are commonly worn in serious drama and sophisticated comedy, such as it is; I might also mention that they are not worn in most of the minor forms, such as mime or story dance, unless called for by the plot, as in the case of brigands, and so on; farce, on the other hand, represents an interesting case for in it some characters commonly wear masks and others do not; the Comic Father, the Pedant, usually depicting a member of the Scribes, and the Timid Captain, for example, are usually masked, whereas the young lovers, the Golden Courtesan, the Desirable Heiress, and others, are not. Some roles, those of saucy free maids, comic servants, and such, may or may not be masked, depending on the troupe. As you may have gathered many of the characters in Gorean comedy and in the minor forms are, for the most part, stock characters. Again and again one meets pompous merchants, swaggering soldiers, fortune tellers, parasites, peasants and slaves.

These stock characters are well known to Gorean audiences and welcomed by them. For example, the Pompous Merchant and the Wily Peasant are well known. The audience is already familiar with them, from numerous performances in dozens of plays and farces, many of them largely improvised around certain standard types of situations. They know generally how the characters will act and are fond of them. They are familiar even with mannerisms and dialects. Who would accept the Comic Father if he did not have his Turian accent, or the Desirable Heiress if she did not speak in the soft accents of Venna, north of Ar? What would the Timid Captain be if he did not, beneath his long-nosed half-mask, have those fierce mustaches to twirl, the formidable wooden sword dragging behind him? Even gestures and grimaces are well known, looked for, and eagerly awaited. This type of familiarity, of course, gives the actor a great deal to build on. The character, even before he greets the audience in the initial parade of the actors, is for most practical purposes established, and in rich, complex detail; furthermore it is anticipated with relish and welcomed with affection. This being the case it is interesting to note that one actor's Merchant is not the same Merchant as that of another actor. Somehow, within the outlines of the role, and the traditional business associated with it, these actors manage to make their versions unique and special onto themselves. I suspect that there are no purely interpretative arts; all arts, I suspect, are ultimately creative.

"Please, Master," whimpered the girl holding my arm, pressing herself against me. "Please, Master."

I looked to one side, to the ground at the side of the raised platform. Two girls were there, standing back, waiting. Judging from the brevity of their bell-like skirts, given that shape doubtless by a lining of crinoline, and their bare arms, with puffed, short sleeves, I took them to be Saucy Maidens, probably a Bina and a Brigella. The Brigella, in particular, was lovely. I had little doubt if I should tip those skirts to the side I should encounter slave brands. The skirts, incidentally, are made to tip. This is utilized in various sorts of stage business. For example, one comic servant may pretend to inadvertently drop larmas, one by one, off a platter, which the girl, one by one, bends over to retrieve, another servant behind her. Then, while the girl chides them for their clumsiness, they change places and, to her feigned exasperation, repeat the trick. The skirt may also be lifted up, for example, by the wily Peasant, reportedly looking for a lost ox, and so on. The audience, of course, generally has the same preferred coign of vantage as the lucky servant or the Wily Peasant.

With the two girls was a rather paunchy, harassed-looking fellow, with long sideburns and a rimless cap. Another fellow, a sailmaker, I think, was negotiating with him for his Golden Courtesan. The paunchy fellow was shaking his head. He did not wish, surely, to sell her off the stage during a performance. The sailmaker was willing to wait. Then it seemed that the paunchy fellow, though sorely tempted, decided to hold on to the girl. Doubtless he needed the money, but what would he do without a Golden Courtesan? She probably also played the role of the Desirable Heiress. The same girl is often used for both roles. I looked back to the stage. The Golden Courtesan was probably unaware that she had nearly changed hands.

"Master," whimpered the girl beside me.

"Kneel," I told her.

"Yes, Master," she moaned, and knelt beside me. I did not wish her to interrupt the performance.

I looked back to the paunchy fellow and saw him, with his swaying belly, looking out into the crowd, somewhat apprehensively. The two girls with him, the Bina and the Brigella, seemed somewhat ill at ease, too.

I returned my attention to the stage.

The Golden Courtesan, facing away, was now feigning indifference to the suits of both the Comic Father and the Pedant. Two servants, Lecchio and Chino, are also in attendance. Chino, usually the servant of the Comic Father or the Merchant, is willowy and mischievous, with a black half-mask, with slanted eye holes, with red-and-yellow diamond-figured tights and pullover. Lecchio, usually the servant of the Pedant, is short and fat, a willing dupe of Chino and a sharer in his fun. He wears a brown tunic with a hood which he sometimes pulls over his head to hide embarrassment. The Comic Father and the Pedant pursue their suits. Chino and Lecchio conspire. Chino kicks the Comic Father and then looks away, studying clouds. In a moment Lecchio kicks the Pedant. This is repeated several times. Soon the Comic Father and the Pedant, each thinking the other is the assailant, are in furious controversy. It seems they will fight. Chino, followed by Lecchio, points out that their rich garments might be soiled, that their wallets might even be lost in such a scuffle. The Comic Father and the Pedant then give their robes and wallets to the servants and begin to berate one another and pull beards. The servants, of course, immediately don the garments and, swinging the wallets on their strings, meaningfully parade in front of the Golden Courtesan who, of course, taking them for rich suitors, goes away with them. The Comic Father and the Pedant, now without their robes and wallets, soon discover the trick. Crying out they give chase to the servants.

The girl kneeling beside me held my leg and pressed her cheek against my thigh. She kissed me. She looked up at me. "Please take me to a pleasure rack, Master," she said.

"Be patient," I told her.

"Yes, Master," she moaned.

The next performance, following on the heels of the first, was a love-potion farce, a form of farce with many variations. In this one the principal characters were the Golden Courtesan, Chino, the Merchant and the Pedant. The Merchant was played by the harassed, paunchy-looking fellow I had seen earlier. The Pedant, this time, was depicted not as a member of the Scribes but as a member of the Physicians. In brief, the Merchant, intending to visit the Golden Courtesan, sends Chino for a love potion. Chino, of course, obtains not a love potion but a powerful laxative from the Physician. The Merchant takes the potion and visits the Golden Courtesan, with Chino in attendance. Predictably, the Merchant must continually interrupt his initial advances which, of course, are bumbling and clumsy, and not much to the liking of the courtesan, to rush hastily to the side of the stage where, conveniently, may be found a great pot. Chino, meanwhile, exaggeratedly, in these interstices, is assuring the courtesan of the merchant's prowess as a lover. He is so successful that the courtesan soon begins to pant and call the merchant, who, eagerly, rushes back, only in a moment, unfortunately, to be forced to beat a new retreat to the pot. Chino then again begins to reassure the confused, uncertain courtesan. Soon he is demonstrating, even, with caresses and kisses, all in the name of the merchant, just how skillful the merchant would be. The courtesan becomes more and more helpless and excited. Meanwhile the Physician comes by to check up on the efficacy of his potion. His conversation with the merchant provides ample opportunity for *double-entendres* and talking at cross-purposes. The physician, in departing, puzzled that the potion has not yet taken effect, assures the merchant, sitting on the great pot, that he should allow it a little more time, that doubtless he will soon feel its effects. The merchant, however, convinced that this is not his day, now hobbles home, clutching the great pot. Chino grins and shrugs. He then leaps upon the Golden Courtesan. The time, after all, has been paid for.

In a moment the actors had returned to the stage, bowing. With them, too, were some of the actors from the earlier farces, usually presented in rounds of four or five. Some tarsk bits rattled to the boards. These were gathered in by the Chino and Lecchio. The Bina and Brigella, too, were now passing through the crowd with copper bowls. They were both very lovely, in particular, the Brigella. Such girls, like the other actresses with a small troupe, usually serve also as tent girls. It helps the troupe to meet expenses. I placed a tarsk bit in the bowl of the Brigella. "Thank you, Master," she said.

The paunchy fellow, his belly swinging, now out of character as the merchant, was informing the audience that a new round of farces, all different, would be performed within the Ahn. I saw his eyes momentarily cloud and, glancing back, I think I detected a possible cause for his distress. In the crowd was an officer of the Master of Revels, with two members of the Council Guard.

I drew the girl beside me to her feet. "Oh, yes," she breathed, "now," holding me, pressing her naked, collared beauty piteously against me, "take me to a pleasure rack. Now, please. I am so ready. I am so hot!"

"Not yet," I told her.

I then bought her a pastry from a vendor. "Eat it," I told her, "slowly, very slowly. Make it last a long time."

"Yes, Master," she said.

When a woman is ordered to eat a pastry in this fashion, she knows that she is barely to touch it, and then only once in a while, with her small teeth. Rather, primarily, almost entirely, she is to address herself to it with her tongue. This puts her under a good discipline, is a good exercise for the tongue and tends to increase sexual heat. In the case of the free woman the tongue is usually something which serves rather conventional purposes, for example, it helps her to talk. In the case of the slave girl, however, it serves other purposes, as well.

I moved along the front of the stage, through the crowd, the slave, the pastry clutched in her hands, at my elbow.

I paused only a yard or two from the end of the stage, before a kaissa booth.

I saw a large figure walking by. It might have stalked off one of the long, narrow, roofed stages of Ar, such as serve commonly for serious drama, spectacle and high comedy. It wore the *cothornoi*, a form of high platformlike boots, a long robe padded in such a way as to suggest an incredible breadth of shoulder, a large, painted linen mask, with exaggerated features, which covered the entire head, and the *onkos*, a towering, imposing headdress. Such costumes are often used by major characters in serious dramas. This exaggeration in size and feature, I take it, is intended to be commensurate with their importance. They are, at any rate, made to seem larger than life. I did not know if the fellow were an actor or simply someone adopting such a costume, all in the fun of carnival. As he walked away I noted that the mask had a different expression on the back. That device, not really very common in such masks, makes possible a change of expression without having recourse to a new mask.

A fellow, a pulley-maker I recognized from the arsenal, and the arsenal kaissa champion, rose to his feet, from where he had been sitting cross-legged before the kaissa board in the kaissa booth. "A marvelous game," he said, rubbing his head, bewildered. "I was humiliated. I was devastated. I do not even know how he did it. In fourteen moves he did it! In fourteen moves he captured three pieces and it would have been capture of Home Stone on the next! Perhaps there were illegal moves. Perhaps I did not see everything he did!"

"Try another game," encouraged the paunchy fellow, he who had been associated with the stage and who, it seemed, had an interest also in the kaissa booth. "Perhaps your luck will change!"

But the pulley-maker, almost reeling, made his way away, through the crowds.

"Why did you do that?" asked the paunchy fellow of the man sitting behind the board.

"He thought he knew how to play kaissa," said the man behind the board.

"How much have you taken in tonight?" asked the paunchy fellow, angrily, pointing to the copper, lidded pot, with the coin slot cut in its top, chained shut, near the low kaissa table.

The fellow behind the table began to move the pieces about on the board.

The paunchy fellow seized up the pot. He shook it, assessing its contents. "Four, five tarsk bits?" he asked. Judging from the timing and the sounds of the coins bounding about inside the pot there was not much there.

"Three," said the fellow behind the board.

"You could have carried him for at least twenty moves," said the paunchy fellow. He replaced the copper coin pot, chained shut, beside the kaissa table.

"I did not care to do so," said the fellow behind the board.

Interestingly the man behind the board wore black robes and a hoodlike mask, also black, which covered his entire head. He did not wear the red-and-yellow-checked robes of the caste of players, He was not, thus, I assumed, of that caste. Had he been of the players he would doubtless have worn their robes. They are quite proud of their caste. His skills, however, I conjectured, must be considerable. Apparently the arsenal champion, one of the best twenty or thirty players in Port Kar, had been no match for him. Perhaps he had engaged in illegal moves. That seemed more likely than the fact that he, a fellow like him, associated with actors and carnival folk, and such, could best the arsenal champion. It was carnival time, of course. Perhaps the champion had been drunk,

"If the game is not interesting for them, if they do not think they are really playing, seriously, they will not want a second or a third game," said the paunchy fellow. "We want them to come back! We want the board busy! That is how we are making the money!"

The price for a game is usually something between a tarsk bit and a copper tarsk. If the challenger wins or draws, the game is free. Sometimes a copper tarsk, or even a silver tarsk, is nailed to one of the poles of the booth. It goes to the challenger if he wins and the game is free, if he draws. This is because a skillful player, primarily by judicious exchanges and careful position play, can often bring about a draw. Less risk is involved in playing for a draw than a win, of course. Conservative players, ahead in tournament play, often adopt this stratagem, using it, often to the fury of the crowds and their opponents, to protect and nurse an established lead. A full point is scored for a win; in a draw each player obtains a half point.

"You must manage to lose once in a while," said the paunchy fellow. "That will bring them back! That way, in the long run, we will make much more money!"

"I play to win," said the fellow, looking at the board.

"I do not know why I put up with you!" said the paunchy fellow. "You are only a roustabout and vagabond!"

I noted the configuration of pieces on the board. The hooded fellow had not begun from the opening position, arriving at that configuration after a series of moves. He had simply set the pieces up originally in that position. Something about the position seemed familiar. I suddenly realized, with a start, that I had seen it before. It was the position which would be arrived at on the seventeenth move of the Ubara's Gambit Declined, Yellow's Home Stone having been placed at Ubara's Builder One, providing red had, on the eleventh move, departed from the main line, transposing into the Turian line. Normally, at this point, one continues with the advancement of the Ubara's Initiate's Spearman, supporting the attack being generated on the adjacent file, that of the Ubara's Builder. He, however, advanced the Ubar's Initiate's Spearman in a two-square-option move, bringing it to Ubar's Initiate Five. I wondered if he knew anything about kaissa. Then, suddenly, the move seemed interesting to me. It would, in effect, launch a second attack, and one which might force yellow to bring pieces to the Ubar's side of the board, thereby weakening the position of the Ubara's Builder's File, making it more vulnerable, then, of course, to the major attack. It was an interesting idea. I wondered if it had ever been seriously played.

"You must learn to lose!" said the paunchy fellow.

"I have lost," said the hooded fellow. "I know what it is like."

"You, Sir," said the paunchy fellow turning to me, "do you play kaissa?"

"A little," I said.

"Hazard a game," he invited. "Only a tarsk bit!" He then glanced meaningfully at the hooded fellow, and then turned and again regarded me. "I can almost guarantee that you will win," he said.

"Why is your player hooded?" I asked. It did not seem the kind of disguising that might be appropriate for carnival.

"It is something from infancy, or almost from infancy," said the paunchy fellow, shuddering, "from flames, a great fire. It left him as he is, beneath the mask. He is a disfigured monster. Free women would swoon at the sight. The stomachs of strong men would be turned. They would cry out with horror and strike at him. Such grotesquerie, such hideousness, is not to be tolerated in public view."

"I see," I said.

"Only a tarsk bit," the paunchy fellow reminded me.

"Do not fear that you will not win," said the hooded fellow, in fury, placing the pieces in position for the opening of play. He then, imperiously, removed his Ubar, Ubara, and his Builders and Physicians, from the board, six major pieces. He looked angrily at me, and then, too, he threw his tarnsmen into the leather bag, with drawstrings, at the side of the table. He spun the board about so that I might have Yellow, and the first move. Thus I would have the initiative. Thus I could, in effect, for most purposes, choose my preferred opening. "Make your first move," he said. "I shall then tip my Ubar and the game will be yours."

"Can you not be somewhat more subtle?" inquired the paunchy fellow of the hooded man.

"I would not consider playing under such conditions," I said.

"Why not?" asked the paunchy fellow, pained. "You could then say truthfully that you had won. Others need not know the sort of game it was."

"It is an insult to kaissa," I said.

"He is right," said the hooded fellow.

The slave girl whimpered, looking up at me. The pastry, which she had been diminishing, bit by minuscule bit, flake by tiny, damp flake, with her tongue, was clutched in both her hands. As she ate thus, the placement of her arms constituted a provocative modesty, one terminable, of course, at my will. Similarly, her small, delicate wrists were close together, so close that they might have been linked by slave bracelets.

"Please, Master," she whimpered.

"Hazard a game," suggested the paunchy fellow.

I looked down into the eyes of the slave girl. She looked up at me, and slowly and sensuously, with exquisite care, licked at the sugary, white glazing on the pastry. She might be helpless with need, but I saw she had had training.

"I have another game in mind," I said.

She looked up at me, flakes of the pastry and glazing about her mouth, and kissed me. "I want to love you," she said. I tasted the sugar on her lips.

"I can understand such games," said the paunchy fellow. "It is pleasant to have a naked slave in one's arms."

"Yes," I agreed.

"Put them all in collars," he said. "Teach them what they are for, and about. No woman is worth anything until she is put in a collar. None of them have any worth until they are made worthless."

"What do you think?" I asked the slave.

"It is true, Master," she said.

"Now that fellow," said the paunchy fellow, gesturing to the hooded fellow, "is different from us. He lives only for kaissa. He does not so much as touch a woman. To be sure, it is probably just as well. They would doubtless faint with terror at the very sight of him."

"Do you wish to play, or not?" asked the hooded fellow, looking up at me.

"Under the conditions you propose," I said, "I would not accept a win from you, if you were Centius of Cos." Centius of Cos was perhaps the finest player on Gor. He had been the champion at the En'Kara tournaments three out of the last five years. In one of those years, 10,127 C.A., he had chosen not to compete, giving the time to study. In that year the champion had been Terence of Turia. In 10,128 C.A. Centius had returned but was defeated by Ajax of Ti, of the Salerian Confederation, who had overcome Terence in the semifinals. In 10,129 C.A., last En'Kara, Centius had decisively bested Ajax and recovered the championship.

At the mention of the name Centius of Cos, the hooded player had stiffened angrily. "I assure you I am not Centius of Cos," he said. He then, angrily, thrust the pieces into the leather bag, tied it to his belt, put the board under his arm, and, limping, withdrew.

"It is still early!" called the paunchy fellow after the hooded man. "Where are you going?"

But the hooded fellow had disappeared between the booths, going somewhere to the rear.

"I am sorry," I said. "I did not mean to upset him."

"Do not worry about it," said the paunchy fellow. "It is always happening. He is a touchy fellow, impetuous, arrogant and reckless. Doubtless the ground should be grateful that he deigns to tread upon it. His kaissa, on the other hand, seems strong. It is probably too good, really, for what we need."

"Perhaps he should apply for membership in the caste of players," I suggested.

"He does not seem interested in that," he said.

"Oh," I said.

"Besides, he is a grotesque monster," he said. "Even the slaves fear him."

"I understand," I said.

"Too, if he were really any good, honestly speaking, between you and me, he would not be with us."

"I see," I smiled. To be sure, there was more money to be made in the kaissa clubs and on the high bridges. It was interesting to me that the fellow had limped. I had once known a kaissa player who had done that. To be sure, it was long ago.

"Have you, yourself, ever played him?" I asked.

"No," said the fellow. "I do not play kaissa."

"I see," I said.

"You are Boots Tarsk-Bit?" asked a voice.

The voice came from behind us. The paunchy fellow with me turned white.

I turned about.

"Greetings, Captain," said the man.

"Greetings," said I to him. It was the officer of the Master of Revels. Behind him were the two members of the Council Guard.

"Hold," said the officer to the paunchy fellow, who, it seemed, had backed away, turned, and was about to disappear between the stage and the kaissa booth.

"Did you call?" asked the paunchy fellow, pleasantly, turning. A meaningful gesture from the officer, pointing to a spot in front of him, brought the paunchy fellow alertly back into our presence. "Yes?" he inquired, pleasantly.

"I believe you are Boots Tarsk-Bit," said the officer, "of the company of Boots Tarsk-Bit."

"He must be somewhere about," said the paunchy fellow. "If you like, I shall attempt to search him out for you."

"Hold," said the officer.

The paunchy fellow returned to the spot in front of the officer.

"That is he," said one of the guards with him.

"No offense meant, good sir," said the paunchy fellow. "A mere jest!"

"You are Boots Tarsk-Bit," said the officer, consulting an

inked handbill, clipped with other papers, "Actor, Entrepreneur, and Impresario, of the company of Boots Tarsk-Bit?"

"At your service," said the paunchy fellow, bowing low. "What may I do for you?"

The girl was now kneeling beside me, with her head down. She had assumed this position immediately upon the appearance of the officer and the guards.

"We are here in connection with the matter of a license," said the officer.

"Yes?" said the paunchy fellow, Boots Tarsk-Bit, pleasantly.

"Do you have one?" asked the officer.

"Would you care to come to my quarters?" asked Boots. "We have some lovely larmas there, and perhaps you and your men would like to try my Bina and Brigella."

"In the license," said the officer, "there is the provision that girls associated with companies such as yours, if slaves, may be commanded to the apartments and service of whomsoever the council, or a delegated officer of the council, directs."

"I scarcely ever read all the provisions of the licenses," said Boots. "Such things are so tedious."

"Do you have a license?" asked the officer.

"Of course!" said Boots, indignantly. "They are required, as is well known. No fellow with the least sense of ethics would think of being without one."

"May I see your license?" inquired the officer.

"Certainly," said Boots, fumbling about in his robes. "It is right here—somewhere." He examined his wallet. "Somewhere," he assured the officer. "Alas," he said, after the second ransacking of his robes, and his third examination of the wallet, "it must be in my quarters, perhaps in the wardrobe trunk. I shall return in a nonce. I trust that I shall not discover that I have been robbed!"

"Hold!" said the officer.

"Yes?" said Boots, turning back.

"According to our records," said the officer, "you have no license. You did not petition to perform, and you did not obtain a license.

"I remember distinctly obtaining the license!" said Boots.

The officer glared at him.

"Of course, it might have been last year," said Boots. "Or maybe the year before?"

The officer was silent.

"Could I have neglected such a detail?" asked Boots, horrified. "Could such a thing have slipped my mind? It seems impossible!"

"It is not really so hard to believe," observed the officer. "It has happened three years in a row."

"No!" cried Boots, in horror.

"It is folks like you who give scoundrels and rogues a bad name," said the officer.

"What are you writing?" asked Boots anxiously.

"A disposition order," said the officer.

"To what effect, may I inquire?" pressed Boots.

"Your properties," said the officer, "including your actresses, will be confiscated. They will look well in state chains. You yourself will be publicly flogged in the piazza, and then, for five years, banished from Port Kar."

"It is carnival time," I said to the officer.

"Captain?" he asked.

"What is owed?" I asked.

"The licensing fee is a silver tarsk," he said.

"Surely," I said to Boots Tarsk-Bit, "your players have taken in a silver tarsk?"

"No," he said. "We have, so far tonight, taken in only ninety-seven tarsk-bits, not even ten copper tarsks." Coinage on Gor varies considerably from city to city. In Port Kar, and generally in the Vosk Basin, there are ten tarsk bits to a copper tarsk and one hundred copper tarsks to a silver tarsk.

"Surely you have some money saved," I said.

"Not enough," he said. "We live from day to day. Sometimes there is nothing to eat."

"More than a silver tarsk is actually involved, Captain," said the officer. "There is the matter of the last two years, as well, considerations of interest, and the customary emoluments."

"I am ruined," said Boots Tarsk-Bit.

"Let us not be hasty, officer," I said. "Boots Tarsk-Bit is an old friend of mine, a friend from long ago."

Boots looked at me, startled. Then he nodded, earnestly. We had known one another for quite some time now, at least ten Ehn.

"If you wish, Captain," smiled the officer, "I shall not pursue the matter further." He knew me. He had been with the fleet on the 25th of Se'Kara.

"Boots, of course, as is well known," I said, "is an honest fellow."

Boots looked startled.

"He always pays his debts," I assured the officer.

"I do?" asked Boots. "I do!" he then said quickly, firmly, to the officer.

"So pay the man," I said.

"With what?" inquired Boots, speaking to me in an intense whisper.

"With your earnings," I told him.

"They are not even ten tarsks!" hissed Boots to me, his eyes bulging.

"Check the pots of your Bina and Brigella," I said.

"I have checked them," he said.

"Check them again," I said.

He turned away, and then turned back, to stoop down and pick up the copper pot by the kaissa table.

"Leave it," I said.

He shrugged and then, straightening up, took his leave.

"He will doubtless be back for it," smiled the officer.

"He cannot, in any event, escape from the city," said one of the guards.

I reached down and picked up the pot from beside the kaissa table.

I looked down at the slave kneeling on the tiles of the piazza beside me, naked and in her collar, clutching the pastry. "You may now eat the pastry,"I said. "You may now finish it."

"Thank you, Master, she said, happily. She had now been under my total command for something like half of an Ahn.

I put three silver tarsks into the pot. "These cover the licensing fees for three years," I said. I then put another silver tarsk into the pot. "This," I said, "should more than cover any interest due on the debts outstanding."

"More than enough," granted the officer.

"This tarsk," I then said, slipping it into the pot, "is for the Master of Revels."

"You are most generous, Captain," said the officer, impressed. "That is more than is normally expected."

"And this tarsk," I said, "is for you and your men."

"That is not necessary, Captain," protested the officer.

The coin dropped into the pot. "It is carnival," I smiled.

"Thank you, Captain," said the officer.

"Thank you, Captain," said the guards.

I replaced the copper pot beside the kaissa table.

I looked down at the slave. "Have you finished the pastry?" I asked.

"Yes, Master," she smiled.

"Clean your fingers. Suck and lick them," I said.

"Yes, Master," she said. I was growing hot for her. I must soon get her to a rack.

"It is no use, kind sirs," said Boots Tarsk-Bit, returning, carrying the two empty coin bowls. "They are empty."

"What of that pot?" asked the officer, indicating the one beside the kaissa table. "That contains earnings accruing to your troupe, does it not, from your kaissa booth?"

"Alas, it contains only three tarsk bits," lamented Boots Tarsk-Bit.

"Do you trust him?" asked the officer of one of the guards.

"Not I, Sir," responded the guard.

"Open it," said the officer.

"Very well," shrugged Boots. Then, as he picked up the kettle, a strange look suddenly came over his face. He shook it. From within it came the unmistakable clink of several coins.

Feverishly he drew a key out of his wallet. In a moment he had unlocked the padlock on the chain and drawn it, sliding through the handles, rattling, free. He removed the lid from the kettle.

"Sly scamp, rotund rogue," scolded the officer. "You have been holding out on us."

Boots, his eyes wide, sorted through the coins in the pot.

"What is there?" asked the officer.

"Three tarsk bits," said Boots, "—and five silver tarsks."

"Three silver tarsks for licensing fees, present and past, one for interest, and one for the Master of Revels," said the officer.

Boots counted out the coins and handed them to the officer.

"Is there nothing for myself and my men?" asked the officer.

Boots drew the last silver tarsk out of his sleeve and, sheepishly, handed it to the officer. I had not seen him place it there. He had done it very skillfully.

The girl at my feet now held my leg in her arms and kissed at my leg, whimpering.

"It seems a slave is ready for pleasure," grinned the officer, looking at me.

"Perhaps," I said, as though nonchalantly.

"The rack, Master," she whimpered. "Please take me to a rack!"

"I see that you wear the favor of a free woman," observed the officer. He referred to the rich, light, colorful scarf thrust through the eyelet of my robes.

"Yes," I said. I recalled the richly robed, veiled, wheedling free woman whom I had permitted to place it there. What a churl I would have been, considering how prettily she had begged, and she a free woman, not to have accepted it.

"Take me to the rack, Master, please, I beg it!" said the girl at my feet.

"I see that you, too, have accepted the favor of a free woman," I said.

"Yes," he said, grinning. The favor he wore was different from mine, both in border and color. In the game of Favors, of course, the favors are supposedly unique to the given woman, in pattern, material, texture, color, shape, decoration, and so forth. If they were not unique in this fashion they could not act as practical counters in the game. Similarly, of course, they would be less efficient in manifesting the results of the deeper competitions involved, those competitions in which women desperately strive against one another, each to prove themselves more desirable to men than the others. Each woman desires to be more pleasing to men than the others. This is significant. It is in their nature.

"It is interesting to me that free women play the game of Favors," I said.

"It gives them a way of flirting," he said. "Too it gives them an opportunity to put themselves, in a way, at the mercy of the male, to engage in petitioning behavior, suing for his indulgence. In this it is not difficult to see a form of symbolic submission, a making of themselves dependent on his will. Too, of course, it gives them a way of testing their desirability and publicly proclaiming, or advertising, it."

"Luscious, vain creatures," I observed. I myself had earlier speculated along these lines. To be sure, the game of Favors, like most games, customs and practices, was undoubtedly complex and multiply motivated. Too, sometimes things take on additional meanings and values as they are enriched in a historical tradition or more deeply or variously interpreted in different contexts.

"It also, of course, gives them a way of establishing rankings among themselves," said the officer, "which is probably about the best they can do until they find themselves enslaved, put naked on blocks and priced."

"I agree," I said. That certain games, such as that of Favors, provided a mechanism for establishing desirability rankings among females, something in which they seemed much interested, seemed clear.

"What do you think of free women?" asked the officer.

"I didn't know there were any, really," I said. Goreans have a theory that there are only two sorts of women, slaves and slaves.

"You know what I mean," he said.

"I suppose they are all right," I said. They were all right, I supposed.

"Slaves are incomparably superior," he said.

"That is true," I said. There was no comparison.

"Please, Master, take me to a rack," begged the girl at my feet.

Freedom, with its inhibitions, inertnesses and hostilities, tends to produce a blockage to the emergence of the depth female. In bondage this blockage is removed, freeing the woman to find her natural fulfillment, her fulfillment in the order of nature, that of a slave at the feet of her master.

"Please, Master," begged the girl. "I beg to be taken to a rack."

I pulled her by the arm to her feet.

"Happy carnival," I said to the officer.

"Happy carnival!" said he.

"Happy carnival," said I to Boots Tarsk-Bit.

"Happy carnival," said he.

I thrust the slave ahead of me, and we pressed through the crowds. In a few Ehn we had crossed the piazza and come to the racks. There were two sorts, refined, adjustable strap racks, with beddings of flat, soft, criss-crossed straps, with sturdy stud-and-eyelet securing straps, and simple net racks, little more than sturdy wooden frames within which was slung a netlike webbing of rope. In these racks, if one wishes to secure the woman within the webbing, simple cords are used. There were also some trestles. I took the slave to one of the net racks. The strap racks were all in use.

I saw the free woman who had worn the brief cloth about her hips near the racks.

I threw the slave on her belly on the netting and then turned her to her back. I had her place her wrists and ankles through the netting in certain fashions. I did not bother securing her in position. I then joined her on the netting. In moments, gasping, looking at me wildly, gratefully, she was in the throes of slave orgasm. To arouse a free woman to the point of orgasm, even the sort of which she is capable, takes, usually, from a third to a quarter of an Ahn. The reflexes of the slave, on the other hand, for psychological reasons, and because of her training, can be much more easily, profoundly and frequently activated. This is not really surprising. The free woman, after all, is a free woman, and the slave is a slave.

"Buy me," said the slave, intensely. "You have money. Buy me, please! I will serve you well!"

I kissed her, and withdrew from her; in a moment I stood beside the rack, adjusting my robes.

"May I break position, Master?" she asked.

"Yes," I said.

She removed her hands and feet from the netting, slipped from the rack and came to kneel before me. She put down her head, and kissed my feet. The marks of the rope, where she had lain on the netting, were on her body. She then looked up at me. "I did not mean to be forward, before," she said. "Please, forgive me. Beat me, if you wish."

I lifted her to her feet, and kissed her. "It is all right," I said.

She looked at me.

"Go, seek out your own master," I said. "See that you give him even more pleasure than you did me."

"Yes, Master," she smiled, and turned, disappearing into the crowd. A slave girl's first duty is to her own master.

"Paga?" invited a fellow, reeling by.

We exchanged swigs from our botas, I from his, he from mine.

I saw the free woman standing, watching, she with the brief bit of cloth about her hips. I looked at her. It was interesting, I thought, that she had now come to the vicinity of the pleasure racks. Our eyes met. I looked imperiously to the rack. She shrank back, in terror. When I looked back again she was half crouched over, her head in her hands, her body shaken with fear and sobs. I then left the area of the racks. It was about that time that I caught sight, once again, of Henrius and Vina. In a small space, with Henrius and some men about, to the music of some nearby musicians, the men clapping and keeping time, she was dancing. She did well. She might have been a nude, leashed, harnessed street dancer, one of the lowest forms of dancer on Gor. Soon, I suspected, Henrius would take her to a rack, or perhaps back to his holding. She was an incredibly lovely young slave, and loved him from the depths of her heart. Her perspiration had run in trickles through the paint on her body. I watched her for a moment. How real and alive she was, the slave.

I turned away, troubled by some thought, but I could not, at the moment, determine what it was. It was now growing late and I thought that perhaps I should consider returning to my holding. It was then that I recalled my earlier conversation with Henrius. He had told me that someone was looking for me. I wondered who this might be. Perhaps it had to do with Samos. Surely

Samos, the last time I had been in his holding, had been evasive.
Someone wished to see me, as I recalled, in Booth Seventeen. I
turned my steps, curious as to what might be involved, toward
the purple booths. The purple booths are normally maintained by
slavers, used as locations in which girls, usually higher-quality
slaves, more expensive merchandise, may be inspected and tried
by bonafide buyers or their agents. Such booths are usually set
up in the courtyards of slavers' houses and at special times,
generally in the neighborhood of holidays and festivals. At other
times, of course, such girls may be examined and tested in
private chambers in the slavers' houses. The purple booths set up
now in the piazza, however, had to do with the time of carnival.
They were, in effect, good-will and promotional devices, do-
nated to the festivities, for the pleasures of free men, by the
houses of various slavers. The house of Samos, for example,
provided the first five booths, each complete with its furnishings,
including a charming occupant. His fifth booth, as I had heard,
contained the slave, Rowena. He wished to bring her along
quickly. As I recalled, he intended to soon sell her, with several
others, at the Fair of En'Kara, near the Sardar. Some men think
that the girls in the public purple booths are much the same as
those vended from the private purple booths on other occasions.
Generally, however, as most men know, this is not the case. For
example, Rowena was a new slave. Thus, even though she was
very beautiful, she would probably not, in virtue of her
inexperience, even be considered for a private-booth showing for
several months or a year. It takes time for a girl to develop
adequate skills.

I walked along the line of the booths until I came to Booth
Seventeen. Most of the booths had the curtains drawn, and the
lining of the booths and curtains is usually opaque. In two booths
the threshold curtains were partly open. In one I saw a slave,
naked, writhing slowly in chains before a man, his hands upon
her. In another I saw a slave and her lover-master of the moment
in one another's arms, half off the large, soft cushion on which
the slave, customarily, kneeling, in obeisance, greets the booth's
entrant. Outside most of the booths two or three men were
waiting. Interestingly enough, on Booth Seventeen, there was a
sign pinned on the front of the booth, near the entrance curtain.
It said, "Closed." The curtain itself was drawn shut, but it did
not appear, from the look of it, from its lack of tautness, to be
secured from the inside. I looked about. There were men about,
some with carnival masks, but none seemed concerned with this
booth. I waited outside the booth for a few moments. No one,

however, approached me. To be sure, I was supposed to meet the individual in Booth Seventeen, according to what Henrius had been told. I wondered who had spoken to him. I wondered if this matter had to do with Priest-Kings. To be sure, it seemed mysterious. Any normal business, I supposed, would have been conducted in more normal fashions.

I brushed aside the curtain and entered the booth, permitting the curtain, not much drawn on its rings, to fall shut behind me. A small tharlarion-oil lamp lit the interior of the booth. The booth was the only one furnished by the house of Vart, once Publius Quintus of Ar, a minor slaver in Port Kar. I had not seen him around outside. I wondered why the booth was closed. He had perhaps rented the space to someone for an Ahn or so. Perhaps the whole matter was a mistake. On the large cushion, soft, and some five feet in diameter, toward the back of the booth, there lay a small, lovely body. It was a tiny, luscious redhead. She lay terribly still, extremely still. I approached her and, crouching down beside her, put my fingertips to the side of her throat, by the collar. She was alive. I pulled her to a seated position on the cushion and smelled her mouth and lips, and, gently, carefully, delicately, touched her lips with my tongue. I detected nothing. There was a smear of Ka-la-na wine at the left side of her mouth. Tassa powder had doubtless been used on her. It is traceless, and effective. I did not think she would awaken for hours. The lamp flickered slightly. Her wrists had been thonged behind her; her ankles, too, had been crossed and thonged. The thongs were narrow, dark and tight. I put her back on the cushion.

I jerked my body suddenly to the side, to evade the grasping left arm, seeking to hold the target in place for the short, low right-handed thrust of the knife, or the throat attack, if the assailant was right-handed, and of the assassins or the warriors. The small tharlarion-oil lamp had been placed in such a way that no shadow would be cast by it of a figure entering through the curtain. Warriors notice such things. Too, in permitting the curtain to fall shut behind me, I had not interfered with the natural closure of the booth. Had it not closed in this fashion I would have adjusted it shut. It is difficult to move such a curtain, heavy and lined as it is, customary in purple booths, without a rustle of fabric, or the scraping of one or more of the rings. Too, of course, the air in the booth changes slightly as the curtain is moved, admitting it. The flame of the tiny lamp had flickered, too, in this shifting of air. The knife and arm, however, descending, passed over my body. The high stroke has various

disadvantages. It begins from farther back and thus makes it
difficult to use the left hand or arm to secure the target. It is
easier to block. It does not have the same power as the short
blow. The blade that has only six inches to move, with a full
weight behind it, other things being equal, effects a deeper
penetration than a blade which must move farther and has behind
it primarily the weight of a shoulder and arm. Too, of course,
the stab from a shorter distance at closer range, point-blank
range, so to speak, is likely to be more accurate. The target,
after the initiation of the blow, even if it is not held in place, has
very little time, given the mathematics of reflexes, to shift its
position. My assailant, I gathered, was neither of the assassins or
warriors.

I rolled to the side, my hand going instinctively for the blade
in my sheath, but the sheath, the weapon earlier surrendered at
the check point through which I had entered the piazza, was
empty. The man adjusted quickly, very quickly. He was fast. He
wore a half mask. The blade had cut into the cushion. Before I
could rise to my feet he was upon me. We grappled. I caught his
wrist, turning the blade inward. Suddenly he relaxed. I left the
blade in him. I was breathing heavily. I pulled away the half
mask. He was the fellow whom I had seen at the check point.
Too, we had spoken together near the magician's stage.

I rifled through his robes. I could find no identification.
Probably he had seen me throw the golden tarn disk to the stage.
His motivation, doubtless, had been robbery. Yet I had seen him
earlier at the check point. That could have been a coincidence, I
supposed. I opened his wallet. It was filled with golden staters,
from Brundisium, a port on the coast of Thassa, on the mainland,
a hundred pasangs or so south of the Vosk's delta, one reported
to have alliances with Ar. Robbery, then, did not seem a likely
motivation. I knew little about Brundisium. Supposedly it had
relations with Ar. I wondered if this were the fellow who had
arranged to meet with me in Booth Seventeen. I did not think
Vart, the slaver whose booth this was, was likely to be involved.
He had probably just rented the booth. If he was involved he
would have been stupid to use his own booth. Too, I suspected
he had little love for Ar, and perhaps thus for Brundisium. He
had once been banished from Ar, and nearly impaled, for the
falsification of slave data, misrepresenting merchandise as to its
level of training and skill.

I, too, had once been denied salt, bread and fire in Ar, and
banished from the city. I did not think, however, that Marlenus,
of Ar, her Ubar, he who had banished me, would be likely to

send a covert assassin from Brundisium against me, from Brundisium perhaps to make the connection with Ar seem unlikely or tenuous. If he wished to have it out with me, presumably he would do so, with his own blade. Marlenus was too direct and proud for such deviousness. Too, we were not really enemies. Too, if he had wished to send an assassin against me, presumably he would have done so long ago. Too, the fact that the staters in the fellow's wallet were from Brundisium did not mean that he himself was from that city. Anyone might have paid him in the staters of Brundisium. What enemies did I have? Perhaps, after all, robbery was the fellow's motivation.

I shuddered. I did not understand what had happened. I did not like what had happened.

I looked to the slave. I turned her to her belly on the cushion, putting her head to the side. I was disturbed, shaken and tense. I untied her ankles. Too, I had made a kill. I must calm myself. It is one of the things women are for. She whimpered, pounded, her small hands twisting in the tight leather thongs. I then tied her ankles together again, and then, this time, fastened her wrists to her ankles. I then tied the wallet, filled with the golden staters of Brundisium, about her collar. That would give Vart some consolation, I suspected, for the scandal he would find in his booth.

"Tarl," I heard, a voice speaking softly, outside the curtain. It was the voice of Samos.

"Enter," I said.

"I have been looking all over for you," he said. "I saw Henrius. He suggested you might be here." Samos' eyes opened widely. "What is going on here?" he asked. "Who is that?"

"Do you know him?" I asked.

"No," said Samos, examining the body.

"He tried to kill me," I said.

"Why?" he asked. "The slave?"

"No," I said. "I think perhaps robbery."

"His robes seem rich," said Samos.

"In his wallet were several staters, of gold, from Brundisium," I said.

"That is a valuable stater," said Samos. "It has good weight."

"He knew I was carrying gold," I said. "I had given evidence of this in rewarding a magician in the carnival."

"Even so," said Samos, "it would seem, from what you say, that he stood in no need of money."

"I do not think so," I said. "Yet robbery seems the only likely explanation."

"I do not know," said Samos. "Perhaps you are right."

"You sound doubtful," I observed.

"Thieves, my friend," said Samos, "seldom carry gold on their persons."

"Perhaps he had stolen it this evening," I said.

"No considerable theft has been reported this evening," said Samos, "as far as I know. It was not in the recent reports of the guards."

"Perhaps he slew the individual from whom he stole the coins and then thrust the body into a canal," I suggested.

"Perhaps," said Samos. "But his mode of garb does not suggest that of the elusive, quick-moving thief."

"It might make it easier to approach a victim," I suggested.

"Perhaps," said Samos.

"Too, robes would make it easier to get a knife through the check points at carnival," I said.

"Perhaps," said Samos.

"You do not seem convinced," I said.

"I am not," said Samos.

"This booth is closed," I said. "I gather that you did not rent it and close it."

"No," said Samos.

"Henrius," I said, "told me that someone wished to see me here."

"Was that before this fellow saw you throw gold to the magician?" asked Samos.

"No," I said. "Afterwards."

"Perhaps that is the explanation, then," said Samos.

"I do not think so," I said. "It was really not very long after I left the magician's platform that I saw Henrius. I do not think it likely that the arrangement could have been made that quickly. Too, Henrius, as I recall, did not speak as though he had just been contacted."

"He did not deny it, either, did he?" asked Samos.

"No," I said. "But if the fellow was a stranger, a common thief, how would he be likely to know my name, or of any connection between myself and Henrius, or others?"

"That is true," said Samos.

"The booth, too, presumably would have to be rented, and the slave drugged," I said.

"I see," said Samos. "It seems likely then, if he is a common thief, that he would have merely followed you here, and is not the fellow who spoke to Henrius, or who would be connected with the booth in some way."

"Yes," I said, "but then who would have rented the booth, who would have wanted to see me here?"

"What have we there?" asked Samos, gesturing to the girl, bound hand and foot on the cushion, the wallet tied at her collar.

"A drugged slave," I said.

"Was she unconscious when you entered the booth?"

"Yes," I said.

"Then she probably would not be able to give helpful witness," he said.

"She might know who drugged her," I said.

"Presumably she would only know that it was some fellow in a mask," said Samos. "Too, it may very well have been done to her by her master, Vart, whose booth this is, he doing this under instructions."

"We could contact Vart," I said.

"The fellow to whom he rented the booth would presumably have been masked," said Samos. "It is, after all, carnival time. I doubt that Vart would be able to help us. Besides he is not noted, anyway, for his excessive concern for scrupulosity in his business dealings."

"What, then, do you think?" I asked.

"The signs, it seems to me," said Samos, "suggest a calculated ambush and one in which your friend here was probably implicated."

"I agree," I said. "You are thinking, then, in terms of a carefully planned robbery?"

"Not really," said Samos. "All things considered, such as the coins in his wallet, robbery seems to me, at least, to be a very unlikely motive for this attack."

"What could have been the possible motivation then?" I asked.

"I do not know," he said. "Who do you know who might wish to have this done?" he asked.

"I do not know," I said. "What did you wish to see me about?"

His face clouded.

"You wish to speak to me," I said.

"Yes," he said.

"Let us leave the booth," I suggested.

"No," he said. "Not now. I must speak to you privately in any case. This place is as good as any. Then we will leave the booth separately. It would not be good for us to be seen together at this time."

"Why not?" I asked.

"I fear spies," he said.

"The spies of Kurii?" I asked.

"No," he said.

"Of whom, then?" I asked, puzzled.

"Of Priest-Kings," he said.

"I do not understand," I said, puzzled.

"I think there is a new order in the Sardar," he said. "I suspect it."

"That is possible," I granted him. I remembered the tale of Yngvar, the Far-Traveled.

"Twice, rather recently, I have heard from the Sardar," he said, "once some ten days ago, and once yesterday."

"What is the import of these messages?" I inquired.

"They pertain to the arrest and detention of one who is reputed to be an enemy of Priest-Kings."

"Who is he?" I inquired. "Perhaps I can be of assistance in his apprehension."

"His name," said Samos, "is Tarl Cabot."

"That is absurd!" I said.

"When the first message arrived, some days ago, I was certain there was some grievous error involved. I sent back to the Sardar for confirmation, if only to buy time."

"It is no wonder you were so uneasy when I was in your holding," I said.

"I wanted to speak to you," he said, "but did not know if I should do so. I thought it best, finally, not to do so. If the whole thing turned out to be a mistake, as I was sure it would, we could then, at a later date, no harm done, have a fine laugh over the matter."

"But yesterday," I said, "the confirmation arrived."

"Yes," he said, "and the terms of the orders are unmistakable."

"What are you going to do?" I asked. "I am unarmed. Doubtless you have men outside."

"Do not be silly," he said. "We are friends and we have stood together with blades before enemies. I would betray Priest-Kings before I would betray you."

"You are a brave man," I said, "to risk the wrath of Priest-Kings."

"The most they can take is my life," he said, "and if I were to lose my honor, even that would be worthless."

"What are you going to do?" I asked.

"I am sure," he said, "that this whole business is founded on some mistake, that it can be rectified, but the orders are clear. But I will need time."

"What are you going to do?" I asked.

"I shall send a report to the Sardar tomorrow," he said, "dated tomorrow. I shall inform the Sardar that I am unable to carry out their orders for I am unable to locate you, that you have apparently left the city."

"I see," I said.

"In the meantime," he said, "I shall press for further clarifications, and a full inquiry into the matter, detailed explanations, and so on. I shall attempt to get to the bottom of things. Some terrible mistake must surely be involved."

"What are the charges?" I asked.

"That you have betrayed the cause of Priest-Kings," he said.

"How can I have betrayed their cause?" I asked. "I am not really an agent of Priest-Kings. I have never pledged a sword to them, never sworn a fidelity oath in their behalf. I am my own man, a mercenary of sorts, one who has, upon occasion, as it pleased him, labored in their behalf."

"It may be no easier to withdraw from the service of Priest-Kings than from that of Kurii," said Samos.

"In what way have I frustrated or jeopardized their cause?" I asked. "How have I supposedly subjected them to the insidiousness of betrayal?"

"You saved the life of Zarendargar, War General of the Kurii, in the Barrens," said Samos.

"Perhaps," I said. "I am not really sure of it."

"That was your avowed intention, was it not, in entering the Barrens?" asked Samos.

"Yes," I said. "I wished to warn him of the Death Squad searching him out. On the other hand, as it turned out, he anticipated the arrival of such a group. He might have survived anyway. I do not know."

"Also, as I understand it," said Samos, "you had dealings with him in the Barrens, and ample opportunity there to attempt to capture or kill him."

"I suppose so," I admitted.

"But you did not do so," said Samos.

"That is true," I said.

"Why not?" asked Samos.

"Once we shared paga," I said.

"Is that what I am to tell the Sardar?" asked Samos, ironically.

"I see your point," I said.

"The Sardar, by now," said Samos, "probably views you as an agent of one of the parties of Kurii, and as a traitor, and one who probably knows too much."

"Perhaps I should turn myself in." I smiled.

"I do not think I would recommend that," smiled Samos. Rather I think you should conveniently disappear from Port Kar for a time, until I manage to resolve these confusions and amibiguities."

"Where shall I go?" I asked.

"I do not want to know," said Samos.

Do you think you will be successful in straightening this matter out?" I asked.

"I hope so," he said.

"I do not think you will be successful," I said. "I think the Sardar has already acted."

"I do not understand," said Samos.

"You received the first message some ten days ago," I said.

"Yes," he said.

"I expect its terminology, and such, was clear," I speculated. Samos shrugged. "I suppose so." he said.

"You may have endangered yourself by your delaying," I said.

"How is that?" asked Samos.

"The Sardar transmits a clear message," I said. "Instead of an acknowledgment and compliance report it receives a request for clarification or confirmation, and that from an agent of high intelligence and proven efficiency. This informed the Sardar that you were reluctant to carry out the orders. Furthermore, our friendship is not unknown, I am sure, to the Sardar. It is not difficult to conjecture the nature of the response in the Sardar. Presumably it has been decided that you are not to be relied upon in this matter. Indeed, you yourself, by virtue of your response, may now be suspect to them."

"I received the confirmation yesterday," said Samos, lamely.

"That may have been to conceal from you any apprehensions existing in the Sardar as to your loyalty."

"Perhaps," he whispered.

"In any event the delay between the messages has given independent agents of Priest-Kings time to arrive in Port Kar. It may also have been noted you did not act immediately upon the receipt of the confirmation."

"What are you saying?" asked Samos, aghast.

"I think I have an explanation which makes sense of this little affair in the booth," I said.

"No!" said Samos.

I looked down at the fellow in the rich robes, the knife protruding from his chest.

"I think I have just killed an agent of Priest-Kings," I said.

"No!" said Samos. "No!"

I shrugged. We could hear the sounds of carnival outside.

"If anyone," said Samos, "Kurii must have sent him."

"Perhaps," I said.

"Priest-Kings would not behave in such a way," said Samos.

"Perhaps," I said.

"Leave the city," he said.

"In his wallet were staters of Brundisium," I said. "Do you know anything about Brundisium, anything having to do with either Priest-Kings or Kurii?"

"No," said Samos.

"Then the Brundisium staters are probably meaningless," I said.

"I would suppose so," said Samos. "They are, of course, a valuable stater. There would be nothing incredible about their use being specified in a given transaction."

"Why not the coinage of Ar," I asked, "or that of Port Kar, or of Asperiche, or Tharna, or Tyros, or Schendi or Turia?"

"I do not know," said Samos.

"How will I know if it is safe to return to Port Kar?" I asked.

"From time to time," said Samos, "presumably you yourself, incognito, or an agent acting on your behalf, might be in the city. Do you know the slave chains I have hanging behind the banner on the banner bar to the left of my threshold, where the bar meets the wall, those that have tied there with them a bit of scarlet slave silk?"

"Yes," I said.

"When it is safe for you to again appear publicly in Port Kar, when it is safe for you to again make contact with me, the scarlet slave silk will be replaced with yellow."

"I understand," I said.

"I wish you well," he said. We clasped hands.

"I wish you well," I said.

Samos then withdrew from the booth. I remained inside for a few Ehn. It would not be well for him to be seen with me at this time. I looked at the man on the rug, that flooring the booth, spread over the tiles of the piazza, he in whose heart I had left his own knife. I recalled the tale of Yngvar, the Far-Traveled. There was a new order, I surmised, in the Sardar. I did not regret what I had done in the case of Zarendargar. Once we had shared paga.

I listened to the merriment of the revelers outside, to the cries, the horns and music.

I must leave Port Kar tonight. I would go to my holding; I would make arrangements; I would obtain weapons, moneys, letters of credit. I could be gone in two Ahn, on tarnback, before Priest-Kings discovered the failure of their plans.

I looked back at the small, lovely redheaded slave bound hand and foot on the large cushion, the wallet filled with the staters of Brundisium tied at her collar. Throughout all that had transpired in the booth she had not regained consciousness. Tassa powder is efficient.

I then left the booth. In a moment I was again making my way through the crowds of carnival.

I was bitter.

I would take no men with me. I had no wish to endanger them, nor to involve them in the dark matters of warring worlds. Too, the best guarantee of the safety of Samos, it seemed to me, was my departure from the city. He was my friend. He had risked much for me. I could be gone in two Ahn, on tarnback, before Priest-Kings discovered the failure of their plans.

"Paga?" inquired a fellow.

"Of course," I said. It was carnival.

We exchanged swigs, I from his bota, he from mine. Then he turned aside, to offer paga to another. I stepped back, while one of the gigantic fellows, on stilts, stalked by. I was jostled. I checked my wallet. It was intact.

I then continued on my way, pressing through the throngs.

"Master," said a woman, kneeling before me. She put down her head and kissed my feet, and then looked up at me.

I recognized her. She was the free woman whom I had seen earlier, she masquerading as a slave, with the brief bit of cloth about her hips.

"What do you want?" I asked.

"I have been in agony for two Ahn," she said. "I am now ready, of my own free will, to go to a rack."

I looked down at her. Women are very beautiful on their knees.

"Please," she said, "—Master."

"Precede me," I said.

She rose to her feet and, frightened, trembling, I behind her, made her way through the crowds.

At one point we were literally stopped in the press.

"Paga?" asked a fellow, waiting beside me. We exchanged swigs. Then, in a few moments, the crowd loosened and, once again, I followed the female.

She came to the foot of a rack and stopped, regarding it. It was one of the strap racks, not a simple net rack, or rope rack. It was now open. Frightened, she crawled upon it, and then lay on it, on her back, on the broad, soft, flat, smooth, comfortable interlaced straps.

"I have never been on a rack before," she said.

"Not all of them are this comfortable," I assured her.

"I do not doubt it," she smiled. The comfort of the slave may or may not be taken into consideration by the master, as it pleases him. They are only slaves.

"You are a free woman," I said. "You need not go through with this."

"Touch me," she said.

"Paga?" asked a fellow. We exchanged swigs. Then he was on his way. He had not concerned himself with the woman. He had assumed she was a slave. She was, after all, half naked, in a collar and on a pleasure rack.

"I had to wait," she said, wonderingly.

"If you are going to masquerade as a slave," I said, "you should grow accustomed, at least in some respects, to being treated as a slave."

"Yes," she said.

"Suppose it were not a masquerade," I said.

"I understand," she said. Her eyes briefly clouded. I saw that she was frightened. I saw that she had just had some inkling as to what it might be to be truly a slave, to be truly, utterly, at the mercy of masters.

"Leap up," I suggested. "Flee the rack. Hurry home. If the straps are fastened upon you, it will be too late."

"No," she whispered.

"But what of respect and dignity?" I asked. "Surely you desire these, desperately."

"I have had respect and dignity for years," she said, "and they are empty! I have had my fill of respect and dignity! For years I have been betrayed and deluded by those trivializing, vacuous, negative verbalities! I do not want respect and dignity! Obviously they are not the answer. If they were, I should be happy, but I am not! I do not want respect and dignity! I want fulfillment, and truth!"

I saw that her sexual drives were far too strong to be appropriate for those of a free woman. In her there was an eager, succumbing slave.

"Now I want to be overwhelmed, dominated. Now I want to take my place in the order of nature. Now I want to be what I am, and have always been, truly, a woman!"

In every woman, of course, Goreans think, there is a slave. Perhaps, in the end, there is no difference.

She looked at me, pleadingly.

"You are a free woman," I told her.

She moaned.

"It would seem thus," I said, "at least according to some, that you are entitled to respect and dignity."

"I have never encountered a convincing proof to that effect," she said. "Have you?"

"No," I said.

"Oh, would that I were a slave," she smiled. "Then I would not have to concern myself with such matters. Then I would only have to mind my manners and make certain that I pleased my masters, totally."

"To be sure," I said, "many of the matters with which the free woman must concern herself are simply irrelevant to the slave."

"Such as dignity and respect," she said.

"Yes," I said.

"Under those names I have gone hungry for years," she said.

"And yet, now," I said, "you have come, and of your own free will, to a rack."

"There comes a time," she said, "when the slogans no longer suffice, a time when the myth is seen to be meaningless."

"And such a time came for you?" I said.

"Yes," she said.

"And then you put on a collar and came to carnival."

"Yes," she said, "and to a rack!"

"Interesting," I said.

"Are you going to touch me?" she asked.

"I do not know," I said.

"You would use me without a second thought if I were a slave," she said. "You are putting me through this because I am a free woman. That is why you are making me suffer! That is why you are torturing me! Do you want me to beg?"

"Surely that would be unseemly in a free woman," I said.

"If I were a slave," she smiled, "I would beg quickly enough."

"I do not doubt it," I said. I could sense that she was quite hot, for a free woman. To be sure, as a free woman, she could not even begin to suspect what it might be to be in the throes of slave need, to be slave hot, so to speak.

"Are you going to touch me?" she asked.

"I do not know," I said, musingly.

She twisted her head angrily, in fustration, to the side, on the surface of broad, soft, interlaced straps.

"You are free to leave, of course," I said. "You have not yet been fastened in place."

"And what if I were fastened in place?" she asked.

"Then you would not be free to leave," I said.

"I see," she said. She lay back on the straps, and lifted her knees, and put her hands above and behind her, hooking her fingers in the interstices of the broad straps. She looked at me.

"I think there may be a slave in you," I said.

"Very well," she said. "You win. I beg rape."

I regarded her.

"Do you find me attractive?" she asked.

"Yes," I said.

"Do you want me?" she asked.

"Yes," I said.

"Then take me," she said. "I am yours."

"You are a free woman," I said. "Thus, it would doubtless be improper for me to subject you to powerful uses. It is up to me, doubtless, to see that you are protected from, indeed, shielded from, powerful sexual insights and experiences. You do not need to know what it is to be under male dominance. It is doubtless best that you never learn. It might change your life. Similarly, it is probably best that you learn nothing of helpless obedience, of submission and total surrender. It is difficult to tell where such things might lead. All in all, you had best remain on the superficial levels of sexuality, those appropriate to a free woman, unaware that anything deeper and more profound exists."

She looked at me, angrily.

"It seems, thus," I said, "that I must refrain from responding to your needs, real and urgent though they may be."

"Do you think that I will respect you for falsifying your manhood," she cried, "for denying it, for pretending it does not exist! No! Ultimately I would only despise you for your self-betrayal! Is honesty too much to ask from men? If you will not be a man, how can I be a woman? If I were a man, I would be a true man, and I would never betray my manhood! It would be precious to me! I would rejoice in it! And I would teach women, which is what we want, what it is to be women! I would be merciless with them! I would be their master!"

"That is what you want?" I asked.

"Yes," she said, "for without it, we cannot be women."

I reached to one of the straps. It was a holding strap. These straps are adjustable. I would take it twice snugly about her wrist and then, angling it, press the cap-topped stud at the end of the strap, from the bottom, up through one of the small, sturdy, suitable eyelets on the same strap. No buckles are used. The occupant of the rack, of course, because of the nature of the cap-topped stud and the eyelet, cannot, from her position, free herself. She is helpless. The arrangement, thus, is not only such that the girl finds herself, when the straps are on her, held in perfect custody, but this custody, in virtue of the nature of the studs and eyelets, may be easily imposed or removed, a convenience to the handler. "If I fasten these upon you, you will be helpless," I said.

I began with her wrists, and then I secured her ankles.

"Free yourself," I suggested.

She struggled. "I cannot," she said. She looked at me, frightened. "I am as helpless as a slave," she said.

I regarded her. She was extremely attractive.

"What are you doing?" she cried. My hands were at the string holding the cloth about her hips.

"I am going to lay aside your veil," I told her.

"No!" she begged.

I undid the string.

"I shall cry out!" she threatened.

"Then it will only be necessary to gag you," I said.

"Please," she begged. "I have changed my mind! Release me!"

"It is too late for that," I said.

"Please," she pleaded.

"I am only human," I told her.

"Please," she pleaded.

"No," I told her.

Then she lay back on the soft, broad straps, moaning. The cloth at her hips, now freed, had been brushed to the sides. No longer now between us lay the least impediment. She was now, as it is sometimes said on Gor, slave naked.

She looked at me. I put down my head and began to kiss her, and lick her, slowly about the belly.

"Oh!" she said.

And then, in a few moments, she was trying to move her body beneath my mouth, trying to bring me to other positions on her body. Her movements were mute pleas.

"Ohhhh!" she said suddenly, softly.

"Now," I said, "you must restrain yourself. You must try not to move."

"I cannot help myself," she said.

"It would be easy enough for me to desert you now," I said, "leaving you in the straps."

She moaned.

"You will not move now," I said, "until you receive permission."

"I will try," she said.

I then continued to lick and kiss at her, softly. She began to whimper and moan. I looked at her. Her eyes were wild, pleading. I put my hands on her belly. It was tense and hot, throbbing with blood and need. "Do not move," I told her.

"No," she said, "no!"

I then resumed my ministrations to her body. They were such as might be inflicted upon a woman who was no more than a slave.

"Please!" she whimpered. "Please! Please!"

"Very well," I said. "You may move."

She cried out and seemed to explode under me, sobbing with joy and helplessness. Then she looked at me wildly, still held in the straps, disbelief in her eyes. Then I entered her and took her, not gently. "Oh," she cried. "Master! Master!" Then again she lay back on the straps, helpless.

"I have business to attend to," I said. Indeed, I must soon make away from Port Kar.

"Tarry but a moment," she begged. She was in a position to do no more than beg, secured as she was.

I lay beside her and kissed her, and held her, for a moment.

"Thank you," she breathed.

"I think there is a slave in you," I said.

"I know. I know, Master," she whispered.

"Perhaps you should consider the collar," I said.

"Such thoughts are not new to me," she said. "I have had them for years."

"It must be a difficult choice for a woman," I said, "the choice between freedom and love."

I rose from the rack, and drew my robes about me.

"I have business to attend to," I said. I should soon leave the city. I adjusted my wallet.

"Yes, Master," she said.

I freed her from the flexible, efficient restraints, and helped her courteously from the rack.

"Thank you," she said. "You are very kind." I restrained her from kneeling. She was, after all, a free woman. "Was I pleasing?" she asked.

"That question seems more appropriate to a slave than a free woman," I said.

"I ask it," she said.

"Is it important to you?" I asked.

"Yes," she said.

"Yes," I said. "You were pleasing."

"Wonderful!" she said.

"For a free woman," I added.

"Oh," she said.

"Certainly you did not think to be able to compete with a slave," I said. "You would not have her experience, her skills, her training. You have not been forced to live with and endure slave heat. You have not been forced to learn submission, obedience, service, passion and love. You have not yet been sensitized to her collar."

"Suppose I became a slave," she said. "Do you think I might become a pleasing slave?"

"You have generated a great deal of heat," I said. "That is an excellent sign."

"Do you think, in time, I might make an adequate slave?" she asked.

"Yes," I said, "and perhaps, in time, even a superb one."

"That is high praise," she smiled.

"You had better wear this," I said, handing her the brief bit of cloth which she had worn about her hips. "If men see you without it, they may be stimulated, and you may be raped several times on the tiles before you manage to leave the piazza. Many men are drunk here tonight and they may be careless. They may not think to check your body for brands. You might be had before they determined their error."

Smiling, she tied the cloth about her hips.

"Farewell," said I, "Free Woman."

"Will I see you again?" she asked.

"It is not likely," I speculated.

"Do you wish to know my name?" she asked.

"No," I said, "nor is it needful for you to know mine."

"I see," she said.

"It was only a touching at carnival," I said.

"I see," she said.

"Happy carnival," I said.

"Happy carnival," she said. Then she turned about and, sobbing, fled away. I watched her go. Her body was hormonally rich. That was evident in the configuration of her beauty and in her dispositions and reflexes, exhibited on the rack. Too, she was profoundly feminine. She had now disappeared among the revelers. Her body, I thought, would make the decision for her.

"I see that you have won the favor of a free woman," said a man.

"What?" I asked. I thought he referred to the free woman, she who had just disappeared among the revelers.

"That," he said, indicating the silken favor in the eyelet of my robes.

"Oh!" I said. "Yes, it would seem so." I looked at the favor. I had forgotten it.

"Paga?" said he, extending his bota.

"Surely," I said. We exchanged swigs of paga.

"It must be nice to have won the favor of a free woman," he said.

"I and a few hundred other fellows," I said.

"That particular favor," he said.

"Alas," I said, "even there I fear I am but one out of ten."

"One out of fifteen," he said.

"Oh?" I said.

"Yes," he said.

I shrugged. The game of favors can be played with any number of favors and contestants, but the usual number of favors distributed is ten.

"Happy carnival," he said.

"Happy carnival," I said.

I turned to proceed to the check point where I would turn in my numbered receipt and reclaim my weapons. The crowds had thinned now, but the piazza was still, for the most part, crowded.

I stumbled, and then straightened myself. Surely I had not had that much paga.

I took another step or two, and then I slipped to one knee. The piazza seemed to move beneath me. I caught my balance. I was conscious of masks and costumes swirling about.

"What is wrong?" asked a voice.

"He has had too much paga," said another voice.

I wanted to rise to my feet, but I slipped to the tiles.

"It is all right," said a voice.

Things began to grow dark. I fought to retain consciousness. It was difficult to move. I could not speak.

"Put a mask on him," whispered a voice.

I felt a carnival mask fastened on me.

"No," I seemed to say, but no sound escaped my lips.

I felt myself lifted to my feet, each of my arms held about the shoulders of a man.

"What is wrong with him?" asked a voice.

"Too much paga," responded a voice.

"Is he all right?" asked a voice.

"Yes," said a voice.

"No!" I wanted to cry, but could not.

"Do you require help?" asked a man.

"No," said a voice, that of one of the two men supporting me.

"Are you sure?" asked the man.

"Yes, citizen," said the other fellow supporting me. "We will manage quite well. Thank you."

I then sensed we were alone.

"Put him in the boat, with the others," said a voice. It was a woman's voice.

I then lost consciousness.

3

LADY YANINA

"That one," she had said. "Have him brought to my tent."

"Go in," said the guard.

I lowered my head and entered the tent. I moved my hands upon my wrists. They were ringed and sore where the manacles, too closely fitting, had clasped them. I straightened my body.

The tent was one of rich cloths, supported by five poles. It was rich with hangings and, about its interior circumference, furnished with suitable appointments, including vessels, cushions, a low inlaid table, cases and trunks. These, with the various materials for the tent, and its poles, had been disembarked from a large, high-wheeled wagon. I, with several others, in harness, some others chained by the neck behind, had drawn this wagon for the past two days.

I, and others, had been awakened to the blows of spear butts three days ago.

"On your knees," we had been told, "heads to the dirt! You are in the presence of your Mistress!"

We had struggled to our knees. Our hands were manacled behind our backs. There seemed the stench of fish on us. We were connected by the neck, by collars and chains.

I had been aware of someone stopping before me.

"Lift your head," had said a woman's voice.

I looked up. She was veiled, and clad, too, in robes of concealment, sumptuous robes which seemed incongruous in the open terrain, the grassy field, in which I found myself. I looked about, seeing what guards I could. I saw five. I felt her tharlarion quirt at the side of my face, indicating I should keep my head forward. Then it pressed up, under my chin. I lifted my head higher, obedient to the quirt, looking up at her. "That is better," she said. She looked at me. "It seems I have won the game of favors," she said.

"At least for now," I said.

"In the distribution of my favors in the piazza in Port Kar," she said, "I had two major criteria in mind. Would you like to know what they were?"

"Of course," I said.

"First," she said, "the males must be large and strong. They must be suitable for inclusion in a work chain. They must be capable, with their bestial strength, of sustaining indefinitely so onerous a servitude."

"And what is your second criterion," I asked, "that which they must also meet, what is that?"

"I must find them, personally, of some sexual interest," she said.

"I see," I said.

"We are going to get on splendidly, aren't we?" she asked.

"On whose terms?" I asked.

"On mine," she said.

"I do not know," I said.

"Do you know how to obey?" she asked.

"Yes," I said.

"Then I am sure we will get on splendidly—on my terms," she said.

"Perhaps," I said.

She withdrew the quirt from beneath my chin. "Put your head down," she said, "—to the dirt."

I did so. And, in a moment, she had continued on down the line, pausing here and there to order another fellow to lift his head, to be commanded and interrogated, and then to resume a posture of abject obeisance.

"Approach," she said.

Within the tent there was an inner sanctum, or private area, formed of diaphanous, white hangings. It was rather like a small tent, or walled room, within the larger tent. It was within this area that I could see her, vaguely. There was a tiny lamp on a stand, near her, to one side. She was sitting on a curule chair.

"Approach," she invited me.

I brushed back the hangings and let them fall closed behind me. I then stood before her, a few feet away, within the sanctum.

On the floor there were cushions and silk. I stood straight, my arms folded, surveying her.

I could detect perfume.

"You have my permission to kneel," she said.

I regarded her.

"There are guards, just outside," she said.

I knelt. I put my hands on my thighs.

"You have broad shoulders," she said, "a narrow waist. You have strong thighs. Your hands are large and strong."

I said nothing.

"You are a large, strong, handsome-looking fellow," she said, "very animal-like. If you were not in my total power, I might be uneasy."

"You have me at a disadvantage," I said, "as you are veiled, and fully clothed."

"At least you no longer smell of fish," she said.

"No," I said.

"That is how you and your fellows were smuggled out of Port Kar," she said. "We took you, one by one, drugged, to the boat. There we stripped and chained you. You were each packed in a barrel with salted parsit fish, and over your heads these barrels had a false bottom, which was covered with more parsit fish. Tiny holes in the upper sides of the barrels would permit you to breathe. The barrels were then sealed."

"The captures were smoothly and cleverly effectuated," I observed.

"Thank you," she said.

"Are you a female slaver?" I asked.

"No," she laughed, "though I think I might have been successful in such a profession."

Most female slavers, incidentally, are not involved in field captures. It is, on the whole, too dangerous for them. Too, there is always the danger that they might be added to the catch by their men. Most female slavers, accordingly, are established in cities, where they own or manage houses. There they buy and sell slaves, board or rent them, train them, and so on. Statistically, there are very few female slavers. Most Gorean women tend to be attractive, and most Gorean men tend to be strong, for example. Accordingly, in a business such as slaving it is not unusual that the female slaver sooner or later, in one way or another finds the collar on her own throat. That, then, she then helplessly under the whip like any other female, is that.

"I am rather," she said, "only the humble mistress of a small work chain."

"Surely it is unusual for an individual in your line of work to procure laborers as you did," I said.

"It is cheaper than buying them," she said.

"That is doubtless true," I admitted. I did not believe this woman was actually the mistress of a work chain. There were many reasons for this. First, there are very few women involved in such things. Secondly, she did not seem skilled in the handling of men. For example, in our present situation, I could reach her and kill her or capture her and make use of her to effect a probable escape. Thirdly, she did not seem to have the hardness of a woman likely to be efficient in such a post. Fourthly, the tent did not suggest the tastes or appointments of such a woman. Fifthly, her garmentry revealed clearly a vanity and taste for sumptuous luxury, a penchant for self-indulgence and ostentatious elegance, also unlikely to be characteristic in such a woman. The number of guards on hand, too, which was five, was really too small to manage a normal work gang, not because of the ratios involved, but because of the necessity of maintaining night watches. Similarly, she really had no work gang but the fifteen men she had picked up in Port Kar. A work gang usually consists of fifty to one hundred men, and some contain as many as five hundred or a thousand men. If she were really the mistress of a work gang we presumably would not have constituted the work gang but would merely have been added to it. Even more obviously we did not have the equipment of a work gang with us, the implements and tools pertinent to the work of such gangs, such as levers, picks, hammers and shovels.

"What was used to drug us?" I asked.

"Tassa powder," she said. "I put enough of it in the botas of my men to stun a kailiauk."

"How long were we unconscious?" I asked.

"With tube feedings, of broth mixed with tassa, five days," she said.

"Where are we?" I asked. I knew. I wished to see what she would say.

"I think it more amusing to keep you in ignorance," she said.

"As you wish," I said. From the location of our camp, indeed, from our chain line, between two stakes, we could see the Sardar Mountains in the distance. They were unmistakable. I assumed this woman must be an agent of Priest-Kings. Yet she did not seem to recognize me. Too, I was only one of fifteen men captured. If she was an agent of Priest-Kings, it did not seem, ironically enough, that she realized who it was, so to speak, who was on her chain.

That we were so near the Sardar, incidentally, after a presumed five days of unconsciousness, followed by two days of travel on foot, drawing her wagon, further suggested that she was not likely, really, to be the mistress of a work chain. We could not have come this far from Port Kar in so short a time, presumably, if we had not been brought most of the way by tarn, probably in tarn baskets. Common laborers are seldom transported in this fashion. But then, two days ago, we had been awakened, and had then proceeded on foot. This was presumably to make it appear, at least in the vicinity of the Sardar, that we were truly a work chain. The woman, I assumed, must be working for Priest-Kings. On the other hand, it did not seem that she knew who I was. Perhaps, then, she was not an agent of Priest-Kings. Perhaps she was a slaver, of sorts, after all, and intended to sell us, her catch, at the Fair of En'Kara. But then, if that were so, I wondered why she was having recourse to this elaborate pretense of being merely the mistress of a common work chain. I decided not to seize her, at least not yet.

"What is your name?" she asked.

"I have been called various things," I said, "at different times, in different places."

"Ah, yes," she said, "I know you fellows of Port Kar. You are all rogues, all pirates, thieves and slavers. I think I shall call you—Brinlar."

"And how shall I address you?" I asked.

"As 'Mistress,' " she said.

"How is it that you made your strike in Port Kar?" I asked.

"I was in Port Kar on business," she said, "and, with the carnival, matters were convenient."

"I had thought you might be of Tyros or Cos," I said. Those two island ubarates were at war with Port Kar.

"No," she said.

I was now more sure than ever that she was of the party of Priest-Kings.

"To be sure," she said, "my sympathies lie with Cos and Tyros, Thassa's foremost citadels of enlightenment and civilization. A certain amusing fittingness was thus manifested in my choice of a location for my predations, a choice fully vindicated, incidentally, by the catch of lovely males I acquired there." She looked at me. "Would you like a rag for your loins?" she asked.

"Whatever you wish," I said.

She laughed.

"Am I, and my fellows, to be enslaved?" I asked.

"That would certainly seem to be in order, would it not?" she asked.

"Of course," I said.

"Somewhere, sometime, I would suppose," she said, "at my convenience, at a site of my choosing."

"Of course," I said.

She smiled.

"What, then, afterwards, is to be our fate?" I asked.

"Perhaps I will sell you then, somewhere," she said, "perhaps even at the Fair of En'Kara."

"I see," I said. This confirmed my conjecture that we were not truly intended to be kept as members of a work chain. She presumably had a rendezvous to keep at the fair. Her rendezvous kept, and her cover still intact, but then no longer needed, she could dispose of us in the En'Kara markets.

"You and your fellows remain legally free, of course," she said, "though totally in my power, as complete captives, until a sign of bondage is burned into your pretty hides, or you are appropriately collared, or otherwise legally enslaved."

"I understand," I said.

"Do you recall the two major criteria I used in selecting my captures in the piazza?" she asked.

"You wanted strong, large fellows, as I recall," I said, "suitable for inclusion in a work chain."

"Yes," she said. "Do you recall the other criterion?"

I was silent.

"It was," she said, "that I must, personally, find them of some sexual interest."

"Yes," I said.

"Spread your knees," she said.

I did so.

"Excellent, Brinlar," she said, "indeed, excellent."

I did not speak.

"How does it feel to be a free man, but one who is in the total power of a woman?" she asked.

I shrugged. I did not really regard myself as being totally in her power.

"Am I beautiful?" she asked.

"I do not know," I said.

"But surely you men conjecture about such matters," she said.

"I would suppose you might be beautiful," I said. "There seem the suggestions of the lineaments of a beautiful woman, particularly as you have belted and arranged them, beneath your garments."

"I like pretty clothes," she said, "and I wear them well."

"Doubtless you would be even more beautiful in the rag of a slave, or naked in a collar," I said.

"Bold fellow," she said. But I could see she was pleased. All women are curious to know how beautiful they might be as slaves. This is because all of them, in their heart, are slaves.

She regarded me for a time, not speaking. I knelt there, knees spread. She seemed in no hurry to disclose her will with respect to me. Her eyes roved me, glistening.

"Are you not curious to know why you were brought to my tent?" she asked.

"Mistress has not yet explained it to me," I said. My heart began to race. I feared she would now announce to me that she knew my true identity, that she was going to put me to her pleasure, and rape me, and then turn me over, a woman's catch, to the Sardar. It did not seem appropriate to me to attack her, and perhaps kill her. She might be an agent of Priest-Kings. So, too, for all I knew, might be her men. I recalled the fellow in the booth, he in whom I had left his own knife, in the piazza at Port Kar.

"But surely you can guess," she said.

"Perhaps," I said.

"Spread your knees more widely," she said, coldly.

I did so.

"Now perhaps you can guess," she said.

"Yes," I said.

"You seem relieved," she said, puzzled.

I shrugged. I was indeed relieved. She had again only been toying with me. It seemed clear to me now, as it had before, that she did not know who I was. The man in the booth, I recalled, had tried to kill me. Thus, if she had truly known my identity, she might, by now, have had me killed. That would have been easy enough to have done while I was drugged. Too, the nature of my capture did not suggest anything special about me. I had merely been one of fifteen brought into her chains.

"There is something else," she said.

"Oh?" I asked.

"I am interested in being assessed," she said.

"Assessed?" I asked.

"Yes, objectively," she said. "I have been curious about it for a long time. The richness of your garments in the piazza, the weight of your purse, suggests to me that you might have had

experience in such matters, that you had the means to be intimately familiar with the doings in markets, and so on.''

I was silent.

"Let me remind you," she said, "that it is you who kneel
before me, with your knees spread like an imbonded girl!"

"I understand," I said.

Her hand went to the pins at the left side of her veil.

"I think you will find me extraordinarily beautiful," she said,
"perhaps even slave beautiful."

"Perhaps," I said.

She unpinned her veil at the left side, and let it fall, and
brushed back the silken hood of her tent robe, shaking her head,
freeing a cascade of long, dark hair. She looked at me, amused.
"I see that you find me beautiful," she said.

"Yes," I said.

She stood. "Are you familiar with the duties of a silk slave?"
she asked. As she spoke, she began to casually disrobe.

"I am a free man," I said.

"But you have some conception of their duties, do you not?"
she inquired.

"Yes," I said.

"Such duties, and others," she said, "will be yours."

"I understand," I said.

I caught my breath. She stepped from her robes, softly dropped,
as though from a pool of silk at her feet.

"Well?" she asked.

She was stunningly beautiful. She would bring a high price.
She then reclined, on cushions, and strewn silks. These were
near the back of the small inner sanctum, near the white hangings forming its rear wall. She regarded me, amusement in her
eyes. She leaned on one elbow.

"Well?" she asked.

"You are quite beautiful," I said.

"Do you think I would sell easily?" she asked.

"No," I said.

"Oh?" she asked.

"Your price would be much too high," I said. "Most men
would not be able to afford you."

"But if I were put at a reasonable price," she said.

"Then, doubtless," I said, "you would be snapped up
immediately."

"You do regard me then," she said, "objectively, as being
quite beautiful?"

"Yes," I said.

"Even slave beautiful?" she asked.

"Your beauty," said I, "at least in its external lineaments might well be the envy of many slaves, and if it were to become itself a slave's beauty, with the inward transformations bondage effects in a woman, it might, in time, in my opinion, attain at least the minimum standards of being slave beautiful."

"Then only a slave can be slave beautiful?" she asked.

"I would not wish to make it a matter of meanings," I said, "but, empirically, it does seem to be pretty much a matter of the condition, a function of its fulfillments, and such."

"Free women are more beautiful than slaves," she said.

"That is false," I said. "Furthermore, every woman, in her heart, knows it is false. Any beauty a free woman has, for example, is enhanced a thousandfold when she becomes a slave."

"I hate slaves!" she said.

"That is because you are not one of them," I said. "You envy them."

"Beware," she said. "I am a free woman!"

"I know," I said.

"And you are totally in my power," she said.

"I understand," I said.

"Approach me, on all fours," she said. "Perhaps I will forgive you, if you are skillful."

I approached her.

"You see me more closely now," she said. "Have you assessed free women before?"

"Yes," I said.

"Assess me," she said.

"As a free woman?" I asked.

"Of course," she said. "That is what I am."

"You are an incredibly beautiful free woman," I said.

"Your body obviously agrees with you," she said.

"Indeed," I admitted.

"And free women," she said, "are a thousand times, and more, above a mere slave."

"Yes," I said. "There is no comparison. A free woman is inordinately precious. She is a thousand times, and more, above a mere slave."

"Your status here," she said, "is that of a servant, a total servant, until I have you enslaved."

"I understand," I said.

"I think it will be amusing to apply a free man to the duties of a silk slave."

"Doubtless," I said.

"Indeed, I may dally somewhat, as it pleases me, or not, in the matter of your enslavement."

I said nothing.

"And perhaps, if I find you quite good, after you are enslaved, with your fellows, I might not even sell you at the Fair of En-Kara. I might keep you—as a silk slave."

I did not speak.

"You will touch me if, and only as, and exactly as, I direct," she said. "I am total Mistress. I shall obtain considerable gratification from you, and you will obtain gratification, if any, only as it pleases me."

"I understand," I said.

"To the silks, my brawny, helpless servant," she said. She then put her small hands in my hair. She drew me to her. "Please me," she said.

I then began to address myself to her pleasures.

I immersed myself in the exciting, intimate, marvelous, powerful odors of the aroused female.

"Oh, Brinlar," she gasped, suddenly, "you are an excellent servant!"

I took her wrists in my hands and pulled them from my hair, and held them to her sides, meanwhile alternately forcibly and aggressively, and delicately and tenderly, continuing my service.

Her wrists were helpless in my grip. She pressed herself piteously against me.

She began to moan and squirm.

Suddenly she said, "I am helpless! I am being held, helplessly!"

"Forgive me, Mistress," I said, unhanding her, as though my grip upon her might have been an inadvertence.

She seized me again by the hair, drawing me closely to her.

"Oh, Brinlar," she whispered. "Yes, Brinlar! It is marvelous, Brinlar! Do not stop! Yes, Brinlar! Yes!"

In such a manner can one subdue a female, turning her into an object totally helpless with pleasure.

"Yes, Brinlar," she whispered. "Yes! Yes!"

I did not think it was necessary to remind her that I was not really according her the polite courtesies and gentle dignities appropriate to the pleasures of the free woman, but was, in effect, of my own will, by my own decision, subjecting her to attentions more commonly reserved for the imbonded female, the woman who has no choice but to submit to a lengthy and authoritative ravishing, one which well teaches her the meaning of her collar, and what it is to be in the hands of a man, and as he wants her.

"Oh, Brinlar!" she whispered.

Her responses were such that it was difficult to conjecture what her experiences might have been had she truly been a slave, and had she known herself helplessly in my power, and had she known that she must yield totally and without reservation in the last fiber of her very being.

"Brinlar!" she cried, surging against me. "Yes, Brinlar!"

"What is your name?" I asked.

"Yanina!" she cried. "Lady Yanina!"

"Of what city?" I asked.

"Brundisium!" she cried. "Brundisium!"

4

FLAMINIUS

"Drink, Mistress?" I asked.

"Yes, Brinlar," she said. She lifted the veil delicately, almost flirtatiously, drinking behind it. She looked at the man across from her.

"Drink, Master?" I asked.

"No," he said. I then withdrew a yard or two and knelt in the grass, holding the vessel of light Ka-la-na. I wore a tunic of white silk.

She dabbed at her lips with a napkin, under the veil, and then let the veil fall again into place.

"This is a pleasant spot," she had said earlier. "Spread the cloth here, Brinlar, and lay out the things from the basket."

"Yes, Mistress," I had said.

We could see the Sardar Mountains in the distance. I had been her servant for some three days. After the first night she had not commanded me to her intimate service. I think that first night had terribly unsettled her. She had apparently not understood that she could have such feelings. At times she had seemed almost taken out of herself. At times, clearly, she had responded uncontrollably, reflexively, at my mercy, almost as might have a slave. This sort of behavior was inappropriate in her, inexcusably so, she doubtless deemed, as she was a free woman. Roundly had I been scolded for my part in matters. Yet with mixed feelings, it was, I think, that she chastised me. I pretended, of course, to ignorance and innocence, and a perhaps overzealous desire to please. In any event she clearly now feared her feelings.

She had not dared to again order me to her pleasure. I think she was now afraid of herself in a man's arms, and what she might become. Too, I think she clearly understood that what I had done to her might, as a matter of fact, have been done to her by almost any man.

"He is coming now, Brinlar," she had said earlier.

"Yes, Mistress," I had said, shading my eyes.

A rider, mounted on a high tharlarion, flanked by two footmen, had been approaching.

I had little doubt this had to do with her business in the vicinity of the Sardar.

"I must make my identification," said the fellow to her. "Lower your veil."

She unpinned the veil.

"Lady Yanina," he said.

"Yes," she said. I gathered they knew one another.

"You may replace the veil," he said to her.

"It does not much matter, does it," she asked, "as in the course of our work you have, of necessity, several times, seen me face-stripped?"

"Do as you please," he said.

I saw that she repinned the veil. She was extremely modest. She was not a slave. She was a free woman.

The fellow, clad in dark garments, with a cape spread behind him, sitting cross-legged at the edge of the cloth, she kneeling across from him, turned to look at me. I lowered my head.

"I do not care to speak before him," he said. His two footmen were in the background, a few yards away, where the tharlarion was tethered. Two of Lady Yanina's men, from her camp, were also nearby. They were withdrawn several yards to the rear, behind us, as his men were behind him. They were sitting cross-legged in the grass, playing stones.

"Do not mind him," she said. "He is only a servant."

"What sort of servant?" he asked.

"A common sort of menial," she said. "I use him for various things. He waits upon me, he combs my hair, he tidies up the tent."

"I see," he said.

"Does it bother you that I have such a servant?" she asked.

"No," he said. "Of course not."

"You have girls who tend you hand and foot," she said.

"I would rather not speak before him," he said.

"Several times," she said, "we have spoken openly before your slaves."

"That is different," he said. "They are only slaves."

"Would you feel more comfortable if I put him in a collar?" she asked. "It is my intention to do that."

"I despise such servants," he said.

"I shall withdraw, Mistress," I said, making as though to rise.

"Stay, Brinlar," she said, imperiously, coldly.

"Yes, Mistress," I said. I smiled inwardly. My trick had worked. I had been reasonably confident that she would choose to exert her authority in this fashion. She was obviously in some sort of competitive relationship with the male. There was a tautness, a tension, between them. She seemed jealous of him and his power. She was very defensive about her status in his eyes. I conjectured that they were theoretically on the same level, or nearly on the same level, perhaps reporting to the same superior, or superiors, presumably Priest-Kings. If it were acceptable to discuss sensitive matters before his slaves, women like herself, but reduced to a status as negligible as that of furniture or animals, then surely it should be similarly acceptable to discuss such matters before a male, she must have reasoned, one who shared his sex, but was now to her only as total servant. Clearly, of course, she did not understand the differences between men and women. They are not the same. No more fundamental mistake can be made. Too, in making his identification, he had had her face-stripped. This is not a small thing from the point of view of a Gorean woman. I saw that it was important to her to pretend to be his equal. From his point of view, of course, she was only a woman. He must have often conjectured, like any strong man, what she would have looked like at his feet, stripped and in chains. If any roughnesses remained in their relationship after that, they could always be smoothed out with the whip.

"You have brought the materials?" he asked. I was relieved. I saw that he did not choose to contest these matters with her. They were beneath his dignity. She was only a female.

"They are in my tent," she said, airily. "I did not bring them to this meeting, of course. I wished to make certain of the contact first."

"Of course," he said. I wondered what the "materials" were. He seemed to have spoken somewhat guardedly. I assumed that was because of my presence.

"I have them ready for delivery whenever and wherever you wish," she said.

In tidying up her tent, I had taken the opportunity to examine, in so far as I could, its contents. Certain of the trunks were kept locked. In one of those, I supposed, lay the "materials" in question. I did not know the location of the keys to these trunks. I supposed most were locked in one of the trunks, and the key, say, to that trunk, or trunks, was carried about her person, probably concealed in her robes. I could not investigate these matters in detail at night as at night I was hooded and chained to a stake just within the entrance to her tent. In this way she kept me near her. Also, in this way, I did not have to be put with the other captives. It was feared they might harm me in their resentment or anger, given the nature and lightness of my duties.

"I think it was a mistake to have routed them through Port Kar," he said.

This speculation had to do, I supposed, with possible recent misgivings on the part of Priest-Kings pertaining to the loyalty of Samos.

"Not at all," she said. "Dour Babinius held passage with me. I had to deliver him to Port Kar, that he might there, in accord with his sealed orders, conduct his affairs."

She had told me earlier that she had had business in Port Kar. That, I supposed, had been the business. While there, of course, she had taken advantage of carnival to expeditiously accomplish her captures, among which I, like a fool, must be counted.

"Do you know the nature of those orders?" he asked.

"No," she said.

"I do," he said.

"Oh," she said, irritatedly. I gathered he must stand somewhat higher than she in some hierarchy of power.

"He was to have made a strike in Port Kar," he said.

"His target?" she asked.

"An admiral," he said, "one called 'Bosk.' "

"I have heard of him," she said.

"He failed," he said.

"Oh," she said, surprised.

"He was found in one of the purple booths, in his heart his own knife."

"This 'Bosk' did that?" she asked.

"Presumably," he said.

"Where is this 'Bosk' now?" she asked.

"His whereabouts are now unknown," he said. "It is even suspected that he has fled from Port Kar."

"So the entire matter came to naught?" she asked, scornfully.

"Yes," he said.

"It would have been better for Belnar to have entrusted the

entire matter to me," she said. Belnar, I supposed, might be
their common superior.

"You?" he asked, skeptically.

"Yes," she said.

"How might you have succeeded where Babinius failed?" he
asked. "With a bludgeon? With a quicker dagger?"

"With no means so crude," she said.

"Then, how?" he asked.

"I am a woman," she said, straightening her body, making
clear the indications of considerable beauty concealed beneath
her silk. "I could present myself to him. I could allure him. I
could win his interest. I could win his confidence. I could make
him desperately eager for so much as a touch or kiss. Then,
when, in effect, I could twine him about my tiny finger, when I
could do with him as I wished, I could drug or poison him."

I wondered what she would look like, naked and in a collar, in
the shadow of a whip. When a woman is absolutely powerless it
is easy to teach her her sex.

"Doubtless it is Belnar's mistake," said the guest, drily, "not
to entrust you with greater matters."

"In Port Kar," she said, "on my own initiative, and by
means of my own plan, I took fifteen men!"

"Doubtless you had some help in this," he said.

"I command my subordinates, as you command yours," she
said, angrily.

"You are a woman," he said.

"Serve us, Brinlar!" she said, angrily, lifting and holding her
goblet, not looking at me.

"Yes, Mistress," I said, rising and approaching with the
vessel of Ka-la-na.

"Is this one of the 'men' you captured?" inquired the guest.

I poured the Ka-la-na for them.

"At least fourteen are true men," she said, angrily. "You
may withdraw, Brinlar."

"Yes, Mistress," I said, and returned to where I had knelt
before.

"Do you know where lies the old inn of Ragnar, on the old
west road?" he asked.

"Yes," she said. "It is now abandoned, is it not?"

"It is not now in use," he said, "though it is occasionally
reopened when there is an overflow of folks from Torvaldsland,
come for the fair."

Some two years ago the merchants and builders had opened
the road of Cyprianus, named for the engineer in charge of the

project, which led to the fairs rather from the southwest. This had considerably reduced the traffic on the road of Clearchus, now to its north, which had approached the fairs in such a way as to favor the traffic from the northwest, with the result that several of the establishments on the road of Clearchus had been abandoned or relocated. One advantage of the more southern route is that it passes through less rough terrain, terrain which provides less cover for highwaymen. In particular, it does not pass, for several pasangs, through the woods of Clearchus.

As rumor has it, Clearchus was a famous brigand of some two centuries ago who decided to legitimize and regularize his brigandage. He proclaimed his area of operations a ubarate, proclaimed himself its ubar, and then proceeded to impose taxes and levy tolls. Interestingly enough, in time, several cities accorded this ubarate diplomatic recognition, generally in return for concessions on the taxes and tolls. Finally a large force of mercenaries, in the hire of the merchant caste, in a campaign that lasted several months, put an end to the spurious reign of Clearchus, driving him from the forest and scattering his men. It is generally conceded, however, that had Clearchus had more men he might have turned out to be the founder of a state.

It is not altogether clear what happened to Clearchus but some historians identify him with Clearchus of Turia, an immigrant, with followers, to Turia, now chiefly remembered as a patron of the arts and philanthropist. The woods of Clearchus, incidentally, to this day, remain a haunt of brigands.

In the old days the road of Clearchus was often referred to as the "west road." This designation became less useful after the recent opening of the road of Cyprianus. It is not unusual, now, to refer to the road of Clearchus as the "old west road" and that of Cyprianus as the "new west road." Neither of these roads, incidentally, are "great roads," in the sense of being mounted in the earth several feet deep, built of stone like a sunken wall, the sort of roads which are often intended to last a thousand years, the sort of roads which, typically, are found in the vicinity of large cities or are intended to be military roads, speeding directly to traditionally disputed territories or linking strategic points. These roads are both secondary roads, so to speak, generally graveled and rutted; occasionally they are paved with such materials as logs and plated stone; they can be almost impassable in rainy weather and in dry, warm weather, they are often dusty. Tertiary roads, so to speak, are often little more than unfrequented, twisting trails. There is often talk of improving the secondary

roads, and sometimes something is done, but generally little is
accomplished. The major consideration, of course, is money.
Too, many roads, for great portions of their length are not
clearly within the jurisdiction of given states. Power in Gorean
cities tends to vary with the power of the Home Stones, which
tends to fluctuate with the military and economic fortunes of the
city. The notion of the fixed and absolute border is not a typical
Gorean notion.

"I understand," she said.

"Meet me there, with the materials, tomorrow evening," he
said.

"Very well," she said.

"At the fifteenth Ahn," he said.

She lifted her veil, delicately, and sipped Ka-la-na behind it.
He regarded her.

"That is rather early," she observed.

"The fifteenth Ahn," he said.

"That time does not seem to me convenient," she said. She
set down the goblet.

"I do not understand," he said.

"I must prepare myself. I must arrange the materials," she
said. "I have a busy schedule."

"What time would be convenient for you?" he asked, with
mock solicitude.

"I am certain I do not know as yet," she said. "I am a busy
woman."

"You know where I am staying at the fair," he said.

"Yes," she said.

"Perhaps you will then be good enough to transmit word to
me, as to when you might find it appropriate to transact this
urgent business."

"Of course," she said.

He rose, angrily. He spoke not further then but turned and,
cape swirling, strode to his tharlarion. In moments he and his
footmen were taking their leave.

"I showed him, did I not, Brinlar?" she asked, on her feet
now, looking after them.

"Yes, Mistress," I said.

"I shall make him wait upon my convenience," she said.

"Yes, Mistress," I said.

"I shall make him understand my importance," she said.

"Yes, Mistress," I said. I gathered that she must indeed be
somewhat important. For example, he had not stripped her and
led her away, chained by the wrists to his stirrup.

"It is a bit chilly here now, Brinlar," she said. "You may put my wrap upon me."

"Yes, Mistress," I said. I lifted her light cloak about her shoulders and she fastened it beneath her chin, under the veil. I did not throw it over her head and then belt it tightly about her waist, effectively hooding her and confining her arms and hands within it.

"We will return to camp shortly," she said. "You may now pick up the things."

"Yes, Mistress," I said, and knelt down, near her feet, replacing things in the basket.

"May I speak, Mistress?" I asked.

"Of course, Brinlar," she said.

"I gather from what I have heard," I said, "that those of your party, whatsoever it might be, might have some interest in him called 'Bosk' of Port Kar."

"Perhaps," she said.

"I can recognize him," I said.

"Oh?" she said, suddenly interested.

"Furthermore, I have reason to believe," I said, "that he may be even now at the fair, or in the vicinity of the fair."

"Why should you think so?" she asked.

"I have a feeling in the matter," I said. "Perhaps it is based on something I heard in Port Kar. At any rate, he sometimes attends the fair."

"That is interesting," she said. "Do you think yourself capable of pointing him out to us?"

"I do not think I would have any trouble in doing so," I said.

"Lift your head, Brinlar," she said.

I looked up into the eyes of the Lady Yanina. I could see that her mind was racing.

"Tomorrow, under guard," she said, "you will go to the fair. If you see this Bosk, inform my men."

"But I know him," I said. "If he were to see me under guard, might he not be suspicious? Too, foul play, if that be your intent, is not to take place on the fairgrounds. They are truce grounds. Besides, what if he is in the presence of retainers?"

"I see," she said, angrily. "It is merely a plan on your part to escape."

"The inn of Ragnar is outside of the fairgrounds," I said. "What if I could get him to come there, alone?"

"How could it be done?" she asked, eagerly.

"I would wish your help," I said.

"Yes?" she said.

"Some think he finds women too excruciatingly desirable," I said.

"Yes," she said, "yes!"

"I could approach him and tell him that I am acting as the agent of a rich, free woman, one who is much attracted to him and desires to serve him, even as a slave."

"I understand," she said.

"Do you think you could disguise yourself as a mere slave?" I asked.

"Not to the collar!" she said.

"Of course not," I said. "Indeed, it is a premise of my plan that Mistress be understood to be a free woman."

"You would then have him come to the inn of Ragnar," she said, "supposedly to a secret rendezvous."

"Mistress penetrates swiftly to the core of my plan," I said.

"The entrapment might best take place in an alcove," she said, musingly, "wherein I might lie as bait."

"An interesting idea," I granted her.

"He enters the alcove, puts aside his weapons," she mused, "and then my men, in the small quarters, he confined on three sides, set upon him."

"I salute the brilliance of Mistress," I said.

She clenched her small fists. "What a triumph!" she cried. "What a victory! Getting Bosk of Port Kar in my chains! Then delivering him, almost in passing, as a casual surprise, to Flaminius."

Flaminius, I gathered, was the name of her recent guest at this picnic and meeting. The name suggested the city of Ar, or one of her allies. I had once known a physician by the name of Flaminius, who was of Ar. They were not the same individual, of course. There are many common names on Gor, as, I suppose, in most civilizations. Tarl, for example, my name, tends to a familiar one on Gor, particularly in the northern areas, such as Torvaldsland and its vicinity. The commonness of names is even more acute with slave names. For example, common slave names on Gor are Tuka, Lana, and Lita. There are probably hundreds of girls on Gor answering to those names, and others, almost as familiar, which are similarly luscious. Earth-girl names, incidentally, as is well known, are often used on Gor as slave names.

"Why should he listen to you?" she asked, suddenly, looking down at me.

"I am sure he trusts me," I said.

"Can you do this?" she asked.

"You must understand," I said, "that he may not even be at the fair."

"That is true," she said, angrily. "Too, he might be there, and you might miss him."

"If he is there, I think I will be able to determine it," I said.

"How so?" she said.

I shrugged. "I know him," I said. "Too, I think I know certain of his favorite places."

"Excellent!" she said. "It might just work!" She regarded me. "If I let you out of my sight," she said, "I think I shall put you in close chains. It should then be easy to recover you."

"In such chaining I could barely move," I said. "It would certainly not facilitate my inquiries at the fair."

"Then two of my men must accompany you, surreptitiously," she said.

"This Bosk, I assure you," I said, "is commonly an observant fellow. I doubt that he would fail to detect the presence of two loiterers in our vicinity."

"Then it is the chains for you, Brinlar!" she said, angrily.

"As you wish," I said, "but it would not seem likely to Bosk, surely, that a well-intentioned compatriot of Port Kar would be likely to approach him in close chains, would it?"

"No," she said, irritably, "it would not."

I shrugged.

"Too, in many of the places Bosk might frequent," I said, "it would even be difficult to gain admittance in chains. I would be dismissed as no more than a slave."

"If I permit you this service," she asked, "what would you wish in return?"

"Perhaps Mistress might consider granting me freedom from her captivity," I suggested.

"No," she said. "It is my intention to enslave you, with the others. But if you perform this service for me you might find favor in my eyes. I might even be tempted to treat you with somewhat greater indulgence than you might otherwise deserve. I might even keep you as a personal tent slave. I might even give you pretty clothes to wear."

"Mistress is generous," I said.

"What assurance have I," she asked, "that you will, whether successful or not, keep the rendezvous?"

"You have my word on it," I said, "as a free man."

"I think we can do better than that," she said. "If you do not return, your fourteen compatriots, one by one, one each Ahn, will be slain."

"I will return," I said.

"Word of your treachery will reach Port Kar," she added. "Men will hunt you. Too, sleen will be put upon your trail. Too, in the vicinity of the fair, your description will be circulated, as that of an escaped slave."

"Mistress has surely given me many reasons to return," I said.

"I think so," she said.

"But surely she, in her modesty, has overlooked at least one significant motivation," I said.

"What is that?" she asked.

"That I would wish to look once more upon her beauty," I said.

"You flatterer, Brinlar!" she laughed. "But you are not the first man who has been entrapped in the toils of my beauty. I have lured many, as it pleased me, to their downfall."

"Mistress is so beautiful," I said, "that she could almost be a slave."

"It is true," she said.

"In the morning, then," I said, "I shall go to the fair, to see if I may find this Bosk of Port Kar."

"Arrange with him, if you should encounter him," she said, "to be at the inn of Ragnar at the eighteenth Ahn. I shall, in the meantime, send word to Flaminius to meet me there at the nineteenth Ahn. That will give me time to effect the capture, strip and chain the captive, and change into my prettiest clothes, ready to welcome Flaminius as though nothing out of the ordinary had happened."

"And tonight, Mistress?" I asked, anxiously.

"Tonight," she said, imperiously, "you will be hooded and chained, as usual, within the entrance to my tent. I am to be touched only if I please, and exactly as I please."

"Yes, Mistress," I said. I saw that she still feared me, and herself, and, I think, men generally. She had not yet been able to cope with the sensations which I had induced in her. This is not surprising in a free woman. To be sure, such sensations can be terribly frightening to a free woman. They whisper to her of slavery. She is terrified to say "yes" to them, with all she knows this means, but aches and longs to do so, and will not be whole until she does.

"Hurry, Brinlar!" she said. "Hurry! Pick up the things!"

"Yes, Mistress," I said.

"Until tomorrow!" she said. "Until tomorrow!"

"Yes, Mistress," I said, "until tomorrow."

5

WHAT OCCURRED IN THE INN OF RAGNAR; I WILL RETURN TO THE CAMP OF THE LADY YANINA

I pounded on the door of the old inn of Ragnar, now closed, on the old west road. It lies in the midst of certain other buildings, mostly now, too, closed and dark. I heard a movement behind one of the boarded-up windows. It was a bit past the seventeenth Ahn. The door opened a crack.

"It is Brinlar," said a voice, that of one of the men of the Lady Yanina. "I did not think you would return," he said to me.

"He is a fool," said another of her men, from just within.

"He fears the sleen," said another.

"Let him in! Let him in!" said the voice of the Lady Yanina.

I was admitted into the dark vestibule of the inn, and the door was closed behind me.

"Were you successful?" asked the Lady Yanina, anxiously.

"Yes," I said.

"Marvelous!" she whispered.

"He is intrigued," I said. "He is eager to meet you. He is particularly impressed that you are so attracted to him that you, though a free woman, will serve him in the modalities of the slave."

"Superb!" she said. "The gullible fool!"

"He will be here at the eighteenth Ahn," I said.

"Marvelous, Brinlar," she said. "Marvelous! It is all going perfectly!" As my eyes became accustomed to the darkness, I could see that her five men were here. I had thought they would be. I knew they were not at the camp. I had stopped at the camp on the way back from the fair. I had wished to pick up some things. The "work chain," heavily chained, secured between two trees, had not been guarded. They were unimportant to her now, I supposed. She wanted all of her men here. I could see, too, that she wore some form of belted robe. She was not veiled. "What are you carrying?" she asked.

"Some wine, and things," I said. "I took the liberty of stopping by the camp on the way back from the fair. I thought perhaps you might care for some refreshments. The wait until the nineteenth Ahn, and the arrival of your colleague, Master Flaminius, might be long. You might be hungry."

"You are a dream, Brinlar," said the Lady Yanina. "You are a treasure!"

"May I make a suggestion, Mistress?" I inquired.

"Of course," she said.

"I would, if I were you, light a small lamp or two, illuminating the main hall and perhaps the selected alcove. This should suggest an atmosphere of delicate openness to Bosk of Port Kar, encouraging him to believe that he is eagerly awaited. The darkness of a seemingly deserted inn might appear ominous, perhaps suggesting a trap."

"Light two lamps," said the Lady Yanina to one of her men, "one in the main hall and one in the first alcove."

He set about to accomplish her bidding.

"You are very clever, Brinlar," she said.

"I would further suggest," I said, "that you leave the door to the inn ajar, but that you make no particular effort to conceal your men."

She looked at me, puzzled.

"I have informed Bosk," I said, "that you might have men in attendance. After all, a free woman cannot very well be expected to traverse the old west road unattended. She might fall to a slaver's noose and his iron. The men, however, while not attempting to hide themselves, are expected to remain unobtrusive. Thus the door is to be left tactfully ajar. In this fashion we will not have to devise hiding places for them, nor risk the loss of time, and perhaps the noise, perhaps alerting Bosk of Port Kar, of their emergence from concealment."

"Oh, splendid, Brinlar," she said. "Splendid!"

The man was now completing the lighting of the second lamp. In a moment he had emerged from the alcove.

"I would now encourage my men to sit about the table, there," I said, indicating one of the large rough-hewn tables, with benches, in the main hall. "I would further encourage them," I said, "to sit there as naturally as possible, perhaps even partaking of the refreshments which I have brought."

"Do it," she said.

"Good," said one of the men, taking the sack from me which I had stocked at the camp.

"Does Lady Yanina care to partake?" asked one of the men.

"Not now, not now," she said.

The men sat about the table, reaching into the sack, pulling out the flagon of wine, the goblets, the viands. One of them kicked aside some chains under the table, lying in the vicinity of a stout ring in the floor. The men of Torvaldsland sometimes chain naked bond-maids in such a place.

"I think there is at least one thing more," I said.

"What is that?" she asked.

"May I inspect Lady Yanina?" I asked.

"Inspect me?" she asked.

"Yes," I said. "Bosk is not a fool. He may be dismayed, or become suspicious, if he detects even the least inaccuracy or imperfection in your disguise."

"Turn away," she said to her men.

They did so.

"Look," she said to me, opening her robe. Her body, now clad in slave silk, was incredibly lovely. She would doubtless, as I had earlier thought, bring a high price in a slave market.

"It is as I feared," I said.

"What is wrong?" she asked.

"You have a lining beneath the silk," I said.

"Of course!" she said.

"Remove it," I said.

"Brinlar!" she protested.

"Do you think a master would be likely to permit such a thing to a slave?" I asked.

"But I am not a slave," she said. "I am a free woman!"

"But supposedly you are bringing Bosk here, to serve him as a slave," I said.

She looked at me.

"Do you think he would not note so glaring a discrepancy in your costume?" I asked.

"Look away," she said.

I saw the wine slosh from the flagon I had brought into the goblets of the men.

"You may now look again," she said.

"Ah!" I said.

"I am more naked than naked," she said.

"Mistress is quite beautiful," I said. There was no doubt about that slave-market price.

"It must be somewhere near the eighteenth Ahn," I said. "I think it is time for Mistress to go to the alcove." I turned her about and conducted her to the alcove. "Lie down there," I said, pointing to the furs. She did so. She looked well at my feet.

"Doubtless Mistress has arranged a signal with her men," I said.

"It is quite simple," she said. "I shall merely cry out. They will then rush forward and seize Bosk of Port Kar. In moments, then, he will be stripped and in chains, my helpless prisoner."

"I see," I said.

"Do you think he will come?" she asked.

"Be assured of it," I said. "He will be here."

"But perhaps he will be suspicious," she said.

"Have no fear," I said. "He trusts me. He trusts me like I trust myself."

"What are you doing?" she asked, trying to draw back. I had taken her left ankle in my left hand. It was helpless in my grip.

"Completing your disguise," I said. I took the ankle ring, heavier than was necessary for a female, from the side of the alcove, on its chain, and, with my right hand, clasped it, locking it, about her left ankle.

She jerked at it. "I am chained!" she said.

"Yes," I said.

"Where is the key?" she asked.

"Just outside, on its hook," I said. I had made this determination earlier in the day, in scouting the inn, before she and her men had arrived.

"Can I reach it from where I am?" she asked.

"In no way," I said.

She looked at me, frightened.

"Do not be afraid," I said. "Your men are just outside."

"Yes," she said. "Yes." She examined the ring and the chain, her hands on the chain, frightened, fascinated. She looked up at me. "I'm chained," she said, "truly chained."

"Your men are just outside," I reminded her.

"Yes," she said.

"Is this how you intend to receive Bosk of Port Kar?" I asked.

"What do you mean?" she asked.

"The first moments may be crucial," I said. "You will wish to disarm his suspicions. What if he does not immediately put aside his weapons?"

"I do not understand," she said.

"Lie more seductively, Lady Yanina," I said. "Think slave."

"Brinlar!" she said.

"That is better," I said.

"Your hands!" she said.

"Part your lips slightly," I said. "Look at a man as a slave, feel your helplessness, feel burning heat between your thighs."

"You are posing me as a slave!" she said.

"You are not the first woman who has lain chained in this alcove," I said.

"But they were slaves!" she said.

"Most of them, probably," I said, "but perhaps not all."

She looked at me, frightened.

I rose to my feet.

"What time is it?" she asked.

"It must be quite near the eighteenth Ahn," I said.

"What are you going to do now?" she asked.

"I am going to withdraw from the alcove," I said. "I shall draw the curtains behind me."

"Then I must simply wait," she said, "wait for a man!"

"Yes," I said. "It would seem so."

She squirmed, angrily.

"Many women have done so, of course," I said, "particularly women in such places, in such a bond."

"Of course," she said, angrily.

"And many of them," I said, "would not have known who it was who would come through the curtains, only that they must serve him, and exactly according to his dictates, and marvelously."

"Yes!" she said, angrily.

"You are very beautiful," I said. "Slave silk and a chain become you."

"Oh!" she said.

"It is difficult to conjecture how beautiful you might be, if you were truly a slave."

"Do you think I would be a beautiful slave?" she asked, interested.

"Yes," I said.

"I thought I might be," she said, cuddling down in the furs, "but let men despair, for I shall never be a slave."

I then withdrew from the alcove, closing the curtains behind me. I heard a small sound of the chain, from within, as she moved her ankle.

I conjectured that it must now be about the eighteenth Ahn. Flaminius, probably with his men, would be arriving in the neighborhood of the nineteenth Ahn. This did not give me a great deal of time for all I wished to do. I looked about the inn. The Tassa powder which I had placed in the wine had already, mostly, taken its effect. One of the Lady Yanina's men lifted his head from the table, looking at me, groggily, and then tried to rise to his feet. His legs failed him and he sprawled back, over the bench, and then, half catching himself, slipped to the tiles of the inn floor. I had had little difficulty in locating the Tassa powder. It had been contained among the belongings of the Lady Yanina. I had discovered it on my first full day as her servant, while tidying her tent. It had been contained in a small chest of capture equipment, such as weighted slave nets, ropes, hoods, gags and manacles. Similarly I had had access to the general stores of the camp, that I might more conveniently wait upon and serve her and her guards. With the aid of the lamp taken from the table, about which the guards now lay sprawled, I soon located, in one of the farther alcoves, what I was looking for.

I then returned to the table about which the guards lay and replaced the small lamp on its surface. The things I had taken from the alcove I put to one side. I then went to the curtained threshold of the alcove wherein lay the Lady Yanina. I jerked apart the curtains.

"Brinlar!" she said, startled, drawing back on the furs, her legs under her, with a movement of chain, against the back wall of the alcove.

I regarded her.

"You startled me," she said.

I did not speak.

"Is he here?" she whispered.

"Yes," I said. "He is here."

"Where?" she asked, in a whisper.

"Just outside the alcove," I said. "I suggest you compose yourself. I suggest you prepare yourself for him. I suggest you invite him to your arms."

"Yes," she whispered, frightened. "Yes."

I stepped back a bit, as though to yield the threshold, that it might admit the entrance of another.

The Lady Yanina now lay seductively on her side. She was quite beautiful in the slave silk, and the chain, in the light of the tiny lamp. She gathered together her powers of concentration. Then she extended one hand. "I love you, Bosk of Port Kar," she called, softly. "I have loved you from the first moment I saw you. At the very thought of you I am helpless and weak. Do not be dismayed that someone whom you do not know and whom you have perhaps never even seen is madly in love with you! I have fought my passion for you! But it has conquered me! I am yours!"

She looked at me. "Very good," I said, nodding.

"Permit me to confess my love for you," she called. "Permit me, too, the dignity, as I am a free woman, of using your name in my doing so, before perhaps, if it pleases you, you impose upon me the discipline of a slave."

I nodded.

"I love you, Bosk of Port Kar," she cried. "I love you!"

There was silence.

"What is wrong?" she whispered to me.

I shrugged. "Perhaps he intends to make you wait a moment or two," I said.

She made a small movement of impatience.

I frowned.

She then again composed herself, seductively. Again she extended her hand. "I lie here panting with passion," she called, "as submitted as a slave."

Many of the things which she had said, incidentally, were not different from the genuine, heartfelt declarations of women in love, particularly those so much in love that they find themselves, in effect, the slaves of masters. On the other hand, of course, the Lady Yanina was acting. It is not difficult for a skilled master, incidentally, to discriminate between such declarations which are genuine and those which are not, usually in virtue of incontrovertible body cues. The lying female is then punished. Soon she learns that her passion must be genuine. She then sees to it, with all the consequences, physical, psychological and emotional, attendant upon it, consequences which, at first, are sometimes found horrifying or disturbing but which, ultimately, because of their relation to her depth nature, when she surrenders to this, are found joyfully and gloriously fulfilling. She is then herself, fully.

"Hurry to me, Bosk of Port Kar!" she cried. "I desire your touch! I desire to serve you! I beg to please you! I plead to please you! Take pity on me! Do not torture me so! Do not make me wait longer! Hurry to me, Bosk of Port Kar, my lover, my master!''

"Good," I said.

"Enter my alcove!" she cried. "I am yours!"

I entered the alcove. I did not have a great deal of time.

"Brinlar," she cried, drawing her legs under her, "what are you doing!"

"What do you mean, 'What am I doing!'?" I asked.

"Where is Bosk of Port Kar?" she asked.

"He is here," I said.

"Where?" she asked.

"Here," I said, jerking my thumb toward my chest. "I am he."

"Do not be absurd!" she said.

"Kneel," I said.

"Is this some form of mad joke, Brinlar?" she asked. "Have you taken leave of your senses?"

"I believe you received a command," I said.

"Men!" she cried, leaping to her feet. "Men! Men!"

I let her run to the threshold of the alcove, where the shackle on her left ankle held her up short. She looked wildly out into the main hall. From where she stood, at the curtains, in the light, and shadows, of the small lamp on the table, she could see the slumped, fallen, senseless figures of her guards.

"Tassa powder," I explained. "It was your own. I believe you are familiar with its effects."

I then took her by the upper arms and hurled her back into the alcove, with a rattle of chain, onto the furs.

She scrambled about, and looked at me, wildly. "You are not Bosk of Port Kar!" she cried. "You cannot be Bosk of Port Kar!"

"I am Bosk of Port Kar," I assured her.

"You have gone mad, Brinlar!" she cried. "This is an outrage! Release me!"

I smiled.

"Sleen! Sleen!" she wept.

"You are a female," I said, "and you are in slave silk, and chained. I suggest you keep a respectful tongue in your head, unless you wish to have it removed."

She looked at me, frightened.

"Do you recall having received a command earlier?" I asked.

She knelt.

"How does it feel to be kneeling before a man?" I asked.

She clenched her fists.

"You are wearing slave silk," I said.

"Yes," she said.

"Remove it," I said.

"No," she said.

I reached to the wall and took a slave whip from its hook. Such things are common in the alcoves of inns and taverns on Gor. They help a girl be mindful of her duties.

"Now," I said.

She jerked the silk angrily from her body.

"You are quite beautiful," I said, "for a free woman."

She tossed her head, angrily. "Thank you," she said.

"Kiss the whip," I said.

"Never!" she said.

"You will kiss it now, or after you have felt it," I said. "It does not matter to me."

"I will kiss it," she said angrily.

"More lingeringly," I said, "and lick it, as well."

She complied.

"Now, kiss it again," I said.

She complied.

"Now say, 'I have licked and kissed the whip of a man,' " I said.

"I have licked and kissed the whip of a man!" she said. "Now what are you going to do with me?"

"I do not have much time," I said.

"I do not understand," she said.

"Turn about," I said, "and lean forward, resting on the sides of your forearms."

"No!" she cried.

"Assume the position, as instructed," I said.

"No!" she protested.

I lifted the whip.

She complied.

A few moments later, having freed her ankle from the shackle, I dragged her by her right arm out of the alcove, to the side of the table about which her men lay sprawled. Her lovely dark hair was down about her face. I forced her down on her knees, under the table. I put her over the ring, in the midst of the chains. I clasped the ankle rings about her ankles, locking them. I thrust the short, attached chain, attached to the ankle-ring chain at one end, and the wrist-ring chain at the other, and the wrist rings, on their short chain, between her legs and through the sturdy floor ring. I then, close to the floor, locked her wrists snugly into the wrist rings. She was now held helplessly in place beneath the table. "In such a fashion," I told her, "the men of Torvaldsland sometimes secure their bond-maids. Thus they have them at hand and may use them, to some extent, to please them under the table. In this fashion, similarly, it is easy to feed them by hand and throw them scraps of meat. It is a useful arrangement in their training and, too, even a skilled, experienced girl, even one who is highly esteemed, is sometimes confined so, when it pleases the master to do so."

Her eyes were glazed. Her hair was down before her face. She pulled at the chains, weakly.

"But perhaps you are not interested in the lore of Torvaldsland," I said.

"What you did to me," she said.

"Perhaps you are hungry," I said.

She looked at me, angrily. She moved her head to the side, trying to free her face of hair. I took her hair and, arranging it, put it back over her shoulders. "You are quite beautiful in chains," I said. "Perhaps you should be a slave."

She did not respond.

"You look well chained under a table," I said.

"Thank you," she said, angrily.

I took a piece of meat from the table, one of the viands I had brought from the camp, a small tidbit of roast tarsk.

I held it out to her.

"No," she said.

"Eat," I said.

Her wrists pulled upward, against the wrist rings, but her hands, chained as they were, could lift but a few inches from the floor. "I cannot reach it," she said.

"I am not a patient man," I said.

"I am a free woman!" she said.

"I am well aware of that," I said. "If you were a slave, you would probably have received at least two beatings by now."

She extended her head.

"Excellent, Lady Yanina," I said. "You take food well on your knees, from a man's hand."

The next few pieces of meat I scattered on the tiles. She must take them without touching them with her hands. While she was doing this I disarmed the guards, slinging their weapons about my shoulder.

I then came back to regard the Lady Yanina.

"Have you finished the meat, Lady Yanina?" I inquired.

"Yes!" she said.

I picked up the things, lying to one side, which I had taken from the farther alcove. Her eyes suddenly widened, and she regarded me with terror.

"This key," I said, "I found concealed in your robes. It is, I assume, the key to one of the chests, which contains, doubtless, the keys to certain other chests, and perhaps other keys, as well, such as those pertinent to the shackles of your work chain. If it does not, of course, I may have to make use of certain tools in your camp."

She began to tremble in the chains.

"Among your belongings," I said, "there are also doubtless other things of interest, such as rings, and moneys, and such, pilfered from your captives. I alone am missing a considerable wallet. Too, I think I may count on your having independent stores of coins and notes, and, given your apparent wealth and elegance, a suitable measure of costly cloths, gems and jewelries. These materials I shall distribute among the members of the work chain, to compensate them somewhat for their inconvenience and loss of time. These weapons I carry, too, save for those I reserve for my own use, I shall give to skillful, worthy fellows. We shall then, still free men, make our way to the fair. At the fair, as you know, fighting, enslavement, foul play, and such, are not permitted. After some days of sport and recreation at the fair, we may then, if we wish, from the fairgrounds themselves, take tarns to Port Kar, an expensive proposition to be sure, but one which your resources will doubtless prove sufficient to fund. If you see a light in the sky later, it may be your camp burning."

"Do what you wish," she pleaded, in her chains. "Free the men, take the gold, burn the camp, but do not touch that packet!"

"Oh, yes, this," I said, lifting the leather packet which I had taken from the farther alcove. "This contains the materials, doubtless, which you were to deliver to your dear friend, Flaminius."

"Leave it!" she said.

"Why?" I asked.

"I am a courier," she said. "I must deliver that to Flaminius!"

"I gather that that will be difficult for you to do," I said, "chained as you are."

"Please," she said. "Do not even think of taking that! Leave it! I beg you! I beg you!"

"It must be very important," I said.

"No," she said, quickly, moving in the chains, drawing back. "No. No."

"Then its loss will be negligible," I said.

"The materials will be meaningless to you!" she cried. "They will mean nothing to you!"

"Where are they from?" I asked.

"From Brundisium," she said.

"Who are they from?" I asked.

"From Belnar, my Ubar," she said. I assumed that was a lie. Presumably there was no Belnar who was a Ubar in Brundisium. Still, I did recall that she had referred to a "Belnar" at yesterday's rendezvous with Flaminius.

"And you were to deliver them to Flaminius?" I asked.

"Yes," she said. "Yes!"

"And what is he supposed to do with them?" I asked.

"He is to deliver them to the appropriate parties in Ar," she said.

"In Ar?" I asked.

"Yes," she said.

That surprised me. I wondered if she knew the true destination of the materials. I assumed they must actually be transmissions to the Sardar. Presumably it was merely her intention to mislead me.

"They are state papers," she said. "They must not fall into the wrong hands!" I assumed they were not state papers, of course. On the other hand, I was prepared to believe that they had their origin in Brundisium, and that there was some fellow named Belnar associated with them. He would be, I supposed, an agent of Priest-Kings. I was curious. I considered waiting for Flaminius and his men. Yet I had no special wish to kill them, and particularly if they were agents of Priest-Kings. I had already killed one fellow who, I took it, was an agent of Priest-Kings, the fellow, Babinius, in Port Kar. I had once served Priest-Kings. I did not wish now, whatever might be their current attitudes toward me, to make a practice of dropping their agents. To be sure, I did not know for certain that this Belnar, and Flaminius, the Lady Yanina, and those associated with them were agents of Kurii.

"Do you serve Priest-Kings?" I asked the Lady Yanina.

"I do not understand," she said.

"Do you serve Beasts?" I asked.

"I do not understand," she said.

"Whom do you serve?" I asked.

"Belnar," she said, "my ubar, Ubar of Brundisium."

"Why should this Belnar, whom I do not know, supposedly the Ubar of Brundisium, a city with which I have never had dealings, find me of such interest? Why should he send a killer against me, or desire my apprehension?"

"I do not know," she said.

I smiled.

"I do not!" she said.

It could be, of course, that she, for all her beauty, was only a lowly counter in an intricate, complex game beyond her understanding. She might not even know, ultimately, whether she served Priest-Kings, or Kurii. That was an interesting thought.

"I am going now," I said.

"Don't go!" she cried.

"On the other hand, I recommend that you remain where you are, waiting for Flaminius."

She shook the chains, in helpless frustration.

"He will be along shortly," I assured her.

"Leave the packet!" she begged.

"Do you beg it naked, on your knees, chained, as might a slave?" I asked.

"Yes!" she cried. "I beg it on my knees, naked, in chains, as might a slave!"

"Interesting," I said.

"Leave it," she begged.

"No," I said.

She looked at me, aghast.

"But you did beg prettily," I said, "and had the matter been otherwise, for example, had you been begging to serve my pleasure, I would truly have been tempted to give you a more favorable response."

"I am a free woman," she said. "How can you, a free man, deny me anything I want?"

"Easily," I said.

She looked at me, angrily.

"Many free women believe they can have anything they want, merely by asking for it, or demanding it," I said, "but now you see that that is not true, at least not in a world where there are true men."

She shook the chains in frustration. "You make me as helpless and dependent on you as a slave!" she cried.

"Yes," I said.

"Wait!" she said.

"Yes?" I said, turning.

"What will they do with me?" she asked.

"I do not know," I said.

"Belnar will not be pleased," she said. "In Brundisium we

do not look lightly on failure. At the least I shall be considerably reduced in rank. I will be denied the use of footwear. My pretty clothes will be taken away. I will be permitted only plain robes, and shortened so that my calves may be seen by men. I may even be forced to go publicly face-stripped. I may even be expelled from the palace. It could even mean the collar for me!"

I wondered if she were truly of the household of the palace. If so, then perhaps this Belnar might be a resident of the palace. Perhaps he was an official or minister of some sort in the government of Brundisium. It did not seem to me likely that he would be the Ubar of Brundisium. So important a personage as a Ubar would not be likely to have much of an interest in a captain of Port Kar. On the other hand, I supposed it was possible. He might, I supposed, be both a Ubar and an agent of Priest-Kings, or of Kurii. If he were indeed so prominent then it seemed to me more likely that he might serve Kurii than Priest-Kings. The Priest-Kings, at least on the whole, it seemed to me, seldom picked prominent, conspicuous personages for their agents. Samos had been in their service before he had become the first captain in the Council of Captains in Port Kar. Perhaps then Flaminius, and the Lady Yanina, and those associated with them, did serve Kurii.

"I see then," I said, "that you will have much to think about while awaiting the arrival of Flaminius."

"Flaminius!" she laughed bitterly. "Dear Flaminius! He will shed few tears, I assure you, over my plight!"

"That would be my impression," I said.

"He will find my downfall amusing, relishing it," she said.

"Perhaps if your punishment is enslavement," I said, "you might aspire to be one of his girls."

"Perhaps," she said, bitterly.

"He seems the sort of a man who would know how to make a woman crawl beneath his whip," I said.

"That, too, is my understanding," she said. "Wait! Wait!"

But I had then withdrawn from the inn of Ragnar. Then I was making my way back to her camp.

6

I RENEW AN ACQUAINTANCE; I AM CONSIDERING VENTURING TO BRUNDISIUM

"Disgusting! Disgusting!" cried the free woman, one veiled and wearing the robes of the scribes, standing in the audience. "Pull down your skirt, you slave, you brazen hussy!"

"Pray, do withdraw, noble sir, for you surprise me unawares, and of necessity I must improvise some veiling, lest my features be disclosed," cried the girl upon the stage, Boots Tarsk-Bit's current Brigella. I had seen her a few days earlier in Port Kar.

"Pull down your skirt, slut!" cried the free woman in the audience.

"Be quiet," said a free man to the woman. "It is only a play."

"Be silent yourself!" she cried back at him.

"Would that you were a slave," he growled. "You would pay richly for your impertinence."

"I am not a slave," she said.

"Obviously," he said.

"And I shall never be a slave," she said.

"Do not be too sure of that," he said.

"Beast," she said.

"I wonder if you would be any good chained in a tent," he said.

"Monster!" she said.

"Let us observe the drama," suggested another fellow.

"Though I be impoverished and am clad in rags, in naught but the meanness of tatters," said the Brigella to Boots Tarsk-Bit, he on the stage with her, he in the guise of a pompous, puffing, lecherous merchant, "know, and know well, noble sir, that I am a free woman!"

This announcement, predictably, was met with guffaws of laughter from the audience.

"Take the scarf from about her throat!" hooted a man. "See if there is not a steel collar beneath it!" On Gor, as I have perhaps mentioned, most of the actresses are slaves. In serious drama or more sophisticated comedy, when women are permitted roles within it, the female roles usually being played by men, and the females are slaves, their collars are sometimes removed. Before this is done, however, usually a steel bracelet or anklet, locked, which they cannot remove, is placed on them. In this way, they continue, helplessly, to wear some token of bondage. This facilitates, in any possible dispute or uncertainty as to their status or condition, a clear determination in the matter, by anyone, of course, but in particular by guardsmen or magistrates, or otherwise duly authorized authorities.

This custom tends to prevent inconvenience and possible embarrassment, for example, the binding of the woman and the remanding of her to the attention of free females, that she may be stripped and her body examined for the presence of slave marks. In such an event, incidentally, it behooves the girl to swiftly and openly confess her bondage. Free women despise slaves. They tend to treat them with great cruelty and viciousness in general, and, in particular, they are not likely to be pleasant with one who has been so bold as to commit the heinous crime of impersonating one of them. There is no difficulty in locating or recognizing the slave mark in a girl's body. It, though small and tasteful, is prominent in her flesh. It is easily located, perfectly legible and totally unmistakable. It serves its identificatory purposes well. It, in effect, is part of her. It is in her hide.

Normally when a girl plays upon the stage, even if she is nude, the brand is not covered. Usually, if she is playing the role of a free woman it is simply "not seen," so to speak, being ignored by the audience, by virtue of a Gorean theatrical convention. If a great deal is being made of the freedom of the woman in the play, as is not unusual in many dramas and farces, the brand is sometimes covered, as with a small, circular adhesive patch. The removel of this patch, conjoined perhaps with a collaring, for example, may then suggest that the female has now been suitably enslaved. The covering of the brand, thereby suggesting that for the purposes of the play and the role it does not exist, or does not yet exist, is another Gorean theatrical convention.

There are many such conventions. Carrying a tarn goad and moving about the stage in a certain manner suggests that one is riding a tarn; a kaiila crop, or kaiila goad, and a change of gait suggests that one is riding a kaiila; a branch on the stage can stand for a forest or a bit of a wall for a city; standing on a box or small table can suggest that the hero is viewing matters from the summit of a mountain or from battlements; some sprinkled confetti can evoke a snow storm; a walk about the stage may indicate a long journey, of thousands of pasangs; some crossed poles and a silken hanging can indicate a throne room or the tent of a general; a banner carried behind a "general" can indicate that he has a thousand men at his back; a black cloak indicates that the character is invisible, and so on.

"Are you truly free?" inquired Boots Tarsk-Bit, with exaggerated incredulity, in the guise of the merchant, of his Brigella.

"Yes!" she cried, holding her skirt up about her face, it clenched in her small fists, to veil herself with it. There was laughter then, doubtless not only at the preposterousness of the situation but, too, at the incongruity of so obvious a slave, such a lovely Brigella, enunciating such a line.

Boots puffed across the stage, as though to obtain a better vantage point.

"Tal, noble sir," she said.

"Tal, noble lady," said he.

"Is there anything wrong?" she inquired.

"I would say that there is very little wrong, if anything," he said.

"Have you never seen a free woman before?" she asked.

"This farce is an insult to free women!" cried the free woman in the audience, she in the blue of the scribes.

"Have you never seen a free woman before?" repeated the Brigella.

"Generally I do not see so much of them," Boots admitted, as the merchant.

"I see," said the Brigella.

"Often not half so much," said Boots.

"Insulting!" cried the free woman.

"But I expect I see more of you than most," he said.

"Insulting! Insulting!" cried the free woman.

"Are you dismayed that I do not receive you properly?" asked the Brigella.

"I should be pleased," Boots assured her, "if it were your intention to receive me at all, either properly or improperly."

"What lady could do otherwise?" she inquired.

"Indeed!" Boots cried enthusiastically.

"I mean, of course," she said, "that I apologize for having to veil myself so hastily, making such swift and resourceful use of whatever materials might be at hand."

"I effect nothing critical," he assured her.

"Then you do not think the less of me?" she asked.

"No, I admire you. I admire you!" he said, admiring her.

"And thus," she said, "do we free women show men our modesty."

"And you have a very lovely modesty," affirmed Boots admiringly.

"Oh!" she cried, suddenly, as though in the most acute embarrassment, and, crouching down, hastily pulled her skirt down about her ankles.

"I thought you were a free woman," exclaimed Boots.

"I am!" she cried. "I am!"

"And you go face-stripped before a strange man?" he inquired.

"Oh!" she cried, miserably, leaping up, once more pulling her skirt up, high about her face, using it once more to conceal her features.

"Ah!" cried Boots, appreciatively.

"Oh!" she cried in misery, thrusting her skirt down as though in great embarrassment.

"Face-stripped!" cried Boots, as though scandalized.

Up went the skirt.

"Ah!" cried Boots. "Ah!"

Down came the skirt.

"Face-stripped," said Boots, reprovingly.

"What is a poor girl to do!" cried the Brigella. "What is a poor girl to do!"

The skirt's hem, clutched in her small hands, she moaning with misery and frustration, leapt up and down, again and again, in ever-shortening cycles until she held it, frustratedly, between her bosom and throat. In this fashion, of course, to the amusement of most of the crowd, it concealed neither her "modesty," so to speak, nor her features.

It must be understood, of course, to fully appreciate what was going on, that the public exposure of the features of a free woman, particularly one of high caste, or with some pretense to position or status, is a socially serious matter in many Gorean localities. Indeed, in some cities an unveiled free woman is susceptible to being taken into custody by guardsmen, then to be veiled, by force if necessary, and publicly conducted back to her home. Indeed, in some cities she is marched back to her home stripped, except for the face veil which has been put on her. In these cases a crowd usually follows, to see to what home it is that she is to be returned. Repeated offenses in such a city usually result in the enslavement of the female. Such serious measures, of course, are seldom required to protect such familiar Gorean proprieties. Custom, by itself, normally suffices.

Social pressures, too, in various ways, contribute to the same end. An unveiled woman, for example, may find other women turning away from her in a market, perhaps with expressions of disgust. Indeed, she may not even be waited upon, or dealt with, in a market by a free woman unless she first kneels. It would not be unusual for her, in a crowded place, to overhear remarks, perhaps whispers or sneers, of which she is the obvious object, such as "Shameless slut," "Brazen baggage," "As immodest as a slave," "I wonder who her master is," and "Put a collar on her!" And if she should attempt to confront or challenge her assailants, she will merely find such remarks repeated articulately and clearly to her face.

Slaves, incidentally, are commonly forbidden facial veiling. Their features are commonly kept naked, exposed fully to public view. In this way they may be looked upon by men, even casually, whenever and however they might be pleased to do so. That the Earth girl commonly thinks little of this exposure of her features, incidentally, is one of the many reasons that many Goreans think of her as a natural slave. For a Gorean girl that she is now, suddenly, no longer entitled to facial veiling, unless it pleases the master to grant it to her, is one of the most fearful and significant aspects of her transition into bondage. Her features, in all their sensitivity and beauty, so intimate, personal and private to her, so revelatory of her deepest and most secret thoughts, feelings and emotions, are now exposed to public view, to be looked upon, and read, by whomsoever may be pleased to do so.

It is interesting to note that even some Earth girls on Gor, after a short while, tend to become sensitive to this sort of thing. It is usually interpreted by both sorts of girls, then, for a time, as a part of the "shame" of the collar. In a little longer while, of course, neither sort of girl, the Gorean girl or the Earth girl now sensitive to the subtler implications of facial exposure, thinks anything more about it, or at least not normally. Both have now learned that they are now naught but slaves, and that that is all there is to it. No longer do they aspire to the prerogatives of the free woman. Their exposure, their human legibility, so to speak, like their obedience, service, love and discipline, is part of their condition. In a sense they find it liberating. It frees them from the temptations of deceit, pretense and restraint. Seldom now do they think, among themselves, of the "shame" of the collar. Rather, now, in their place in the perfection of nature, yielded fully, helplessly, choicelessly, if you like, submitted at the feet of men, their deepest sexuality and needs recognized, attended to and fulfilled, they tend to think of its joy. No longer now do they aspire to the privileges and prerogatives of the free woman; let her continue to live in her house of inhibition and convention; let her have her frigidities, jealousies and shams; they have found something a thousand times more precious, their meaning, their significance, their happiness, their joy, their fulfillment, their collars.

"What am I to do?" called the lovely Brigella to the crowd, the hem of her garment clutched up about her neck. Her lovely lips pouted. It seemed she was almost in tears. How seemingly distraught she was, how seemingly dismayed she was with her dilemma!

"Kneel down!" called a man jovially.

"Take off your clothes!" called another.

"Lick his feet!" suggested another.

"Slave!" said the free woman, coldly, imperiously, obviously addressing the Brigella, and in no uncertain terms.

"Mistress," responded the girl immediately, frightened, breaking out of character, turning about and kneeling down. She had been addressed by a free woman.

"Head to the boards!" snapped the free woman.

Immediately the girl put her head down to the boards. She trembled. Such women are totally at the mercy of free persons.

"Are you the owner of this slave?" asked the free woman of Boots Tarsk-Bit.

"Yes, Lady," he said.

"I suggest that she be beaten," she said.

"Perhaps an excellent suggestion," said Boots Tarsk-Bit, "as she is a slave, but have you any special reason in mind, not that one needs one, of course."

"I do not care for her performance," said the free woman.

"It is difficult to please everyone," Boots admitted. "But I assure you that if I, her master, am not fully satisfied with her performance, I will personally tie her and see that she is well whipped.''

"I find her performance disgusting,'' she said.

"Yes, Lady,'' said Boots.

"And I find it an insult to free women!'' said the free woman.

"Yes, Lady,'' said Boots, patiently.

"Let's see the rest of the play,'' said a man.

"So beat her!'' said the free woman.

"I see no reason to beat her,'' said Boots. "She is doing precisely what she is supposed to be doing. She is obeying. She is being obedient. If she were not being obedient, then I would beat her, then I would see to it that she were suitably and lengthily lashed.''

"Beat her!'' demanded the free woman.

"Shall I beat her?'' inquired Boots of the crowd.

"No!'' called a man.

"No!'' shouted another.

"On with the play!'' shouted another.

"Have you a license for this performance?'' inquired the free woman.

"Have mercy on me, Lady,'' said Boots. "I am come on hard times. Only yesterday I had to sell my golden courtesan, just to make ends meet.''

It is difficult to run a Gorean company of Boots's sort without a golden courtesan. That is one of the major stock characters in this form of drama. That character occurs probably in fifty to sixty percent of the farces constituting the repertory of such a company. It would be like trying to get along without a comic merchant, a Brigella, a Bina, a Lecchio or a Chino. I already knew of Boots's difficulty. I had learned of it yesterday evening. Indeed, I had already seen fit, for reasons of my own, to engage in certain actions pertinent to the matter.

"Have you a license?'' pressed the free woman.

"Last year I did not have one, admittedly, due to some fearful inadvertence,'' admitted Boots, "but I would not risk that twice at the Sardar Fair. I have settled my debts here. Indeed, no sooner had I settled one than it seemed that a thousand creditors, guardsmen at their backs, descended upon me, like jards upon an unwatched roast. At the point of their steel I became enamored with the satisfactions attendant upon the pursuit of punctilious honesty. And destitution, when all is said and done, is doubtless a negligible price to pay for so glorious a boon as the improvement of one's character.''

"You do have a license then?" she asked.

"I had to sell my golden courtesan to purchase one," said Boots.

"You have one then?" she asked.

"Yes, kind lady!" said Boots.

"It is my intention to see that it is revoked," she said.

"Good," said one of the men. "Go off, and see to it."

"Get on with the play!" called another.

"Have mercy, kind lady," begged Boots.

"I do not think that I will see fit to show you mercy in this matter," she said.

"Take off the clothes of the scribe female and put her under the whip," said a man.

"Enslave her," growled another.

"Silence, silence, rabble!" she cried, turning about, facing the crowd.

"Rabble?" inquired a fellow. Assuredly the crowd was composed mostly of free men.

"Rabble!" said another fellow, angrily.

"Beasts and scum!" she cried.

"Enslave her!" said a man.

"Get her a collar," said a man. "She will then quickly mend her ways."

"Take off her clothes," said another. "Bracelet her. Put her on a leash."

"I have bracelets and a leash here," said a man.

"Put them on her," said another. "Conduct her to an iron worker."

"I will pay for her branding," said another.

"I will share the cost," said another.

"I am Telitsia, Lady of Asperiche," she said. "I am a free woman! I am not afraid of men!"

I smiled to myself. She was perfectly safe, of course, for she was within the perimeters of the Sardar Fair. How brave women can be within the context of conventions! I wondered if they understood the artificiality, the fragility, the tentativeness, the revokability of those subtle ramparts. Did they truly confuse them with walls of stone and the forces of weaponry? Did they understand the differences between the lines and colors on maps and the realities of a physical terrain? To what extent did they comprehend the fictional or mythical nature of those castles within which they took refuge, from the heights of which they sought to impress their will on worlds? Did they not know that one day men might say to them, "The castle does not exist,"

and that they might then find themselves once again, the patience
of men ended, the folly concluded, the game over, struck to their
place in nature, gazing upward at masters? Asperiche, incidentally,
is an exchange island, or free island, in Thassa. It is south of
Teletus and Tabor. It is administered by merchants.

"Let us continue with the play," suggested a man, irritably.

"Yes, yes," said others. "On with the play!" "Continue!"
"Get on with the play!"

"I understand that your Brigella is good," said a man. "I
want to see her, fully."

The Brigella trembled, but she, still kneeling, could not lift
her head from the boards. She had not yet received permission to
do so. She did not, accordingly, know who it was who had
expressed interest in her. I had little doubt, however, that she
would now perform marvelously, that she would now play superbly to the entire crowd, that she would now make a special
effort to be as deliciously skillful and juicily appealing in her
role as possible. Someone was out there, doubtless with money
in his wallet, who might be interested in spending it on her,
buying her. This doubtless thrilled her, and pleased her vanity. It
is a great compliment to a woman to be willing to buy her. It is
then up to the girl to see that the man gets a thousand times his
money's worth, and more. I licked my lips in anticipation.

"With your permission, Lady Telitsia?" inquired Boots,
addressing himself politely to the haughty, rigid, proud, vain,
heavily veiled, blue-clad free female standing in the front row
below the stage.

"You may continue," she said.

"But you may find what ensues offensive," Boots warned
her.

"Doubtless I will," she said. "And have no fear, I shall
include it in my complaint to the proper magistrates."

"You wish to remain?" asked Boots, puzzled.

"Yes," she said, "but do not expect a coin from me."

I smiled. The Lady Telitsia was obviously as interested in
seeing the rest of the play as the rest of us. I found this
interesting.

"The simple beneficence of your presence, that of a noble free
woman, is in itself a reward far beyond our deserving," Boots
assured her.

"What is he saying?" asked a man.

"He is saying that she is more than we deserve," growled a
fellow.

"That is true," laughed a man.

"She could be taught to be pleasing," said a man.

"True," said a man.

"That might be amusing," said a man.

"You may continue," said the Lady Telitsia, loftily, to Boots Tarsk-Bit, ignoring these remarks.

"Thank you, kind lady," he said. He then turned to the Brigella. "Girl!" he snapped. His demeanor toward the Brigella was quite different from that toward the free woman. She, of course, was a slave. She leaped to her feet, clutching her skirt's hem again up about her neck.

"Shameless," said the free woman.

The Brigalla anxiously surveyed the crowd, trying to guess who it might be who had expressed interest in her. It could, indeed, have been any one of several men. Then she smiled prettily and flexed her knees. It was very well done. I think she probably made every man in the audience want to get his hands on her. She then, pouting and affecting her expression of dainty, ladylike consternation, resumed her character in the interrupted farce.

"Continue," signaled Boots Tarsk-Bit, himself returning to his comedic role.

"If I lift my skirt it seems I must reveal my modesty to a stranger," she wailed to the audience, "whereas should I lower it I must then, it seems, face-strip myself before him as brazenly as might a hussy! Oh, what is a poor girl to do?"

"I myself, putatively lovely lady, have in my pack the answer to your very problem," announced Boots.

"Pray, tell, good sir," she cried, "what might it be?"

"A veil," said he.

"That is just what I need!" she cried.

"But it is no ordinary veil," he said.

"Let me see it," she begged.

"I wonder if you will be able to see it," he said.

"What do you mean?" she asked.

"But, of course, you will be able to see it," he said, "for you are obviously a free woman!"

"I do not understand," she said.

"It is a veil woven by the magicians of Anango," he said.

"Not them!" she cried.

"The same," he agreed solemnly. Anango, like Asperiche, is an exchange, or free, island in Thassa, administered by members of the caste of merchants. It is, however, unlike Asperiche, very far away. It is far south of the equator, so far south as to almost beyond the ken of most Goreans, except as a place both remote and exotic. The jungles of the Anangoan interior serve as the setting for various fanciful tales, having to do with strange races, mysterious plants and fabulous animals. The "magicians of Anango," for what it is worth, seem to be well known everywhere on Gor except in Anango. In Anango itself it seems folks have never heard of them.

"And it is the special property of this veil," Boots solemnly assured the girl, "that it is visible only to free persons."

"It would not do then to wear it before slaves," she said.

"Perhaps not," said Boots, "but then who cares what slaves think?"

"True," she said. "Let me see it! Let me see it!"

"But I have it here in my hand," said Boots.

"How beautiful it is!" she cried. There was much laughter. The device of the invisible cloth, or invisible object, a stone, a sword, a garment, a house, a boat, supposedly visible only to those with special properties, is a commonplace in Gorean folklore. This type of story has many variations.

Boots held the supposed cloth up, turning it about, displaying it.

"Have you ever seen anything like it?" asked Boots.

"No!" she said.

"It is so light," he said, "that one can hardly feel it. Indeed, it is said that slaves cannot even feel it at all."

"I must have it!" she cried.

"It is terribly expensive," he warned her.

"Oh, woe!" she cried.

"Perhaps you have ten thousand gold pieces?" he asked.

"Alas, no!" she cried. "I am a poor maid, with not even a tarsk bit to her name."

"Alas, also," said Boots, gloomily, proceeding to apparently fold the cloth. He did this marvelously well in pantomime. He was very skillful. "I had hoped to make a sale," he added.

"Could you not cut me off just a little piece," she asked.

"A thousand gold pieces worth?" he asked.

"Alas," she wept. "I could not afford even that."

"To be sure," he said, "the veil is quite large, containing easily enough cloth to conceal an entire figure."

"I can see that," she said.

"Stinting on their work is not allowed by the magicians of Anango," he said.

"Everyone knows that," she said.

"In any event," said Boots, "surely you would not be so cruel, so heartless, so insensitive, as to suggest that I even consider using the scissors, that cruel engine, those divisive knives, upon so wondrous an object.''

"No!" she cried.

"I wish you well, lady," said Boots, sadly, preparing to return the veil to his pack.

"I must have it!" she cried.

"Oh?" asked Boots.

"I will do anything to obtain it!" she cried.

"Anything?" asked Boots, hopefully.

"Anything!" she cried.

"Perhaps," mused Boots. "Perhaps—"

"Yes!" she cried. "Yes?"

"No, it is unthinkable!" he said.

"What?" she begged, eagerly.

"Unthinkable!" announced Boots.

"What?" she pressed.

"For you are a free woman," he said.

"What?" she cried.

"It is well known that men have needs," he said, "and that they are lustful beasts."

"I wonder what he can have in mind?" asked the girl of the crowd.

"And I have been a long time upon the road," he said.

"I grow suspicious," she said.

"And I know that you are a free woman," he said.

"My suspicions deepen with every instant," she informed the crowd.

"And that the beauty of a free woman is a commodity beyond price."

"My mind races," she kept the crowd informed. There was laughter. In a sense what Boots was saying was correct. The beauty of a free woman was a commodity beyond price. This was not because there was anything special about it, of course, but only because it was not for sale.

"And so I wonder," said Boots, "if in exchange for this wondrous veil I might be granted the briefest of peeps at your priceless beauty."

"It is far worse than I thought," cried the girl in dismay to the crowd.

"Forgive me, lady!" cried Boots, as though in horror at the enormity of what he had suggested.

"Yet," said the girl to the crowd, "I do desire that object mightily."

"I must be on my way," said Boots, resignedly.

"Stay, good sir. Tarry but a moment," she called.

"Yes?" said Boots.

"Would a glimpse of but an ankle or a wrist do?" she inquired.

"I hesitate to call this to your attention," said Boots, "but as you may not have noticed, as you are not hosed and gloved, such bold glimpses are already mine."

"My beauty, as that of a free woman, is priceless, is it not?" she asked.

"Of course," he said.

"Suppose then," she said, "that for your briefest of peeps you give me the ten thousand gold pieces of which you spoke, as a mere gesture of gratitude, of course, as the values involved are clearly incommensurate, and the veil, as well."

"Your generosity overwhelms me," cried Boots, "and had I ten thousand gold pieces I would doubtless gladly barter them for such a vision, but, alas, alack, I lack that mere ten thousand pieces of gold!" Boots turned to the crowd. "So near," he said, "and yet so far."

There was much laughter.

The free woman in the audience turned to me. "That line," she said, "was well delivered."

"Yes," I agreed.

"Can you see the veil?" one of the men in the audience asked her.

"Of course," she said. I saw that the female had an active wit. She had not fallen into his trap. There was laughter. She seemed highly intelligent. I supposed, then, other things being equal, that she might be capable of attaining at least the minimum standards of slave adequacy. I wondered if she were attractive. It was not easy to tell, robed and veiled as she was. It would have been easier to tell had she been in slave silk, or nude in a collar.

Boots, I saw, had followed this small exchange from the stage.

"Nine thousand pieces of gold, then," called the Brigella to Boots.

He returned his attention to the stage.

"Eight thousand?" she asked, hopefully.

Boots, with a great flourish, shook out the magic veil and displayed it shamelessly, so cruelly tempting her, awing her with its splendors.

"How marvelous it is!" she cried. "Oh! Oh!"

"Well," said Boots, seemingly folding the cloth, "I must be on my way."

"No, no!" she said. "Five thousand? One thousand!"

"Oh, curse my poverty," cried Boots, "that I cannot take advantage of so golden an opportunity!"

"I must have it," she wailed to the audience, "but I do not know what to do!"

Many then were the suggestions called out to the bewildered Brigella from the audience, not all of which were of a refined nature. This type of participation, so to speak, on the part of the audience is a very familiar thing in the lower forms of Gorean theater. It is even welcomed and encouraged. The farce is something which, in a sense, the actors and the audience do together. They collaborate, in effect, to produce the theatrical experience. If the play is not going well, the audience, too, is likely to let the actors know about it. Sometimes a play is hooted down and another must be hastily substituted for it. Fights in the audience, between those who approve of what is going on and those who do not, are not uncommon. It is not unknown, either, for the stage to be littered with cores and rinds, and garbage of various sorts, most of which have previously, successfully or unsuccessfully, served as missiles. Occasionally an actor is struck unconscious by a more serious projectile. I do not envy the actor his profession. I prefer my own caste, that of the warriors.

"May I make a suggestion?" inquired Boots.

"Of course, kind sir," she cried, as though welcoming any solution in her dilemma.

"Disrobe in private," he suggested, "and while disrobing, consider the matter. Then, if you decide, in your nobility, to deny me even the briefest of peeps, what harm could possibly have been done?"

"A splendid suggestion, kind sir," she said, "but where, in this fair meadow, at the side of a public road, will I find suitable privacy?"

"Here!" said Boots, lifting up the veil.

"What?" she asked.

"As you can see," said Boots, "it is as opaque as it is beautiful."

"Of course!" she said.

"You can see it, can't you?" he asked, suddenly concerned.

"Of course! Of course!" she said.

"Then?" asked Boots.

"Hold it up high," she said.

Boots obliged. "Are you disrobing?" he asked. The men in

the audience began to cry out with pleasure. Some struck their
left shoulders in Gorean applause.

"Yes," called the Brigella.

She was quite beautiful.

"I shall mention this in my complaint to the proper magistrates,"
said the free woman from her position near the stage.

"Are you absolutely naked now?" asked Boots, as though he
could not see her.

"Totally," she said.

"A silver tarsk for her!" called a fellow from the audience.
The Brigella smiled. It must have been he, then, who had
expressed an interest in her.

"A silver tarsk, five!" called another fellow.

"A silver tarsk, ten!" called another.

These offers clearly pleased the Brigella. They attested her
value, which was considerable. Many women sell for less than a
silver tarsk. Too, the fellows bidding all seemed strong, handsome fellows, all likely masters. There was not one of them who
did not seem capable of handling her perfectly, as the slave she
was. I suspected that this Brigella was not destined to long
remain a member of the troupe of Boots Tarsk-Bit.

"Do not interrupt the play," scolded the free woman.

"And not a tarsk-bit for you, lady," laughed one of the men.

The Lady Telitsia of Asperiche stiffened angrily and returned
her attention to the stage. "You may continue," she informed
the players.

"Why thank you, lady," said Boots Tarsk-Bit.

"Are you being insolent?" she asked.

"No, lady!" exclaimed Boots, innocently.

"She should be whipped," said a man.

The Lady Telitsia did not deign to respond to this suggestion.
She could afford to ignore it, disdainfully. She was not a slave.
She was a free woman, and above whipping. Too, she was
perfectly safe. She was on the protected ground, the truce ground,
of the Sardar Fair.

"Here I stand by a public road, stripped as naked as a slave,"
said the Brigella, confidently, to the audience, "but yet am
perfectly concealed by this wondrous veil."

"Are you truly naked?" asked Boots.

"See?" she said to the crowd.

"To be sure!" called one of the men, one of the fellows who
had bidden on her.

"Yes," she called out to Boots.

"But how can I know if you are truly naked?" inquired Boots, ogling her.

"You may take my word for it," she said, haughtily, "as I am a free woman."

"With all due respect, noble lady," said Boots, "in a transaction of this momentous nature, I believe it is only fair that I be granted assurances of a somewhat greater magnitude."

"What would you wish?" she asked.

"Might I not be granted some evidence of your putative nudity?" he inquired.

"But, sir," she said, "I have not yet decided whether or not to grant you your peep, that moment of inutterable bliss for which you will, willingly, surrender the wondrous veil to me in its entirety."

"Do not mistake me, kind lady," cried Boots, horrified. "I had in mind only evidence of an ilk most indirect."

"But what could that be?" she inquired, dismayed.

"I dare not think on the matter," he lamented.

"I have it!" she cried.

"What?" he asked, winking at the crowd.

"I could show you my clothing!" she cried.

"But of what relevance might that be?" asked Boots, innocently.

"If you detect that I am not within it," she said, "then might you not, boldly, infer me bare?"

"Oh, telling stroke, bold blow!" he cried. "Who might have conjectured that our problem could have succumbed to so deft a solution!"

"I bundle my clothing," she said, "and place it herewith beneath the edge of the veil, that you may see it."

There was much laughter here, at the apparent innocence of this action. This was extremely meaningful, of course, in the Gorean cultural context. When a female places her clothing at the feet of a man she acknowledges that whether or not she may wear it, or other garments, or even if she is to be clothed at all, is dependent on his will, not hers. Boots, in effect, in the context of the play, had tricked her into placing her clothing at his feet. This is tantamount to a declaration of imbondment to the male.

"Hold up the veil," said Boots to the Brigella.

"Why, good sir?" she asked.

"I must count the garments," said Boots, seriously.

"Very well," she said. "Oh, the veil is so light!"

"It is exactly like holding nothing up at all," Boots granted her.

"Exactly," she said. Boots then made a great pretense of

counting the garments. The Brigella turned to the audience, as though holding up the cloth between herself and them. "He is so suspicious, and has such a legalistic mind," she complained. Meanwhile Boots thrust the garments into his pack.

"I trust that all is in order," said the Brigella.

"It would seem so," said Boots, "unless perhaps you are now wearing a second set of garments, a secret set, which was cleverly concealed beneath the first set."

"I assure you I am not," she said.

"I suppose even in matters this momentous," said Boots, "there comes a time when some exchange of trust is in order."

"Precisely," said the Brigella.

"Very well," said Boots.

"I do not see my clothing about," said the Brigella to the crowd, "but doubtless it is hidden behind the veil."

"Then!" cried Boots.

"Yes," she said, "you may now, if you wish, infer, and correctly, sir, that behind this opaque veil I am bare."

"Utterly?" he asked.

"Utterly," she said.

"Oh, intrepid inference!" cried Boots. "I can scarcely control myself!"

"You must struggle to do so, sir," she said.

"Hold the veil higher," said Boots. "Higher, lest I be tempted to peep over its rippling, shimmering horizon, daring to look upon what joys lie beyond. Higher!"

"Is this all right?" she asked.

"Splendid!" said Boots.

She now stood with the veil raised high above her head with her arms spread. This lifted the line of her breasts beautifully. Women are sometimes tied in this posture in a slave market. It is a not uncommon display position.

"Ah!" cried Boots. "Ah!"

"The sounds you utter, sir," she said, "would almost make me believe, could I but see them, which, of course, I cannot, that your facial expressions and bodily attitudes might be those of one who looked relishingly upon me."

"Yes," cried Boots, "it is my active imagination, conjecturing what exposed beauty must lie perfectly concealed behind the impervious barrier of that heartless veil."

"And I am a free woman," said the girl to the crowd, "not even a slave." There was laughter. All that she wore now, in actuality, not in the context of the play, of course, in which she was, by convention, understood to be utterly naked, was her collar, concealed by a light scarf, and a circular adhesive patch on her left thigh, concealing her brand.

"Ah!" cried Boots.

"I had best not permit him more than the briefest of peeps," she said, to the audience, "lest he perhaps in rapture go out of his senses altogether."

Boots pounded his thighs.

"Imagine what it might be if he could truly see me," she said.

"Let me, dear lady," said Boots, "hold the veil. Though it be as light as nothing itself, yet, by now, your arms, if only from their position, must grow weary."

"Thank you, kind sir," she said. "Do you have it now?"

"Of course," said Boots, as though astonished at her question.

"Of course," she said, lightly. "I just did not wish you to drop it."

"There is little danger of that," he said. "I mean, of course, I will exercise considerable caution in its handling."

He now held the cloth up between them.

"Have you given some thought to the matter of whether or not you will permit me the peep of which we spoke so intriguingly earlier?" he asked.

"Keep holding the veil up high," she said. "Perhaps I will consider giving some thought to the matter."

Suddenly, with a cry of apprehension, looking down the road, Boots snapped away the cloth and whipped it behind his back, seeming to stuff it in his belt, behind his back. "Oh!" she cried in horror, cringing and half crouching down, trying to cover herself as well as she could, in maidenly distress. "What have you done, sir? Explain yourself, instantly!"

"I fear brigands approach," he said, looking wildly down the road. "Do not look! They must not see the wondrous veil! Surely they would take it from me."

"But I am naked!" she cried.

"Pretend to be a slave," he advised.

"I," she gasped, in horror, "pretend to be a slave?"

"Yes!" he cried.

"But I know nothing," said the Brigella, in great innocence, to the audience, "of being a slave."

There was laughter.

"What you know nothing of," said the free woman to her, "is of being a free woman, meaningless slut."

The Brigella at one time or another had doubtless been a free woman. Accordingly she would presumably know a great deal about being a free woman. On the other hand she did not dare respond to the free woman, for she was now a slave.

"Would you rather be apprehended by the brigands?" inquired Boots of the Brigella. "They might be pleased to get their capture cords on a free woman."

"No!" she cried.

"Kneel down," he said, "quickly, with your head to the dirt!"

"Oh, oh!" she moaned, but complied.

"That way," he said, "they may take you for a mere slave, perhaps not worth the time it might take to put you in a noose and the time it might take to transport you to a sales point, and me for a poor merchant, perhaps not worth robbing. Here they come. They are fierce looking fellows."

"Oh," she moaned, trembling, "oh, oh."

"Do not look up," he warned her.

"No," she said.

"No, what, Slave?" he said, sternly.

"No, Master!" she said.

There was laughter. He now had her kneeling naked at his feet, addressing him as "Master." In the Gorean culture, of course, this sort of thing is very significant. Indeed, in some cities such things as kneeling before a man or addressing him as "Master" effects legal imbondment on the female, being interpreted as a gesture of submission.

There was now great laughter for, strolling across the stage, swinging censers, mumbling in what was doubtless supposed to resemble archaic Gorean, in the guise of Initiates, came Tarsk-Bit's Lecchio and Chino. In a moment they had passed.

"Those were not brigands," cried the girl, angrily, looking up. "They were Initiates!"

"I am sorry," said Boots, apologetically. "I mistook them for brigands."

She leaped to her feet, covering herself with her hands, as well as she could. "You may now give me the veil, sir," she said, angrily.

"But you have not yet given me my peep," protested Boots.

"Oh!" she cried angrily.

"Consider how you are standing," said Boots, "half turned away from me, half crouched down, and holding your legs as you are, and with your hands and arms placed as they are, such things seem scarcely fair to me. Surely you must understand that such things constitute obstacles uncongenial, at the least, to the achievement of a peep of the quality in question."

"Oh! Oh!" she cried.

"It is a simple matter of bargaining in good faith," said Boots.

"Sleen!" she cried.

"Perhaps we could get a ruling on the matter from a praetor," suggested Boots.

"Sleen! Sleen!" she cried.

"I see that I must be on my way," said Boots.

"No!" she cried. "I must have that wondrous veil!"

"Not without my peep," said Boots.

"Very well, sir," she said. "How will you have your peep? What must I do?"

"Lie down upon your back," he said, "and lift your right knee, placing your hands at your sides, six inches from your thighs, the palms of your hands facing upwards." He regarded her. "No," he said, "that is not quite it. Roll over, if you would. Better. Now lift your upper body from the dirt, supporting it on the palms of your hands, and look back over your shoulder. Not bad. But I am not sure that is exactly it. Kneel now, and straighten your body, putting your head back, clasping your hands behind the back of your head. Perhaps that is almost it."

"I hope so!" she cried.

"But not quite," he said.

"Oh!" she cried in frustration.

"Sometimes one must labor, and experiment, to find the proper peep," he informed her.

"Apparently," she said.

Boots, then, it seemed always just minimally short of success, continued dauntlessly to search for a suitable peep. In doing this, of course, the female was well, and lengthily, displayed for the audience.

She was incredibly beautiful. The men cried out with pleasure, some of them slapping their thighs.

"Disgusting! Disgusting!" cried the free woman.

I myself considered bidding on the Brigella. She was incredibly, marvelously beautiful.

"Disgusting!" cried the free woman.

"It is you who are disgusting," said one of the men to the free woman.

"I?" she cried.

"Yes, you," he said.

The free woman did not respond to him. She stiffened in her

robes, her small hands clenched in her blue gloves. How antibiological, petty, and self-serving were her value judgments.

"Look," cried Boots to the Brigella, in his guise of a merchant. "Someone is coming!"

"You will not fool me twice, you scoundrel, you cad!" she replied from her knees.

"I think it is a woman," said Boots.

"What?" she cried, turning about, half rising, and then collapsed back in confusion, in misery, to her knees. She looked up at Boots, wildly. "It is Lady Tipa, my rival, from the village," she said. "She cannot be allowed to see me like this. What, oh, what, shall I do? Where can I hide?"

"Quickly," cried Boots, "here, beneath my robes!"

Swiftly, on her knees, wildly, knowing not what else to do, the girl had scrambled to Boots. In a moment she was concealed beneath his robes, on her knees, only her calves and feet thrust out from beneath their hem.

"I see, sir," said the newcomer, who was understood to be the free woman, the Lady Tipa, but was presumably Boots's Bina, usually the companion and confidant of the Brigella, "that you well know how to put a slave through her paces."

"Why, thank you, noble lady," said Boots.

"I did not get a good look at her as I approached," said the Bina. "Is she pretty?"

"Some might think her passable," said Boots, "but compared to yourself her beauty is doubtless no more than that of a she-urt compared to that of the preferred slave of a Ubar."

The Brigella churned with rage beneath Boots's robes. She dared not emerge, of course.

"What is wrong with your slave?" asked the Bina.

"She burns with desire," said Boots.

"How weak slaves are," said the Bina.

"Yes," said Boots.

"I am looking for a girl from my village," said the Bina. "I was told, by two fellows, peddlers, I think, whom I take to be of the merchants, that she may have come this way."

"Could you describe her?" asked Boots.

"Her name is Phoebe," said the Bina, "and were she not veiled it would be easier to describe her to you, as she is frightfully homely."

The girl under Boots's robes shook with fury.

"Still," said the newcomer, "you might have been able, nonetheless, to recognize her. She is too short, too wide in the hips and has thick ankles."

At this there was more churning beneath Boots's robes.

"Surely there is something wrong with your slave," said the Bina.

"No, no," Boots assured her.

"What is she doing under there?" asked the Bina.

"She begged so piteously to be permitted to give me the kiss of a slave that I, in my weakness, at last yielded to her entreaties."

There was much furious stirring then beneath the robes.

"How kind you are, sir," said the Bina.

"Thank you," said Boots.

There was a muffled cry, as of rage and protest, from beneath the robes.

"Did she say something?" asked the Bina.

"Only that she begs to be permitted to begin," said Boots.

The robes shook with fury.

"Surely there is something wrong with her," said the Bina.

"It is only that she is suffering with need," said Boots.

"Though she is naught but a meaningless slave," said the Bina, "she is yet, like myself, a female. Please be kind to her, sir. Let her please you."

"How understanding you are," marveled Boots. "You may begin," he said to the concealed girl.

The robes shook violently, negatively.

"What is wrong?" asked the Bina.

"She is shy," said Boots.

"The slave need not be shy on my account," said the Bina. "Let her begin."

"Begin," said Boots.

His robes again shook violently.

"Begin," he said.

Again there seemed a great commotion beneath his robes.

Boots then, with the flat of his hand, with some force, cuffed the girl concealed under his robes. Instantly she knelt quietly. "Lazy girl, naughty girl," chided Boots. The tops of her toes, as she knelt, beat up and down in helpless frustration. "I see that I shall have to draw you forth and beat you," he said.

"Look!" cried the Bina. "She begins!"

"Oh, she does, doesn't she?" said Boots. "Oh, yes!"

"What a slave she is!" cried the Bina. "How exciting! How exciting!"

"To be sure," agreed Boots. "Ah! Yes! Ohhh! To be sure! Eee! Yes! Quite! Oh! Yes! Oh! Oh! To be sure! Eee! Yes! Oh! Yes! Yes! Yes! Yes! Yes! Ohhhh, yes, yes, yes." Boots then wiped his brow with his sleeve.

"Has she gone?" called out the Brigella, after a time, her voice muffled from beneath his robes.

"Yes," said Boots.

The Brigella, as the Lady Phoebe, extricated herself, on her knees, from the robes of Boots Tarsk-Bit. She turned about, still on her knees. "Tipa!" she cried in horror.

"I thought you had gone," said Boots.

"Phoebe!" cried the Lady Tipa.

"Tipa," moaned Phoebe, in misery.

"Phoebe!" cried the Lady Tipa, in delight.

"Tipa!" pleaded Phoebe.

"Phoebe on her knees, as naked as a slave, on a public road, crawling out of a man's robes!" laughed the Bina, pointing derisively at her. "How shameful, how outrageous, how marvelous, how delicious, how glorious!"

"Please, Tipa," pleaded Phoebe.

"You are the sort of girl who should have been whipped and collared at puberty!" said the Bina.

The free woman in the audience stiffened at these words. These words seemed to have some special meaning for her. She shook her head and clenched her small fists in the blue gloves.

"You have always been a slave," said the Bina.

"I am a free woman," wailed the Brigella.

"Slave, slave, slave!" laughed the Bina. "This story will bear a rich retelling in the village," she said, hurrying away.

"I am ruined," wailed the Brigella, rising to her feet, wringing her hands. "I cannot bear now to return to the village and, if I did, they would put a chain on me and sell me."

"Perhaps not," said Boots, soothingly.

"Do you not think so, sir?" she asked.

"It might be a rope," he said.

"Ohhhhh," she wailed. "Where can I go? What can I do?"

"Well," said Boots, "I must be on my way."

"But what shall I do?" she asked.

"Try to avoid being eaten by sleen," said Boots. "It is growing dark."

"Where are my clothes?" she begged.

"I do not see them about," said Boots. "They must have blown away."

"Take me with you!" she begged.

"Perhaps you would like to kneel and beg my collar?" he asked. "I might then consider whether or not I find you pleasing enough to lock it on your neck."

"Sir," she cried, "I am a free woman!"

"Good luck with the sleen," he said.

"Accept me as a traveling companion," she urged.

"And what would you do, to pay your way on the road?" he asked.

"I could give you a kiss, on the cheek, once a day," she said. "Surely you could not expect more from a free woman."

"Good luck with the sleen," said he.

"Do not go," she begged. "I am willing, even, to enter into the free companionship with you!"

Boots staggered backwards, as though overwhelmed. "I could not dream of accepting a sacrifice of such enormity on your part!" he cried.

"I will. I will!" she cried.

"But I suspect," said Boots suspiciously, musingly, regarding her, "that there may be that in you which is not really of the free companion."

"Sir?" she asked.

"Perhaps you are, in actuality, more fittingly understood as something else," he mused.

"What can you mean, sir?" she asked.

"Does it not seem strange that you would have fallen madly in love with me at just this moment?"

"Why, no, of course not," she said.

"Perhaps you are merely trying to save yourself from sleen," he mused.

"No, no," she assured him.

"I fear that you are tricking me," he said.

"No!" she said.

"In any event," he said, "you surely cannot expect me to consider you seriously in connection with the free companionship."

"Why not?" she asked, puzzled.

"A naked woman," he asked, skeptically, "encountered beside a public road?"

"Oh!" she cried in misery.

"Do you have a substantial dowry?" he asked. "An extensive wardrobe, wealth, significant family connections, a high place in society?"

"No!" she said. "No! No!"

"And if you return to your village I think you will find little waiting for you there but a rope collar and a trip in a sack to the nearest market."

"Misery!" she wept.

"Besides," he said, "in your heart you are truly a slave."

"No!" she cried.

"Surely you know that?" he asked.

"No!" she cried.

"I do not even think you saw the wondrous veil," he said.

"I saw it," she said. "I saw it!"

"What was its predominant color?" he asked, sharply.

"Yellow," she said.

"No," he said.

"Red!" she said.

"No!" he said.

"Blue, pink, orange, green!" she cried.

"Apparently you are a slave," he said, grimly. "You should not have tried to masquerade as a free woman. There are heavy penalties for that sort of thing."

She put her head in her hands, sobbing.

"I wonder if I should turn you over to magistrates," he said.

"Please, do not!" she wept.

"I will give you another chance," he said, reaching behind his back, to where he had supposedly hidden the veil at the first sight of the supposed brigands. "Now," he said, thrusting forth his hands, "in which hand is it?"

"The right!" she cried.

"No!" he said.

"The left!" she wept.

"No," he said, "it is in neither hand. I left it behind my back!"

"Oh, oh!" she wept.

"On your knees, Slave," he said, sternly.

Swiftly she knelt, in misery.

"Do not fret, girl," said Boots. "Surely you know that you have slave curves."

"I do?" she asked.

"Yes," he said. "In any event, you are far too beautiful to be a mere free companion."

"I am?" she asked.

"Yes," he said. "Your beauty, if you must know, is good enough to be that of a slave."

Here several of the men in the audience shouted their agreement.

"It is?" she asked, laughing.

"Yes," said Boots, struggling to keep a straight face.

"Good!" laughed the Brigella.

There was more laughter from the audience.

"Mind your characterizations!" called the free woman in the audience.

"Forgive me, Lady," said Boots, trying not to laugh.

"Forgive me, Mistress," said the Brigella.

"Continue," said the free woman.

"Are you in charge of the drama?" inquired a man.

The free woman did not deign to respond to him.

"Will you not then accept me as a free companion, noble sir?" called the Brigella to Boots, in his guise as the merchant.

"It is the collar for you, or nothing," said Boots, grandly.

There was a cheer from the men in the audience.

"Though I may be a slave in my heart," cried the Brigella, leaping to her feet, "I am surely not a legal slave and thus, as yet, am bond to neither you nor any man!"

"Many are the slaves who do not yet wear their collars," said Boots, meditatively, and then, suddenly, turned about and, to the amusement of the men in the audience, to sudden bursts of laughter, stared directly at the outspoken, troublesome, arrogant free woman standing in the front row, below the stage. He could not resist turning the line in this fashion, it seemed.

"Sleen! Sleen!" she cried.

There was much laughter.

"Is it true that you are as yet merely an uncollared slave?" asked a man of the free woman.

"He is a sleen, a sleen!" cried the free woman.

"I must soon be on my way," said Boots to the Brigella, chuckling, trying to return to the play. He was well pleased with himself.

"Go!" she said, grandly, with a gesture.

"If you wish," he said, "you may kneel and beg my collar. I might consider granting it to you. I would have to think about it."

"Never!" she said.

"What are you going to do?" he asked.

"I shall return to the village and take my chances," she said.

"Very well," he said, "but watch out for those two fellows approaching. I fear they may be slavers."

"They appear to be peddlers, merchants, to me," she said.

"They do seem so," admitted Boots. "But that may be merely their disguise, to take unwary girls unaware."

"Nonsense," she said. "I know a peddler when I see one."

"At any rate," he said, "let us hope that they are no worse than slavers."

"What do you mean?" she asked.

"I heard there were two feed hunters in the vicinity," he said.

"What is a feed hunter?" she asked.

"Why one who hunts for feed, of course," said Boots.

"Feed?" she asked.

"Usually for their sleen," he said. "They are pesky, careless, greedy fellows, little better than scavengers, in my opinion. They will settle for almost anything. They are particularly pleased when they can get their ropes on a juicy girl."

"Surely there are better things to do with a girl than feed her to sleen," she said.

"It probably depends on the girl," said Boots.

"No!" she cried.

"You are just saying that because you are a girl," he said.

"No!" she said.

"I am inclined to agree with you, though," said Boots, "all things considered, but then, of course, I am not a feed hunter."

"You are trying to frighten me," she said.

"Have it your own way," said Boots.

"You have fooled me already today, perhaps many times," she said. "Do not seek to do it again!"

"Have it your own way," said Boots.

"I wish that my clothes had not blown away," she said.

"Yes," said Boots. "That was too bad."

"I am on my way," she announced.

"Good luck!" he called.

She then, in accordance with a common Gorean theatrical convention, trekked about the stage in a circle, while Boots withdrew to one side. In a moment, of course, she had come into the vicinity of the two aforementioned fellows, they entering from the other side of the stage. So simply was the scene changed. These two fellows, of course, were Boots's Chino and Lecchio, now largely garbed in tatters of yellow and white, the colors of the merchants.

"Greetings, noble merchants," said the girl.

"Hah!" snarled the Chino to his fellow, Lecchio. "Our disguises are perfect! She takes us for merchants!"

"Would you please step aside, good sirs," she said. "I desire to pass."

"It is warm today," said Chino.

"True," she said.

"But even so," he said, "it seems you are somewhat lightly clad."

"My clothes, I fear, blew away," she said.

"That is what they all say," said Chino.

"That is not really what they all say," said Lecchio, scratching his head, through the hood. "Some say other things. One said her clothes were dissolved by magic in the bushes. That must have been frightening for her, to have had her clothes dissolved by magic in the bushes.''

"No," protested the girl.

"Doubtless they were torn from your body in a recent hurricane," said Chino.

"No!" she cried.

"Removed from your body by an ardent suitor, then, who neglected to replace them?" asked Chino.

"No!" she cried.

"Eaten in a moment by ravenous insects?"

"No!"

"You were attacked by cloth workers with scissors, who desired to replenish their stores?"

"No!"

"Magic?" asked Lecchio.

"No, no!" she cried. "It is as I told you. They just blew away!"

"Do not lie to us, Girl," said Chino, sternly.

"Girl?" she asked.

"This morning," said Chino, "you were simply sent forth stripped."

" 'Sent forth'?" she asked.

"Yes," said Chino, folding his arms.

"I think that you are under a grave misapprehension, sirs," she said, righteously. "Simply because I might be somewhat lightly clad this evening, do not mistake me for a slave."

"Do I understand you correctly?" asked Chino. "Have we the honor of being in the presence of a free woman?"

"Yes," she said.

"You mean that no one owns you, that you are totally unclaimed?"

"Yes," she said, proudly.

"Excellent!" said Chino.

"Wonderful!" said Lecchio.

"Sirs," she asked, "why is it that you are drawing forth coils of stout ropes from beneath your robes?"

"Why to bind your pretty arms to your sides, and to put a good rope on your neck, my dear," said Chino.

"I do not understand!" she said.

"She will make a juicy morsel for our sleen, will she not, Lecchio, my friend?" inquired Chino.

"That she will," agreed Lecchio.

"You are feed hunters!" cried the girl in horror.

"What is a feed hunter?" asked Lecchio of Chino.

"That is exactly right, my dear," Chino confirmed her darkest suspicions.

"But you cannot feed me to sleen!" she cried.

"You are free to be taken," Chino informed her. "It is all perfectly legal. You are neither claimed, nor owned."

"But I am a slave in my heart!" she cried.

"That is not good enough," said Chino. "All free women are merely uncollared slaves."

At this line more than one man in the audience turned to look at the veiled free woman in the audience, she of the scribes. She, however, of course, her back stiff, pretended not to notice that she was the object of this rather obvious attention.

"Oh, misery, misery!" cried the Brigella.

"You do not have a legal master," said Chino. "Thus you are eminently qualified for sleen feed. Come now. Do not be difficult. Let us get these ropes on you."

"No, no!" she cried, and, turning, sped away. As she again retraced the circle on the stage, this time hastily, suggesting her journey, Chino and Lecchio watched her depart. "We must soon begin our fierce pursuit," Chino informed the audience.

In a moment or two the Brigella had again reached the vicinity of Boots Tarsk-Bit who turned about, congenially enough, effecting some surprise at the sight of her. "Greetings," he said.

"I kneel before you as a naked slave," cried the girl. "I beg your collar! I beg your collar!"

"Your head is rather high," said Boots.

Immediately the girl put her head to the ground.

"I wonder how you would look on your belly," said Boots.

Immediately she lay on her belly before him.

"My sandals are rather dusty, from the road," said Boots.

Immediately the girl began to lick his feet and sandals, cleaning them.

"You may kiss them, as well," Boots informed her.

Immediately the girl began to add fervent kisses to her ministrations.

"Did you wish to speak to me?" inquired Boots.

"I beg your collar!" she said hoarsely. "I beg your collar!"

"You may kneel before me, with your knees spread," said Boots.

The men in the audience cried out with pleasure. The Brigella was so beautiful! Too, a woman is so marvelously vulnerable and attractive in this position. It is no wonder that it is a portion of a common position of a Gorean pleasure slave.

"Now," said Boots, "what was it that you wanted to speak to me about?"

"I want your collar," she said. "I beg it!"

"I have given some thought to this matter," said Boots, "and I have decided against it."

"No!" she cried.

"Yes," he said. "I have decided that, after all, you are a free woman."

"No, I am not," she said. "I am only a miserable slave, a rightful slave, one pleading for her collar."

"How can I know that you speak the truth?" he asked, thoughtfully.

"I am prepared to offer any evidences that you might suggest," she said.

There was a cheer from the men in the audience.

The Brigella laughed.

"Are you?" asked one of the men in the audience to the free woman in the audience.

"Get her on her knees naked, too," said another man of her.

"With her knees spread, and well," added another.

"Collar her," said another.

"Give her a taste of the whip," said another.

"Teach her quickly to lick and kiss," said another.

"Teach her what being a woman is all about," said another.

"Did you not see?" asked the free woman. "She laughed! She lost her characterization!"

"It is sometimes hard to keep one's characterization in such a play," I said.

"Perhaps," she said.

"Do not be too hard on her," I said. "She is only a slave."

"Slaves are to be shown no mercy," said the free woman coldly.

"Do I detect that you are critical in some respects of her performance?" I asked. The Brigella seemed to me to be very talented.

"She is undoubtedly quite good," said the free woman, "but many of her lines, I think, could have been better handled, or at least differently handled, particularly in this form of farce, more broadly, both verbally and gesturally."

"Interesting," I said.

"May we have Lady Telitsia's permission to continue," inquired Boots, not too pleased with the interruption.

"You may continue," she said.

"Thank you," he said. "You are very kind." He then returned

his attention to the Brigella. "No," he said. "I am sure you are a free woman, not a slave."

"No, no!" she said. "I am a slave! I swear it! I swear it!" She cast a wild glance back over her shoulder. As yet, supposedly, Chino and Lecchio were not in sight.

"It is true," said Boots, "that at one time I thought you might be a slave."

"Yes!" she said.

"But I think I was wrong," said Boots.

"No, no," she said. "You were right! You were right!"

"You are a slave, really?" asked Boots.

"Yes," she said. "I am really a slave! I swear it!" Again she looked over her shoulder.

"You do have slave curves," admitted Boots.

"Yes, yes!" she cried.

"Very well," said Boots. "I acknowledge, unqualifiedly, with no reservations whatsoever, uncompromisingly, that you are a slave."

"Collar me!" she cried.

"I think," said Chino to Lecchio, at the other side of the stage, "that it is nearly time for us to begin our fierce pursuit."

"Surely you must understand," said Boots to the Brigella, "that two quite different matters are under consideration here. One is whether or not you are a slave, a matter which has now been settled in the affirmative, and the other is whether or not I might be interested, in the least, in having you as my own slave."

She looked at him in disbelief.

"Not every man wants to own every slave," he said, "or, at least, it would not be too practical for a fellow to own every slave, for that would be a great many slaves."

"Please," she begged.

"Too, slaves can be expensive. One must feed them and, if one wishes, find them a rag to wear."

"Our fierce pursuit begins," announced Chino to the audience, and Lecchio began to describe a circle about the stage, carefully, bending over, hesitating now and then, apparently tracking the lovely fugitive.

"Disciplinary devices, such as whips and chains, too, can be expensive," said Boots.

"I fear they are coming!" she cried, turning back from looking over her shoulder.

"Who?" asked Boots.

"Oh, no one," she said.

"Oh," said Boots.

"I am at your feet, a naked supplicant," she said. "I entreat you, implore you, to show me mercy! Deign, in your graciousness, to consider my humble petition!"

"What was it again," asked Boots. "I fear it may have slipped my mind."

"Make me your slave!" she cried. "I beg to be made your slave!"

"Oh, yes," said Boots. "That is it. Have you had any experience?"

"That is her, up there, ahead, I think," called out Chino to Lecchio.

"No!" she wept.

"Then perhaps you should apply to another master," said Boots.

"Train me!" she said. "We must all start somewhere! I will be zealous and obedient!"

"I think you are right," said Lecchio to Chino, looking in the direction of Boots and the Brigella.

"Put your collar on me, please!" cried the Brigella. "There is little time!"

"I will give you my answer in the morning," said Boots.

"No," she cried. "No, please, no!"

"Or next week," he said.

"No!" she cried.

"Yes," said the Chino. "I am sure it is she. Let us hurry. We can have our ropes on her in a moment!" They then, apparently, began to hurry. To be sure, their new haste was largely a matter of marking time in place. Yet one had the distinct impression, in the lovely conventions involved, that they were getting closer and closer.

"Do you think you can be pleasing?" asked Boots. Free companions, after all, can be anything. But slaves must be pleasing.

"Yes," she cried, "yes!"

"Good," said Boots. "I shall let you know in the morning or in a few days."

"No!" she cried.

"Why not?" asked Boots.

"Then you would miss a night's pleasure," she said, desperately, wildly, "or perhaps even my use, at your slightest whim, for a few days!"

"That is true," mused Boots.

"Yes! There she is!" cried Chino to Lecchio. "Let us rush upon her! In an instant we will have her helpless in our bonds!"

"Oh, collar me, Master!" she cried. "Please, please, Master!"

"What did you call me?" asked Boots.

" 'Master, Master'!" she cried.

"Oh, very well," said Boots.

Swiftly she thrust her neck forward, lifting her chin. Boots stood between her and the audience and seemed to reach into his pack. He seemed then to withdraw something from the pack and, in a moment, to fasten it on her neck. In this instant, of course, he had removed the scarf from about her neck, that concealing her collar. He then stepped back. Lo, there was steel on her neck! There was a cheer from the men in the audience.

"We have you now!" cried Chino, he and Lecchio arriving on the scene, ropes in hand.

"Who are you fellows?" called Boots. "What do you want?"

The Brigella, now collared, trembling, cowered beside Boots, clinging to one of his legs.

"Do not question us," said the Chino. "Our profession is a dark one. I dare not mention it lest you faint in fear."

"Assassins!" cried Boots.

"Far worse," said the Chino.

"Feed hunters!" cried Boots, aghast.

"The same," said Chino.

"The very same," said the Lecchio, grimly.

"I am surprised, actually," said the Chino, "that you have heard of our profession, as it is not well known."

"I myself," said the Lecchio, "heard of it but moments ago."

"I heard that two such rascals as yourselves were about," said Boots. "What do you want here?"

"Her!" said the Chino, pointing dramatically, menacingly, at the Brigella. She shrank back in fear.

"Her?" inquired Boots.

"Yes!" said the Chino. "Now if you will be so kind as to step aside, we will get our ropes on her."

"Hold, rogues!" said Boots.

"What is wrong, sir?" inquired Chino.

"You cannot have her," said Boots.

"We have been hunting her for some time," said Chino. "She is our legitimate prey. It is all quite legal. We are honest fellows. We are entitled to her. Now please do not interfere. Come now, little vulo, put your head in this noose."

"Desist!" cried Boots.

"What is wrong now?" asked Chino.

"Apparently," said Boots, "you are under the delusion that this is a free woman, one that may simply be picked up, like a larma in a field, for whatever purposes you might please."

"Of course," said Chino.

"She is not a free woman," said Boots.

"What!" cried Chino.

"Observe her pretty neck," said Boots.

"It is collared!" cried Chino.

"Yes!" said Boots.

"She is a slave!" said Chino.

"Yes," said Boots.

"Ah, well, an unclaimed slave is almost as good as a free woman," said Chino, reaching forth again with the noose.

"Stop!" cried Boots.

"What now?" inquired Chino.

"Yes, what now?" inquired Lecchio.

"This woman is both claimed and collared," said Boots.

"What!" cried Chino.

"What?" asked Lecchio.

"Are you thieves?" asked Boots.

"No!" cried Chino.

"No?" asked Lecchio.

"No!" cried Chino.

"No!" said Lecchio, righteously.

"Then desist, scoundrels," said Boots, "for this woman is my property!"

"Is it true?" asked Chino.

"Yes, Masters," she said, "it is true. I am his property. He is my master. He owns me. I belong to him, legally and completely, in all ways, fully!"

"There are, of course, two of us," said Chino, menacingly.

"I do not fear you!" said Boots. "Be off, you scurvy scamps, lest I feed you to your own sleen!"

"I did not know we had any sleen," said Lecchio to Chino.

"Be gone, scamps, scoundrels, rogues!" cried Boots, with a vast, wild threatening gesture. Immediately Chino and Lecchio, in apparent terror, scampered away.

"You have saved me!" cried the Brigella.

"Yes," said Boots.

"I wear your collar," she said. "I am now yours, truly, you know."

"Why, yes," said Boots, interested. "That is true, isn't it?"

"Yes, Master," she said.

"And then anything may be commanded of you," mused
Boots, "absolutely anything, anything whatsoever, and you must
obey, instantly and perfectly."

"Yes, Master," she said.

"Assume," said he, "standing, partly crouching, the position
of a free woman, zealous to conceal her beauty."

"Yes, Master," she said. There was much laughter as she, the
already-so-much-exposed slave, assumed this coy, silly position,
one often associated with timid, scandalized, shocked, surprised
free women. Indeed, it was the same as that which she had often
assumed earlier in the farce, when she had supposedly been such
a free female.

"Now, for the merest instant," said Boots, "move your hands
away, and then replace them, instantly, immediately, as they
were."

She complied. If one had not been watching closely, one
might have missed the action.

"Yes, yes!" cried Boots ecstatically. "Oh, bliss! Bliss! That
is it! That is it!"

"What?" she asked.

"A peep!" cried Boots. "A marvelous peep!"

"That is all?" she asked.

"Yes!" he cried, joyfully.

"Give me then," she cried, suddenly, "the wondrous magic
veil!"

"Alas," cried Boots. "I cannot. It would be incorrect to do
so."

"How so?" she asked.

"What I negotiated for, as you may recall," said Boots, "was
a peep at the beauty of a free woman, not a peep at the beauty of
a mere slave."

"Oh, oh!" she said, in misery.

"If that were all one wished," said Boots, "one could go to
the nearest market, to see girls naked in their chains." That was
true, I supposed. That is how girls are normally displayed in
such markets, incidentally, that and in cages.

"But I am the same woman!" she protested.

"That is not really true," said Boots, "for you are now a
slave." That sort of thing, incidentally, in its way, is true. A
woman collared is quite different from a woman uncollared. The
collar works a wondrous tranformation in a woman, psycho-
logically, sexually and humanly. She is then vulnerable; she
must then obey. She is no longer the same. She has then no

choice but to be a total female. She becomes a thousand times more interesting, exciting and desirable.

"Even though I am a slave, Master," she said, "yet do I strongly desire it. I have been through so much! Please let me have it!"

"My benevolence may perhaps yet prove my undoing," said Boots, reaching into his pack.

"I begin already," said the Brigella to the audience, "to sense that slaves may have ways and wiles wherewith to achieve their ends which are denied to free women."

"I have it here," said Boots, supposedly withdrawing it from his pack, "but you, of course, now that you are a slave, will not be able to see it."

"To be perfectly honest, Master," she said, "for I am your slave and no longer dare lie to you, I could not see it before either."

"No!" cried Boots.

"Yes," she said, putting down her head, "it is true."

"It is perfectly fitting then," he said, "Slave, that you are now in your collar."

"Yes, Master," she said.

"Even though you are a slave, yet still do you desire the wondrous veil?" he asked.

"Yes, Master!" she said. "Now," she said to the audience, "I am at last to have my way. You see, in the end, it is I who win. What does it matter that I am a slave? I am to obtain the wondrous veil."

Boots seemed to be folding up the veil, neatly.

"How clever I am," said the Brigella to the audience. "My patience is now to be rewarded. How simple are men! How easy it is to obtain my way with the wiles of a slave! I did not know that before. The wondrous veil is now to be mine! Thus it is that I, with my beauty, can conquer men!"

"Here," said Boots.

She, still on her knees, rising from her heels, reached eagerly for the veil. "Oh!" she cried, in disappointment, for Boots, at the last moment, had jerked it back.

"I forgot," said Boots.

"What is wrong?" she asked.

"I cannot give you the veil," he said.

"Why not?" she wailed.

"You are a slave," said Boots. "You can own nothing. It is you who are owned."

"Oh!" she cried, in misery.

"Back on your heels," he snapped. "Spread your knees! Hands on thighs! Back straight! Chin up!"

"Oh, oh," she moaned, but swiftly complied. "He reminds me well that I am a slave," she said to the audience. "I had thought to conquer men but instead I find that it is I who am helpless, that it is I who am conquered, and totally."

At this moment Chino and Lecchio reappeared, now with their peddler's packs.

"Beware, Master," cried the girl. "The feed hunters have returned!"

"Greetings, Boys," said Boots.

"Greetings," said Chino and Lecchio to Boots.

"Do you know these men, Master?" asked the girl, not daring to rise from her knees.

"I mistook you for feed hunters earlier," said Boots to the new arrivals. "I see now you are my old buddies, with whom I have been traveling these roads for weeks."

"The collar is locked on my neck!" said the girl to the audience, struggling with the collar. "It is truly on me. I cannot remove it!"

"A pretty vulo," said Chino, scrutinizing the girl.

"A juicy pudding," said Lecchio.

"I am now only a slave!" cried the girl to the audience.

"I am now going to toss this wondrous veil up into the air," said Boots. "Let it blow away on the winds, traveling to I know not where." He then tossed it up, lightly, into the air.

"Master!" protested the girl.

"There it goes!" said Boots.

"Master!" said the girl.

"It was in such a fashion that I received it," said Boots. "Surely it is only right that I should let it fly away, back into the clouds and winds, perhaps even back to Anango."

"But why would you let it go?" asked the girl, in misery.

"It has served its purpose," said Boots.

"Its purpose?" asked the girl.

"Yes," said Boots. "It has served to catch me a pretty, greedy little slave, one who by tomorrow morning will be in no doubt as to the nature of her many utilizations."

"Surely you have not tricked me!" she cried.

"Shoulder my pack," said Boots.

"And mine," said Chino.

"And mine," said Lecchio.

The girl, then, with great difficulty, struggling, bending under the weight, staggering, shouldered the three packs.

"Hurry, lazy girl!" called Boots, leaving the stage with Chino and Lecchio. "I did not know we had any sleen," Lecchio was saying to Chino. "Where could they be?"

"I wonder if I have been tricked," said the girl to the audience. There was much laughter. "In any event," she said, "I am now in the collar, and that is all there is for it!"

"Hurry, hurry, lazy girl!" called Boots from off-stage.

"I must go now," said the girl. "Oh, these packs are heavy. But I must bear them as best I can. I am a slave now, and if I am not pleasing, I will be beaten!"

She then turned about and, staggering under the weight of the packs, left the stage.

In a moment Boots, smiling, reappeared on the stage, with Chino and Lecchio, and the Brigella, too, now freed of her preposterous burden. "Noble free woman, and noble gentlemen, of the audience," said Boots, "the Magic Veil of Anango, presented by the players of Boots Tarsk-Bit, actor, promoter and entrepreneur extraordinary! We thank you for your consideration!" There was much applause. Boots, and the Chino and Lecchio, smiling, bowed, again and again. The Brigella, at a sign from Boots, knelt on the stage. She would take her bows on her knees, of course, for she was a slave.

"Bina!" called Boots, gesturing to the side of the stage. The Bina, then, in her garments of a free woman, she who had played the brief role of the Lady Tipa, the fellow villager of the Lady Phoebe, emerged onto the stage. "Off with those absurd impediments to our vision," said Boots, jollily, to her. She removed her veil and threw back her hood, shaking loose her dark hair. She was an exquisite little slave, but not a match for the Brigella in beauty. She would not, at least, I supposed, have brought as much as the Brigella on a slave block. I remembered her, too, from Port Kar.

"Come, come," said Boots, her master. She then pulled down her robes, about her shoulders, and then stripped herself to the waist. She had small, well-formed, exquisite breasts. On her neck was a collar of steel. "Off with them, now, completely," said Boots, gesturing to the robes she had clutched about her hips. "Kneel." She thrust the robes down about her ankles and knelt then on the boards, beside the Brigella, before the audience. Boots gave her an almost unnoticeable kick with the side of his foot and she spread her knees before the audience. I could see that she was reluctant to do this. Perhaps she had been a slave less long than the Brigella. But now both of them knelt identi-

cally before the audience, backs straight, back on their heels,
chins up, stark naked in their collars, their knees spread, slaves.

"Our little Bina!" said Boots, showing her off. "Thank you,
noble free woman and noble gentlemen! Remember poor Boots
and his company! Be generous!" Some coins, mostly copper,
rattled to the stage. I myself gave a couple of copper tarn disks. I
had much more money, my own, and some more I had helped
myself to at the camp of the Lady Yanina, before I had freed her
prisoners and burned the camp, but I had no wish to advertise the
current weight of my purse at the fair. It is one thing to do this in
a city where one, and one's financial status, is reasonably well
known, and quite another, as you may well imagine, to do it in a
strange place before strangers.

"Thank you, noble people, splendid patrons of the arts,"
called Boots. "Thank you!" The Chino and Lecchio gathered up
the coins, handing them to Boots, who took them and deposited
them somewhere inside his robes, perhaps into the lining or a
hidden pocket. The girls, here at the fair, were not passing
through the crowd with copper bowls, perhaps because they had
both been in the play. At any rate, even when they had done this
in Port Kar, they had not, of course, been handling or touching
the coins, only the bowls in which the coins were collected. The
only female performers who customarily gather up the coins
thrown to them for their masters are dancers, who usually perform alone, except for their musicians. They tuck the coins in a
bit of their silk, if they have been permitted any. Given the
nature of their silk, which is usually diaphanous, and the general
scantiness of their garb, and the publicness of their picking up
the coins, there is little danger that they could conceal a coin,
even if they dared to do so. A slave girl, you see, is generally
forbidden to so much as touch a coin without permission. This
does not mean, of course, that they may not be sent to the
market, and given coins for errands, and such. For an unaccounted-
for coin to be found in a slave girl's possession, or among her
belongings, can be a cause for severe punishment. She might
even be fed to sleen.

"Lout!" called the free woman.

"Yes, noble lady?" said Boots, coming forward.

"Your plays are insulting to free women!" she cried. "I have
never been so insulted in my life!"

"Have you seen them all?" asked Boots. "There are more
than fifty."

"No," she said. "I have not seen them all!"

"We cannot perform them all without a full company, of

course," said Boots. "I am short-handed at the moment. I do not even have a golden courtesan. There are frequent changes in the repertory, of course. We make up new ones, and sometimes we feel it best, temporarily or permanently, to drop out old ones, ones that do not then seem as good or which do not seem to play as well any longer. One improvises about given ideas or themes, and then, performance by performance, a play is built. To be sure, much always remains open to invention, to innovation, to constant revision, to impromptu spur-of-the-moment contributions, and so on. One must always be ready, too, to capitalize on such things as local color, current happenings, the current political situation, popular or well-known figures, the prejudices of a district, and so on. Local allusions are always popular. They can occasionally get you in trouble, of course. One must be careful about them. It would not do to be impaled. You seem highly intelligent. Perhaps you could help us."

"Do you think that all free women are no better than slaves!" she cried.

"I would suppose that women are all pretty much of a muchness," said Boots.

"Oh!" she cried in fury.

"Take yourself," he said. "How would you look stripped and in a collar, and under a whip? Do you think you would behave much differently, then, than any other slave? Indeed, have you ever stopped to think about it? Have you ever wondered, secretly perhaps, whether or not you might have what it takes to prove to be even an adequate slave?"

"I am a free woman," she said, icily.

"Forgive me, Lady," said Boots.

"I will, before nightfall, and you may depend upon it," she said, "lodge my complaint with the magistrates. By tomorrow noon, you will be closed, forbidden to perform at the fair."

"Show us mercy, Lady," said Boots, "we are a traveling company, a poor troupe in desperate straits. I have had to sell even my golden courtesan!"

"I do not care," she said, "if you must sell all your sluts!"

"The Fair of En'Kara is the greatest of all the fairs," he said. "It comes but once a year. It is important to us! We need every tarsk-bit we can make here."

"I do not choose to show you mercy," she said, coldly. "Too, I shall see to it that you are fined and publicly whipped. Indeed, if you are not gone from the fairgrounds by tomorrow evening, I shall also see to it that your troupe is disbanded, and that your goods, your wagons, your clothes, your sluts, everything, is confiscated!"

"You wish to see me ruined?" he said.

"Yes!" she said.

"Thank you, gracious lady," he said.

She spun about, and with a movement of her robes, lifting them a bit from the dust, took her leave. She had on golden sandals. Boots Tarsk-Bit and myself, as she left, considered her ankles. I did not find them bad, and I suppose Boots Tarsk-Bit did not either. They would have looked well in shackles.

"It seems I am ruined," said Boots Tarsk-Bit to me.

"Perhaps not," I said.

"How shall I make even enough money to clear my way from the fair?" he asked.

"Sell me, Master," said the Brigella, kneeling on the stage, radiant, flushed and excited. There were several fellows, some five or six of them, standing before the stage, some of them leaning forward with their elbows upon it. Any one of them, I supposed, as I had conjectured earlier, would be capable of handling her superbly. Gorean men do not compromise with their slaves; the girls obey, and perfectly. She knew she was valuable; how straight she knelt; how proud she was, naked and in her collar.

"What am I offered?" asked Boots, resignedly.

"Two silver tarsks," said a man.

"Two?" asked Boots, surprised, pleased. The girl cried out with pleasure. That is a high price for a female on Gor, where they are plentiful and cheap.

In a few moments the Brigella, her small wrists braceleted behind her, had taken her way from the area, eagerly heeling, almost running to keep up with him, her new owner, a stalwart, broad-shouldered, blond-haired fellow. The first thing he had done after making her helpless in his bracelets had been to pull the small, circular adhesive patch from her left thigh. She wore the common Kajira brand, the tiny staff and fronds. She had gone for five silver tarsks.

"A splendid price on her," I congratulated Boots.

He stood there, dangling her collar in his right hand. "I am ruined," he said, glumly. "Whatever shall I do without a Brigella?"

"I do not know about your Brigella," I said, "but I think I might be able to help you with another of your problems."

"Do I not know you from somewhere?" asked Boots.

"We met some days ago, briefly, in Port Kar," I said.

"Yes!" he said. "The carnival! Of course! You are a captain, or officer, are you not?"

"Sometimes, perhaps," I said.

"What do you want of me?" asked Boots, warily.

"Do not fear," I smiled. "I am not in hire to pursue you, nor am I interested in collecting bills."

"I fear," said Boots, "that I may be indebted to you in the matter of five silver tarsks in Port Kar. I have them here." He held out his hand with the five silver tarsks, accrued but moments earlier from the sale of the Brigella.

"It was six, not five," I said.

"Oh," said Boots.

"If I had anything to do with them," I said, "to which I do not admit, of course, let us consider them merely as copper-bowl coins, coins such as might be gathered in the pursuit of your normal activities."

"But six silver tarsks," he said.

"You may consider them, if it makes it easier for you," I said, "as a gratuitous contribution to the arts."

"I accept them, then, in the name of the arts," said Boots.

"Good," I said.

"You have no idea how that arrangement assuages the agonies of conscience with which I might otherwise have been afflicted," said Boots.

"I am sure of it," I said.

"Thank you," said Boots.

"It is nothing," I said. "Happy carnival."

"To be sure," he said. "Incidentally, did you enjoy the show?"

"Yes," I said.

"I wonder if you forgot to express your appreciation," asked Boots, rather apologetically.

"No," I said.

"It was an excellent performance," he said.

"Here is another copper tarsk," I said. "That makes three."

"Thank you," he said.

"You are quite welcome," I said. I watched the tarsk disappear somewhere in his robes.

"Now," he said, "as I recall you were mentioning that you might be able to help me with some problem."

"Yes," I said. "As I mentioned, I do not think I can help you with your Brigella problem, at least certainly not now, but I think I do know where you might be able to get your hands on a splendid candidate for a 'golden courtesan.' "

"A slave?" asked Boots.

"Of course," I said.

"Can she act?" asked Boots.

"I do not know," I admitted.

"My girls must double as tent girls," he said.

"About her potentiality as a tent girl," I said, "I have no doubt."

"My girls, you must understand," said Boots, "are not ordinary girls. They must be extraordinarily talented."

"She is blond, and voluptuous," I said.

"That will do," said Boots.

"You could always teach her to act," I said.

"That is true," said Boots. "And fortunately I am a master teacher. And if she should prove sluggish in her lessons, I will unhesitantly encourage her with the whip."

"Exactly," I said.

"Where is she?" he asked.

"Perhaps she has been sold by now," I said. "I do not really know."

"Where is she?" he asked.

"One advantage to getting her," I said, "is that I think that she, being a relatively new slave, may be fairly cheap. I doubt that she would cost you, at the most, even given her beauty, more than two silver tarsks. You would then have three silver tarsks left over."

"Where may I find this slut?" he asked.

"She is for sale, I believe, at this very fair," I smiled.

"This is the Fair of En'Kara," he said. "There are thousands of girls for sale here, in the care of hundreds of owners."

"I know the very platform on which stripped, and in her collar and chain, she awaits her first buyer," I said.

"Perhaps you would be so good as to impart this information," said Boots.

"It would probably be difficult for you, by tomorrow evening, by which time, I gather, you may be taking your leave from the fair, to locate her."

"Particularly," said Boots, "if we are attempting to get in an extra performance or two."

"Precisely," I said.

"What do you want?" asked Boots.

"You have a fairly regular itinerary in your travels, do you not?" I asked.

"Sometimes," said Boots, warily. "Sometimes not. Why?"

"Surely you have some notion of your plans for the next few months," I said.

"In what way?" asked Boots.

"You have some notion of the villages, the towns, the cities you plan to visit," I said.

"Perhaps," said Boots.

"I am interested particularly in one given city," I said, "a port on the coast of Thassa, one south of the Vosk's delta."

"Yes?" he said.

"Brundisium," I said.

"She is a staunch ally of Ar," he said. "We will be visiting her late in the summer."

"Good," I said.

"Why?" he asked.

"I am interested in joining your company," I said.

"What could you do?" he asked.

"Odd jobs, heavy work," I said.

"Security at Brundisium is very tight," he said. "They have become, in the last two years, for some reason, very suspicious of strangers. It is difficult to get access into the city, other than her closed-off wharves and trading places."

"A troupe such as yours might do so, however," I speculated.

"We have performed in the main square," he admitted, "once even in the courtyard of the palace itself."

"Let me join your company," I said.

"You are merely interested in obtaining admittance to Brundisium," he said.

"Perhaps," I said.

"Where might I get my chain on this female," he asked, "she whom you think might be found acceptable as a 'golden courtesan'?"

"Among the hundred new slaves of Samos of Port Kar," I said, "chained on the Shu-27 platforms in the southwestern sections of the Pavilion of Beauty."

"Has she a name?" asked Boots.

"Probably not now," I said. "But she had been given a name, or at least a house name, in the house of Samos, in Port Kar."

"What was it?" asked Boots.

"Rowena," I said.

"Thank you," said Boots. "You have been very helpful."

"Now, what about my proposal," I said.

"What proposal?" he asked.

"About my joining your company," I said.

"That?" he said.

"Yes," I said.

"Out of the question," he said.

7

THE TENT;
I SLIP FROM THE TENT

"Oh!" she wept, clutching me, squirming, helplessly pressing her imbonded flesh against mine. "Yes! No, don't let me go!" she cried. "Don't spurn me, I beg you. Hold me! Hold me! Please!" Her creamy flesh was hot. She was covered with sweat. Even her long blond hair, cut somewhat shorter now, half covering her face, was wet. Her body, broken out and mottled, was like a map, one recollective of my attentions. It was covered with an intense, irregular geography of scarlet patches, the capillaries near the surface of the skin swelled with blood, the red color suffusing upward as though from a light within her, as though fires raged within her, just beneath her exposed, yielding, eager softness, witnessing her excitement and arousal. She clutched me, helplessly. "What you can do to me!" she cried. "What men can do to me! I love it. I love it! Please, Master, do not stop!" She threw back her head, her lips parted, her eyes closed. "Ohh!" she gasped. "Yes! Ohhh! Yes! Yes! Oh! Oh! Yes, Master! Yes, Master! Continue, I beg you, with all my heart! I plead with you not to stop! Oh, Master! Yes, Master! Yes, Master!" I heard the sound of the chain on her ankle. "Oh, Master! Yes, Master!" she said.

The chain was about a yard long. It ran between the ankle ring, locked snugly on her ankle, and a long, heavy stake. The stake was driven deeply into the ground. About five inches of it showed above the surface. It was placed about a yard within, and to the left of, facing outward, the entrance to the small, striped tent. The girl was stripped, save for her ankle ring and collar. She lay on a mat, spread on a blanket, spread over the grass. She awaits within, to see who will open the flaps of the tent. That will be he who has paid her current use fee, that set by her master. We were some two hundred pasangs west of the fairgrounds. at the edge of the woods of Clearchus, just off the road of Clearchus.

"Oh, yes," she wept, clutching me. Her collar was a simple one. It read, "If you find me, return me to Boots Tarsk-Bit. Reward." Boots used such collars for all his slaves. "Aii!" she cried, suddenly. My touch had been light. I saw that she was ready for more. She was in a condition of slave arousal. She looked at me, wildly. "Yes," I said. "There is more." She began to squirm and shudder. "We now begin again," I said. "How can I feel more?" she wept. "You have not yet even experienced the fullness of a slave orgasm," I said. Then, in moments, building on her earlier sensitivity, I conducted her perforce to a height where she might sense, but not yet experience, a new horizon. I held her there, on the brink, for a time, as it pleased me, sometimes permitting her to subside a bit, and then again, when I wished, with the cruelty of the master, almost as though beckoning her, a command she could not refuse, bringing her back to the edge, where, almost in madness, she quivered and pleaded for release.

"Not yet," I told her.

"Yes, Master," she wept. The decision was mine. She was totally in my power. She was a slave.

"In any event," I had said to Boots Tarsk-Bit, a few days ago, "let me show you the girl."

"That would be very nice of you," he had said.

"Perhaps, too," I said, "you will change your mind."

"Never," he had said.

I had then conducted Boots to the area where the agents of Samos had his hundred girls on sale, sent out from Port Kar for vending during the Fair of En'Kara. I had checked the location earlier in the afternoon. It was among the southwestern sections of the Pavilion of Beauty, more specifically on the Shu-27 platforms. The girls were all on their hands and knees on the long, narrow platforms, uniformly positioned, facing outwards, a short chain on the neck of each, running down to individual rings anchored in the thick planks. They had been forbidden to speak among themselves. Agents of Samos walked here and there among them, with whips. "There is the girl," I said. She had not yet been sold. A white "holding disk" was wired to her collar. Some of the collars which had held women near her earlier were empty.

"You!" she had said, earlier, around noon, when I had first seen her there.

"You remember me?" I had said.

"A girl never forgets the first man who puts the whip to her," she had smiled.

"How are the sales going?" I had asked her.

"I do not really know, Master," she had said, "as we are kept in separate slave boxes, and are usually brought forth only to be exercised or exhibited. I myself was first put on display only this morning."

"I have seen some empty collars about, on the other platforms," I said.

"Perhaps the sales, then, are going well," she said. "I dare not turn my head to look. One girl was beaten fearfully for that, only an Ahn ago."

The matter of the empty collars was not an easy one to interpret. If there are no empty collars then customers may think that no one else is interested in the merchandise, perhaps that something might be wrong with it, and then go elsewhere. If there are only a few girls left, and many empty collars, they may get the impression, perhaps mistakenly, that nothing much of interest is likely to be left. The ideal impression to convey to the customer is perhaps that you have marvelous merchandise for sale, that even now many people are interested and buying, that it is moving fast, and that if he sees a girl he wants, perhaps he should snatch her up before someone else does. If you see a female locked in her platform collar, with its chain, of course, and in a while you see the collar empty, it is not irrational to suppose that she has been sold. Sometimes a woman who has been sold is not immediately removed from the platform but only, in one way or another, marked "Sold." There are several ways in which this can be done. For example, she may be placed in a white hood bearing the word "Sold" in red letters, a red tag, bearing the inscription, "Sold," may be wired to her collar, or the word "Sold" may be simply written in grease pencil on her body, usually, by convention, on her left breast.

"I think the sales are not going as well as they might," I said.

"Master?" she asked, frightened.

"You were put out only this morning," I said. "That suggests that the goods are not moving as rapidly as they might. Too, it is my impression, from what I have seen here and elsewhere, that

there is an unusual amount of high-quality merchandise available
this spring. I suspect that many of the lots, even large lots, literal
bevies of luscious slaves, chained together forty or fifty in a lot,
may end up being simply purchased by slavers at rock-bottom
prices, for purposes of later speculation."

She groaned. "I am afraid the masters will be displeased,"
she said.

Her apprehension was understandable. She was a slave.

"Are you interested in this slave?" asked one of the men on
the platform, coming over, his whip in hand. I did not think he
was of the house of Samos. I did not, at any rate, know him. He
was probably a slaver's agent, licensed for work at the fair.
There are many fellows who, seasonally, do this work. At other
times they normally work in slavers' houses. He may, of course,
have been one of the fellows on the fairs' permanent staff. There
are four such fairs, administered by the merchants, held annually
in the vicinity of the Sardar, those of En'Kara, En'Var, Se'Kara
and Se'Var. The girl was immediately very still, and very quiet,
on all fours.

"I think I can find a buyer for her," I said.

"Who?" he asked.

"Come now," I said. "Let us not be naive."

"Do you want a commission?" he asked. "We are very
careful about that sort of business."

"No," I said.

"Ah," he said, pleased. What he feared, of course, particularly since he did not know me, is the trick of two friends
cooperating in the purchase of a slave. One attempts to obtain a
finder's commission from the merchant which he then, of course,
turns back to his friend, the buyer. In this way, the slave is
purchased more cheaply. As it was, since I was not bargaining
for a commission with him, he presumably supposed that I
would obtain a finder's fee from the buyer. Some people actually
make their living in this way, acting as buying agents, providing
services such as locating rare slaves for collectors and filling the
"want lists" of rich men.

"I would appreciate it, however," I said, "if you would put a
'hold' on her until, say, the eighteenth Ahn."

"Impossible," he said. "Look at her. See the curves, the
lines." He tapped her with the whip. "Superb slave meat."

"I cannot get the buyer here until then," I said.

"Ten copper tarsks, to hold her until then," he said.

"Absurd," I said.

"It is refundable," he said.

"Under what conditions?" I asked.

"That you bring your buyer to the platform before the eighteenth Ahn," he said.

"What if he doesn't want her?" I asked. Actually, I was pretty confident he would want her.

"I will not hold you responsible for that," he said. "I will still give you back your tarsks."

"Good," I said. I then gave him the ten copper tarsks. His reasonableness in this matter, I suspect, was due at least in part to the slowness of the market. Indeed, some of the girls in the market, I suspected, would go for as little as that same ten copper tarsks.

"Hold still, Girl," said the man to the girl. I watched him while he, crouching down beside her, wired a circular, white tag, a holding disk, to her collar. He had placed his whip behind her. Some men place the whip where the slave can see it, noting its heavy-leather blades or coils, that she may understand its menace. Others, like this fellow, place the whip behind her, where she does not know precisely where it is, but knows very well that it is there. The second placement is perhaps, generally, somewhat more to be dreaded by the female. There are no hard-and-fast rules in this sort of thing. Much can depend on the girl, on her intelligence and imagination, on the stage of her training, on the specific occasion in question, and so on. Sometimes it is desirable to have the female look very closely and clearly on the whip and, at other times, it is better for her merely to understand that it is in her immediate vicinity, somewhere, and that she may not, now, turn about to determine its specific location.

The tag on its wire now dangled some four inches below her collar. It had been one of several such tags in a small bag hooked to his belt. It had an inked "Eighteen" on it. Some of the white tags were blank, and might be written on. The red tags carry the inscription "Sold." A black tag is sometimes used to indicate that a girl is ill. A yellow tag sometimes indicates that a girl is not to be sold without prior consultation with the slaver. Tags are sometimes, too, used to indicate distinctions among slaves, at least among slavers themselves, being correlated to the classes or grades of slaves. For example, a brown tag commonly signifies a low slave, such as a mere kettle-and-mat girl or a pot girl, little more than female work slaves, and so on, whereas a gold tag commonly signifies a much higher grade of slave, usually a trained pleasure slave or a dancer. There is, however, to be perfectly honest, no absolutely uniform color coding in these matters. Different houses have their own conventions. It is unusual, incidentally, for a woman to be tagged in a regular market, except in so far as she might be marked "Sold" or have a "Hold" put on her. It is not hard in a Gorean market, for example, where the women are usually stripped, or will be stripped for the buyer's inspection, to see who is most beautiful or interesting. Too, of course, women in such a market can be literally made to display their beauty and pose and perform in various ways for the viewers. This, too, makes it easier to make choices amongst them.

One form of tagging is fairly common, however, during sales, and that is tagging during auctions, or in preparation for large sales, as when the girls are in exhibition cages, before being brought, usually serially, later, before the public. This form of tagging is in sales disk. It bears the girl's lot number on it. It is usually wired to her collar. This not only provides the seller with a convenience, helping to make certain his records remain clear, but it can be helpful to the buyer also, who may then, presumably already having established his interests, perhaps by virtue of commands earlier addressed to the lovely chattels in the exhibition cages, simply bid by number.

I regarded the girl. She was quite beautiful, on all fours on the platform, the short chain on her neck descending to its ring in the heavy planks. There was a white disk dangling from her collar. She would be held until the eighteenth Ahn. The slaver's man was now again on his feet. He had retrieved his whip.

I turned away.

"I now wear a holding tag, Master," she said to the slaver's man. "May I break position?"

I heard the lash fall upon her. "Forgive me, Master!" she cried.

How stupid her question had been. Did she not know that the prospective buyer might not prove to be interested in her, and that she might in the meantime, by lax postures or attitudes, be discouraging other occurrences of interest; too, what of the other slaves and the aesthetic integrity of the display line; too, the prospective buyer might appear earlier than was anticipated. Too, did she think her discipline would be relaxed because someone might be interested in her? No! It would be trebled!

"Ah!" had cried Boots, later, about the seventeenth Ahn, when he had first seen her. "But wait! She wears a holding disk!"

"Do not fear," I said. "It is for your inspection that she is being held."

"Oh?" said Boots.

"I arranged it," I said.

"Let us take a look at her," said Boots.

In the end Boots got her for two silver tarsks. This is a high price for an untrained slave but, to be sure, all things considered, she was an excellent buy. Too, she seemed ideal for Boots's purposes. She would doubtless make a splendid "golden courtesan" and, after performances, there was little doubt but what she would prove popular in the sex tents. Too, getting her for two silver tarsks, though perhaps somewhat more than Boots cared to pay, left him a full three silver tarsks, the residue of his profit from the sale of the Brigella. Three silver tarsks would surely tide him over, and his company, until the next performances, presumably to take place somewhere other than on the fairgrounds.

"I do not know what I shall do without my Brigella," moaned Boots, preparing to pay the slaver's man.

"Look at it this way," I said. "You are at least getting a golden courtesan."

"There are more Brigella roles," said Boots.

"Well, this girl is not a Brigella," I said.

"True," lamented Boots.

"Perhaps you should not have sold your Brigella," I said.

"I needed the money," said Boots.

"Two silver tarsks," said the slaver's man.

"The price is steep," said Boots. "Could we not reconsider the matter?"

"Two silver tarsks," said the man.

"Would you care to make it double or nothing, on the basis of some wager of your choosing, such as in cups and pebbles?" he asked.

"Two," said the man.

"I have the cups and a pebble, by some stroke of luck, in my wallet," said Boots.

"Two," said the fellow. This game, like many such games, of various types, involves guessing. Small, inverted metal cups are used. A coin, pebble, or small object is supposedly placed beneath one of the cups. They are then moved about, rapidly. The odds are with the "house," so to speak, particularly if the coin or pebble is not placed under one of the cups. I was already familiar with Boots's skill in slight-of-hand manipulations from Port Kar. "Two," repeated the man. Boots then paid him. The slaver's man, of course, was well pleased with the sale. It was a good price, and it was a particularly good one for a slow market.

I had no difficulty in recovering my ten copper tarsks, put down to hold the girl for Boots's later inspection.

"Are you pleased with your buy?" I asked Boots later, when we were leaving the market, the girl following behind us, heeling us, her wrists tied behind her back with a string.

"She was pretty expensive," said Boots.

"But you are pleased, are you not?" I asked.

"Yes," he said.

"Are you grateful?" I asked.

"Eternally, undyingly," he assured me.

"Perhaps you would consider granting me a favor," I said.

"Just ask," he said.

"I would like to join your troupe," I said.

"No," he said.

"I thought you just said to 'just ask,' " I said.

"You are correct," said Boots. "That is exactly what I had in mind, that you should just ask, only that, just that, and nothing more. Now, where are my wagons?"

"You are a hard man," I said.

"Yes," he said, "I am a grim fellow. But one does not attain my heights by being soft."

"Your wagons are in that direction," I informed him.

"Thank you," he said.

"You will not reconsider?" I asked.

"No," said Boots, "and what am I to do without a Brigella?"

"I do not know," I said.

"I am ruined," said Boots.

"Perhaps not," I opined, hopefully.

"Are you a business man?" he asked.

"No," I said.

"I will thank you, then," said Boots, "to have the decency to refrain from forming an opinion on the matter."

"Sorry," I said.

"Do you know where I can find a Brigella?" he asked.

"Perhaps you could buy one," I said.

"Not just any girl can be a Brigella," he said.

"I suppose not," I said.

"I am ruined," he said.

"At least you now have a golden courtesan," I said, "and I expect that she will prove profitable in the tent as well."

"Perhaps," said Boots.

"I would like to join your troupe," I said.

"It is out of the question," said Boots. "Now, where are those wagons?"

"That way," I said.

"Thank you," he said.

"More to the left," I said.

"Thank you," he said.

"You would not have to pay me!" I called out, after him.

"No, no," he said, waving his hand, "it is out of the question." He then continued on his way, muttering about Brigellas, expenses, free women, fate, elusive wagons and the woes that sometimes afflict honest men.

Security in Brundisium, I had learned earlier from Boots, was tight. I wondered why this might be. I was curious to know, too, why at least some in that city seemed to have an interest in Tarl Cabot, or Bosk, of Port Kar. Much seemed to me mysterious in Brundisium. It might be an interesting place to go visiting, I thought. Too, it had been a long time since I had gone hunting. I was sorry that I had not been able to join Boots's troupe. None, I thought, would be likely to suspect a lowly member of a group of strolling players. It would have been a superb cover. Tomorrow, before nightfall, I suspected, Boots's wagons would leave the fair, probably heading west, probably on the road of Clearchus. It is a dangerous road. There was no law against two traveling it. Boots had disappeared now among the booths and stalls of the fair.

"Please, let me yield!" she whispered. "I beg to be permitted to yield! Please, Master, let me yield! Please, Master! Please, Master!"

I looked down into her eyes. She looked up at me, through her hair, wildly, piteously.

"No," I said.

She moaned. She tried to control her breathing. Her beauty was held tense, rigid, almost motionless. I heard the tiniest sound of the chain on her ankle. The collar, the flat, snug, unslippable band on her throat, locked behind the back of her neck, was lovely.

We were some two hundred pasangs west of the fairgrounds, at the edge of the woods of Clearchus, just off the road of Clearchus. I had traveled for the last few days in the vicinity of the troupe of Boots, but not really with it. We had traversed the woods of Clearchus, Boots losing little time in the business, without incident. He had, this afternoon, at the edge of the woods, for local villagers, given his first performances since the fair, from which, as we had anticipated, he had been duly expelled, that following from various complaints lodged with the

fair's board of governance by a certain free woman, the Lady
Telitsia of Asperiche. He had also, given the supposed gravity of
his offenses, been fined three silver tarsks and publicly flogged.

He had not been in a good mood that evening. Such things, of
course, are not that unusual in the lives of players. Worse,
perhaps, two of his company had joined another troupe, taking
advantage of an opportunity at the fair, the fellows who commonly played the comic father and the comic pedant. Boots was
now trying to make do with his Chino and Lecchio, two other
fellows, his Bina and his new "golden courtesan." Things were
so bad that he had, this afternoon, actually interspersed his
dramatic offerings with what were more in the nature of variety
or carnival acts. One must make do as one can.

Fortunately his Chino was an accomplished juggler and his
Lecchio was excellent as a comic tight-rope walker. Boots himself was very skillful in the matter of slight-of-hand and magic.
Indeed, his delapidated, oval-roofed wagon seemed a veritable
repository for all sorts of wondrous paraphernalia, much of it
having to do with matters of illusion and legerdemain. This
multiplicity of skills, incidentally, is not all that uncommon with
players. Most of them, too, it seems, can do things like play the
flute or kalika, sing, dance, tell jokes, and so on. They are
generally versatile and talented people.

Boots's player, incidentally, the kaissa player, the surly, masked
fellow, called usually "the monster" in the camp, remained,
too, with the troupe. He remained, as far as I could tell, from
what I had heard this afternoon, consistently and insolently
adamant to Boots's pleas that he manage to lose a game once in
a while, if only for the sake of business, or, at the least, make an
effort to play a bit less well. Nonetheless, even as it was, he did
make some contribution to the welfare of the troupe. His kaissa
games, for what it is worth, usually brought in a few coins.
There was something I wanted to talk with him about, sometime.

"Please, Master," whimpered the girl.

"Are you ready?" I asked.

"Yes, yes, yes!" she said, tensely.

" 'Yes,' what?" I asked.

"Yes, Master!" she said, helplessly, tensely.

"Very well," I said. "You may yield."

"Aiii!" she screamed, wildly, inarticulately, in release, in
relief, in animal gratitude. Then she cried, "Oh! Oh!" and
thrashed beneath me. "Oh!" she cried. "Oh!" She clutched me,
desperately. Her legs, with a rattle of the chain, locked about
me. "Oh!" she cried. Her fingernails dug deeply into my back.

Then again she could speak. "I yield me!" she cried. "I yield me to you, Master! I am yours! I am yours, yours, yours! Oh, yes, I am yours, yours." She clung then to me, sobbing and gasping. I heard the chain on her ankle.

"Your yielding," I said, "was satisfactory—for a new slave."

She looked at me wildly, and then moaned softly, continuing to cling helplessly to me.

"There are, of course," I said, "infinite horizons and varieties of such responses, ranging from ravishings in which the slave, by one means or another, is driven almost to the point of madness by the pleasures inflicted upon her, ravishings in which the master, in his cruelty, and despite her will, forces her relentlessly and helplessly to, and beyond, ecstasy, giving her no choice but to accept total sexual fulfillment, to putting her helplessly to lengthy and gentle services, warm and intimate, in which her slavery and condition are well brought home to her."

"Sometimes, too, I gather," she whispered, "the slave must serve in varieties of manners regardless of her desires of the moment or will."

"Of course," I said.

"She is at the master's disposal, completely, for all forms of work and duties."

"Yes," I said.

"She is to be diligent and obedient in all things," she said.

"Yes," I said.

"That, too," she whispered, "is rewarding and gratifying."

"Really?" I said.

"Yes," she whispered. "Very much so."

"Interesting," I said.

"The being of the slave, like the being of the master," she said, "is a totality."

I lay on my back, looking up at the ceiling of the tent. She was right, of course. These things are totalities, modes of being. Too, I knew, from my own experience, that nothing fulfils maleness like the mastery. He who would be a man must be a master. He who surrenders his mastery surrenders his manhood. I wondered what those who flocked like sheep to their own castration received in recompense for their manhood. I supposed it must be very valuable. But if this were so, why did they feel it necessary to shrill so petulantly at others, those who scorned them and had chosen different paths?

I could hear Boots outside the tent. He was a few yards away, around the campfire with Chino and Lecchio. "Lamentations!" cried Boots. "Surely we are ruined! Surely we shall all starve!

There are not two copper tarsks in the coin kettle! What hope is
there these days for artists such as we! That the skilled and
famous company of Boots Tarsk-Bit, actor, promoter and
entrepreneur, that company whose performances are commanded
by high cities and ubars, the finest theatrical company on all
Gor, should be forced to resort to mere carnival acts, that it
should have to stoop to jugglery and somersaults, to mere tricks
and illusions, to entertain village bumpkins, solid, noble fellows
though they may be, is almost too much to bear. What shall be
our fate first, I wonder, to merely starve in simple dignity or to
perish in shame from such humiliation?"

"You are wrong about at least one thing, Boots," said Chino.

"Can it be?" asked Boots.

"Yes," said Chino. "There are more than two copper tarsks
in the coin kettle."

"Oh?" said Boots.

I heard coins shaking in a metal kettle. "Listen," said Chino.
"There is at least a silver tarsk's worth here."

"Are you sure?" asked Boots.

"Count it yourself," said Chino.

"Yes," said Boots. "Ah! Ah, yes. I did not realize my skills
with magic were still that mysterious and baffling. Very good.
Excellent, excellent. Excellent, indeed! You did well also, of
course, Chino, my friend, and you, too, Lecchio. Well, it is as I
always say, a bit of variety is a good thing. And one cannot
always be too serious about art, you know. Upon occasion one
should take a respite from even high drama. Too, excessive
significance is not always good for the digestion. Also, we still
need a Brigella, and desperately. I think, accordingly, that it will
not be amiss if, upon occasion, particularly in somewhat less
enlightened and more remote locations, we intermix a dash of
legerdemain and prestidigitation, as well as a bit of carnival
hilarity, prankery, and such, the sort of things that you folks are
good at, with our nobler offerings. To be sure, we will still
remain fundamentally true to the theater, for we are primarily,
when all is said and done, serious actors. Too, our reputation
depends upon it. What do you think? I am glad that you agree."

I lay on my back, looking up at the ceiling of the tent. I felt
the girl's cheek against my thigh. I remembered when she had
been the free woman, Rowena of Lydius, whom I had first seen
in the house of Samos. How proud she had been! She was now a
contented slave, a girl who had been named "Rowena," at a
man's thigh.

"The somersault on the rope was very good," Boots was telling Lecchio. "You should try to do it twice."

Boots's little Bina was chained in another tent. I thought perhaps I might try her sometime.

"Perhaps even three times, and backwards," Boots was saying.

I smiled to myself. He was talking, of course, about Lecchio's somersaults. The little Bina was very pretty, but I thought, rather clearly, she had not yet been brought to slave heat. I had gathered, from various tiny indications, back at the fair, and this afternoon, that Boots was not altogether satisfied with her. As a collared slave, I feared, she had much to learn. Too, she seemed to have a nasty streak in her. More than once I had heard her deride the "monster." In this I think she showed little judgment. He, at least, was free, whereas she, though she seemed not to fully understand it, was imbonded.

"It was funny, too," said Boots, "when you fell off the rope. Perhaps you should include that in the act."

"I did not do it on purpose," said Lecchio. "I am out of practice. I nearly broke my neck."

I supposed I might as well soon depart from the neighborhood of Boots's company. Surely there seemed little point in continuing any longer in its vicinity. My own small camp was within two hundred yards. To be sure, there was little there but a bedroll, some supplies and weapons, purchased at the fair. I had not seen fit to purchase a shield or spear, or even a bow, with sheaf arrows. Such things, I feared, might mark me as one to be reckoned with, or watched, one perhaps familiar with weapons. I supposed I would arouse enough suspicion in the neighborhood of Brundisium as it was, coming to their city as a lone male with no obvious business. I did have a sword and I had also purchased a set of Tuchuk quivas, their famed saddle knives. The set consists of seven knives, one for each of the seven sheaths in the Tuchuk saddle. They are balanced for throwing. I was rather skillful with them. I had learned their use long ago in the lands of the Wagon Peoples, or, as some think of them, on the plains of Turia. I must soon leave the tent. I must return to my own small camp. I must get a good night's sleep, and start out early in the morning.

"Ho!" I heard Boots call, suddenly. "Who is there?"

I was suddenly alert. It was a bit late now. The performances had been over for some hours. I was not at all sure that villagers or travelers would be about at this time.

"What is wrong?" asked the girl, sensing the change in me.

"Be silent," I said.

"Who are you?" called Boots. There was no answer. Who-
ever it was had not identified themselves.

I slipped into my tunic and picked up my sword, in its
scabbard, the belt looped about the scabbard.

"Come forward," called Boots. "I know you are out there.
Do not be afraid. Identify yourselves. Come into the light."

"If they wish to know if one was with you," I said to the girl,
"tell them that he fled."

"What is going on?" she said.

I cautioned her to silence, holding my finger across my lips.
This is a very natural gesture. I do not know if the gesture,
considered as a Gorean gesture, had an independent development,
or if, specifically, somewhere in the remote past, it had an Earth
origin. There are many Gorean gestures, of course, some of
which are very similar to Earth gestures and some of which are
not. Another way of warning an individual to silence, incidentally,
is to touch the fingers twice, lightly, to the lips. The origin of
that gesture, as far as I know, is uniquely Gorean. I looked back
at the female. Her lip trembled. She was frightened. She wanted
desperately to speak. She could not speak, of course. She was a
slave. She had been silenced. I lifted up the back of the tent, and
inspected the terrain behind it. I would take my leave in this
fashion. I looked back once more at the girl. She was kneeling,
looking after me, frightened. She would remain, of course,
exactly where she was. The chain on her ankle would see to that.
How beautiful they are in collars. I then slipped from the tent.

8

I MAKE MYSELF USEFUL TO BOOTS TARSK-BIT; I WILL ALSO SHOW HIM WHAT I HAVE FOUND IN THE WOODS

"Release us!" demanded Boots Tarsk-Bit, on his knees, near the campfire, his arms roped to his sides.

The leader of the brigands, a bearded fellow, with a cloth wrapped about his head, lashed him across the mouth with the back of his hand. This was inappropriate as Boots was a free person.

"Your conduct," sputtered Boots, "is deplorable. I am Boots Tarsk-Bit, actor, promoter and entrepreneur. Doubtless you have heard of me. I am not a slave. I demand to be treated with civility and courtesy."

"Shall I cut his throat?" asked one of the brigands, taking Boots by the hair and pulling his head back.

"Not yet," said the leader of the brigands.

"Where are the keys to the ankle rings of your tent sluts?" inquired the leader of the brigands.

Boots grunted as his head was jerked farther back. The blade of the fellow's knife pressed against his throat.

"You had only to ask," said Boots.

"Where are they?" asked the leader of the brigands.

"On a nail, inside of the door of my wagon, the large wagon with the red roof, on the left," said Boots.

"Bring the two tent sluts here, bound, to the edge of the fire," said the leader of the brigands. "We shall then see if they are worth keeping or should be left here, with the others."

"What are you going to do with us?" asked Boots.

I saw two of the brigands exchange glances, grinning at one another. I saw another fellow start toward Boots's wagon, presumably to fetch the keys to Bina's and Rowena's ankle rings. I gathered if they were found sufficiently beautiful, or sufficiently desirable, they might be spared. It is in the modality of slavery, on the terms of masters, that females historically have sought, and sometimes have been granted, at least provisionally, their survival.

"Do you call this money?" asked the leader of the brigands, shaking the coin kettle under Boots's nose.

"Why, yes," said Boots, looking into the kettle.

The leader of the brigands again struck him.

"There is scarcely a silver tarsk here," snarled the leader of the brigands.

"I agree," said Boots. "It is a piteous sum, not even worth taking. Leave it, if you wish." He then shrank back, but the chief of the brigands lowered his hand, angrily.

The fellow who had gone to fetch the girls now returned. He had the two girls with him. The hands of each, by a cord knotted about their waist, were tied before their bodies. He drew them after him, in leading position, each bent over, by the hair. He then twisted them about and flung them to their backs in the dirt, by the fire. The leader of the brigands then took a flaming brand from the fire and holding it over the girls passed it back and forth, over their bodies, scanning them, examining them in the dancing light. He tossed the brand back into the flames. "We will keep them," he said.

The girls shuddered with relief. They had been found acceptable.

"Tie them," said the leader of the brigands, "kneeling, left ankle to right ankle, right ankle to left ankle."

In a moment this was done. They were knelt, back to back. Two cords are used. One cord fastens the first girl's left ankle to the other girl's right ankle, the same cord looped tight about both ankles, binding them closely together. The other cord, similarly, fastens her right ankle to the other's left ankle. It is a lovely, efficient tie, fastening both girls helplessly in a posture of submission. In this tie they will not leap to their feet and flee away. They will remain, waiting, where they have been placed.

"What moneys are there here?" demanded the chief of the brigands of Boots.

Boots was silent.

The chief of the brigands looked down, near the fire. There the other male members of Boots's company lay on their stomachs, bound, sly, agile Chino, simple Lecchio, Petrucchio, the tall, doleful "captain," and Publius Andronicus, supposedly the most famous actor in the company, saving perhaps the incredible Boots Tarsk-Bit himself. I had not yet, as a matter of fact, seen Publius Andronicus act. I supposed that he was capable of doing so. He was quite impressive, in a ponderous way, rather like a mountain range, in figure and visage. He also had a deep bass voice, which, when he wished, he could make boom like thunder. Boots was quite impressed with him. He was apparently holding himself in reserve for major leads, such as those of tragic statesmen, tormented poets, confused ubars, and such. I thought that perhaps he was in the wrong company. At any rate it did not seem that the repertory of Boots's company, as I was familiar with it at least, was richly or unusually endowed with roles of such a nature. Too, bound, still hooded, the player, he called the "monster," lay with the others.

"Take what you want," said Boots. "Then be gone."

"That one," said the chief of the brigands, indicating Chino, "kill him."

"No!" cried Boots. "Hold! You cannot be serious! Such an act would desecrate the theater! That is the finest Chino on all Gor!"

"I do not like the idea either," said Chino, "on independent grounds."

"If only I had my sword!" cried Petrucchio. I really doubted that Petrucchio's huge, clumsy wooden sword, no more than a comic theatrical prop really, would be likely to turn the tide of battle. Still his courage I found admirable.

"Cut his throat," said the leader of the brigands.

"No," said Boots. "In my wagon, in the right-hand corner of the tray in my trunk there is a knotted sock which contains coins and there are some coins, too, thrust in the toe of a slipper at the side of the trunk."

"Fetch them," said the leader of the brigands.

The fellow who had seized Chino thrust him back to the dirt. He then made his way to Boots's wagon.

"What else?" demanded the leader of the brigands.

"I know of little else that might be of value to you," said
Boots. "You may look about and take what you like. I cannot
speak for the others."

"Where is Bort?" asked the leader of the brigands.

"He was keeping watch, at the road," said one of the men.

"We have them now," said the leader of the brigands. "We
have called the guards in. Where is he?"

"Doubtless he will be in in a moment," said one of the men.
He was mistaken.

"Bort! Bort!" called a fellow.

I had counted, all told, counting the leader, seven brigands. It
is important, for obvious reasons, to be as clear as possible on
such matters.

"Bort!" the man called out, again, more loudly.

I had made the acquaintance of Bort, briefly, near the road.
He had not had a great deal of time, however, to savor the
relationship. His attention had been distracted by a tiny sound,
the sound of a falling pebble, to one side. I had then approached
him from the opposite direction.

"Bort!" called out the man.

The brigands were now six in number. They did not realize
this, as yet.

"Where is he?" said one of the men.

"Sleeping at his post," said a man.

"Lost," said another.

"Let him go," said a fellow. "There will be more loot for us
that way."

"Go find him," said the leader of the brigands.

Interestingly enough, only one man, he who had been calling
Bort, came forth to locate him.

"Bort?" he inquired, warily, peering into the darkness. "Is
that you?" I killed him. "No," I said.

I then circled about the camp, approaching from the other side
of the wagons. The leader of the brigands, and one other fellow,
were near the prisoners. The others were rummaging through the
wagons and goods. They were intent only on their loot. I caught
one from behind and dragged him back into the darkness. I left
him there. I used the same quiva I had on the other two.

"Titus!" called one of the brigands, emerging from a wagon,
pausing on the steps at the rear. "See what I have found!" He
brandished a large inlaid cup. I had seen such cups before.
"Titus!" he called. "Titus?"

"Where is Crassius?" called the leader of the brigands to him.
"Is he with you?"

"No," said the man. "Has he not yet returned?"

"No," said the leader.

The man lowered his arm with the cup.

"He should be back with Bort by now," said the man on the wagon steps.

"Bort!" called the leader into the darkness. "Crassius!" He then turned about. "Titus!" he called. "Titus!" He regarded the fellow with him. "I do not like it," he said.

"What is wrong?" asked another fellow, emerging from one of the wagons.

"Bort is missing," said the leader. "Crassius has not yet returned. We have called Titus. He does not respond."

The men looked about themselves, apprehensively.

"Sleen," said one of the men.

It is true that sleen sometimes make kills swiftly and silently.

"It could be a panther come from the woods, or a strayed larl," said one of the men. This was less likely than a sleen attack. Though panthers and larls can be extremely dangerous to men they will usually attack men only if they are disturbed or other prey is not available. Sleen, which tend to be fine hunters and splendid trackers, which are swiftly moving, aggressive, serpentine, generally nocturnal animals, particularly in the wild state, are less fastidious about their eating habits.

"It could be urts," said a man. "It is near the time of the year for their movements." Certain species of urts migrate twice a year. At such times, annually, it is usually necessary only to avoid them. People usually remain indoors when a pack is in their vicinity. There is little danger from these migrations unless one finds oneself in their direct path. The urt, on the whole, most species of which are quite small, large enough to be lifted in one hand, does not pose much direct threat to human beings. They can destroy Sa-Tarna fields and force their way into granaries. Similarly urts of the sort which live on garbage cast into the canals will often, unhesitantly, attack swimmers. Certain forms of large, domesticated urt, incidentally, should be excepted from these remarks. They are especially bred for attacking and killing. Such animals, however, are inferior to sleen for such purposes. They also lack the tracking capabilities of the sleen. Similarly they lack its intelligence. There was at least one good additional reason, incidentally, for supposing that whatever might be perplexing the brigands was not urts. The urts do not make their kills neatly and silently. They normally attack in a pack. It is usually a messy business. There is usually much blood and screaming.

"Gather in what you can," said the leader of the brigands. "Then we will be on our way." He looked about himself. Then he threw some more wood on the fire. The fire, of course, would be useful in keeping sleen at bay. It also, from my point of view, was useful in illuminating the camp area.

The two men at the rear doors of the wagons, on the steps, looked across at one another.

"Get busy," said the leader.

"You are near the fire," said one of the men on the wagons.

"We have enough," said the other.

"Cowards," said the brigand near their chief, near the fire.

"Let us be on our way," said the first fellow, holding the cup in his hand.

"Do you dispute me?" asked the leader.

The fellow put down the cup. His hand went to the hilt of his sword. I was pleased that the cup had been put down. I would not have wanted it to be dropped.

"Perhaps you are right," said the leader. "Come here, by the fire."

The fellow descended from the steps of the wagon, warily.

"You are right," said the leader. "We have enough."

"Good," said the fellow.

"Fetch the cup," said the leader.

As soon as the man turned about, however, the leader leaped toward him, seized him from behind, his arm locked about his throat, and plunged a dagger, to the hilt, into his back.

"Teibar!" cried the other fellow on the steps.

The leader, his knife bloody, whirled to face him. "Do you gainsay me in this?" he asked.

"No, no!" said the other fellow, quickly.

"Put leashes on the females," said the leader, straightening up, "and then untie their legs, to make it possible for them to move." This is common Gorean practice, to place one bond before removing another.

"You shall be led as befits slaves, as befits animals, as chattels," said the leader to the girls.

"Yes, Master," said Rowena.

"Yes, Master," said pretty Bina.

"What of the wagons and the men?" asked the fellow who was near the leader.

"We will burn the wagons," said the leader. "We will cut the throats of the men."

"Excellent," said his fellow.

"Fetch the cup," said the leader to the fellow who had now descended from the steps of the wagon.

"I do not want it," said the fellow, shakily, looking at his fallen fellow, near the fire.

"Coward," laughed the leader. He then moved past the fellow, proceeding toward the wagon.

The leader had not noticed, it seemed, that although the fellow's voice had surely suggested uncertainty and fear, his hand had been perfectly steady. The fellow's draw was swift and smooth. The leader had barely time to turn, taking the blade, descending, diagonally across the neck. He fell away from the blade, his head awry. The girls screamed. The assailant turned to face the other brigand.

"Do not strike!" cried the other brigand.

Momentarily the assailant hesitated. For an instant he was indecisive. He had not considered matters, it seemed, beyond the slaying of the leader. That had perhaps been short-sighted on his part. Surely the other man should have been included, in one way or another, in his original plan. Obviously he was going to be there, after the original blow. Obviously, in some fashion, he would have to be dealt with or related to. At any rate he had hesitated for a moment. Such dallience can be costly. The other fellow now had his own blade free of its sheath.

"Let us not fight," said the fellow who had just drawn his blade. "I am with you! There is enough loot for two."

I now revised my estimate of the intelligence of the fellow who had struck down the leader. It seemed reasonably clear, from the voice and attitude of the fellow who had just drawn his weapon, that he was clearly alarmed. I did not think he was acting in this matter. At any rate it seemed to me that his fear was genuine.

"Sheath your sword," said the fellow who had struck the leader.

"Sheath yours," invited he who had been with the leader.

It was now my assessment of the situation that he who had struck the leader had been confident of his capacity to deal with the other fellow. It was thus, apparently, that he had been willing to postpone, for a moment or so, at least, his decision as to how to deal with him. He was now, it seemed, considering it.

"Let us not quarrel," urged the fellow who had been the confidant of the leader. "There may be sleen about."

The first fellow, scarcely taking his eyes off the other, glanced uneasily about. He could not see me, as I stood back in the darkness. Both were within the cast of a quiva. I turned the blade in my hand.

"Put away your sword," urged the fellow who had been the confidant of the leader.

"I do not trust you," said the other.

"Let us not fight," said the fellow who had been with the leader. "There is little enough here to justify our war."

"There is enough," said the fellow who had struck the leader. I saw that his decision had now been made.

"It is enough for two!" said he who had been with the leader.

"It will be more for one," said he who had struck the leader. "What is wrong?"

The fellow facing him had suddenly stiffened, drawing his shoulders close together. Then his hand fell, lowering the blade. He stumbled forward a step. The other, he who had struck the leader, tensed, his sword poised to fend any possible blow. Then the other, he who had been the confidant of the leader, pitched forward, falling near the fire. The girls, slaves, kneeling, still bound helplessly, naked, their small hands jerking at the cords holding their wrists tight to their belly, screamed. Men, too, bound, cried out. From the fellow's back there protruded the handle of a knife, the hilt of a particular sort of knife, that of a saddle knife, that of the sort common in the land of the Wagon Peoples, that commonly known as a "quiva." I had not thrown it hard enough, intentionally, to bring the point fully through the body. It is not necessary. The cast, as recommended, had been easy and smooth. The quiva itself, in its sharpness and weight, does the work. I turned another blade in my hand.

The fellow leaped backward from the fire. Perhaps, after all, he was not as intelligent as I had supposed. He had not destroyed the fire. He had only retreated from it. I could still see him. Understandably, of course, he was unwilling to flee headlong, blindly, from the camp, into an unknown, unexplored darkness, one in which the number and position of enemies was unknown.

"Who is there?" he cried.

Only the night noises of the nearby woods answered him.

"If you are magistrates," he cried, "know that I have come on this camp of brigands and, in cognizance of my jeopardy, was making ready to defend myself!" He looked about, wildly, drawing back another pace or so. "Show yourself," he cried, "as befits your office, that of those who courageously do war with brigands, that of those who do nobly defend and support the law, or as plain honest men, if that you be, that I may ally myself with you, that we may then offer to one another, no, then pledge to one another, mutual protection and succor on these dark and dangerous roads.''

It was very quiet, save mostly for the rustling and clicking of insects. Too I heard, intermittently, from somewhere far off, the cries of a tiny, horned gim.

"You do not show yourselves," called the man. "Good! Know then that I am a brigand, too! I feared you might be magistrates. It was thus that I spoke as I did. A falling out occurred here in which I was forced to defend myself. I am Abdar, who was of the band of Ho-Dan. Perhaps you have heard of me. I am wanted in five cities. Approach. Though the loot here is meager I am pleased to share it with you, or, if you wish, surrender it to you, as a token of my good faith. Consider the females, if you can see them. Both, I am sure, you would find acceptable as slaves. If you desire them, I give them to you. Show yourselves! Let us enmesh our destinies. I desire to enleague myself with you. Who are you! Show yourselves!''

I did not respond to him. I measured the distance between us.

"Are you still there?" he cried. "Are you still there?''

Then, suddenly, with a cry of misery, the fellow spun about and broke into a run. I took one step and released the blade. He grunted and fell forward, sprawling to the dirt, and then lay on his stomach, a few feet from the fire. He rose to his knees and crawled a pace or two, and then again sank to his stomach. Then he lifted his upper body and head, and then fell forward again. He squirmed. He tried, vainly, clutching with his hand behind him, to reach the blade in his back. He could not do so. Then he shuddered and lay still.

I came forward and regarded the body. I removed the knife from it, cleaning it on his tunic. Then I resheathed the blade, in one of the seven sheaths sewn on the common, supple leather backing, slung now from its shoulder strap, at and about my left hip. Someone, as it had turned out, had been still there.

"You!" cried Boots Tarsk-Bit.

I regarded the two slaves. They knew that they were now being scrutinized as females, basically and radically. It is a fundamental sort of inspection. The girl must hope that she passes it. They straightened their bodies. They did not dare to meet my eyes. It is important for slaves to be pleasing. Their lives depend upon it.

I looked at Boots. He swallowed, hard.

I then crouched down near him. I began to free his arms, where they were bound to his body. His sigh of relief was audible.

"Where are the other brigands?" he asked.

I freed his arms. "They are here and there," I said. "Do not fear. They are all accounted for."

"How many are with you?" he asked.

"I am alone," I said.

"By yourself you did this?" he asked.

"Yes," I said.

"Where did you learn to throw a knife like that?" he asked.

"In the south," I said, "far in the south."

"You have saved our lives," he said. "Those rascals, I fear, had no intent to spare us."

"Except the slaves," I said.

"Of course," he said. They, after all, were usable, beautiful, salable animals.

We then began to free the others, all but the slaves.

"We are grateful," Boots assured me.

"Thank you," said the player, surlily, begrudgingly, as I freed his hand from behind his back. He then bent quickly, angrily, to untie the ropes on his ankles.

"Do not mind him," said Boots. "He is a puzzling chap. He would probably have preferred to have had his throat cut."

"But you are grateful?" I said to Boots.

"Yes," he said. "I am grateful."

"Eternally, undyingly?" I asked Boots, smiling.

"Of course," he said. "Eternally, undyingly!"

"I think I may be of further service to you," I said.

"How is that?" asked Boots, interested. We finished untying Chino, Lecchio, Petrucchio and Publius Andronicus. We left the girls, for the time, of course, as they were, as they were slaves. They would await our pleasure, that of free men.

"Come with me," I said. "And bring a torch."

"What is it?" asked Boots.

"It is something I would like to show you," I said. "I found it nearby in the woods, when I returned to my camp, to fetch weapons, a few Ehn ago."

"What is it?" he asked.

"Come with me," I said. "I will show you."

"Very well," he said.

"Bring a torch," I said.

"Very well," he said.

9

TWO WOMEN, ONE FREE, ONE BOND; I JOIN THE COMPANY OF BOOTS TARSK-BIT

"Here," I said. "See?"

We were in a small clearing in the woods, not far from the road.

"Yes!" said Boots, appreciatively.

"Lower the torch," I said. "Look more closely."

The two women whimpered, looking up, blinking against the light. The torch, Boots crouching down, was passed slowly over their bodies. One wore a long gown, sleeveless and white. It was all she wore, however, and it was thin. I did not think it was what she would have chosen to wear. It had apparently been picked out for her. The fullness of her beauty, at any rate, in its delicious amplitudes, was not difficult to conjecture beneath it. The other was excitingly curvaceous, too. About her beauty, however, there could be no possible mistake. She was absolutely naked. Both were bound tightly, helplessly, hand and foot.

"Pretty," said Boots.

"Yes," said Chino.

"Yes," said Lecchio.

Petrucchio and Publius Andronicus, too, voiced their assent. The surly, hooded player was not with us. After he had finished freeing himself from the ropes on his ankles, he had hurried to recover the cup which had been of such interest to the brigands. It seemed he did not wish others to see it, or understand its meaning. He had then, taking the cup, gone into his wagon. It seemed then that he had chosen, at least for the time, to remain there. He had not, at any rate, come with us. It seemed he was not particularly appreciative of what had been done for him. Perhaps he was too proud a man. Perhaps he resented fiercely the thought that he might owe anything to another. Perhaps, on the other hand, given his hatred, and the shame in which he seemed to live, he might not have found the cruelty of a brigand's knife that unwelcome.

I looked down at the woman in the long, thin white gown. "Have you been branded?" I asked.

"No!" she said, tensely. "I am free!" This seemed to me probably true, as she had been put in the gown, doubtless, at least for the time, to protect her modesty.

"You must understand," I said, "that we must make a determination on that matter."

"Of course," she said. The results of this determination could make an important difference in how she was treated and what might be, as a matter of course, expected of her. A free woman is one thing, and a female slave is quite another.

I put her on her side and thrust up her gown, and turned her about, from one side to the other. In a moment or two I had checked the normal brand sites for a Gorean female. The most typical brand site is high on the left thigh, high enough, under the hip, to be covered even by the brevity of a typical slave tunic. In this way one often does not know what brand the girl wears. In this way a bit of mystery, I suppose, might be thought to be added to her.

The mystery in most cases, however, if one is truly interested, is usually no more than temporary. It is only necessary to lift her skirt. Sometimes bets are made on this matter. In such bets, of course, the odds are with he who wagers on the graceful, cursive Kef. This is the most common Kajira brand. "Kef" is the first letter in "Kajira," the most common expression in Gorean for a female slave. It is sometimes, too, spoken of as the "Staff and fronds." This is doubtless because of a fancied resemblance to such objects. Also, of course, this involves an allusion to beauty under discipline, indeed, to helpless beauty under absolutely uncompromising discipline. I also checked certain less common brand sites, such as the lower left abdomen, the interior of the left forearm and the high instep area of the left foot. If there is such a mark on a girl, it would not be well to miss it. Imagine the embarrassment of relating to a woman as though she were free and then discovering only later that she had been a legally imbonded slave all the time! Too, how dreadfully perilous would such a deception be for the female! I would surely not wish to be the female who might be found out in such a deception.

"Her body seems clear of brands," I said. "Apparently she is free."

"Yes," she said. "Yes!"

I pulled her gown down from where I had thrust it up, above her breasts, for my convenience in examining her body for brands, and then I worked it down, inching it, carefully, over her body and hips. It was thin and fit her closely. I did not wish to tear it. I then pulled its hem down to where it was supposed to be, at about her ankles. I then made my final adjustments of the gown, that her modesty might be as well protected, or about as well protected, as such a flimsy garment permitted. To be sure, I did, here and there, pull it a bit more snugly about her body than was perhaps necessary. This was excusable, of course. She was beautiful and bound.

I had made a stop at my own camp, incidentally, before coming to this place in the woods.

"As she seems to be free," I said, "I will claim her, she in the modality of the free captive."

"No!" she cried.

"Very well," said Boots.

"No, no!" she wept, struggling in the ropes.

I knew this female.

I pulled her to a seated position. I looked into her eyes. "You are my captive," I said.

"Please, no!" she said.

"It is up to you, at least for the time," I said, "to decide what sort of captive you will be."

She looked at me, frightened.

I removed some metal from my pouch, that which I had brought from my camp, but moments ago, to this clearing in the woods. I dangled it, in its small, sturdy rings and four heavy, close-set links, before her eyes. "Do you desire it?" I asked.

"Yes," she whispered. "Close-chains."

I put the shackles on her ankles. Her ankles were now shackled only some four inches apart. She had decided that she wished to be kept in honor and modesty. To be sure, aside from the obvious consideration of the inflexible efficiency of the shackling itself, given the large number of ways in which a woman may be used for a man's pleasure, the matter was primarily symbolic. The ankle rings snug on her I removed the bonds of the brigands from her ankles. Her ankles parted, to the brief extent permitted by the chain linkage of my shackles. Her wrists were still tied behind her. "How did you come to be captured by the brigands?" I asked.

"My superiors were dissatisfied with me," she said. "My lackeys were removed from me. I was put in a brief tunic, almost as though I might be a slave. I was forbidden even to wear a veil. I was given a small purse of coins, one sufficient for my projected expenses, and instructed to report back to my headquarters, alone and on foot."

"Alone, and on foot?" I asked.

"Yes," she said, bitterly.

"It is my conjecture," I said, "that they did not expect you to complete your journey successfully."

"It seems they were right," she said, bitterly.

I smiled. I did not think that her superiors were likely to be any more unaware of the dangers of Gorean highways than anyone else. A lovely woman, scantily clad, not even veiled, alone, on foot, did not seem a likely candidate to travel the Gorean wilderness with impunity. Their instructions, it seemed, had been, for most practical purposes, tantamount to an enslavement sentence. I did not think they expected to see her again, unless it might be in the rag of a slave and a collar.

"I was caught by the brigands last night," she said.

"You do not appear to be clad as might be a slave," I said.

"The garments in which my superiors had placed me," she said, "were removed by the brigands. They regarded them as inappropriate for a free woman. They put me, instead, in the gown in which you now see me."

"That was thoughtful of them," I said.

"But it is so thin and flimsy!" she protested.

"Of course," I said.

"I suppose it does mark me as a free woman," she said, "and in that sense might perhaps raise my price somewhat in case they were readying me for sale to a slave merchant."

"Too," I said, "with all due respect it is, in spite of its length and nature, rather flattering and revealing. Doubtless, too, it would give the merchant pleasure to remove it from you in your assessment, thereby revealing your beauty, that then of a potential slave."

"Yes," she said, bitterly.

"Have no fear," I said. "I will find you something else to wear."

"Thank you," she said.

"Is there another camp about, or somewhere," I asked, "used by the brigands?"

"No," she said. "There was one, but they broke it this morning. This afternoon they surreptitiously met a fellow in the woods. He had a wagon. They sold most of their loot to him."

"Apparently they did not sell all of it to him," I said, regarding her, glancing, too, at the other bound woman, she naked in the dirt.

"No," she said. "He was not a slaver. Too, I do not think he wanted any obvious connection to be noted between himself and the brigands, such as might be furnished by handling their slaves."

"Where were you enroute?" I asked.

"I do not know," she said. "I was told only that we were being taken somewhere where we could be sold to a proper slaver."

"Besnit, Esalinus or Harfax," suggested Boots.

I shrugged. "Perhaps," I said. These towns were all within a hundred pasangs of our present location. Such women could be disposed of almost anywhere, of course. Slave markets, like slaves, are common on Gor. Given the large number of slaves on Gor it is only natural that there should be an abundance of outlets for their handling and processing.

"You apparently made camp here," I said, "several Ahn ago."

"We stopped early, I think," she said. "I think they had discovered another camp, one on which they intended to perpetrate a raid."

"That is correct," I said.

"We were left here, helplessly trussed, females, to await their return," she said.

"They will not be coming back," I said.

"I see," she said, shuddering.

"Where are the other valuables, the moneys, in the camp," I asked, "their accruals from the fellow with the wagon, or otherwise?"

"It is all there," she said, indicating it with her head, "in those packs. The gold is in a small coffer, one bound with bands of iron, one studded with silver, that closed with a heavy golden-plated lock, in the first pack."

"It is all yours," I told Boots.

"All of it?" asked Boots, incredulously.

"All of it," I said.

"Thank you!" said Boots, fervently. "It will be put to good use."

"Perhaps you could use it in support of the arts," I suggested.

"My intention exactly," admitted Boots.

"It might be used, for example," I suggested, "in support of some worthy but struggling theatrical company."

"That is a sound and brilliant suggestion." Boots congratulated me.

"Perhaps you have some company in mind," I said.

"I have just the company in mind," he said.

"Us," said Lecchio.

"A bit abruptly and crassly put," said Boots, reprovingly, to Lecchio, "but that would indeed seem to capture the gist of the matter."

"Are you grateful?" I asked.

"Yes," said Boots.

"Eternally, undyingly?" I asked.

"Surely," said Boots.

"There is then something you can do for me," I said.

"Name it, Brother," said Boots.

"I am still interested in joining your company," I said.

"Out of the question," said Boots. "Impossible."

"Come now," I said.

"Come now," said Chino.

"Come now," said Lecchio.

"Come now," said Petrucchio.

"Come, come now!" insisted Andronicus.

"My mind is made up," said Boots.

"Perhaps you could unmake it, and start in all over again," I suggested, reaching to the multiple sheath of saddle knives slung at my hip.

Boots eyed me, closely.

"My dear Boots, do not be an ungrateful dolt," scolded the ponderous Andronicus.

"I have spoken," announced Boots, grandly.

I drew one of the blades, and turned it in my hand. "Perhaps you could speak again," I suggested.

"Never," said Boots.

"Oh?" I asked. I turned the knife again, now holding it by the handle. The point idly seemed to focus on Boot's throat.

"What could you do?" asked Boots uneasily, watching the knife point.

I flipped the blade in my hand, holding it now again by the blade. I looked at Boots, evenly. "I do a knife throwing act," I said. "Remember?"

"And a good one, too," admitted Boots.

"Let him join the company," pressed Chino.

"Yes," urged Lecchio.

"By all means," urged Petrucchio.

"It is little enough for all he has done," said Andronicus.

"We cannot take in every stray sleen who comes whining about the wagons," said Boots. "Are we a refuge for homeless waifs, a food wagon for improvident wayfarers, a training ground for amateurs, a nomadic inn for stage-struck aspirants, an itinerant shelter for every awed, hopeful bumpkin desirous of donning the thespic mantle, and on our stage, that of the theater's titans, of sharing our riches, tangible and intangible, our glory and largesse, that of Gor's finest theatrical aggregation? What of our professional standards? What of our reputation?"

"Urt droppings," said Chino.

"Urt droppings?" inquired Boots.

"Yes," said Chino.

"Perhaps you are ready to reconsider your position on this matter," I said. I flipped the knife meaningfully about. The point now, again, was looking at Boots.

"You are skillful," said Boots. "There is no doubt about it. You are not an experienced, professional actor, of course."

"That is true," I granted him. The point was now an inch or so from his neck.

"There are, of course, many other things you might do, simple work, heavy work, say, unsuitable for more skilled personnel."

"True," I said.

"Perhaps you could help the monster," he mused.

"Yes," I said.

"The stage must be set up," he said, "the tents put up, and so on."

"Yes," I encouraged him.

"Do not be ungrateful, Boots," said Andronicus. "We owe him our very lives."

"And you still could," I pointed out.

Boots swallowed, hard. "I am not a stern, inflexible fellow," he said. "It is well known that I am resilient and supple, as well as complex, subtle and talented. That Boots is a broad-minded fellow, I have often heard it said. He is easy-going and tolerant, as it is said, and, indeed, perhaps sometimes too much so for his own good, as it is also said. Yes, that Boots is a good fellow, one always ready to listen to arguments, to consider carefully the claims of reason, as they say.''

"I take it you are reconsidering your position," I said.

"I am taking its reconsideration under consideration," said Boots.

"Let him join the company," said Andronicus.

"I am weakening," said Boots. "The arguments of Andronicus are swaying me."

"If you do not permit him to join us," said Andronicus, "I shall resign from the company."

Boots regarded him, aghast.

"Yes," said Andronicus, firmly.

"We would be devastated!" objected Boots.

Andronicus regarded him, his arms folded adamantly.

"I am swayed," said Boots.

Swiftly I reversed the blade I held and tucked it under my arm that I not wound Publius Andronicus who, victorious, was heartily reaching for my hand. Chino, Lecchio and Petrucchio, too, moved about me, slapping me on the back and congratulating me. Lastly Boots himself seized my hand, warmly. "Welcome to the company of Boots Tarsk-Bit," he said. "Remember, however, this is no ordinary troupe. In joining us you have undertaken a grave responsibility and a most serious charge. See that you struggle to live up to our high standards."

"I will try," I assured him.

"We do have a problem, however," said Boots to the others in the troupe.

"What is that?" asked lanky Petrucchio.

"Where will he stay?" asked Boots. "I have no intention of sharing my wagon with someone who can handle a knife like that."

"He can use my wagon," said Petrucchio. "I myself, if he be amenable, will lodge with my friend, Andronicus, with whom I have lengthy discussions on the craft of the actor."

"On the art of the actor," said Andronicus.

"Craft," said Petrucchio.

"Art," said Andronicus.

"Is it all right?" asked Petrucchio.

"Of course, and welcome," said Andronicus. "It will give me an opportunity to train you in the one hundred and seventy-three movements of the head."

"I thought it was one hundred and seventy-one," said Petrucchio.

"In a text by Alamanius, I have discovered two new movements," said Andronicus, "each with its several variations."

"Fascinating," said Petrucchio.

"It is settled then," said Boots.

"Yes," said Petrucchio.

"Yes," said Andronicus.

"Thank you," I said to Petrucchio and Andronicus.

"It is nothing," they assured me.

"Do you wish to share my wagon?" I asked my captive.

"No!" she said.

"You may lock her in the girl wagon, chained in her place, with Rowena and Bina," said Boots, generously.

"No," I said. "Do not bother. I will simply chain her by the neck under my own wagon."

"Very well," said Boots.

She regarded me angrily, and squirmed in her bonds.

"Gather up those boxes and packs, and that which might seem to be of any value here," said Boots to his fellows. "In particular do not neglect a small coffer, bound with iron, studded with silver, closed with a golden-plated lock, reputed to be in the first pack. These things we shall transport back to our own camp. Victory has been ours. The loot, thus, in its various items, of which I shall keep a careful list, in its various natures, quantities and qualities, is also ours."

"No!" protested the other woman, she who lay in the dirt, absolutely naked, helplessly bound, hand and foot, next to my own captive.

"Did you speak, my dear?" asked Boots Tarsk-Bit.

"Yes!" she said. "Free me!"

"Why should I do that?" asked Boots.

"I am a free woman!" she cried.

"Chino, bring a torch closer," said Boots.

Chino came from the area of boxes and packs, with one of the torches.

"As you are perfect gentlemen, you will free me," she said. "I can count on that as a free woman!"

I smiled. Goreans tend to be less gentlemen, than owners and masters of females. In the order of nature they tend to acquire and dominate them, making them uncompromisingly their own.

"Who are you?" asked Boots.

"I am the Lady Telitsia of Asperiche," she said.

"Ho, ho, ho!" cried Boots, gleefully, triumphantly, rubbing his hands together.

"I do not understand," said the woman.

"Hold the torch closer," said Boots to Chino.

"Oh!" cried the woman, as I turned her roughly to her right side in the dirt, this exposing her left thigh.

"Aha!" cried Boots, triumphantly.

"I have never been collared!" she cried. "I have never worn a collar!"

"That can be remedied," Boots informed her.

"I am not a slave!" she cried.

Her thigh, however, belied her protestation. It bore, clearly, indisputably, unmistakably, a brand, the common Kajira brand. It was as clear on her body as on that of any other slave. The brigands, it seemed, had, or had had her, reduced to slavery.

"It is only a mark!" she cried.

"I think it is a little bit more than that," said Boots. "It is a slave brand."

"It means nothing!" she cried.

"It means a great deal, as I am sure, sooner or later, you will agree," said Boots.

"No!" she cried.

"You are a slave," said Boots.

"Free me!" she begged. "I beg you to free me!"

"You will be the first item on my loot list, Lady Telitsia, as I may choose to call you for a time," said Boots.

"Surely you jest! Surely you will free me!" she said.

"Do I seem a fool to you?" asked Boots.

"No!" she said, hastily.

"Only fools free female slaves," said Boots. "Surely you are familiar with the saying."

"I am of high caste, and am rich!" she said.

"Once perhaps," said Boots, "but neither is true any longer. "With your branding you became only an animal, a property. With the iron's first touch you ceased to be a legal person. You are now casteless. You now own nothing. Rather it is now you yourself, slave, who are subject to being owned, as much as any other object or property."

"No, no!" she cried, squirming in the thongs that bound her. She was attractive, doing so. She could not free herself, of course. She was absolutely helpless. She had been bound by Gorean men.

"I think we can find some chains for you in the girl wagon," said Boots. "Perhaps, on occasion, I will have you come to my own wagon."

"No, no, no!" she wept, struggling.

Boots looked down upon her, beaming.

"Surely you have no intention of keeping me!" she cried.

"Your body, as I now see," said Boots, "now that you are naked, now that the pesky, interfering, obscuring robes of the scribe have been totally removed from it, not inconceivably might be of interest to a male."

She regarded him with horror. Too, he had surely understated the case. I had little doubt but what she would bring a fine price in a slave market. Indeed, those slave curves of hers, even routinely put up for sale on a block, would be almost certain to elicit active and serious bidding.

"Too," said Boots, "I think you are highly intelligent, and, if I am not mistaken, you have also, at the fair, earlier, given us some subtle indications of possessing a great deal of talent."

"I do not understand," she stammered.

"Gather around, everybody," called Boots.

Petrucchio, Andronicus, and Lecchio joined Boots, myself and Chino near the bound woman.

"On your knees, my dear," said Boots to the bound woman. She, moaning, struggled to her knees.

"Gentlemen," said Boots, "may I present Lady Telitsia, as, for the time, as it pleases me, I shall refer to her."

"Greetings," said Lecchio.

"Greetings," she whispered.

"Perhaps you remember her from the fair," said Boots.

"Yes," said Chino. "We remember her—well."

The slave shuddered.

"Behold her," said Boots, cheerfully. He took her by the hair and pulled her head back. Yes, I thought, she would bring a high price.

"Pretty," said Chino.

"Pretty," agreed Lecchio.

"That we have acquired her," said Boots, "we may account a stroke of great good fortune."

"How is that?" asked Lecchio.

"She comes to us, does she not," asked Boots, "at a peculiarly opportune time, at an instant when we are struggling in desperate straits, at a time when we find ourselves in agonizing and desperate need."

"She does?" asked Lecchio, a golden necklace draped about his neck, taken from the loot of the brigands.

"Yes!" said Boots.

"Ah, yes!" mused Chino.

"I have consented to Lady Telitsia's joining our company," announced Boots.

"No!" she cried, her head back, wincing, her hair in Boots's grasp.

"Yes!" reaffirmed Boots. "Too, she comes to us just in time to solve one of our most pressing problems."

"Yes, indeed," agreed Andronicus.

"I do not understand," said Lecchio.

"Is the matter not clear?" asked Boots.

"No," said Lecchio.

"Behold, Gentlemen," said Boots, pulling her head back a bit more and indicating her, displaying her, expansively with the palm of his left hand, "we have found our Brigella!"

"No!" cried the girl.

The fellows applauded Boots, admiringly, striking their left shoulders in Gorean applause.

"No!" she cried. "Never!"

"She is even prettier than the last," said Lecchio.

"I think she will do very nicely," said Chino.

"An excellent choice," said Andronicus.

"I refuse!" she cried. "The very thought of it! The outrage! The indignity! How dare you even think of such a thing! I am of high caste! I am of the scribes! Wait until I bring this matter to the attention of magistrates!"

"As I may remind you, my dear," said Boots, patiently, "you are no longer of high caste nor of the scribes. Similarly, as I am sure you will recognize, at least upon reflection, you now have no standing before the law. You are now of no more interest to magistrates, in their official capacities, as opposed to their private capacities, than would be an urt or a sleen."

She regarded him, frightened.

"Your days of making a nuisance of yourself are now over," said Boots. "Indeed, I speculate that those very same magistrates whom you have so often inconvenienced would be quite pleased to learn that you are now, at last, no longer capable of pestering them with your inane, time-consuming nonsense. I doubt that they would wish to see you again, unless perhaps it would be to return you naked and bound to your master, with the blows of a whip on your body, or perhaps, say, to have you serve them in a tavern, helpless in the modality that would then be yours, that of the total female slave."

"Please!" she begged.

"Hitherto you have sought to use men for your purposes," said Boots. "That is now changed. It is now you who will be used for their purposes, fully. In the past you have made many demands on men. Henceforth it will be your hope rather that they will find you pleasing, in all respects.''

"I am a free woman!" she cried.

"You will soon learn differently," said Boots.

"I am free!" she wept.

"That is not true," said Boots, "as you will soon come to understand."

"I am not a slave," she wept. "I cannot be a slave!"

"Silence, Slave," said Boots.

"Please!" she wept.

"It has been a busy day," said Boots. "Chino, would you please untie the slave's ankles?"

"Surely," he said.

Boots then drew her to her feet and held her head, bent down, by the hair, at his waist, in leading position. Her hands were still tied behind her. "Lecchio, Chino, Andronicus, Petrucchio, if you would," said Boots, "bring along these other things, whatever seems of value."

"Very well," they assented.

"It is growing late, and I am weary," said Boots to Lady Telitsia. "It will be time enough in the morning to whip you."

"Whip me?" she gasped.

"I will then be fresher and can lay the lash to you more roundly," he said.

"The lash?" she queried.

"Yes," he said.

"You're joking!" she said.

"You may ponder that tonight, while chained in the girl wagon," he said.

"But why?" she asked.

"You have not been pleasing," he said, "not that that matters that much. As you know, no excuse, explanation, defense or reason is required to justify the whipping of a female slave. She may be beaten for any reason, or for no reason, whenever the master wishes. She may be whipped even, if he wishes, on the outcome of the spinning of a wheel or the cast of a die."

I crouched down beside my own prisoner, the free female, she whom I had shackled, she whose beauty seemed to strain protestingly against the long, thin gown put upon her by the brigands, as though calling for a man to tear it from her.

"You look upon me boldly," she said.

"You are a captive," I reminded her.

"But I am to be kept in honor!" she said.

"Of course," I said, "or at least for a time."

"I wear your gyves," she reminded me.

I regarded her fair ankles, snug in their metal fastenings, linked by the short chain. They could not now be parted, unless I chose to do so.

"Perhaps it is your intention to remove them?" she asked, apprehensively.

"Perhaps I shall occasionally remove them," I said, "perhaps for the purposes of exercise."

"Exercise?" she asked.

"Yes," I said. "For example, I might wish to take you—"

"Take me?" she asked.

"Say, for a run on a leash," I said.

"I see," she said.

"We must soon return to our camp," said Boots, his fist in the bent-over Lady Telitsia's hair.

"Surely you will remove my fetters at least to permit me to walk to your camp," suggested my captive.

I saw that she wanted the fetters off. I wondered if this was because she desired to escape, or if she wished to be caressed.

"Otherwise," she said, "I fear the journey will be both lengthy and painful. I do not even know if I can stand in them."

"You can stand in them," I said. "It is only that it would be difficult to move in them without falling."

"I see," she said.

"You could always crawl," I said, "dragging yourself forward, say, on your hands or elbows."

"Perhaps if your camp is close, I might, dragging myself through the underbrush, arrive there by morning."

"Perhaps," I said.

"If I did not get lost, or fall to sleen," she said.

"Perhaps," I speculated.

"Doubtless you will now, for your convenience, remove them," she said.

"No," I said.

"I do not understand," she said.

"They were not put on you to be removed so soon," I said.

"How then shall I get to your camp?" she asked, apprehensively.

"I have another mode of transportation in mind for you," I said, "a mode which I trust you will find instructive."

"No!" she begged.

"Yes," I said.

"Head forward," she pleaded.

"No," I said, "you shall be carried to the camp on my shoulder, your hands tied, your ankles helpless in their fetters."

"My head forward," she begged.

"No," I said, "to the rear."

"As a slave!" she cried, angrily.

"Yes," I said.

"Even she there, she who is naked and bound, she who is a true slave, is permitted to walk!"

"I do not think you will long envy her," I said.

Lady Telitsia, now a slave, whimpered, frightened.

"You treat me as a slave," said my captive. "Perhaps you will soon make me a slave!"

"Perhaps," I said.

"Your eyes rove me brazenly, I note," she said, angrily, "as though I might be a slave."

"Yes," I admitted. To be sure, she was quite beautiful. I had no doubt but what she might, if collared and trained, and brought into touch with her feelings, prove to be not only an adequate slave, but perhaps even a quite marvelous one.

"You said," she said, "that you would get me something else to wear."

"Have no fear," I said. "I shall."

"Let us be on our way," said Boots.

I scooped up the woman and threw her over my shoulder, her head to the rear. She was not heavy. I looked out, into the shadows of the woods. I did not think she would be likely to forget this nocturnal journey, being carried helplessly through the darkness into captivity.

"Back at the fair," said Boots to me, "as I recall, you expressed your eagerness to join our company."

"Yes," I said.

"As I recall, as well," said he, "you were willing to work without pay."

"True," I grinned.

"That seems a suitable arrangement from my point of view," said Boots.

"Boots," warned Andronicus, sternly.

"But, of course, even though it might be difficult, we shall struggle to manage some small renumeration—somehow," Boots assured me.

"Thank you," I said.

"It is nothing," said Boots, generously.

"And if you are not careful, it will be," said Chino, cheerfully.

Boots then set off confidently through the woods.

"Your camp," I said to him, "is more to the right. That's it."

Boots led the way, Lady Telitsia stumbling along, bent over, held, beside him, in approximately the right direction. He was followed by his fellows, carrying various articles taken from the brigands' camp. I then brought up the rear, on my shoulder the Lady Yanina.

10

A PLEASANT MORNING IN CAMP; THE LADY YANINA WILL OBEY

"Are you comfortable, Lady Telitsia?" asked Boots.

"Yes," she said. She knelt, her wrists tied together over her head, fastened by a short strap to a transversely mounted, sturdy wooden bar. It was about five feet from the ground. It was the morning after he had acquired her.

"Surely you are bluffing, and you have no intention of going through with this," she said. She was naked, except for a collar. The legend on the collar said, "If you find me, return me to Boots Tarsk-Bit. Reward." It was the same collar as was worn by Boots's other girls. He had put it on her immediately after returning to the camp last night. He had then chained her in the girl wagon, on one of the open, steel-floored, steel-sided kennels, and retired. This morning, early, he had dragged her forth and bound her in her present position. He had then had a large breakfast. Doubtless she was quite hungry. Still she had not yet been fed. That was just as well, considering what was to be done to her.

Boots shook out the blades of a five-stranded Gorean slave whip.

"As I recall," said Boots, "you said, at the fair, that you were not afraid of men."

She was silent.

"How proudly you said that," marveled Boots, swinging the freed lash blades loosely. "To be sure, at that time, you probably had never had any reason to be afraid of men. Now that you are a slave, however, you will find that you do have reason, and ample reason, and not only to fear men, but, indeed, any free person."

"I am hungry," she said. "Am I to be fed?"

"Perhaps when you learn to beg for it," he said.

"Never," she said.

"Did you enjoy your night in the girl wagon?" he asked.

"No," she said. "The steel was cold. I did not even have a rag to put between myself and the steel."

"To be sure, the nights are chilly," said Boots.

"I would like to have a blanket in the future," she said.

"There might be a shred of a blanket somewhere about," said Boots. "Perhaps you could beg for it."

"Never," she said.

"I gave you some time last night, while you were chained in the girl wagon," said Boots, "to consider your up-coming beating this morning. Did you give it much thought?"

"No," she said.

"Why not?" asked Boots.

"You would not dare to beat me," she said.

"Why not?" asked Boots, eager to be informed.

"Because of the kind of person I am," she said. "I am above being beaten. That is for low females."

"Such as slaves?" asked Boots.

"Yes," she said.

"I see," said Boots.

"As it turns out," she said, "I am right."

"How is that?" asked Boots.

"If you were going to beat me," she said, "you would have already done so by now."

"I have been giving my breakfast some time to digest," said Boots. "I would not wish to upset my stomach."

"Of course not," she said, ironically.

"But now," said Boots, "I think I will be all right."

"What?" she asked, half turning about.

"You have been a nuisance. Lady Telitsia," he said. "I think I will very much enjoy whipping you."

"You're serious!" she suddenly said, alarmed.

"Yes," he admitted.

"Wait!" she said, twisting in the ropes. "I am prepared to

admit that in some legal sense I am a slave, and that I am theoretically subject to such things!"

"Very much more so than theoretically, my dear," said Boots.

"But I am too refined, too sensitive to be whipped!"

"Nonsense," said Boots.

"It is inappropriate to whip me," she said. "I am a lady of quality."

"You are only another slave," said Boots.

"Wait!" she cried.

"What now?" asked Boots, impatiently.

"I am bound," she wept, twisting in the ropes. "I am naked. I am tied in such a way that I cannot protect myself. I am exposed helplessly, utterly, to your mercy."

"Of course," said Boots.

"But it will hurt," she said.

"Have you ever felt the whip?" asked Boots.

"No!" she said.

"Then how do you know it will hurt?" he asked.

"I have seen girls beaten," she said.

"Perhaps it does not hurt much," said Boots. He himself, of course, earlier, at her instigation, when she was a free woman, had been flogged at the fair. This turnabout then must have been extra delicious for him, in addition to the simple, straightforward pleasure of giving her a good beating. To be sure, Boots had been beaten with a heavy whip, of the sort used on men, whereas she would find herself under only the familiar, common five-stranded Gorean slave lash. Still it is not without reason that that implement is much favored on Gor for the disciplining of females. Without permanently marking the girl it punishes with excruciating, terrible efficiency. The mere sight of such a whip generally inspires terror in any female who has ever felt it.

"Do not whip me!" she cried. "It is not necessary! I admit that I am a slave! I am a slave! I will even obey!"

"Prepare to be beaten," said Boots.

"Mercy!" she cried.

"To quote someone I once heard at the fair," said Boots, " 'I do not choose to show you mercy.' "

The bound female groaned, hearing her own words.

"Prepare," said Boots.

"No! No!" she cried, springing to her feet, her bare feet raising dust, her bound wrists, of course, still tethered to the bar.

"Back on your knees, Lady Telitsia," said Boots, sternly, "or you will add blows to your beating."

Lady Telitsia, in misery, moaning, trembling, sank back to her knees, her wrists again now over her head.

"Would you like me to cross and bind your ankles?" Boots asked, kindly.

"No," she moaned.

I think she could see the shadow of Boots before her. Her back was illuminated by the morning sun.

"I do not want to be whipped!" she cried.

"It will be good for you to be whipped," said Boots. "It will be good for you to know what it is like. It will help you to understand that you are now truly a slave. Too, it will help to make you a more diligent slave, one more anxious to please."

"Mercy!" she wept.

" 'Slaves,' " said Boots, " 'are to be shown no mercy'. I heard someone say that, also, recently, at the Fair of En'Kara. Perhaps you recall it?"

She sobbed, helpless in the ropes, awaiting her beating.

"Slaves are to be shown no mercy," she had said a few days ago at the fair. I recalled it. How uncompromisingly, how coldly, she had said it. Now she herself was a slave.

"Do you recall saying that?" asked Boots.

"Yes," she sobbed.

"Is it true?" asked Boots.

"Yes," she wept.

He then struck her, once, with the lash. She cried out, startled, in pain, in disbelief.

"Yes, what?" he asked.

"Yes—Master!" she cried.

He then struck her again. "No, no!" she cried out. "Please do not strike me again, Master!"

"It will be done with you as your Master pleases," he said.

"Yes, Master!" she sobbed.

He then, with a few blows, concluded her beating. It was neither a long nor a severe beating. Still he had placed the blows diversely and had varied their timing. It was in its way a kindly beating, as Boots was a kindly fellow, but it was also, I think, an efficient beating.

When Boots had finished he untied the strap that had fastened her bound wrists to the wooden bar. She fell to her belly in the dust and reached out, her wrists still bound, to touch his ankles. She put down her head and, lying in the dust before him, pressed her lips, those of a slave, again and again, piteously, to his feet. Boots then turned away and went about his business. She then lay on her belly in the dust, collapsed, near the wooden bar to which she had been tied for her beating. I went to her and turned her over with my foot. She looked up at me. She was in misery and in pain.

"You are branded," I said.

"Yes, Master," she said.

"You wear a collar," I said.

"Yes, Master" she said.

"What are you?" I asked.

"I am a female slave," she said, "a slave girl."

"Anything else?" I asked.

"No, Master," she said. "Only that."

"It is true," I said.

"Yes, Master," she said.

I saw in her eyes that she now knew these things to be true, that she now truly knew that she was a slave girl, that and only that.

"What am I to do, Master?" she asked.

"Go to your Master," I said, "and beg him to forgive you for having been displeasing."

"Yes, Master," she said. She rose painfully to her feet and went slowly, painfully, to where Boots was sitting cross-legged, near the small fire between the wagons. He was now in the midst of enjoying a second breakfast. Chino and Andronicus were with him. She knelt down near him, her bound wrists on her thighs. She dared not speak. After a time, Boots, sucking his fingers, removing the grease from fried tarsk strips from them, turned about. She quickly, under the eyes of her master, put her head down to the dirt. "Did you wish something, girl?" asked Boots.

"Yes, Master," she said.

"You may speak," said Boots.

"I beg your forgiveness, Master," she said, her head still down, "for having been displeasing."

"Mend your ways in the future," cautioned Boots, sternly. "Next time it may not go as easily with you."

"Yes, Master," she said, trembling.

Boots then helped himself to some more rolls and slices of fried tarsk.

Lady Telitsia, as it seemed she would be called now, at least for the time, then lifted her head and straightened her body. She remained kneeling, of course, in the immediate vicinity of her master.

"Good rolls," said Boots to Chino.

"Yes," agreed Chino, helping himself to another, as well.

"Excellent vulo eggs, excellent tarsk," said Boots, his mouth full.

"Quite," agreed Andronicus, wiping his fingers fastidiously on his tunic.

Lady Telitsia eyed the food, hungrily, pitiously. She squirmed. I heard her small, lovely, rounded belly growling.

"Did you say something, my dear?" asked Boots.

"No, Master," she said, quickly.

Boots returned to his repast. I wondered how long it had been since Lady Telitsia had been fed.

More noises emanated from her pretty belly. She put down her head in embarrassment.

"Lady Telitsia," said Boots. "Clean my hands."

She came forward and began to lick his cupped hands and then to suck his fingers, removing the grease from them. Meanwhile he continued to talk with Chino and Andronicus.

"Slowly and more sensuously," said Boots.

"Yes, Master," she groaned. She looked up at him. Their eyes met. Their exchange of glances was quite meaningful. Then she complied, as best she could, given that she had only recently been a free woman. She, apparently half starved, had been too eagerly licking and sucking at the grease on his hands and fingers.

"Better," he said. "Better." Then he dried his hands, partly on her body, partly on her hair, and returned his attention to his companions. As he had touched her body I had noted that she had gasped and, ever so slightly, had pressed against his hand. I do not think, however, this action had been lost on Boots, either. The slave, "Lady Telitsia," had in her, I suspected, superb slave potential. Up to now, of course, as a free woman, given her conditioning and what was expected of her in her culture, she had undoubtedly, possibly even agonizingly, resisted her sexuality, fighting to control and suppress her slave drives. Now, of course, now that she had been freed of the psychological chains, the confining restrictions, the imprisoning inhibitions of the free woman, I had little doubt that she, and perhaps even soon, would prove to be a helplessly arousable, helplessly yielding slave, a joy both to herself and her masters.

"That is enough," said Boots.

"Master," she said.

"Yes?" said Boots.

"May I have permission to speak, Master?" she asked.

"You need only ask—sometimes," said Boots.

"Thank you, Master," she said, gratefully. "Master—"

"Were you given permission to speak?" asked Boots.

"No, master," she whispered. "Forgive me, Master."

Boots regarded her, sternly.

"But you said I need only ask," she whispered, frightened.

"I said, 'You need only ask—sometimes,' " said Boots. "This is not one of those times. You may not now speak."

"Yes, Master," she said. "Forgive me, Master." She then knelt back on her heels, not permitted to speak, a chastened slave.

"Ah," said Boots, seeing me. "Are you hungry? Come join us."

"Thank you," I said, and sat down with them, cross-legged. It was still rather early. Soon I was helping myself to a heaping serving of vulo eggs, tarsk strips and rolls.

"Perhaps you should feed your captive soon," said Boots. He referred to the free woman, the Lady Yanina, shackled and chained by the neck under my wagon.

"Yes," I said. "I will take her a plate of food when I am finished here." One must show concern for her, of course. She was a free woman.

"You are going with us at least as far as Brundisium?" said Boots.

"That is my plan," I said.

"What takes you to Brundisium?" asked Boots.

"Mainly Petrucchio's wagon, I would suppose," I said, "and his tharlarion. He was kind enough to loan them to me. I may walk part of the way, of course."

"Seriously," said Boots.

"I am quite serious," I said. "Walking is an excellent exercise."

"It is early in the morning for wit as scintillating as yours," observed Boots.

"Sorry," I said.

"Have you ever considered a career upon the stage?" he inquired.

"No," I said.

"It is probably just as well," he speculated.

"Perhaps," I admitted, somewhat grudgingly, not altogether convinced.

"What are you going to do in Brundisium?" asked Boots.

"That will depend, I expect," I said, "on what I find in Brundisium."

"Come now," said Boots.

"Business," I informed him.

"I see," said Boots. "I am glad that is cleared up."

I bit on some crisp tarsk strips.

"You are certainly a communicative fellow this morning," said Boots.

"The tarsk is good," I said.

"I am glad you like it," said Boots. "Brundisium, as I have warned you earlier, may be dangerous. They seem quite suspicious of strangers the last year or so."

"You do not know why, though?" I asked.

"No," he said.

"You are a good fellow, Boots," I said. "I appreciate your concern."

"I think I know how you intend to use your captive, at least as far as your participation in our show is concerned," said Boots, "but beware. If she is of Brundisium, or is known in Brundisium, it could be very dangerous for you there."

"In the vicinity of Brundisium, or within her walls," I said, "I could keep her hooded. If it seemed desirable, too, of course, I could always have her reduced to slavery before nearing, or entering, the city. She would then be of no legal interest to anyone, for she would then be only a slave, only chattel."

"Of course," said Boots.

"It was a good breakfast," I said. "I had better take her some food now."

"Yes," said Boots. "You must not keep her hungry. You must show her consideration. She is a free woman."

"Of course," I said.

I slowly, carefully, piled a plate high with rolls, eggs and fried vulo strips. It had probably been a long time since the Lady Yanina had eaten. She had been in the care of the brigands. She was probably quite hungry. I could always watch her feedings later, giving attention to their possible effect on her figure. That would be if I decided, later, to turn her into a love captive, or, if it pleased me, a thousand times lower, nay, a thousand thousand times lower, nay, even uncountably times lower, nay, not even on the same scale, a slave. Boots's slave, Lady Telitsia, eyed the plate hungrily, desperately. I thought I heard her whimper, softly. Certainly there were some piteous noises at any rate which suddenly, unexpectedly, perhaps to her embarrassment, emanated from her pretty belly.

"Did you say something?" asked Boots.

"No, Master," she said, hastily. She had been warned to silence.

I rose to my feet.

"May I have the plate a moment?" asked Boots.

"Surely," I said. I handed it to him.

He held it before Lady Telitsia. "It smells good, doesn't it?" he asked.

"Yes, Master," she said. She leaned forward, her eyes closed. She breathed in, deeply, relishing the odor of the fresh-cooked breakfast. She opened her eyes, looking at her master, piteously.

Boots handed the plate to me, and I carried it between the wagons until I came to my wagon.

There, beneath my wagon, sitting down, her knees drawn up, was the Lady Yanina, once my captor. On her neck was an iron collar. By means of this collar and its chain, the chain fastened about the wagon axle, she was secured in place.

I put down the plate of food. "Ankles," I said.

She turned a little and, angrily, lowering her knees slightly, tugging the hem of her garment closely about her lower calves, extended her ankles toward me. I checked the gyves. All was in order. There was no sign of the metal having been tampered with, for example, scratched about the lock, or marked on the bands, as though having been struck futilely with a stone. Similarly her ankles were not cut or abraided as though she might have tried to slip the iron from her fair limbs. Such an action, of course, would have been ludicrously irrational. The Lady Yanina was not a foolish, panic-stricken Earth girl, new to bondage, its possibility scarcely having earlier entered her ken, frenziedly, absurdly trying to remove fetters from her body, but a Gorean woman. She well knew that females locked in Gorean iron do not escape. Its stern, inflexible clasp is not designed to be eluded by she whom it confines and ornaments. Women in such bonds must helplessly await the pleasure of their captors. I thrust back her ankles.

"As you can see," she said, bitterly, "I continue to be held, perfectly."

Her ankles looked beautiful, confined in the steel. Too, she had spoken the truth.

I then checked her collar, and the attachment points of the chain, both at the collar and at the double loop where it was fastened about the axle.

"I am perfectly secured," she said, angrily.

"I am sorry if chain check distresses you," I said. "You comprehend its rationale, of course."

"Yes," she said, angrily.

"It is procedurally recommended by the caste of slavers," I said.

"I am not a slave," she said.

"Chains, I suspect, do not much care whether it is a noble free woman whom they confine or a mere slave."

"Are you satisfied?" she asked, insolently. "Do I pass chain check?"

"Yes," I said. "You are perfectly secured."

She looked frightened for a moment, and her two hands closed on the chain dangling from her collar. She drew on it a moment, almost inadvertently, and felt the tug at the collar ring. Then she removed her hands from the chain and regarded me, again the free woman, again insolent.

"See what you have given me to wear," she said, angrily lifting the hem of the garment I had fashioned for her last night.

"I gathered you did not approve of the thin white gown the brigands had put you in," I said. "Surely it had little purpose other than to display you well for sale to a slaver and, in its piteousness, to invite its casual removal."

"I am a rich woman," she said, angrily. "I have status and position. In Brundisium I hold high station, being a member of the household of Belnar, her Ubar. I am highly intelligent. I am educated and refined. I have exquisite taste. I am accustomed to the finest silks, the most expensive materials. I have my gowns, my robes, even my veils, especially made for me by high cloth workers!"

"I am not a high cloth worker," I said, "but I did make it especially for you."

"Your skills leave something to be desired," she said.

"You are probably right," I said.

"I wear only the latest fashions!" she said.

"Perhaps you could start a new fashion," I said.

"How dare you dress me as you have!" she said.

"At least it is opaque," I said.

"That is true," she said, ironically.

"And it is long," I said, "and thus protective of your modesty."

"I am certain that I am grateful," she said.

"And so what is your complaint?" I inquired. As she was a free woman, it seemed I should be concerned, at least to some extent, with any complaints which she might have. A slave, of course, in distinction from a free woman, is not permitted complaints. She must try to obtain things in other ways, for example, by humble requests while kneeling or lying on her belly before her master.

She cried out angrily and jerked in frustration at the chain on her neck.

"It conceals your figure, at least to some degree," I said.

"You could at least have given me a belt," she said.

"It will conceal your figure better, unbelted," I said.

"Please," she said.

"No," I said.

She cried out in anger, in frustration.

"Stand up," I said.

"It is difficult to stand in close chains," she said.

"There," I said, not pleasantly, indicating a place beside the wheel, beside the wagon.

"Very well," she said, rising, and clutching the wagon wheel, and pulling herself up, and around it. "One woman has been beaten in this camp this morning. I have no desire to be the second." These words interested me. A woman behaves very differently toward a man whom she knows is capable of disciplining her and may, if it pleases him, do so, then toward one whom she knows she may treat with contempt and scorn with impunity.

"Turn," I said. "Now, turn back."

She clutched the wagon wheel to keep her balance, now again facing me.

"How can I be attractive in this?" she asked.

Last night, after bringing her to the camp, I had removed the offensive, light white gown from her body, that to which she, a free woman, so objected, that in which the brigands to her dismay had insolently clothed her, and, from something I found in the camp, prepared her new garment. I had cut a hole in the material for her head, and two more holes for her arms. I had then had her put her arms over her head and had pulled the garment down over her body. She was then in it. She was then standing there, regarding me with rage. "Excellent," I had said. I had then chained her by the neck under the wagon and had gone to bed.

"I do not know," I said, "but you are managing."

"It is a sack!" she cried. "Only a sack!"

That was true. It was a long, yellow, closely woven Sa-Tarna sack. If there could have been any doubt about it such doubts would have been dispelled by the thick, black, stenciled lettering on the bag, giving a bold and unmistakable account of its earlier contents, together with their grind and grade, and the signs of the processing mill and its associated wholesaler.

"Am I to gather that you are dissatisfied?" I asked.

"Yes," she said, acidly.

"The yellow sets off your hair nicely," I said. Perhaps if I enslaved her, I would put her in yellow slave silk. She was a beautiful woman.

"This makes me look ridiculous," she said.

"It is not unknown for free teen-age girls of poor families, in rural areas, to wear such garments," I said. Also, of course, it was not unknown for such girls to put themselves in the way of slavers, that they might be caught, and carried to cities, to be sold. Too often, however, it seemed they were merely sold to peasants in distant villages as sex and work slaves.

"I am not the simple, dirty, barefoot, unkempt, scrawny teen-age daughter of some destitute peasant in some out-of-the-way place," she said. "I am the Lady Yanina of Brundisium!"

"You are barefoot," I said. Prisoners, as well as slaves, are often kept that way on Gor.

"This garment makes me look ridiculous," she said.

"You might look a little silly," I said, "but you do not look all that ridiculous. Indeed, I have never seen anyone wear a Sa-Tarna sack better."

"Thank you," she said, in fury.

"You're welcome," I said.

"Give me back the white gown," she said, "that in which the brigands put me!" she said. "I prefer that!"

"That garment," I reminded her, "is strikingly attractive. It excitingly sets off your beauty. No free woman would consider wearing such a garment unless she was implicitly begging, pleading, for a collar. The brigands doubtless put you in it because it seemed an appropriate garment for a woman they were preparing for a full enslavement."

"I prefer it," she said, angrily.

"Are you a slave?" I asked.

"No!" she said.

"Why, then, would you wish to wear it?" I asked.

"It is pretty," she said, defensively.

I smiled. It was actually tauntingly, brazenly sensuous. "Why would you wish to wear something pretty?" I asked.

"To look nice," she said.

"Why do you wish to look nice?" I asked.

"I think better of myself then," she said.

"How do you know when something is pretty?" I asked.

"I just see that it is pretty," she said, puzzled.

"Think more deeply," I said.

"When it makes me attractive," she said. "Then it is pretty."

"It seems then that the test for prettiness is the enhancement of your appearance, and this is understood in terms of increasing your attractiveness."

"Perhaps," she said, cautiously.

"Attractiveness to what end?" I asked. "Attractiveness to whom?"

"I do not know," she said, sullenly.

"Come now," I encouraged her.

"I am a full-grown woman," she said, angrily. "I like to be attractive to men!"

"You dress then," I speculated, "in certain ways, in order to be attractive to men."

"Perhaps," she said, angrily.

"She who is concerned with such matters," I said, "she who dresses in certain ways in order to make herself attractive to men, she who dresses herself in certain ways in order that she may be pleasing to them, is in her heart a slave."

"Then all females are slaves at heart," she said, angrily.

"Yes," I said.

"No!" she cried.

"And they will never be fully content," I said, "until they are imbonded."

"No, no, no!" she cried. "No! No!"

I let her cry out in misery, resisting my suggestions. It was good for her.

Then she wiped her forearm across her eyes. "You distract me from the issue," she said. "The issue is my wardrobe."

"Very well," I said.

"Give me something else to wear," she said.

"No," I said.

"I am the Lady Yanina of Brundisium," she said. "I do not wear sacks."

"Oh?" I said.

"I will wear nothing for a garment before I will wear a sack," she said.

"That can be arranged," I said.

"What are you doing?" she asked. "Why are you drawing your knife?"

"To remove the sack from you," I said. "Nakedness in your chains is acceptable to me."

"No," she said, taking a step backward, clinging to the wagon wheel. "I will wear it!"

I sheathed the knife. "Are you hungry?" I asked.

"Yes," she said.

I reached down and picked up the breakfast which I had put to the side before commencing her chain check.

"It is cold," she said. "Take it away, and bring me another."

"This is your breakfast this morning," I said, "and your only

breakfast this morning. Eat it, and as it is, or not, as it pleases
you."

"Are you serious?" she said.

"Yes," I said.

"Give it to me," she said. I handed her the plate. She began
to attack the food voraciously. She might have been a starving
slave. I supposed that she, like Lady Telitsia, had probably both
been fed sparingly by the brigands, perhaps to conserve food,
perhaps to slim their figures somewhat before their projected
sale.

I watched her eat. In the Tahari a woman is often stuffed with
food for days before her sale, even force fed, if necessary. Many
of the men of the Tahari relish soft, pretty, meaty little slaves.

"Why are you looking at my ankles?" she asked.

"They are pretty," I said. Too, the gyves, sturdy and snug,
looked nice on them, both from the aesthetic point of view and
from the point of view of their significance, for example, that
they were mine and that the beauty, confined, wore them. "Too,"
I said, "I was thinking that perhaps I should remove them, that
you could be exercised."

"Doubtless I am to be exercised in the tall grass or in the
brush," she said.

"Do not be apprehensive," I said.

"I am to be held in honor," she reminded me.

"At least for the time," I reminded her.

"Yes," she smiled, "at least for the time."

"If you do not wish to be exercised," I said, "I shall not
force it upon you. You are a free woman. Not a slave."

"I may continue then to wear the shackles," she said.

"Yes," I said, "at least for the time."

"Of course," she said.

"Do you enjoy your breakfast?" I asked.

"It is cold," she said.

"Do you enjoy it?" I asked.

"Yes," she said.

"Later," I said, "I will give you something briefer and
prettier to wear."

"That will be nice," she said.

"While we are performing," I said.

"Performing?" she asked. "In what way?"

"You will see," I said.

"I am not a performer," she said. "I do not know anything
about performing."

"Your role will not be difficult," I said.

"I have had no experience in such matters," she said.

"Do not fear," I said, "you will do just splendidly."

"I am not a slave," she said.

"This role calls for a free woman," I said, "otherwise it would not be nearly so interesting or impressive."

"I see," she said, pleased.

She wiped her plate with a crust of one of the rolls. She did not wish to leave a particle of food on that homely tin surface.

"Do you know the slave in camp, she called Lady Telitsia?" I asked.

"Yes," she said.

"She has not yet eaten," I said.

"So?" asked the lady Yanina.

"She is probably quite hungry by now," I said.

"So?" she asked.

"I do not think her master would permit her to beg food until a certain free woman, a prisoner in the camp, was fed."

"Probably not," said the Lady Yanina. "Why are you bringing the matter up?"

"I thought it might be of interest to you," I said.

"It is not," she said.

"You were common captives of the brigands," I said. "I thought you might have some concern for her."

"No," she said.

"I see," I said.

The Lady Yanina looked at me, and smiled. She put the piece of crust in her mouth and nibbled on it, slowly. "Let her wait," she said. "She is a slave. Slaves are nothing."

I did not gainsay the Lady Yanina, of course. What she had said was true. I had only brought up the matter as a form of test for her, to satisfy my own curiosity. I wished to more exactly ascertain her self-image. It was, as I had expected, that of the lofty free woman, separating herself, at least publicly, by dimensions and worlds from mere slaves. This was particularly interesting to me in view of the fact that she was herself, obviously, a highly appropriate candidate for the collar. Did she think, truly, she was that different from the slave who, but Ehn ago, had been tied and lashed?

The Lady Yanina handed me the cleaned plate. I put it to one side. "If I had not eaten the breakfast, you would have taken it away, and not brought me another, wouldn't you?" she asked.

"Yes," I said.

"And you will keep me in this pathetic, degrading garment as long as it pleases you, won't you?" she asked.

"Yes," I said.

"And if I give you trouble, or inconvenience you in any way, in spite of the fact that I am free, you will whip me, won't you?" she asked.

"Yes," I said.

"I have always had my own way with men," she said.

"Are you sure you were dealing with men?" I asked.

"Perhaps not," she said.

"Some women do not realize what men are until they must kneel before them and obey."

"Do you find me attractive?" she asked.

"Yes," I said.

"I want these shackles off," she said, suddenly.

"Do you understand what you are asking?" I asked.

"Yes," she said.

"Why?" I asked.

She averted her eyes. "I do not want to be chained under the wagon at night," she said. "It is hard to sleep on the ground. It is uncomfortable. Too, it is cold and miserable."

"I see," I said.

She looked up at me. "I am willing to do whatever is necessary to be permitted in the wagon, where it is warm and dry," she said.

"Speak clearly," I said.

"Remove my shackles," she said. "I am ready to be kept as a full prisoner."

With the key from my pouch I removed her shackles and then, too, removed the collar from her neck.

"Precede me up the steps into the wagon," I said.

She preceded me up the several steps. She drew the hem of her dress up about her calves, that she not trip. Then we were inside the wagon. I locked her hands behind her back. I locked them there with slave bracelets. I did not have another form of manacles for her.

"Oh!" she said. I pulled up her garment and drew it up under her arms and over her breasts, and then hooded her with it. "Kneel here, facing the door," I said. "And wait."

She knelt, braceleted, hooded, in the narrow space between the two bunks, facing the door.

I then left the wagon, padlocking it shut behind me. In a moment or so, retrieving the plate, I rejoined Boots near the fire. He was still eating. I am not clear whether this was a third breakfast, or a mere continuation of a somewhat prolonged second breakfast. In the case of Boots, such distinctions would occasionally prove difficult to draw. "The free woman has been fed," I announced.

"It is just as well," said Boots. "It is nearly time for lunch."

Boots was given to such jocular hyperbole. It was actually several Ehn until lunch time.

He gazed at Lady Telitsia. She wavered, slightly, and caught herself. I feared she might faint with hunger.

"May I speak, Master?" she whispered.

"Yes," he said.

She put her head down to the dirt. Her wrists were still tied before her body. "I beg food, Master," she said.

"Are you hungry?" asked Boots.

"Yes, Master," she said.

"How long has it been since you have eaten?" inquired Boots.

"Since dawn, yesterday," she said, "when I, only a lowly slave, and the other woman, she noble and free, were fed in the brigands' camp."

"You probably are hungry then," said Boots.

"Yes, Master," she said.

"Do you beg on your belly?" inquired Boots.

"Yes, Master," she said, putting her bound wrists forward and lowering herself to her belly. She lifted her head. It was at Boots's knee.

"Speak," said Boots.

"I beg food," she said.

"Speak more clearly," said Boots.

"Lady Telitsia begs food at the hands of her master," she said.

"Turn to your side," said Boots.

She then lay on her left side. Boots then, delicately, carefully, bit by bit, by hand, fed her. After a time he let her kneel near him and then he continued, bit by bit, little by little, to feed her from his hand. She looked up at him, from the palm of his hand, which she had been licking. She looked up at him in gratitude. It was on him that her food depended. Boots then piled a plate with food and put it down before her. "Head down," he cautioned her. "Do not use your hands." She then put her head down and ate from the plate, not touching it with her hands. Finally she was even licking at the plate. She, like the free woman, the Lady Yanina, had been ravenous. Boots then took the plate from her. "Kneel there," he said. She knelt immediately, obediently, where he had indicated, facing him. "Thank you, Master," she said, "for feeding me."

"What do you think?" asked Boots.

"A pretty slave," I said.

"Thank you, Master," she whispered, trembling.

From her reaction I conjectured she was a virgin.

"On your back!" said Boots. "Put your hands over your head! Throw your legs apart, widely!"

"What do you think?" asked Boots.

"She is clumsy," I said, "but she is prompt and earnest."

"I cannot even use her in a girl tent now," said Boots, gloomily. "They would demand their money back. She is desperately in need of training."

"I think she will learn quickly," I said.

"She will, or she will be regularly lashed," said Boots.

"You will prove to be an apt pupil, will you not, Lady Telitsia?" I asked.

"I will struggle to learn!" she said "I will try to do my best to please my Masters!"

"You will prove to be an apt pupil, will you not, Lady Telitsia?" I repeated.

"Yes, Master!" she said.

"Kneel," said Boots.

Swiftly she scrambled to her knees.

Boots regarded her. "I suppose you will prove to be troublesome," he mused, grimly.

"No, Master!" she said.

"Or you will fail to be fully pleasing, and it will be necessary to sell you for sleen feed," he said.

"No, Master!" she said.

"You have dared to beg food," he said. "You grow bold. Doubtless next you will wish a scrap of blanket for the girl wagon, or next even, outrageous effrontery, a brief rag to conceal some bits of your beauty, at least provisionally, from the eyes of men."

"Let it be done with me as my Master desires," she said. "I am his slave."

"The slave's response seems suitable," I said.

"Perhaps," admitted Boots, grudgingly. "Lift your wrists," he said to the girl.

She did so, putting her head down, between her then-lifted arms. Boots removed the thongs from her wrists. "Put your hands on your thighs," he said. He then regarded her, kneeling naked, frightened, before him, her hands on her thighs. Her knees were pressed closely together. This is a natural, defensive posture in a new female slave.

"Perhaps, later," said Boots, "when you have had more training, I will permit you to kneel with your knees wide."

"Yes, Master," she said.

"Are you not grateful?" inquired Boots.

"Yes, Master," she said. "Thank you, Master."

"Now seek out Rowena, the blond slave," said Boots. "I am using her now as first girl in the camp. She will put you about your duties."

"Yes, Master," said the girl, rising.

"Slave," called Boots.

"Yes, Master?" said the girl, turning, and dropping again to her knees, addressed by a free man.

"On second thought," said Boots, "go to my wagon, there. Enter it. Inside, facing the front of the wagon, kneel down, putting your head to the floor. I think I will begin your training."

"Yes, Master," she said, frightened, and leaped up, hurrying to his wagon, to obey.

"It seems we will not be leaving this camping area today," I said.

"Tomorrow will be soon enough," said Boots. He then rose to his feet, belched, spit on his hands, wiped them on his tunic, and stalked slowly, ponderously, like a good-natured, rotund draft tharlarion, perhaps having eaten too much, toward his wagon.

In a moment or two I, too, had left the gray, smoldering ashes of the breakfast fire behind me. I then found myself at my own wagon. I climbed the stairs, taking no care to conceal my approach. I noisily removed the padlock from the door, and let it fall back against the side of the door, suspended on its short chain. I would wait a long moment before I opened the door. Within, inside the wagon, the Lady Yanina would be kneeling. Next she would obey.

11

THE LADY YANINA IS INCLUDED IN THE ACT

"You cannot do this to me!" cried the Lady Yanina.

"Behold," called Boots meaningfully to the crowd, "not a slave, but a free woman!"

"Stop!" cried the Lady Yanina. "I am free! Save me! Some-one save me!"

"Should we attempt to rescue her?" asked one stout youth of another.

"Do not be silly," said his fellow. "It is all part of the act."

"Of course," agreed the first. "How stupid of me to fear otherwise."

"Help!" shrieked the Lady Yanina.

I now fastened Lady Yanina's left wrist in its place on the colorful red, trimmed-in-yellow, backboard. I had already buck-led her right wrist in place.

"Gather around, good friends, good people," Boots encour-aged the crowd. "Look closely upon her. Examine her!"

The crowd, thus encouraged, pressed in about us.

"See her throat," cried Boots. "It is innocent of the collar! See her thighs! No brand is upon them!"

The crowd pressed closely about, some of the men skeptically, roughly, examining Lady Yanina for slave marks. Certainly her costume, incredibly brief and brightly spangled, bared most of the common brand sites utilized by Gorean slavers in marking women.

"Help!" cried the Lady Yanina. "Help!"

"You are doing very well," I congratulated her.

"I am not acting!" she cried. "Help! Help!"

One of the men pulled the top edge of her lower garment out and down a bit from her body, peering within. "What are you doing?" she cried.

"She is not branded on the lower left abdomen," he informed the crowd.

I desisted from buckling her right ankle in its place on the backboard while a fellow checked the backs of her legs. She cried out in misery. "There is nothing here," said the fellow. I then fastened her ankle in place.

"Oh!" she cried. The fellow who had checked her lower left abdomen was now expanding his explorations to check her buttocks. "Stop!" she cried.

"There are no brands here," he said.

"Interesting," said a man.

Another fellow was thrusting up the fringe dangling from the narrow, twisted strip of cloth, covered with sequins, which was bound about her breasts, this serving to conceal her nipples. "Take your hands off me!" she cried.

"There is nothing here," said the fellow.

With difficulty I caught her left ankle and buckled it, too, in its place, against the colorful backboard.

Another pulled her head by the hair forward from the backboard and brushed back her hair, on the left.

"Stop!" she cried. "Stop!"

"Nothing here," said the fellow, pushing back her head against the backboard. She was not branded either on the left side of the neck, behind and below the left ear.

"As you can see, Ladies and Gentlemen," said Boots, "on her lovely throat she does not wear the light collar of inflexible steel, that beautiful circlet proclamatory of absolute bondage. Similarly her beauty has not, as yet at least, as you can see, been graced by the imprinting upon it of some delicate emblem indicative of the status of property, some device recollective of the unmistakable, transforming kiss of the blazing iron! As advertised, as proclaimed, as announced earlier, she is a free female!"

"She cannot be a free female," said a man. "Otherwise she would not be used in this fashion."

"Come now," said Boots. "Surely you have all known free women whom you would have enjoyed treating in this fashion."

There was a great deal of laughter. One of the free women in the audience struck the fellow next to her with her elbow.

"Take your hands off me!" cried the Lady Yanina to one of the men standing near her, a fellow who had perhaps decided to resume the discontinued investigations of his peers. She then, to the horror of the crowd, spit virulently in his face. "Sleen! Sleen!" she cried at him. Then she turned her head to the crowd. "Sleen!" she screamed. "You are all sleen!" She spit out at the crowd, twice. Then she stood there in the straps, helpless, sobbing. The crowd observed her, in stunned silence.

"As you can see," said Boots, swiftly, enthusiastically, thinking like lightning, "she is, as advertised, as certified, a free woman! What more proof could you possibly desire? What slave would dare to behave so?" It was an excellent point which Boots was making. No slave would be likely to behave in a fashion like that, or at least more than once. Such a behavior would be likely to be followed by hideous punishments, if not death by torture. How should I put this delicately? Perhaps, thusly: Insubordination in any form, of any sort, in even the tiniest, least significant degree, is not accepted from slave girls by their Gorean masters.

Suddenly, as it had become clear what had occurred, the crowd began to turn ugly. "Give her to us!" called a man. "Let us buy her!" called another. "We will take up a collection!" cried another, looking about himself. "Yes!" said a man. "Yes!" cried another. "I want her!" called a man. "She can pull my plow!" "We will brand her and put her in a collar quickly enough!" cried another. "Sell her to us!" called another. "If he will not sell her, let us seize her by force!" cried another.

"Gentlemen, gentlemen, ladies!" called out Boots, jovially. "Let us remain calm. No harm has been done. Let us get on with the show. Step back, step back, please."

Grudgingly the crowd stepped back a bit, clearing a half circle around the heavy, braced, upright structure of painted planks. I regarded the Lady Yanina. She was now trembling, terrified, in the straps. There were certainly enough fellows in the crowd, if they became unruly, to take her away from us. Also, of course, Boots would never have approved of vigorous altercations with paying customers, and certainly would have frowned upon slaying them, even a few of them. That sort of thing is not good for business.

Boots motioned me forward. I approached, the multiple sheath of saddle knives at my left hip.

"May I present Tarl, he of the Plains of Turia, he of the Lands of the Wagon Peoples, master of the mystic quivas, the famed saddle knives of the southern barbarians, come to us at great expense and in spite of many perils by special arrangement with Kimchak, Ubar San of the Wagon Peoples!"

"That's Kamchak," I said. I thought I owed at least that much to my old buddy of the south. I supposed that if Kamchak had known his name was being used in this fashion, and mispronounced at that, and Boots was within his grasp he might have, as a joke, for Kamchak was fond of jokes, had Boots put in a sack and put out in front of the bosk, curious to see if they would move in that direction on that particular morning. On the other hand, perhaps he would only have challenged him to a spitting contest or one in which the number of seeds in different sorts of tospits were guessed and then, if Boots lost, put him out with the bosk, to see what way they might move that day.

"Is it true," asked Boots, "that you never miss?"

"Well, actually no," I admitted.

"What!" cried Boots, in horror.

"You must understand," I said, "that I have no intention of hitting her. She is, after all, a free woman."

The Lady Yanina regarded me, wildly. "I thought you were an expert!" she cried.

"I have never done this before," I admitted.

"Good," said a man. I am not sure, but I think he was the one she had spit upon. He, at any rate, did not appear pleasantly disposed towards her.

The Lady Yanina regarded me with horror.

"Never," I admitted.

She stood there, buckled in place, against the bright red, yellow-trimmed backboard. She then, suddenly, frenziedly, began to struggle. I did not much blame her. In the end, of course, she stood precisely as she had before. I had not buckled her in in such a way as to permit her to free herself. She was a lovely woman. The costume, too, set her off nicely. Her throat required only a collar. Her thigh required only a brand. She whimpered a bit, pulling at the straps. She knew herself absolutely helpless. It was important, of course, that she was a free woman for this bit of showmanship. Who in the crowd would have been that interested, or concerned, or thrilled with horror, to see a slave in such jeopardy? What sort of take would that have brought in? Not many coins, I feared, would be likely to rattle in the kettle on behalf of so unimaginative an offering. Also, of course, slaves generally have some value, at least to the master, even if not much. They, at least, can be bought and sold. Who would want to risk one in such a foolish manner? Free women, on the other hand, being priceless, have for most practical purposes no value whatsoever.

"Step back, please," warned Boots gravely. "Give him room."

A hush fell over the crowd.

I took my position.

"Let me ask your forgiveness in advance, lady," I said, "should I possibly strike you."

"Why would you do that, in advance?" asked Boots.

"It might be pointless afterwards," I said.

"That is true," he granted me.

Lady Yanina moaned. She tugged weakly at the straps. As she was fastened against the backboard, her wrists were drawn somewhat above her head and far to the sides. Similarly her legs were widely spread. If the board had been laid flat on the ground, the captive then on her back, the position, immediately, would have been recognized as a common binding position, one in which girls are not unoften put for slave use.

"Be quiet," Boots warned the crowd. "We must have absolute quiet."

Some fellow sneezed. I think it was the fellow she had spat upon.

"Please!" begged Boots.

"I have something in my eye," I said.

"Are you all right?" asked Boots.

"Yes," I said. "I am all right now."

"Is it true that you sometimes miss?" asked Boots anxiously.

"Sometimes," I admitted.

Boots regarded me.

"No one is perfect," I told him.

"Throw," said Boots bravely, resolutely.

I unsheathed one of the quivas, and turned it in my hand. I then turned to face the Lady Yanina. "What is wrong with her?" I asked.

"She has fainted," said a man.

12

CONVERSATIONS WITH A MONSTER; THE PUNISHMENT OF A SLAVE

"How did the accident occur?" I asked.

"What accident?" he asked.

There were fourteen pieces on the board, six yellow, eight red. I was playing red.

I had now been with the company of Boots Tarsk-Bit for several weeks. In this time we had played numerous villages and towns, sometimes just outside their walls, or even against them, when we had not been permitted within. Too, we had often set up outside mills, inns, graneries, customs posts and trade barns, wherever an audience might be found, even at the intersections of traveled roads and, on certain days, in the vicinity of rural markets. In all this time we had been gradually moving north and westward, slowly toward the coast, toward Thassa, the Sea.

"As I understand it," I said, "there was a fire."

He regarded me.

"You wear a hood," I said.

"Yes?" he said.

"That accident which destroyed or disfigured your face," I said, "that rendered it such, as I understand it, that women might run screaming from your sight, that men, crying out, sickened and revolted, might drive you with poles and cudgels,

like some feared, disgusting beast, from their own habitats and
haunts.''

"Are you trying to put me off my game?" he inquired.

"No," I said.

"It is your move," he said. "Your next move."

I returned my attention to the board. "I do not think the game
will last much longer," I said.

"You are right," he said.

"Out of the several times we have played," I said, "never
have I enjoyed so great an advantage in material."

"Do you have an advantage?" he asked.

"Obviously," I said. "More importantly I enjoy an immense
advantage positionally."

"How is that?" he inquired.

"Note," I said. I thrust my Rider of the High Tharlarion to
Ubar's Initiate Eight. "If you do not defend, it will be capture of
Home Stone on the next move."

"So it would seem," he said.

His Home Stone was at Ubar's Initiate One. It was flanked by
a Builder at Ubar's Builder One. It was too late to utilize the
Builder defensively now. No Builder move could now protect
the Home Stone. Indeed it could not even, at this point, clear an
escape route for its flight. He must do something with his Ubara,
now at Ubara's Tarnsman Five. The configuration of pieces on
the board was as follows: On my first rank, my Home Stone was
at Ubar's Initiate One; I had a Builder at Ubar's Scribe One. On
my second rank, I had a Spearman at Ubar's Builder Two, a
Scribe at Ubara Two, and another Rider of the High Tharlarion
at Ubara's Scribe Two. On my third rank, I had a Spearman at
Ubar's Initiate Three and another at Ubar's Scribe Three. One
of my Riders of the High Tharlarion, as I indicated earlier, was
now at Ubar's Initiate Eight, threatening capture of Home Stone
on the next move. On his eighth rank he had a Spearman at
Ubar's Builder Eight, inserted between my two Spearmen on my
third rank. His Spearman at Ubar's Builder Eight was supported
by another of his Spearmen, posted at Ubar's Scribe Seven. He
had his Ubara, as I indicated earlier, at Ubara's Tarnsman Five.
This was backed by a Scribe at Ubara's Scribe Four. This
alignment of the Ubara and Scribe did not frighten me. If he
should be so foolish as to bring his Ubara to my Ubar's Builder
One, it would be taken by my Builder. His Scribe could recapture but he would have lost his Ubara, and for only a Builder.
His last two pieces were located on his first rank. They were, as
I indicated earlier, his Home Stone, located at Ubar's Initiate

One, and a Builder, located at Ubar's Builder One. The Builder was his Ubar's Builder.

"How would you choose to defend?" he inquired.

"You could bring your Ubara over to your Ubar's Initiate Five, threatening the Rider of the High Tharlarion," I said.

"But you would then retreat to your Ubar's Initiate Seven, the Rider of the High Tharlarion then protected by your Scribe at Ubara Two," he said. "This could immobilize the Ubara, while permitting you to maintain your pressure on the Ubar's Initiate's File. It could also give you time to build an even stronger attack."

"Of course," I said.

He placed his Ubara at Ubara's Tarnsman Two.

"That is the better move," I said.

"I think so," he said.

Ubar's Initiate Nine, that square from which I might effect capture of Home Stone, was now protected by his Ubara.

"Behold," I said.

"Yes?" he said.

I now moved my Scribe from Ubara Two to Ubara's Tarnsman Three. This brought it onto the diagonal on which lay the crucial square, Ubar's Initiate Nine. He could not take it with his Ubara, of course, sweeping down his Ubara's Tarnsman File, because it was protected now by my other Rider of the High Tharlarion, that hitherto, seemingly innocent, seemingly uninvolved piece which had just happened, apparently, to be posted at Ubara's Scribe Two. Now its true purpose, lurking at that square, was dramatically revealed. I had planned it well. "You may now protect your Home Stone," I said, "but only at the cost of your Ubara." I would now move my Rider of the High Tharlarion to Ubar's Initiate Nine, threatening capture of Home Stone. His only defense would be the capture of the Rider of the High Tharlarion with his Ubara, at which point, of course, I would recapture with the Scribe, thus exchanging the Rider of the High Tharlarion for a Ubara, an exchange much to my profit. Then with my superior, even overwhelming, advantage in material, it would be easy to bring about the conclusion of the game in short order.

"I see," he said.

"And I had red," I reminded him. Yellow opens, of course. This permits him to dictate the opening and, accordingly, immediately assume the offensive. Many players of Kaissa, not even of the caste of players, incidentally, know several openings, in numerous variations, several moves into the game. This is one reason certain irregular, or eccentric, defenses, though often theoretically weak, are occasionally used by players with red. In this way the game is opened and new trails, even if dubious ones, must be blazed. If these irregular or eccentric defenses tend to be successful, of course, they soon, too, become part of the familiar, analyzed lore of the game. On the master's level, it might be mentioned, it is not unusual for red, because of the disadvantages attendant on the second move, to play for a draw.

"You still have red," observed my opponent.

"I have waited long for this moment of vengeance," I said. "My triumph here will be all the sweeter for having experienced so many swift, casual, outrageously humiliating defeats at your hands."

"Your attitude is interesting," he said. "I doubt that I myself would be likely to find in one victory an adequate compensation for a hundred somewhat embarrassing defeats."

"It is not that I am so bad," I said, defensively. "It is rather that you are rather good."

"Thank you," he said.

To be honest, I had never played with a better player. Many Goreans are quite skilled in the game, and I had played with them. I had even, upon occasion, played with members of the caste of players, but never, never, had I played with anyone who remotely approached the level of this fellow. His play was normally exact, even painfully exact, and an opponent's smallest mistake or least weakness in position would be likely to be exploited devastatingly and mercilessly, but, beyond this, an exhibition of a certain brilliant methodicality not unknown among high-level players, it was often characterized by an astounding inventiveness, an astounding creativity, in combinations. He was the sort of fellow who did not merely play the game but contributed to it. Further, sometimes to my irritation, he often, too often, in my opinion, seemed to produce these things with an apparent lack of effort, with an almost insolent ease, with an almost arrogant nonchalence.

It is one thing to be beaten by someone; it is another thing to have it done roundly, you sweating and fuming, while the other fellow, as far as you can tell, is spending most of his time, except for an occasional instant spent sizing up the board and moving, in considering the ambient trivia of the camp or the shapes and motions of passing clouds. If this fellow had a weakness in Kaissa it was perhaps a tendency to occasionally indulge in curious or even reckless experimentation. Too, I was convinced he might occasionally let his attention wander just a bit too much, perhaps confident of his ability to overcome inadvertencies, or perhaps because of a tendency to underestimate opponents. Too, he had an interest in the psychology of the game. Once he had put a Ubara *en prise* in a game with me. I, certain that it must be the bait in some subtle trap I could not detect, not only refused to take it but, worrying about it, and avoiding it, eventually succeeded in producing the collapse of my entire game. Another time he had done the same thing with pretty much the same results. "I had not noticed that it was *en prise*," he had confessed later. "I was thinking about something else." Had I dared to take advantage of that misplay I might not have had to wait until now to win a game with him. Yes, he was sometimes a somewhat irritating fellow to play. I had little doubt, however, that, in playing with him, my skills in Kaissa had been considerably sharpened.

"Do you wish to resign?" I asked him.

"I do not think so," he said.

"The game is over," I informed him.

"I agree," he said.

"It would be embarrassing to bring it to its conclusion," I said.

"Perhaps," he admitted.

"Resign," I suggested.

"No," he said.

"Do not be churlish," I smiled.

"That is a privilege of 'monsters,' " he said.

"Very well," I said. Actually I did not want him to resign. I had waited a very long time for this victory, and I would savor every move until capture of Home Stone.

"What is going on?" asked Bina, coming up to us, chewing on a larma.

"We are playing Kaissa," said the monster.

I noted that she had not knelt. She had not thrust her head to the ground. She had not asked for permission to speak. Her entire attitude was one of slovenly disregard for our status, that of free men. She was not my slave, of course. She belonged to Boots.

"I can see that," she said, biting again into the larma. The juice ran down the side of her mouth.

Her foot was on the edge of the monster's robes, as he sat before the board, cross-legged.

"Who is winning?" she asked.

"It does not matter," I said. I was angry with her animosity towards the monster. It was not my intention to give her any occasion to receive gratification over his discomfiture. She wore light, leather slippers. Boots had permitted footwear to both Bina and Rowena. He was an indulgent master. To be sure, Lady Telitsia had not yet been permitted footwear, but then she had not yet been permitted clothing either, except for her collar, except when it was in the nature of costuming for her performances. "Do you play?" I asked.

"I am a slave," she said. "I cannot so much as touch the pieces of the game without permission without risking having my hands cut off, or being killed, no more than weapons."

"You do not know how to play, then?" I said.

"No," she said.

"Do you understand anything of the game?" I asked.

"No," she said.

"I see," I said. That pleased me. It was just as well if she did not understand the dire straits in which my opponent now found himself. That would surely have amused the slinky little slut. Surely she knew her foot was on his robes. Surely he, too, must be aware of this.

"I have offered to extend to you such permissions, and teach you," he said.

"I despise you," she said.

"Your foot is on the robes of my antagonist," I said.

"Sorry," she said. She stepped back a bit, and then, deliberately, with her slipper, kicked dust onto his robes.

"Beware!" I said.

"You do not own me!" she said. "Neither of you own me!"

"Any free man may discipline an insolent or errant slave," I said, "even one who is in the least bit displeasing, even one he might merely feel like disciplining. If she is killed, or injured, he need only pay compensation to her master, and that only if the master can be located within a specific amount of time and requests such compensation." In virtue of such customs and statutes the perfect discipline under which Gorean slaves are kept is maintained and guaranteed even when they are not within the direct purview of their masters or their appointed agents. She turned white.

"We are playing," said my opponent. "Do not pursue the matter."

She relaxed, visibly, and regained her color. Then she regarded my opponent. "You should not even be with the troupe," she said. "You do not bring us in enough coins to pay for your own suls. You are hideous. You are worthless! You are a fool and a contemptible weakling! All you do, all you can do, is play

Kaissa. It is a stupid game. Moving little pieces of wood about on a flat, colored board! How stupid! How absurd! How foolish!"

"Perhaps you have some duties to attend to elsewhere," I speculated.

"Leave the camp, Monster," she said to my opponent. "No one wants you here. Go away!"

I regarded the female.

"Yes," she said to me, angrily, "I have duties to attend to!"

"Then see to them, female slave," I said.

"Yes, Master," she said. She then tossed her head, and left.

"An insolent slut," I said, "muchly in need of the whip."

"Perhaps she is right," he said.

"In what way?" I asked.

He looked down at the board. "Perhaps it is stupid, or absurd, or foolish, that men should concern themselves with such things."

"Kaissa?" I asked.

"Yes," he said.

"Now," I said, "you are truly being foolish."

"Perhaps that is all it is, after all," he said, "the meaningless movement of bits of wood on a checkered surface."

"And love," I said, "is only a disturbance in the glands and music only a stirring in the air."

"And yet it is all I know," he said.

"Kaissa, like love and music, is its own justification," I said. "It requires no other."

"I have lived for it," he said. "I know nothing else. In times of darkness, it has sometimes been all that has stood between me and my own knife."

"You did not wish for me to discipline the slave," I said.

"No," he said.

"Do you like her?" I asked.

"I live for Kaissa," he said.

"She is a sexy little slut," I said.

"I know nothing of the management of women," he said.

"It is your move," I said.

"Do you wish to continue the game?" he asked.

"If it is all right with you," I said, "I would not mind it."

"I thought you might not wish to do so," he said.

"No," I said. "It is all right with me."

"I will offer you a draw, if you like," he said.

"You are very generous," I said.

He inclined his head, graciously.

"You are joking, of course," I said.

"No," he said, puzzled.

"I have a winning position," I said.

"Ah!" he said, suddenly. "So that is why you would not comment on the game in the presence of the slave. You wished to protect me from her scorn."

"Something like that," I admitted, shrugging.

"That was really very thoughtful of you," he said. "I must insist that you accept a draw."

"With your permission," I said, "I would prefer to play the game to its conclusion."

"This is the first time in my life," he said, "that I have ever offered someone a draw as a gift."

"I am sure I am appreciative of the gesture," I said.

"But you do not accept?" he asked.

"No," I said.

"Very well," he said.

"I have a winning position," I said.

"Do you really think so?" he asked.

"Yes," I said.

"Interesting," he said.

"I have a protected Rider of the High Tharlarion at Ubar's Initiate Eight. When I move him to Ubar's Initiate Nine you can prevent capture of Home Stone only by giving up your Ubara. After that the outcome of the game is a foregone conclusion."

He regarded me, not speaking.

"It is your move," I said.

"That is what you seem to have forgotten," he said.

"I do not understand," I said.

He swept his Ubara down the board, removing the Spearman I had posted at my Ubar's Initiate Three.

"That Spearman is protected," I said, "by the Spearman at Ubar's Builder Two."

"Threat to Home Stone," he said. To be sure, his Ubara now threatened the Home Stone.

"I will permit you to withdraw the move," I said.

"Threat to Home Stone," he said.

"That move costs you your Ubara," I said. "Further, you are losing it for a mere Spearman, not even a Rider of the High Tharlarion. Further, when I remove it from the board, my Rider of the High Tharlarion is but one move from capture of Home Stone."

"Threat to Home Stone," he said.

"Very well," I said. I removed his Ubara from the board, replacing it with the Spearman I had previously had at Ubar's Builder Two. The move was forced, of course. I could not move the Home Stone to Ubar's Builder One because that square was covered by his Scribe at Ubara's Scribe Four. "My Rider of the High Tharlarion is but one move from capture of Home Stone," I reminded him.

"But it is my move," he said.

He then advanced his Spearman at Ubar's Builder Eight to Ubar's Builder Nine. This was now possible, of course, because I had had to open that file, taking the Spearman from it to capture his Ubara, the move forced in the circumstances. One must, as long as it is possible, protect the Home Stone.

"Threat to Home Stone," he observed.

His advancing Spearman, a mere Spearman, now forked my Home Stone and Builder. The Spearman is not permitted retreat. It, after its initial move, may move only one space at a time. This move may be directly or diagonally forward, or sideways. It, like the chess pawn, can capture only diagonally.

I could not move my Home Stone in front of the Spearman, even if I had wished to do so, because of his Scribe's coverage from afar of that square, Ubar's Builder One. Similarly, even if I had had the option in the circumstances, which I did not, I could not have brought my Builder to that square for defensive purposes without exposing it to the attack of the same piece. I now began to suspect that what I had thought had been a rather weak, easily averted threat of capture of Home Stone, the earlier alignment of his Ubara and Scribe on that crucial diagonal, might actually have had a somewhat different, more latent, more insidious purpose. Similarly, even if his Scribe had not been placed where it was, it would not have been rational in this specific game situation, though it would have been a possible move, to place my Home Stone at Ubar's Builder One. If I had done so this would have permitted the diagonal move of the Spearman to his War's Initiate Ten, my Ubar's Initiate One, at which point it would doubtless have been promoted to a Rider of the High Tharlarion, thusly effecting capture of Home Stone. The defense of my Builder, on which I was relying, would in such a case have been negated by the placement of my own Home Stone, which would then have been inserted between it and the attacking piece. But, as it was, because of the Scribe's coverage of Ubar's Builder One, my move was forced. I could move only to, and must move to, Ubar's Initiate Two. It appeared I must lose my Builder. I eyed my Rider of the High Tharlarion at Ubar's Initiate Eight. I needed only a respite of one move to effect capture of Home Stone.

"Your Home Stone is under attack," he reminded me.

"I am well aware of that," I said.

"You have one and only one possible move," he pointed out.

"I know," I said. "I know."

"Perhaps you should make it," he suggested.

"Very well," I said. I moved my Home Stone to Ubar's Initiate Two. A Spearman who attains the rear rank of the enemy has the option of being promoted, if promotion is desired, to either a Tarnsman or a Rider of the High Tarlarion. The Tarnsman is generally regarded as the more valuable piece. Indeed, in many adjudication procedures the Tarnsman is valued at eight points and the Rider of the High Tharlarion at only two. I did not think he would directly advance his Spearman to Ubar's Builder Ten, even though it was now protected, the file opened behind it, by his Builder at Ubar's Builder One. I now began to suspect that the placement of his Builder on that file might not have been an accident, no more than the rather irritating placement of his Scribe at Ubara's Scribe Four. If he did advance it in that fashion, promoting it presumably to a Rider of the High Tharlarion, to bring the Home Stone under immediate attack, and prevent me from advancing my own Rider of the High Tharlarion to Ubar's Initiate Nine, finishing the game, I would take it with my Builder. He would then, of course, retake with his Builder. On the other hand, this exchange would sacrifice his advanced Spearman. I expected him rather, then, to take the Builder and then, with impunity, promote his Spearman to a Tarnsman at his Ubar's Scribe Ten, my Ubar's Scribe One. If he did this, however, it would give me the move I needed to effect capture of Home Stone, by advancing my Rider of the High Tharlarion to the coveted Ubar's Initiate Nine. I mopped my brow. He had miscalculated. The game was still mine!

"Spearman to Ubar's Initiate Ten," he said, moving the Spearman neither to Ubar's Building Ten nor to Ubar's Scribe Ten, taking the Builder. This placed it behind my Home Stone. "Rider of the High Tharlarion," he said, replacing the Spearman now with the appropriate piece. "Threat to Home Stone," he then said.

"I can take it with my Builder," I said.

"Indeed," he said, "you must do so. You have no other move."

I swept my Builder to my left, capturing the new Rider of the High Tharlarion at my Ubar's Initiate One. His career, it seemed, had been a brief one. There was no way he could, in this situation, recapture. It seemed he had done nothing more than deliver his new Rider of the High Tharlarion promptly, and for nothing, into my prison pit. I could not move the Home Stone to either Ubar's Builder One, Two or Three because of the coverage of these squares, all of them being covered by his Builder at his Ubar's Builder One, and Ubar's Builder One being additionally covered by his Scribe, that posted at Ubara's Scribe Four.

"Builder to Ubar's Builder Nine," he said.

I regarded the board.

"Capture of Home Stone," he said.

"Yes," I said.

My Home Stone had been maneuvered to Ubar's Initiate Two. There he had used my own men to trap it and hold it helplessly in position. Then he had swept down the opened file with his Builder, to Ubar's Builder Nine, to effect its capture.

"Every one of your moves was forced," he said. "You never had an alternative."

"True," I said.

"An elementary Ubara sacrifice," he remarked.

"Elementary?" I asked.

"Of course," he said.

"I did not see it," I said, "at least until it was too late."

"I gathered that," he said. "Otherwise you might have resigned several moves ago, thereby perhaps saving yourself a bit of embarrassment."

"I thought I was winning," I said.

"I think you were under a grave misapprehension as to just who was attacking," he said.

"Apparently," I said.

"Undoubtedly," he agreed, unnecessarily, in my opinion.

"Are you sure the Ubara sacrifice was 'elementary,' " I asked.

"Yes," he said.

"I thought it was brilliant," I said.

"Those such as you," he said, "particularly when they find themselves their victims, commonly salute as brilliancies even the most obvious trivialities."

"I see," I said.

"Do not be despondent," he said. "Among those who cannot play the game, you play very well."

"Thank you," I said.

"You're welcome," he said. "Would you care to play again?"

"No," I said. "Not now."

"Very well," he said. He began to put the pieces back in a large leather wallet.

"Would you care to wrestle?" I asked.

"No," he said, pleasantly enough.

"That Ubara sacrifice was not really all that bad, was it?" I asked.

"No," he said, "it was actually not all that bad. In fact, it was rather good."

"I thought so," I said.

I watched the player replacing the pieces in the leather wallet. He was in a good mood. Just as I had thought, that Ubara sacrifice had not been all that straightforward, or elementary. That, at least, gave me some satisfaction. This moment, it then seemed to me, might be a good time to speak to him. I had been wanting to speak to him for several days. I had been awaiting only a judicious opportunity, one in which the topic might seem to be broached naturally, in such a way as to avoid arousing his curiosity or suspicion. He drew the strings on the wallet, closing it. Yes, this seemed like an excellent time to take action. I would arrange the whole business in such a way that it would seem quite natural. It would be easy. Yes, I thought, I could manage this quite nicely.

"I wish that I had recorded the game," I said.

"I can reiterate the moves for you, if you wish," he said.

"From memory?" I asked.

"Of course," he said. "It is not difficult."

I drew forth from my wallet some papers and a marking stick. Among some of these papers, which I would apparently use as a backing surface for the sheet on which I intended to record the moves, were the papers I had taken, long ago, from the Lady Yanina near the fair of En'Kara.

"Ah," said the player. "I see."

"What?" I asked.

"Am I not, now, supposed to say, 'What have you there?' or is that to come later?"

"I do not understand," I said.

"We must have played a hundred games," he said. "Never before have you seemed interested in recording one. Now you seem interested. Why, I wonder. Now you draw forth papers from your wallet. Some of these are papers obviously covered with the notation of Kaissa. Am I not to express curiosity? And are you not then, almost inadvertently, to ask me some question, or questions, in which you are interested?"

"Perhaps," I said, hesitantly.

"Are you really interested in the game?" he asked.

"I am interested in it, as a matter of fact," I said, "but, to be sure, as you seem to have detected, it is possible I have an ulterior motive in mind."

"The moves in the game were as follows," he said. He then repeated them for me, even, occasionally, adding in some useful annotational remarks. There were forty-three moves in the game. "Thank you," I said.

"You're welcome," he said. "Now what are those other papers?"

I handed them to him.

He looked at them, briefly, flipping through them. They appeared to be covered with the notation of Kaissa, as though various games, or fragments of games had been recorded on them.

"Do you have some question, some specific questions, about these?" he asked.

"I am wondering about them," I said.

"I thought you were giving me these in connection with some specific question having to do with Kaissa," he said, "perhaps with respect to the analysis of a position or a suggested variation on a lesser-known opening. I thought perhaps they might be Kaissa puzzles, in which a forced capture of Home Stone in some specified number of moves must be detected."

I said nothing. I was eager to see what he would say.

"What do you make of them?" he asked.

"I am interested in your opinion," I said.

"I see," he said.

"Are they games," I asked. "Parts of games?"

"They might appear to be so," he said, "if not looked at closely."

"Yes," I said.

"Doubtless you have reconstructed the positions, or some of them," he said.

"Yes," I admitted.

"And what do you think?" he asked.

"I think," I said, "that it is highly unlikely that they are games, or parts of games."

"I agree," he said. "They do not seem to be games, or parts of games. Indeed, it seems unlikely that that is even what they are supposed to be. Not only would the general level of play be inferior but much of it is outright gibberish."

"I see," I said.

"I am sorry," he said. "I can be of no help to you."

"That is all right," I said.

"Where did you get them?" he asked.

"I came on them," I said.

"I see," he said.

"You do not know what they are, then?" I said.

"What they are," he said, "seems to be quite clear."

"What do you think they are?" I asked.

"Kaissa ciphers," he said.

"What are Kaissa ciphers?" I asked. I did not doubt that the papers contained enciphered messages. That conjecture seemed obvious, if not inevitable, given the importance attached to them by the Lady Yanina, she of Brundisium, and her colleague, Flaminius, perhaps also of Brundisium. I had hoped, of course, that the player might be able to help me with this sort of thing, that he, ideally, might be familiar with the ciphers, or their keys.

"There are many varieties of Kaissa ciphers," he said. "They are often used by the caste of players for the transmission of private messages, but they may, of course, be used by anyone. Originally they were probably invented by the caste of players. They are often extremely difficult to decipher because of the use of multiples and nulls, and the multiplicity of boards."

"What is the 'multiplicity of boards,' " I asked.

"Do you see these numbers?" he asked.

He indicated small numbers in the left margins of several of the papers. These tiny numbers, in effect, seemed to divide the moves into divisions. In originally looking at the papers I had interpreted them simply as a device for identifying or listing the games or game fragments.

"Yes," I said.

"Those presumably indicate the 'boards,' " he said. "Begin for example, with a Kaissa board, with its one hundred squares, arranged in ten ranks and ten files. Are you literate?"

"Yes," I said. Torm, my old friend, the Scribe, might have expressed skepticism at the unqualified promptness and boldness of my asseveration, as I had always remained somewhat imperfect in writing the alternate lines of Gorean script, which are written from the right to the left, but, clearly, I could both read and, though admittedly with some difficulty, write Gorean. Gorean is written, as it is said, as the ox plows. The first line is written left to right, the second, right to left, the third, left to right again, and so on. I had once been informed by my friend, Torm, that the whole business was quite simple, the alternate lines, in his opinion, at least, also being written forward, "only in the other direction."

"Begin then, on the first square," said the player, "with the first letter of a word, or of a sentence, or even of a set of letters randomly selected. Proceed then as in normal writing, utilizing all available squares. When you come to the end of the initial entry, list all unused letters remaining in the alphabet, in order, again utilizing all available squares. When you have managed that, then begin with the first letter of the alphabet, Al-Ka, and continue writing the alphabet in order, over and over, once more on all available squares, until you arrive at the last square on the board. When you have done this, one board, in effect, has been completed."

"I think I understand," I said. "If, in a given message, for example, the notation 'Ubar to Ubara's Tarnsman Two' occurs, that could mean that, on the board in question, say, Board 7, the square Ubara's Tarnsman Two was significant. On that board, then, we might suppose, given its arrangement, that the square Ubara's Tarnsman Two might stand for, say, the letter 'Eta.' Both the sender and receiver, of course, can easily determine this, as they both have the keys to construct the appropriate boards."

"Yes," said the player.

"The listing of the moves in an orderly sequence, of course, gives the order of the letters in the message," I said.

"Correct," said the player.

"I see how the multiples are effective," I said. "For example, the letter 'Eta,' the most commonly occurring letter, would actually, on any given board, be capable of being represented by any of a number of appropriate squares, each different, yet each corresponding to an 'Eta.' Similarly, of course, one might skip about on the board, retreating on it, and so on, to utilize 'Eta Squares' in any fashion one chose. This would produce no confusion between the sender and the receiver as long as the enciphered notation was in orderly sequence."

"Precisely," said the player.

"But where do the nulls come in?" I asked.

"In my exposition," the player reminded me, "I mentioned 'available squares.' A board key will commonly consist of a given word and a list of null squares. The nulls may frequently occur in the enciphered message but they are, of course, immediately disregarded by the receiver."

"I see," I said. The presence of nulls and multiples in a message, of course, makes it much more difficult to decipher, if one lacks the key.

"The true power of the ciphers come in, in my opinion," said the player, "not so much with the multiples and nulls but with the multiplicity of boards. Short messages, even in elementary

ciphers, are often impossible to decipher without the key. There
is often just not enough material to work with. Accordingly it is
often difficult or impossible to test one's deciphering hypotheses,
eliminating some and perhaps confirming others. Often, in such
a message, one might theoretically work out numerous, and
often conflicting, analyses. The multiplicity of boards thus permits the shifting of the cipher several times within the context of
one message. This obviously contributes to the security of the
communication.''

"These ciphers seem simple and beautiful," I said, "as well
as powerful.''

"Too, if one wishes," he said, "one need not, in filling out
the boards, do so as in the fashion of normal writing. One might
write all one's lines left to right, for example, or right to left, or
write them vertically, beginning at one side or the other, and
beginning at the top or bottom, or diagonally, beginning at any
corner. One might use alternate lines, or left or right spirals from
given points, and so on. Similarly, after the initial entry the
remainder of the alphabet could be written backwards, or beginning at a given point, or reversing alternate letters, and so on.
These variations require only a brief informative addition to the
key and the list of null squares, if any.''

"I see," I said.

"I think you can see now," he said, "why I cannot be of any
help to you. I am sorry.''

"But you have been of help," I said. "You have made it a
great deal clearer to me what may be involved here. I am
deeply appreciative.''

"Such ciphers are, for most practical purposes, impossible to
decipher without the appropriate keys, null-square listings, and
so on.''

"I understand," I said. It seemed, as I had feared, that it
might be difficult or impossible to decipher the messages without pertinent keying materials. These materials, presumably,
would exist in Brundisium, and of course, in Ar, if indeed that
were the intended destination of the messages. I was now prepared to believe that it was likely they were not messages
intended for Priest-Kings.

First, Flaminius, it seemed, who was to have received the
messages from the Lady Yanina, had apparently intended to
deliver them not to the Sardar, but to some party in Ar.

Secondly, I did not think it likely that messages which were to
be transmitted to the Priest-Kings, or among their agents, would
be likely to be in a Kaissa cipher. Such ciphers seemed too

intrinsically, or idiosyncratically, Gorean for Priest-Kings. Priest-Kings, as far as I knew, were not familiar with, and did not play, what Goreans often speak of simply as "the Game." This suggested to me then that the messages might be transmissions of a sort which might occur among the agents of Kurii.

I recalled one message from Kurii or their agents, to Samos of Port Kar, which had been written on a scytale, disguised as a girl's hair ribbon. The girl who had originally worn it to his house, a blond-haired, blue-eyed Earth girl, was now one of his slaves. She had been named "Linda."

I recalled another message, too, which we had intercepted, a well-disguised but simple substitution cipher. It had been re-corded in the ordering of a string of slave beads. It had been carried, too, in its way, by a slave. She had been a poetess, and a lovely, curvaceous wench, one obviously born for the collar. I think she, too, had been of Earth origin, though little of that had remained in her when I saw her. As I recall, her name was "Dina." At that time, at least, she had been owned by Clitus Vitellius, a warrior of Ar.

The nature of the messages, then, in a native-type Gorean cipher, suggested to me that there might be some sort of linkage between Kurii, and their agents, and Brundisium and Ar. This would be natural enough, I supposed, because close relations reputedly existed between the two cities. This would make travel and communication between them practical in a world where strangers are often regarded with suspicion, indeed, a world on which the same word is generally used for both "stranger" and "enemy." Kurii, then, I suspected, must control Brundisium, or be influential there. It might be an outpost for them or a base of operations for them, perhaps, as, I gathered, Corcyrus had been, in the recent past. The Lady Yanina had been of the household of the Ubar of Brundisium, a fellow named Belnar. This sug-gested that he himself, as she seemed to be in his employ, might well be in league with Kurii.

The keying materials for the messages, I suspected, would lie in the palace in Brundisium, perhaps even in the private cham-bers of her Ubar himself, Belnar. I myself was now in hiding from Priest-Kings, presumably to remain under cover until Samos had resolved certain matters with the Sardar, or until some new developments might be forthcoming. I was not now pleased with Priest-Kings. I did not now, any longer, really consider myself as being of their party. At best I had, even in the past, served them or not, as my inclinations prompted. I was perhaps less of a pledged adherent in their wars than a free sword, a mercenary of

sorts, one who accepted one cause or another, as it might please
him to do so.

Still, I recognized that it was the power of Priest-Kings which,
in its way, protected both Gor and Earth from the onslaught of
lurking Kurii, concealed in their steel worlds, hidden among the
orbiting stones and mountains, the small worlds and moons, of
the asteroid belt. There was some point, then, in my being at
least somewhat well disposed toward their cause. If Brundisium
were in league with Kurii, I did not suppose it would do Samos
any harm to learn of it. Yes, upon reflection, it now seemed
quite likely that Brundisium was in league with Kurii, that there
was some sort of connection between the palace at Brundisium
and the subtleties and machinations of the denizens of the steel
worlds. More importantly, I was curious to know the content of
those secret messages. Their keys might well lie in the private
chambers of Belnar. Perhaps I could pay them a visit. It might
be difficult, of course, to gain access to the palace. But perhaps
it could be somehow arranged.

We were now less than five hundred pasangs from Brundisium.
I must soon, in the performances, I feared, hood the Lady
Yanina, or perhaps, better, sell the wench to someone bound in
another direction, and replace her altogether with another girl,
presumably a slave, whom I might purchase somewhere, a girl it
would be safer to take into Brundisium, one not from that city,
one to whom the city would be unfamiliar and strange, one in
which she could not even find her way around, one in which she
would find herself, absolutely, only another slave.

"You are not really a roustabout, or vagabond, are you?"
asked the player.

"I am a member of the troupe of Boots Tarsk-Bit, actor,
promoter and entrepreneur," I said.

"So, too, am I," said the player.

"I thought so," I said.

"We shall leave it at that, then," said the player.

"Yes," I said.

We stood up. It was now near supper. It was being prepared
tonight by Rowena and Lady Yanina, in her sack. It amused me
that she should be used to perform the labors of a slave. I could
see Boots returning now, from a nearby village, to which he had
gone to purchase some food and advertise our show. Behind
him, barefoot and naked, bent under the burden of his purchases,
which were strapped to her back, her legs filthy to her thighs
with dust from the road, came one of his girls, Lady Telitsia. I
could also see the insolent Bina approaching. She was coming

from the stream, bearing on her shoulders a yoke, from which swung two buckets.

"I see that you are a bearer of burdens," I said.

She cast a scornful glance at the player. "Yes," she said to me. "I am a slave." She then continued on her way to the cooking fire where Rowena and the Lady Yanina were busying themselves. Rowena had been appointed first girl in the camp. We had also made it clear to the Lady Yanina that she, even though she was a free woman, must obey Rowena in all things, she, by our decision, having been placed in power over her. The least waywardness in behavior while under the commands of Rowena, or hesitancy in obeying her orders, or insolence shown towards her, we had assured her would constitute an occasion for discipline, and severe discipline, precisely as though she herself might be naught but a mere slave.

"Thank you for the games," I said. We had played five games this afternoon. To be sure, four of them had not taken very long.

"You are very welcome," he said.

"May I not pay you for them?" I asked.

"No," he said.

"Surely you can use the coins," I said.

"We are both members of the troupe of Boots Tarsk-Bit," he said.

"True," I smiled.

"Actor, promoter and entrepreneur," he added.

"Yes," I said.

Boots was now, his girl, Lady Telitsia, behind him, quite near the camp. Doubtless she would be pleased to be soon relieved of her burdens. Bina was near the cooking fire. She had brought water for the kettles. Lady Yanina, kneeling before a pan of water, under the supervision of Rowena, who was tending the fire, was washing and scraping garden vegetables, mostly onions, turnips and suls. These would later be used in a stew.

"Your Kaissa," I said, "is the finest of anyone with whom I have played."

"You have probably not played with skilled players," he said.

"I have sometimes played with members of the caste of players," I said.

He said nothing.

"I think," I said, "that you could play in the same tournaments as Scormus of Ar."

"Upon occasion," he said, "I have done so."

"I had thought you might have," I said.

"You have a very active mind," he said.

"Perhaps you might even, upon occasion, beat him," I said.

"I do not think that is very likely," he said.

"Nor do I," I said.

"Do not speak to me of Scormus of Ar," he said.

"Why?" I asked.

"Scormus of Ar is a traitor to his city," he said.

"How is that?" I asked.

"He failed his city," he said, "and was disgraced."

"In what way did this occur?" I asked.

"He lost in the great tournament, in 10,125 Contasta Ar," he said, "to Centius, of Cos."

"Centius is a fine player," I said. The tournament he referred to was doubtless the one held at the Sardar Fair, in En'Kara of that year. It had occurred five years ago. It was now 10,130 C.A., Contasta Ar, from the Founding of Ar. In the chronology of Port Kar, it was now Year Eleven, of the Sovereignty of the Council of Captains. I had been fortunate enough to have been able to witness that game. In it Centius of Cos, one of Gor's finest players, indeed, perhaps her finest player, had, for the first time, introduced the defense which came subsequently to be known as the Telnus Defense. Telnus was the home city of Centius of Cos. It is also the capital of that island ubarate.

"That makes no difference," said the player.

"I would think it would make a great deal of difference," I said.

"No," he said, bitterly. "It does not."

"Do you know Scormus of Ar?" I asked.

"No," he said, angrily. "I do not know him."

"I think that is true," I said. "I think you do not know him."

"I do not think we need bother playing again," he said.

"As you wish," I said.

"Are you still here?" asked Bina, come from the side of the cooking fire. She carried a pan of water. It was that in which the Lady Yanina had been washing the vegetables. The water was now rather dirty, and in it there floated numerous scrapings from various vegetables. Presumably she was on her way to empty it, outside the camp.

"Obviously," he said, looking down upon her.

"I thought I told you to go away," she said.

"I did not do so," he said.

"Are you being insolent?" she asked.

"I am a free man," he said. "Insolence, if I choose, is my prerogative."

"Well, I, too, can be insolent, if it pleases me," she said.

"An insolent female slave?" I inquired.

"I am not speaking to you," she said. Boots, by now, had returned to the camp. I was certain that the girl did not realize this. I saw that Boots, who had been sorting through his purchases, from the village, now looked up, in surprise. Lady Telitsia, now unburdened and relieved of the carrying straps, their marks still on her body, lay in the shade near the wheel of his wagon, gasping. It had been a long trek back to the camp from the village and the burdens under which she must struggle, bearing them for her master, had been quite heavy.

"I do not want you in the camp," said Bina to the player. "I told you to go away. Having you about makes us sick! You are too ugly. None of us want you here. Go away! You repulse all of us! Go away!"

"You speak boldly to a free man," he said. The player, too, I think, did not realize that Boots had returned to the camp. I could see him from where I stood. He was back, between two wagons, at the side of his.

"You are a monstrosity," she said. "Go away!"

"You are insolent," he observed.

"Yes," she said, "I am insolent!"

"I would not advise you to speak generally in this way to free men," I said.

For a moment she turned pale, but then, as I made no move to correct her behavior, perhaps stripping her and throwing her to her belly, kicking her, thrusting her face into the dirt, or tying her to an elevated, spinning wagon wheel, she turned, again, boldly, to the player. Boots, of course, unbeknownst to either of them, was observing all this.

"Yes," she said to him, "I am insolent! I am insolent to you! I may be insolent to you with impunity, for you are not a man! You are too weak to punish me! You are only a beast, a monster, a cringing, wretched, pathetic, ignoble, spineless, monster! You are not a man at all! You are only some kind of monster, some kind of monstrosity, some kind of contemptible weakling!"

I wondered if she thought she was speaking to a man of Earth, and not a Gorean male.

"Weakling!" she cried. "Weakling!"

She was very small, looking up at him. I considered her angry, curvaceous little form. How inappropriate seemed her anger, given the smallness, the softness, of her body. How absurd it seemed that the little animal should so boldly address itself to the larger, stronger brute. On what artifices, on what weaknesses, did it count? How bravely tiny animals may conduct themselves in the presence of caged larls! But how stupid are larls who will lock themselves in cages, being told to do so. But what if the larl should free itself?"

"Weakling!" she cried.

Did she not know she was a female? Did she not know she wore a collar?

"Weakling!" she cried.

How the little animals would scurry if the larl emerged from its cage! Did she not know how easy it would be for her to be stripped and returned to her place in nature, at his feet? Did she in her heart fear the larl might one day say, "The joke is finished. It is enough." Or did she long for that day?

"Weakling!" she screamed.

The player regarded her, not speaking.

"Go away!" she screamed. "Go away!"

"Have you finished?" he asked.

"Your robes have dust upon them," she said. This was, of course, the residue of dust remaining on them, after she had, earlier in the afternoon, kicked dust upon them. "I am a slave. Let me clean them for you!" She then suddenly, angrily, flung the pan of water upon him, drenching his robes from the chest down.

"Kneel, Slave!" cried Boots in fury, coming up behind her. "Head to the ground!"

Startled, she cried out with misery. Then, immediately, in terror, she dropped the pan and assumed the prescribed position. "Master," she cried, tembling, "I did not know you had returned!"

"Apparently," said Boots.

"Forgive me, Master!" she begged. The other members of the troupe, now, and the slaves, and Lady Yanina, in her gown fashioned from a Sa-Tarna sack, gathered around. Lady Telitsia was white-faced. She had her hand before her mouth. She, now well acquainted with her own condition, that of the collared, female slave on Gor, was terrified as to what might be done to the errant Bina. Rowena, too, trembled.

"What is going on?" asked Boots.

"I suggest that you ask the slave to give an accounting," I said, "completely."

"The master," she said, swiftly, "was mocking you, abusing you with many insults, Master. I could stand it no longer! I took it upon myself, risking my own life, to stop him, to defend your honor!"

"Is this true?" inquired Boots of the player.

How clever was the little she-sleen. She knew the possible penalties for what she had done. She counted on the player to support her story, to protect her from the horrifying reprisals almost certain to be visited on a helpless slave in her position. I wondered how weak he was.

"Is it true?" asked Boots.

"No," said the player.

"Aiii!" she wept, in misery.

"Speak," said Boots.

"I failed to kneel in the presence of free men," she sobbed. "I have spoken without permission. I stepped on the robes of a free man. I kicked dust upon them. I have been insolent."

"Continue," said Boots.

"I spilled water on a free man," she wept.

"Spilled?" asked Boots.

"I threw water on a free man," she sobbed.

"Is there anything else?" he asked.

"Master?" she asked.

"Surely you remember at least one more thing," he said.

"I lied to my master!" she sobbed, trembling. "I lied to my master!"

"And were these various things done inadvertently," asked Boots, "or deliberately?"

"Deliberately, Master," she sobbed.

Certain of these things, such as failing to kneel in the presence of a free man, may be regarded as a capital offense on the part of a Gorean slave girl, even if it is inadvertent. If intent is involved in such an omission, it can be an occasion for death by torture.

"Mercy, Master!" she cried.

"What shall be done with you?" asked Boots. "Shall you be sold for sleen feed? Shall we contrive exquisite tortures for you, say, cutting off bits of your body and cooking them, and forcing you to eat them, until from the loss of blood and tissue, you die, or should we bind you and sew you in a sack, your head exposed, with rabid urts, or shall we merely cut your throat swiftly, in disgust, and be done with it?"

"Please, Master," she wept, throwing herself to her belly before him, clutching at his ankle, putting her forehead down to his foot, "please, please, Master!"

"Perhaps we should be merciful, sparing your miserable life," said Boots, angrily, "and just throw you on your belly under a wagon, your ankles up and projecting out through the spokes, tied there, in order that your feet may be cut off?"

She sobbed, lying before him.

"You are a frigid little slave, and worthless," he cried.

"Spare me, Master," she begged. "I will become hot, dutiful and subservient!"

"What would be a suitable punishment, for a meaningless, nasty little slut like you?" he asked. "Death? A thousand lashes?"

"I beg to be permitted to become a perfect slave, in all things!" she wept.

"Who begs?" he demanded.

"Bina begs!" she wept. "Bina begs!"

"What does Bina beg?" he demanded.

"Bina begs to be permitted to become a perfect slave, in all things!" she wept.

"I know what I shall do," said Boots.

"Master!" she wept.

"I shall ask someone to decide what your punishment is to be," said Boots, "he whom you have most offended, our hooded friend, the player."

"No, Master," she sobbed, "not he, please, not he!"

"Player?" asked Boots.

He looked down upon the prone slave.

She crawled suddenly to him, desperately, sobbing, and lay before him on her belly. She took his sandaled foot in her small hands and, putting her head down, placed it on her head. "Bina begs the forgiveness of master," she wept. "Bina is sorry. Bina lies on her belly before master! Bina acknowledges that she is less than the dust beneath his feet! Bina is only a slave! Be kind to Bina! Please be kind to Bina!"

"The robes will dry," said the player. "I can clean them later."

"What is her punishment to be?" inquired Boots.

"The matter is unimportant," said the player. "I am not concerned with it. It is nothing."

Bina lay quietly, trembling, startled, beneath his foot.

"It is your recommendation, then," asked Boots, "that she be permitted to live?"

"Yes," he said.

"What punishments, in lieu of death, then, do you suggest for her?" asked Boots.

The player lifted his foot from her head, and stepped away from her, smoothing his robes. She put her head up, the palms of her hands in the dust, looking at him; then she again lowered her head, trembling.

"As I suggested," he said, "it is not an important matter. I am no longer concerned with it. It is, accordingly, acceptable to me that she go unpunished.''

Bina sobbed with relief.

"It is not acceptable to me," said Boots, "that she go unpunished."

The girl looked suddenly, wildly, frightened, at Boots.

"She is yours," said the player. "You may, of course, do with her as you wish."

"Kneel here, before me, Slave," said Boots.

Swiftly the girl knelt before him.

"The player has shown you incredible mercy, girl," said Boots.

"Yes, Master," she said.

"I, on the other hand, shall not be so merciful," he said.

"Yes, Master," she whispered.

"Hear your punishment, slave," said Boots.

"Yes, Master," she whispered, trembling.

"First," said Boots, "you will surrender your slippers."

"Yes, Master," she said, delightedly, and, sitting down, slipped them from her feet. She then knelt again before him, and handed him the slippers. In a different situation, of course, this might have constituted a suitable and humiliating punishment, involving a public reduction in her status, particularly before other girls. The removal of her footwear might have served to punish her for some flaw in her performance, such as a crookedly sewn seam or a poorly served meal, or might, say, have indicated some fall on her part from the favor of the master. Similar punishments can involve the changing of a woman's clothing or its removal altogether. In this situation, of course, such a punishment, the removal of her right to footwear, was almost absurdly trivial. Indeed, most Gorean slaves are not permitted footwear at all. They are commonly kept barefoot.

"Your second punishment," said Boots.

"Yes, Master?" said the girl, somewhat apprehensively.

"You have been insolent," he said, "and seem to have forgotten that you are a slave."

"Yes, Master," she said, frightened, putting her head down.

"Accordingly," said Boots, "you are herewith instructed to remove a panel of material, four horts in width, and curved at the top, near your waist, from the skirts of your slave tunics at the sides, thus well revealing both thighs to the waist, or almost to the waist. In this fashion, in a balanced manner, your thighs will be exposed to the view of free men. In this fashion, too, of course, your brand will be always clearly visible. Perhaps in this way you will be more likely to keep it in mind that you wear it, and what it means.''

"Yes, Master!'' she said.

In my opinion, this constituted little, or no, punishment at all. Many slaves are kept in the common camisk, a narrow, poncholike garment, little more than a long, narrow rectangle of cloth, generally cheap cloth, with an opening for the head. It is drawn on over the head and is normally belted snugly with a double loop of binding fiber. It is, of course, open-sided. Many other girls learn swiftly to be grateful for as little as a strip of cloth suspended from a knotted string about their waist. Many other slaves, particularly in their masters' houses, are kept naked. Lady Telitsia, for example, in our own camp, had not yet even been permitted clothing. Yes, her punishment, if punishment it was, seemed light indeed.

"Hereafter,'' said Boots, "you will be expected to mend your ways.''

"Yes, Master,'' she said, humbly, her head down. But I saw her smile, slyly. How easily she had gotten off! How light had been her punishment! I saw her sneak a scornful, victorious glance at the player. He had been too soft, too weak, to have his vengeance on her. He had been too stupid, too weak, it seemed, to seize his opportunity to discipline her. How successful, too, had been her placatory efforts with her master! How indulgent he was! Was he not too easy with his slaves? Did he not spoil them? It seemed now she could do as she pleased with impunity. What had she to fear? She had won!

"There is one other thing,'' said Boots.

"Yes, Master?'' she said.

"Regard the monster,'' she said.

"Yes, Master,'' she said.

She looked at the "monster.'' He, hooded, garbed in black, tall, straight, his arms folded, was, too, looking upon her. She was a nasty little female, but she was a pretty one, too; that could not be denied.

"Until further notice,'' said Boots, "your use is his.''

"No!'' she screamed, wildly. "No! No!''

The other slaves, and even Lady Yanina, gasped, and shrank back in horror.

"No, Master, please!'' cried Bina.

"You will cook, sew and wash for him, and perform for him all the other duties of the female slave. You will be to him in all things as his own slave. You will serve him in all ways, intimate or otherwise, and perfectly, as he may wish or direct.''

"Please, no, Master!" she wept.

"It has been said," said Boots.

"Thank you," said the player.

"It is nothing," said Boots.

"Do I also have full discipline and whip rights over her?" asked the player.

"Of course," said Boots.

"Good," said the player, approvingly.

The girl put her head in her hands and began to sob, hysterically.

"Go now, slave, to the wagon of your use master," said Boots to the girl, "and close yourself inside, awaiting him."

"Yes, Master," she wept and, springing up, hurried to the player's wagon. The other girls looked after her, with horror. None of them, I think, had expected that her punishment would be so grievous.

"The rest of you females," said Boots, clapping his hands sharply, "get back to your work!"

Swiftly the girls scattered from his sight, seeking various labors. Even the Lady Yanina fled from his sight, as promptly as though she, too, might have been only a common slave.

"I will need her, of course, for the performances," said Boots to the player. "I hope that is understood."

"Of course," said the player.

"Do you think little Bina now knows she is a slave?" asked Boots.

"Yes," I said. "I think she now knows it well."

Boots then turned away, making his way back to his wagon.

"Congratulations," I said to the player.

He shrugged.

"You are pleased, surely?" I said.

"I have never even had a woman," he said.

"Try them," I said. "I am sure you will enjoy them."

"Perhaps," he said.

"They make splendid recreations," I said.

"Perhaps," he said.

"They are absolutely delicious properties," I said. "They are the loveliest thing a man can own."

"What has she to do with Kaissa?" he asked.

"Very little, I would suppose," I said.

"In my life, hitherto," he said, "I have been concerned primarily with Kaissa."

"Perhaps you could broaden your interests," I suggested.

"What should I do with such a woman?" he asked.

"For most practical purposes," I said, "she is yours. I would do with her, then, if I were you, whatever I pleased."

"That seems a splendid suggestion," he said.

"You know the sort of woman she is," I said. "Make her grovel, and crawl, and be perfect for you."

"I will," he said.

"Are you strong enough to punish her?" I asked.

He looked across the area of the camp to his wagon. He looked at the door of the wagon, reached by climbing the flight of steps at the back of the wagon. The door was now shut. The girl would be behind it, awaiting him.

"Yes," he said.

13

NIM NIM

I clutched the bars of the narrow cell window, looking out onto the courtyard. I stood on a table which I had dragged to the side of the wall, in order to be able to look out. Behind me, on his straw, crouched the small, narrow-shouldered, spindle-legged representative of the urt people.

"I had warned you," had moaned Boots, in his camp, "but you would not listen!"

Five days ago I had been returning to the camp of Boots Tarsk-Bit, coming back from a nearby village where I had gone to fetch Sa-Tarna grain, from which the girls, back at the camp, using stones and flat rocks, sifters and pans, would produce flour. This was somewhat cheaper than buying the flour directly, for then one must pay the cost of the peasant women's work or that of its millage. I carried the sack across my shoulders. It was not heavy. It weighed only a little more than an average female. I had been surprised to see Lady Telitsia running towards me down the road. She flung herself to her knees before me. "Run, Master!" she had cried. "Run! There are men at the camp, come looking for you!" "Who are they?" I asked. "What do they want?"

Then, it seemed in a moment, while she cried out in misery, high tharlarion, some twenty of them, thundered suddenly about me, the earth shaking, dust rising in billows about me. I was encircled. "Hold!" cried a man. "Do not move!" Crossbows, in the hands of surrounding, shifting riders, aligned themselves upon me. A great billowing cape, like a flag, swirled behind their leader. I had seen the cape before. I had seen the man before.

"Manacle him," said Flaminius, he in the service of Belnar, Ubar of Brundisium.

Men leaped to the ground. The sack of Sa-Tarna grain was dragged from my shoulders. My hands were pulled behind me. I felt them clasped in steel manacles. One end of a long chain leash was tossed to one of the men near me. I felt it locked about my neck. Flaminius looped the other end of the leash twice about the horn of his saddle. "We meet again, Brinlar," he said, "or is it Bosk, of Port Kar?"

"I am Bosk, of Port Kar," I said.

I saw several of the men look uneasily at one another.

"He is manacled and leashed," said Flaminius to his men. Then, again, he looked at me. "We took you as easily as a slave," he said.

I pulled at the manacles. I could not elude them. They were made to hold men, even warriors.

"We saw the fat fellow of the acting troupe speak to the slave," he said. "Later we saw her slip from the camp. It was easy to suppose that it was her intention to warn you. Then we needed only follow her, and, indeed, the naked, pretty little slut led us immediately, unerringly, to you."

"Forgive me, Master" moaned Lady Telitsia.

"It was our original intention to wait for you in the camp, surprising you there," said Flaminius. "Obviously this worked out much better. For example, it has saved us the problem of trying to conceal the tharlarion, the presence of which might have aroused your suspicions."

"Doubtless it would have," I said.

"Please, forgive me, Master," wept Lady Telitsia.

"It is nothing," I said. "Dismiss it from your mind, female slave."

"Master!" she wept.

"Were you given permission to speak?" I asked.

"No, Master," she wept.

"Then be silent," I said.

"Yes, Master," she said.

She put down her head, sobbing. She was still kneeling, of course, being in the presence of free men. I saw tears fall from her eyes, moistening the dust between her knees. I also saw some of the riders looking at her. If Flaminius did not object I was sure, before we returned to the camp, some of them would make use of her. She was, after all, only a slave.

"How did you find me?" I asked.

"You are now in the territory of Brundisium," he said.

"So?" I said.

"We make it our business to concern ourselves with strangers within our borders," he said. I recalled that I had heard from Boots that security, for some reason, was very tight in Brundisium. Apparently it was tighter than even he had understood. It apparently extended well beyond the walls of the city itself.

"I would have thought," I said, "that a troupe of actors would have aroused little suspicion."

"It didn't," he smiled, "but one of your performances was witnessed by one of our agents."

"I was recognized?" I asked.

"No," said Flaminius. "The Lady Yanina was recognized."

"I see," I said. I should, of course, have followed Boots's advice about keeping her hooded this near to Brundisium, or perhaps I should have sold her off altogether. Still, I had thought that we were still far enough from Brundisium to be safe on that score. I had not realized, and I suspected that Boots had not realized it either, the intensity or extent of the security now being maintained by Brundisium. It was probably greater now, for some reason, I suspected, than earlier, else Boots would presumably have known more of it. I wondered why its extent or degree might have been recently increased.

"How is it that she was recognized?" I asked, irritably. "Are most free women in Brundisium so easily recognized?"

"Hardly," said Flaminius, "but our agent in this case, happily, was one of the men who had originally served the Lady Yanina, one who had occasionally, unbeknownst to her, a lusty fellow, spied upon her in her tent when she had unpinned her face veil."

I smiled. It amused me that the Lady Yanina had apparently, upon occasion, been spied upon in this fashion. How furious and indignant, how outraged and shamed, she would have been to have learned that she had been looked upon without her knowledge, looked upon surreptitiously when her face was as bared as that of a slave. To be sure, after her fall in favor, probably to the amusement of those who had been her former men, face veiling had been denied to her, at least, I assumed, until her return to Brundisium. In this way, of course, there might actually have been several fellows here and there who, theoretically, if they had had the chance, might have recognized her. It was for such a reason, if none other, that I would have kept her hooded nearer to Brundisium.

"And it was from the Lady Yanina, of course," said Flaminius, "that we learned of your presence with the troupe."

"Of course," I said.

"Our agent, now my man, reported that she looked well half naked, buckled to a target board."

"She does," I agreed.

"I know," said Flaminius. "After she eagerly informed us of your presence with the troupe, I, curious as to the matter, had her so costumed and displayed."

"It must have given you pleasure to see her exhibited, limbs extended and helpless, in that fashion," I said.

"Yes," he said, "almost as much pleasure as it would be to see her in the collar of a slave."

"I think she would look well in such a collar," I said.

"Yes," he said.

"Where is she now?" I asked.

"Waiting in the camp," he said. "It was a brilliant stroke of yours, incidentally, giving the proud Lady Yanina for a gown only a flour sack."

"Thank you," I said.

"She is now back in it," he said. "She also has her wrists bound behind her back with slave thongs, and has a rope upon her neck."

"Why?" I asked.

"I think it will amuse Belnar to see her thusly," he said.

"Why?" I asked. "Did she not, eagerly, inform you of my presence with the troupe?"

"Of course," he said. "But she is not now in high favor with Belnar."

"Why not?" I asked.

"For many reasons," he said. "For example, she had Bosk of Port Kar in her very grasp and let him escape. She lost important diplomatic communications, permitting herself to be tricked out of them. I even found her chained like a slave under a table near the Sardar fairgrounds. Now I find her the helpless captive of this same Bosk of Port Kar and clad only in a sack!"

"I see," I said.

"She has fallen far from the favor of Belnar," he said. "In Brundisium I am confident she will be permitted only a brevity of skirting, one suitable for slaves. Similarly I am confident she will be denied footwear and face veiling."

"Excellent," I said.

"Many times Belnar has even considered making short work

of her, having done with it, simply putting her in a collar and selling her on the market."

"Excellent, excellent," I said. It seemed the climb to favor in Brundisium would be, at best, a long and difficult one for the proud Lady Yanina.

"We shall now return to the camp," said Flaminius, well pleased. "Thence we shall make our way to Brundisium. On the way, in order to make all haste, you will be tied, still manacled, on the back of a tharlarion. When we reach the gates, of course, both you and the Lady Yanina will be led in afoot, helpless and on tethers."

"Of course," I said.

"By the way," asked Flaminius, "what did you do with the papers you took from the Lady Yanina?"

"They were worthless," I said. "They contained nothing but some puzzling scraps of Kaissa notation. I threw them out, with the packet itself."

"I am not surprised," said Flaminius. "That is what I expected. Indeed, it is as I assured Belnar."

"I had hoped they would contain negotiable notes," I said.

"Had they done so," laughed Flaminius, "you would doubtless not have had to throw your lot in with an itinerant troupe of impoverished players."

"True," I said.

"You were bringing grain back to your camp," said Flaminius, looking down at the sack of Sa-Tarna grain lying in the dust.

"Yes," I said.

"Put it on his back," he said to one of his men.

The fellow lifted the sack up and, as I bent down, he put it on my back.

"Tie it there," said Flaminius.

The sack was tied on my back. Flaminius then turned his tharlarion about. The chain on my neck swung in front of me, then looped up to his saddle horn.

"Captain," said one of Falminius's men to him.

"Yes?" he said.

The man indicated the kneeling Lady Telitsia with his head. She knelt in the dust, small among the great, clawed hind legs of the shifting tharlarion.

"Very well," agreed Flaminius.

Several of the men dismounted. Two of them pulled her to her feet by the upper arms.

"After your uses," Flaminius informed her, "you will follow us back to the camp."

"Yes, Master," she said. She was then dragged to the side of the road.

Flaminius then urged his tharlarion slowly forward and I, his captive, afoot, on his chain, carrying the burden, followed him. Most of his men followed, too, strung out behind us. After a time the other fellows, too, caught up with us. At the crest of a hill I paused and looked back. Several hundred yards behind us, following slowly, moving in pain, awkwardly, her head down, came the slave, Lady Telitsia.

I clutched the bars of the narrow cell window, looking out onto the courtyard. I stood on a table which I had dragged to the side of the wall, in order to be able to look out. Behind me, on his straw, crouched the small, narrow-shouldered, spindle-legged representative of the urt people.

I looked from the window down into the courtyard. There, some thirty feet in width, was a shallow, iron-railed pit. This pit was encircled with several tiers of bleacherlike wooden benches. These benches were filled with colorfully garbed, screaming spectators. I squinted against the sun. The noise was loud, resounding and reverberating as it did within the walls of the courtyard. I myself did not much care for such spectacles. Some men enjoy them. Too, they provide an occasion for betting.

"Look, look?" squeaked the creature on the straw below me. It scratched about on the straw, backwards with its feet, while looking up at me.

I turned about and reached down, extending my hand to it. Agilely it scurried across the stone floor of the cell and leapt to the table on which I stood. Then, clinging to my arm, and boosted by my hand, it seized the bars beside me, thrusting its forearms through and about them, clinging to them, using them to support its weight.

I then returned my attention to the courtyard below.

The three sleen in the pit, snarling, tails lashing, their hunched shoulders scarcely a foot from the ground moved in a menacing, savage, twisting, eager circle about the center of their interest. This object, alert, every nerve seemingly tensely alive, was chained in the center of the pit.

An attempt on my life had been made in Port Kar. That attempt had seemed tied in, somehow, with Brundisium. This speculation had been amply confirmed in my dealings with the Lady Yanina and Flaminius. It had seemed likely, further, to me, that there must then be some connection between Brundisium and either the Priest-Kings, or Kurii. Over the past weeks, for several reasons, it had come to seem more and more likely to me that it was not the Priest-Kings who had any special dealings with, or interest in, Brundisium. I was then forced to the conclusion that it must be the Kurii who were active in Brundisium, that their subversions must be in effect in that city as once in Corcyrus. Now, however, I found myself forced to abandon what had hitherto seemed a coercive hypothesis.

There was a wild scream of a charging sleen below and its sudden, frightened squeal, and I saw it flung, half bitten apart, to the side. The two other sleen charged, too, fastening themselves like eels on the chained creature. The crowd roared. I saw blood in torrents run down the legs and arms of the attacked creature. It rolled in the scattered, bloody sand, twisting and fighting, the sleen hanging to it. I heard the chain, the screams of the crowd, the howls of the beasts.

"Pretty! Pretty! Bet! Bet!" cried the creature next to me, clinging to the bars.

Kurii, it now seemed clear to me, no more than Priest-Kings, held any special privileges of influence or power in Brundisium.

The attacked creature seized the sleen clinging to its leg and, from behind, with one paw, broke its neck. It then tore the other sleen from its arm and thrust its jaws open and thrust its great clawed paw deep into the creature's throat, down through its throat, forcing its way into its body, clawing and grasping and tore forth, up through the creature's own mouth, part of its lungs. It then flung the creature down at its feet, threw back its head, its fangs and tongue bright with fresh blood, and howled its defiance to the hot noonday sun, to the towers of Brundisium, and the crowd.

"Three times!" cried the creature clinging to the bars, beside me, "three times! It lives again!"

This was the third time, apparently, the creature had survived the pit.

"Bet! Bet! Pay me! Pay me!" cried the creature near me, clinging to the bars.

I saw soldiers now, warily, with leveled crossbows, and with spears, approaching the creature. They threw ropes upon it. It now seemed scarcely to notice them. Its head was down. It was feeding on the bodies of one of the sleen before it.

No, it did not seem likely to me that Kurii were in power in Brundisium.

The creature beside me released the bars, slipping down to the table, from the surface of which it leaped to the floor. It then

went back to its straw in the corner, poking about in it for scraps
of food.

I stayed at the window for a time, until, half led, half dragged,
prodded, the creature below was conducted from the pit. It left,
snarling, but apparently docile. It still dragged part of one of the
sleen behind it.

No, it seemed clear now that Kurii were not in power in
Brundisium.

The creature now leaving the pit, bloodied, furrowing the sand
behind it, dragging part of a sleen, was a Kur.

I found this, in its way, of course, quite disconcerting. An
entire architecture of explanatory hypotheses, of judicious
speculations, had collapsed. It seemed now that neither Priest-
Kings nor Kurii had any special connection with Brundisium.
What then could be the explanation for the attempt on my life in
Port Kar, and for the obvious interest of certain parties in
Brundisium in me? What, if anything, could be my importance
to them? What, too, was the meaning of the messages I had
intercepted? They had apparently been intended for certain parties in Ar. I understood nothing. I did not know what to think.
One thing, of course, was quite clear. I was in a cell in Brundisium,
at the disposition of my captors.

I withdrew from the window, and leaped down to the floor. I
looked back again at the high window; then I put the table back
in the center of the cell. I put it between two benches. In such a
cell, a humane one as Gorean cells went, the table and benches
served a practical purpose. They helped to keep food out of the
reach of urts, and, at night, could be used for sleeping.

"Back against the wall, on your knees!" said a voice.

The representative of the urt people and I complied. It was
time to be fed.

The first day in this captivity I had lurked near the bars,
hoping to be able to get my hands on the jailer. I had, in
consequence of this, not been fed that day. I obeyed promptly
enough the next day. I wanted the food. The evening of my
second day in this captivity, which was the fourth following my
capture, the representative of the urt people had been thrust in
with me. I did not much welcome his company. He was, however,
familiar with the routines of the prison.

The jailer looked into the cell. "The table has been moved,"
he said. He could tell this, I assumed, from the markings in the
dust on the floor. It had not occurred to me that there might be
any objection to this. If I had thought there would have been, I
would have posted the representative of the urt people near the

bars and, presumably warned by him in time of any approach on the part of a jailer, replaced the table carefully in its original position. I hoped this new offense, if offense it was, would not result in the withholding of food. I wanted it, what there was of it.

The jailer put the two trays on the floor outside the bars, and, with his foot, thrust them through the low, flat opening, like a flat rectangle, at the base of the latticework of bars. He had not yet left. We could not yet approach the food. "Bosk of Port Kar," he laughed, "kneeling and waiting for food!"

I did not respond to him. I wanted the food. I was pleased that he had not objected to the movement of the table. Then it occurred to me that it was interesting, too, that the table was in the cell. Gorean keepers are not always that considerate of their charges. Why had we not been chained close to the wall, and forced to fight with insects and rodents for our food? Gorean prisoners are seldom pampered, either of the male or female variety. I wondered if the table was in the room for a purpose, perhaps to have permitted me to see what had occurred outside in the courtyard.

The jailer then left.

The representative of the urt people regarded me, narrowly, furtively, fearfully.

I rose to my feet and fetched my food. I put it on the table, and sat down at the table, on one of the benches.

The representative of the urt people then scurried to his food and, by one edge of the tray, with a scraping noise of metal on stone, dragged it quickly over to his straw. He ate hurriedly, watching me carefully. He feared, I suppose, that I might take his food from him. To be sure, it would not have been difficult to do, had I wished to do so.

There was then a growling in the corridor outside of the bars, and a scratching of claws on stone. I also heard several men and the sound of arms. In a moment or two the Kur from the courtyard below, no longer dragging the part of a sleen, perhaps having finished it, or having had it dragged from him, was ushered past our cell, and prodded, its ropes then removed, a chain still on its neck, into a cell down the way. It had moved slowly past us, slowly and stiffly, as though in great pain. It now, now that it was no longer fighting for its life, seemed exhausted and weak. Much of its fur was matted with dried blood. I did not think it would be likely to survive another such bout in the courtyard. As it had passed our cell it had looked in at me. In its eyes there had been baleful hatred. I was human.

I looked back at the representative of the urt people. He suddenly scurried back to his straw, crouching on it, looking up at me. He had been approaching the table quite closely. He had finished his meal. It seemed reasonable to suppose then that he had intended, or hoped, his own food gone, to steal some of mine, that to be accomplished while my attention was distracted by the passage of the Kur in the hall. I smiled. The little creature was doubtless indeed familiar with the routines, the possibilities and opportunities, of prison life.

It turned its eyes away from mine, not wanting to meet them. It pretended to be examining its straw for lice.

It was one of the urt people. It had a narrow, elongated face and rather large, ovoid eyes. It was narrow-shouldered and narrow-chested. It had long, thin arms and short, spindly legs. It commonly walked, or hurried, bent over, its knuckles often on the ground, its head often moving from side to side. This low gait commonly kept it inconspicuous among the large, migratory urt packs with which it commonly moved. Sometimes such packs pass civilized areas and observers are not even aware of the urt people traveling with them. The urt packs provide them with cover and protection. For some reason, not clear to me at that time, the urts seldom attack them. Sometimes it would rear up, straightly, unexpectedly, looking about itself, and then drop back to a smaller, more bent-over position. It was capable of incredible stillness and then sudden, surprising bursts of movement.

I made a small clicking noise, to attract its attention. Immediately, alertly, it turned its head toward me.

I beckoned for it to approach.

It suddenly reared upright, quizzically.

"Come here," I said, beckoning to it.

When it stood upright it was about three and a half feet tall.

"Do not be afraid," I said. I took a slice of hard larma from my tray. This is a firm, single-seeded, applelike fruit. It is quite unlike the segmented, juicy larma. It is sometimes called, and perhaps more aptly, the pit fruit, because of its large single stone. I held it up so that he could see it. The urt people, I understood, were fond of pit fruit. Indeed, it was for having stolen such fruit from a state orchard that he had been incarcerated. He had been netted, put in a sack and brought here. That had been more than six months ago. I had learned these things from the jailer when he had thrust the creature in with me. The creature approached, warily. Then it lifted its long arm and pointed a long index finger at the fruit. "Bet! Bet!" it said. "Pay! Pay!"

"No," I said. "I made no bet with you." It was referring, I gathered, to the Kur baiting which had taken place this morning in the courtyard, visible from our window. It had probably picked up the expressions from the crowd. I did not know if it understood the concepts of betting and paying or not.

"I do not owe this to you," I said. "It is mine."

The creature shrank back a bit, frightened.

"But I might give it to you," I said.

It looked at me.

I broke off a piece of the pit fruit and handed it to him. He ate it quickly, watching me.

"Come here," I said. "Up here." I indicated the surface of the table.

He leapt up to the surface of the table, squatting there.

I broke off another bit of the hard fruit and handed it to him. "What is your name?" I asked.

He uttered a kind of hissing squeal. I supposed that might be his name. The urt people, as I understood it, commonly communicate among themselves in the pack by means of such signals. How complicated or sophisticated those signals might be I did not know. They did tend to resemble the natural noises of urts. In this I supposed they tended to make their presence among the urts less obvious to outside observers and perhaps, too, less obvious, or obtrusive, to the urts themselves. Too, however, I knew the urt people could, and did upon occasion, as in their rare contacts with civilized folk, communicate in a type of Gorean, many of the words evidencing obvious linguistic corruptions but others, interestingly, apparently closely resembling archaic Gorean, a language not spoken popularly on Gor, except by members of the caste of Initiates, for hundreds of years. I had little difficulty, however, in understanding him. He seemed an intelligent creature, and his Gorean was doubtless quite different from the common trade Gorean of the urt people. It had doubtless been much refined and improved in the prison. The urt people learn quickly. They are rational. Some people keep them as pets. I think they are, or at one time were, a form of human being. Probably long ago, as some forms of urts became commensals with human beings, so, too, some humans may have become commensals, traveling companions, sharers at the same table, so to speak, with the migratory urt packs.

"What do they call you here?" I asked.

"Nim, Nim," it said.

"I am called Bosk," I said.

"Bosk, Bosk," it said. "Nice Bosk. Pretty Bosk. More larma! More larma!"

I gave the creature more of the hard larma.

"Good Bosk, nice Bosk," it said.

I handed it another bit of larma.

"Bosk want escape?" it asked.

"Yes," I said.

"Bad men want do terrible thing to Bosk," it said.

"What?" I asked.

"Nim Nim afraid talk," it said.

I did not press the creature.

"Few cells have table," it said, fearfully. "Bosk not chained."

I nodded. "I think I understand," I said. Not being chained, and because of the table, I had been able to witness the cruel spectacle in the courtyard. That I supposed now, given the hints of the small creature, was perhaps intended to give me something to think about. I shuddered. Much hatred must I be borne in this place.

"More larma!" said the creature. "More larma!"

I gave it some more larma. There was not much left. "They intend to use me in the baiting pit," I speculated.

"No," said the creature. "Worse. Far worse. Nim Nim help."

"I don't understand," I said.

"Bosk want escape?" it asked.

"Yes," I said.

"More larma," it said. "More larma!"

I gave it the last of the larma.

"Bosk want escape?" it asked.

"Yes," I said.

"Nim Nim help," it said.

14

THE URTS;
HOW NIM NIM WAS MADE
WELCOME IN THE PACK;
THE WARRIOR'S PACE

"There!" squealed the small creature. "There! There! The people! Nim Nim escape! Nim Nim free!"

We had emerged through a cut between two rocky outcroppings and ascended a small hill. It was near the tenth Ahn, the Gorean noon. We had left the city, emerging well beyond the walls early this morning. We were naked. The lower portion of my body was covered with dirt and blood from our trek through the brush. It, too, had been cut from the stones and sides of the narrow sewers through which we had made our way. "Nim Nim good urt," he had told me. "Urts find way!"

"Strip, enter the cubicle of the bathing cisterns," had said our jailer, five of his fellows, armed, behind him, before dawn. "Wash your stinking bodies, then emerge."

Our chains, in this area below the prison, had been removed.

"Why?" I asked.

"Obey," he had said.

I was puzzled about this. The luxury of baths is seldom permitted to Gorean prisoners, whether they are of the male or female sort. To be sure, a girl will usually be scrubbed up and made presentable before she is brought up for sale.

Perhaps they had something special in mind for us.

I saw the menacing movement of weapons.

We stripped.

"Leave your clothing here," said the jailer. "Enter the cubicle of the bathing cisterns."

We were prodded with the points of spears through a heavy wooden door.

"Wash well," called a man, laughing.

"We would not wish your stink to offend the crowds," laughed another man.

Immediately I thought of the baiting pit, and the screaming, betting, enthusiastic crowds there. But Nim Nim had told me that it was something far worse than this which they had planned for me.

"Have pity on poor sleen," laughed a man.

"You would not want to make them sick, would you?" asked another. That was, I suppose, very funny. The sleen is one of the least fastidious of Gorean animals. It commonly makes the tarsk, usually thought of as a filthy animal, seem like an epicure. I thought again, of course, from these comments, of the baiting pit in the courtyard.

The heavy door of the cubicle of the bathing cistern closed behind us. I heard it locked. It was very dark inside. There was a little light coming from under the door. There was a bit more light coming from somewhere high above, through some sort of narrow, shuttered aperture.

"It is hard to see," I said.

"Nim Nim see," said the small beast, clutching at my wrist with both of its hands. It began to pull me through the room. Once my foot splashed into the shallow concave approach to a cistern. There was a smell in the place. This area, I suspected, was probably more in the nature of a sump beneath the prison than a bath. In a few moments my eyes could make out things reasonably well. The eyes of the urt people, I gathered, adjusted very quickly to darkness. This may be an adaptive specialization, having to do with the fact that urt packs are often active at night.

"Here, here," said the small creature, eagerly. It pulled me to a grating in the floor. "Nim Nim not strong enough!"

I fixed my hands about the bars of the grating. I pulled at it. It seemed very solidly anchored in the cement. It did pull up a bit at one edge. It was extremely heavy. I was not surprised that the small creature could not move it. I wondered if many men could have moved it.

"Pull! Pull!" said Nim Nim.

"I cannot move it," I said.

"Pull! Pull!" said Nim Nim.

I crouched down, getting my legs under me. Then, largely using the force of my legs, pushing up with them, I pulled against the bars. The side which had lifted before a bit, now, a little at a time, to my elation, with small sounds of loosening, breaking mortar, rose upward. The mortar, perhaps, in years of drainage here, if the area did function largely as a sump for the prison, might have been loosened.

"See! See!" whispered Nim Nim.

I thrust the heavy grating, loose now, to the side.

Nim Nim scuttled into the dark, circular crevice. In a moment, half sickened by the stench, my body moving against the slimy sides of the opening, I followed him.

We stood now, in the neighborhood of noon, on a small hill, some pasangs from the walls of Brundisium. We had emerged through rocky outcroppings below. There was much stone in this area. It could have been quarried. Much of this stone, in its great surrounding, irregular alignments, seemed almost to form the cerrated ridge of some vast, ancient, natural bowl, now muchly crumbled and weathered. These outcroppings, with their breaks and openings, encircled an area perhaps more than two pasangs in width. Guided by Nim Nim, who had sometimes ridden upon my back, and other times upon my shoulders, I had come to this place. Now he had leaped down from my shoulders. "Nim Nim safe now!" he cried, pointing downward into the shallow, muchly encircled valley below. In that broad, sweeping, concave area I could see what Nim Nim called the "people." Never before had I seen an urt pack that huge. It must have contained four or five thousand animals.

"Hold!" called a voice, authoritatively.

I turned suddenly, swiftly about.

"Good trick! Good trick!" cried Nim Nim. "Nim Nim good urt! No pit for Bosk! Worse! Much worse! Nim Nim help! Nim Nim help!"

I felt sick. I remembered his words in the cell. I had not immediately understood, I had then supposed that he meant to help me escape, as indeed, clearly, later, seemed to be the intent of his words. Now I understood that it had been no accident he had been put in with me. He had been, from the beginning, the partisan of my enemies.

"Nim Nim help!" he cried, delightedly. "Nim Nim help! Nim Nim good urt! Now Nim Nim free!"

"Kneel, Bosk of Port Kar," said Flaminius. I knelt. With Flaminius were the jailer, and his other fellows. Several had set crossbows trained on me. More importantly, one held the leashes of three snarling sleen.

"He looks well, naked and on his knees, Bosk of Port Kar, before men of Brundisium," said the jailer.

"Are you of Brundisium?" I asked Flaminius.

"I am in the fee of Brundisium," he said. "But I am of Ar."

I did not understand the sort of triumph which seemed to characterize the voice of the jailer. The alliances of Brundisium were with Ar, not Tyros or Cos. I measured the distance between myself and the jailer. I wondered how long it would take to break his neck. I did not think I could reach him before the quarrels of crossbows would lodge themselves in my body. I was not a female, joyfully, rightfully, on her knees before men. The accent of Flaminius, now that I thought of it, did have traces within it which suggested Ar. To be sure, these things are sometimes difficult to determine with accuracy. It was certainly not obviously an accent of Ar. If he was of Ar, he had probably been out of the city for years.

"I thought you were to have had a bath," smiled Flaminius. "Instead it seems you are in desperate need of one."

I did not respond to him.

"Did you enjoy your trip, crawling through the slime sewers of Brundisium?" he asked.

I did not speak.

"To be sure, your journey in the open-air and sun has doubtless removed some of the stink from you."

Several of the men behind him laughed.

"Even now, men are repairing the various gratings which we loosened or removed for your convenience, as well as narrowing several of the conduits."

I regarded him.

"Oh, yes," he said, "this has all been well planned."

"Would it not have been simpler to slay me in the prison?" I asked.

"Simpler, yes," said Flaminius, "but far less amusing."

"I see," I said.

"The arrangements in your cell, its location, and so on, were intended to encourage you to be apprehensive, and to think about escape."

"I do not think I needed much encouragement," I said.

"Apparently not," he said. "We noticed, of course, that you did not use your bedding. That was clever of you. Without something of that sort it is harder, of course, to set sleen on your trail.''

"I thought you might intend to use me in the baiting pit," I said.

"Of course," said Flaminius. "Indeed, it was intended that you should fear that. On the other hand, it did not seem politically expedient, at least at this time, to have Bosk of Port Kar, that being a city theoretically neutral to Brundisium, publicly slaughtered in one of our baiting pits.''

"I would suppose not," I admitted. Some of the men of Brundisium, several functionaries and soldiers, for example, and guards in the prison, were familiar with my identity. Under such circumstances it would surely be difficult to conceal it from a crowd attending a public spectacle.

"Accordingly, we arranged your escape," said Flaminius, "risking nothing, of course."

"Nothing?" I asked.

"Of course not," said Flaminius. "How do you think we followed you so discreetly, allowing you your lead of better than an Ahn, until, at our pleasure, we chose to close the gap and apprehend you here?''

I looked down at the urt pack in the valley below. "I was brought here, deliberately, of course," I said.

"Of course," said Flaminius. "But even if you had not chosen to follow our little friend's advice in this matter, we could have apprehended you easily anywhere in the vicinity, and then brought you here, as we wished.''

"The sleen," I said.

"Certainly," he said. "Look." He signaled to one of the men standing by the fellow with the sleen. He drew forth from a sack the ragged tunic I had worn in the cell.

"Clever," I said.

Outside the entrance to the cubicle of the bathing cisterns, before being prodded within by the spears of our keepers, Nim Nim and I had been forced to strip. We had then been herded into the darkness and the door closed and locked behind us. It had all seemed very natural. I now realized that it had been part of the plan of Flaminius. After the door had been closed behind us the clothing, or at least mine, had doubtless been taken down to the sleen pens. Then it was only necessary, later, to pick up our trail outside the city, at the termination of one of the conduits, where it would empty into one of the long, half-dry drainage ditches about a half pasang outside the walls.

"Look," grinned Flaminius, and he signaled again to the fellow who held the rags I had worn.

He held them near the sleen. Instantly, furiously, snarling, they seized the garment, tugging and tearing at it.

"Enough!" said Flaminius.

The fellow freed the garment from the sleen, shouting at them, half tearing it away from them. Even though he was their keeper and they were doubtless trained to obey him, and perhaps only him, it was not easy for him to regain the garment.

Flaminius then took the garment, and looked at me. "Behold, Bosk of Port Kar," he laughed, "naked and kneeling before us, outwitted, terrified into the desire for escape, then led to believe his escape was successful, then his hopes dashed, now realizing how he was never out of our grasp. Behold the stupid, outwitted fool!"

I was silent.

"Are you not curious as to your fate?" he asked.

"Yes," I said.

Flaminius then threw me the garment he had taken from the sleen keeper. It was in shreds, little more than dangling tatters, from the teeth of the ravaging, contesting sleen. "Put it on," he said. "No, do not rise. Draw it on as you kneel."

The men laughed at me as I knelt before them then, a few dangling tatters about my neck and body. The sleen eyed me eagerly.

"Would not the stroke of the sword be quicker?" I asked.

"Yes, but not as amusing," said Flaminius.

"Perhaps you should draw back, that you not be injured in the charge of the sleen," I suggested.

"Remain kneeling," he warned me.

"I am somewhat mystified about many things," I said. "Perhaps this is an opportune moment to request an explanation. May I inquire, accordingly, what might be your interest in me, or that of your party? Why, for example, was the fellow named Babinius sent against me in Port Kar? What was the point of that? Similarly, why should there have been an interest in Brundisium in my apprehension? Who, or what, in Brundisium, has this interest in me, and why?"

"You would like me to respond to your questions, would you not?" he asked.

"Yes," I said.

"I do not choose to do so," he said.

I clenched my fists. Those with him laughed.

"But do not think that we are not capable of acts of incredible kindness, or that mercy is beyond our ken," he said.

"Oh?" I said.

"We are willing to permit you a choice of fates," he said. "And we are willing to give you a certain amount of time, to agonize over them."

"I do not understand," I said.

"Surely you do not think it is an accident that we used our little friend here in our plans? Surely you do not think it is a mere coincidence that you have been brought to this place?"

"I suppose not," I said. I shuddered.

Nim Nim leaped up and down gleefully. "Nim Nim help. Nim Nim good urt!" he squealed.

"Go, little urt," said Flaminius, kindly. "Run to your people."

"Nim Nim smart!" it cried. "Nim Nim trick pretty Bosk!"

"Hurry home, little urt," said Flaminius, kindly.

Nim Nim looked up at me with his ovoid eyes, set in that small, elongated face. "Worse than pit," he said to me, "worse, far worse. Nim Nim help. Nim Nim trick pretty Bosk. Too bad, pretty Bosk!"

"Hurry, hurry," urged Flaminius.

Nim Nim scampered down the grassy slope toward the huge urt pack in the distance. Flaminius laughed. So, too, did some of the others. The laughter was not pleasant.

"You will now turn about, slowly, on your knees," said Flaminius to me. "You will then rise slowly and slowly descend the hill. You will go to the edge of the urt pack. We will remain, for a time, here on the hill. You will be under our observation at all times. If you should attempt to run or move to one side, as though thinking of skirting the pack, we will immediately release the sleen. You must then, if you wish, enter the urt pack. If you do not wish to do this we will, after a time, release the sleen, and they will set upon you wherever they find you. Is this all clear?"

"Yes," I said.

"I wonder what you will choose," said Flaminius.

"I bet he will enter the pack," said one of the men.

"I wager he will wait for the sleen," said another.

"Do not permit us to sway your decision," said Flaminius, "but it has been our usual experience in similar situations, that the individual involved waits until the sleen are almost upon him and then, seemingly almost uncontrollably, runs into the pack.

To be sure, it would probably have been better for him if he had waited for the sleen."

"Sleen are quicker," said one of the men.

"Few have the courage, however, to wait for them," said another.

"What will you do, Bosk of Port Kar?" asked Flaminius.

"I do not know," I said.

"An excellent answer," said Flaminius. "Many men think they know what they will do, but when the moment comes it seems it does not always turn out as they expected. Sometimes he who thinks he is brave learns he is a coward, and sometimes, too, I suppose, he who thought himself a coward learns that he is brave."

I turned away from them, slowly, on my knees, and then rose to my feet.

"Slowly, slowly now," said Flaminius.

I began to walk slowly down the hill, toward the urt pack. Nim Nim had not yet entered it. I supposed he might be waiting to see what I might do.

I went to within a few yards of the edge of the pack. Most of the animals did not pay me any attention. A few regarded me suspiciously. I did not, of course, infringe the perimeter of their group, or approach within a critical distance. I looked back to the crest of that low hill. I could see Flaminius there, and his men, and the sleen. I had a few Ehn, doubtless, before they were released. I was supposed to be spending that time, it seemed, agonizingly pondering which fate I would choose for myself. Needless to say, I was not enthusiastic about either of the obvious alternatives. I looked at the urt pack. I had never seen one so large. It contained a very large number of animals. The smell of it even was oppressive. I looked to the ends of the pack; they extended for about a quarter of a pasang on either side of me. If I were to run for them the sleen, doubtless, would be immediately freed. They could be upon me in a matter of Ihn. I looked across the pack. It was some two or three hundred yards across. I did not think that even sleen would be able to make it through them. No, it did not seem likely that even sleen could make it through such a dense thicket of large, vicious creatures. I fingered the tattered garment I wore. Sleen, I knew, are indefatigable hunters, fearless, tenacious trackers, very tenacious trackers.

I looked over to Nim Nim, a few yards from me, much closer to the pack. He was obviously prepared, if I approached him, to dart into the pack.

"Nim Nim safe here!" he called. He pointed to the pack. "The people do not hurt Nim Nim!"

I wondered if somewhere in that vast pack of animals there might be other representatives of the urt people. If there were, however, they were keeping themselves concealed. They do not always stay with the pack, of course, but almost always they remain in its vicinity, seldom gone from it for long. Nim Nim, as I recalled, had been netted in a state orchard.

"Are you sure these are your people?" I asked, curious about the matter. Urts looked much alike from my point of view. To be sure, I supposed one could come to distinguish them individually after a time.

"Yes," said Nim Nim proudly. "There is," and he made a whistling sound, "and there is," and there again he made a piping, hissing, whistling noise, pointing out two urts. "And there is" he said, adding in another noise, "our leader!" He had indicated a large, dark-furred, broken-tusked urt, a gigantic creature for this type of animal, with small eyes and a silvered snout.

I did not doubt that Nim Nim knew what he was talking about. This was surely his pack. There could be no doubt about it.

"The people tear Bosk to pieces!" called Nim Nim. "The people do not hurt Nim Nim! Nim Nim is of the people. Nim Nim safe!"

I looked back at the crest of the hill. The sleen had not yet been released.

"Nim Nim trick pretty Bosk!" he said. "Nim Nim smart! Nim Nim free now! Nim Nim safe!"

I wondered how it was that the urt people could travel with the urt packs. I knew that even strange urts were often torn to pieces when they attempted to approach a new pack. How, then, could the urt people, who were obviously human, or something like human, run with impunity with them? It made no sense. But there must be an explanation, a reason, I thought, some sort of empirical, scientific explanation or reason. Perhaps something had been selected for, somehow, in the recognition and acceptance dispositions of the urt people and the packs. I saw the leader of the pack, he identified as that by Nim Nim, looking at me. I doubted that it could see me too well. Urts tend to be myopic. He had his nose lifted toward me. I saw it twitching and sniffing. Suddenly the hair rose on the back of my neck. "Do not enter the pack!" I called out to Nim Nim. "Don't!"

"Pretty Bosk want to hurt Nim Nim!" he cried. He moved toward the pack.

"Don't go into the pack!" I cried out to him. "I am staying

here! I am not approaching! I will not hurt you! Do not enter the
pack!"

Nim Nim had been caught in a state orchard. He had been
imprisoned in Brundisium. That had been at least six months
ago. I remembered the laughter of the men on the hill, as Nim
Nim had hurried down to join the pack. Too, I thought of the
stately, delicate, golden Priest-Kings in their tunneled recesses
and chambers underlying the Sardar Mountains. "Do not enter
the pack!" I cried.

Nim Nim darted into the pack.

"No!" I cried. It seemed almost as though he was wading in
beasts. Then the animals seemed to draw apart about him and he
was left standing as though in a dry pool, an empty place, an
isolated, lonely place surrounded by tawny waters, waters which
seemed somehow, inexplicably, to have drawn back about him,
waters with eyes and teeth, ringing him. I saw that he did not
understand what was going on.

"Come out!" I called to him. "Come out, while you can!"

Eyes regarded him on all sides. I saw those narrow, elongated
snouts lifted towards him, the nostrils twitching and flaring.

Nim Nim began to utter reassuring noises to the urts. He
began to whistle and hiss at them. In this fashion I supposed the
urt people might speak with one another. Perhaps, too, some of
these were signals used by the urts themselves. The animals, I
could see, were becoming more and more excited. They were
now quivering. There was an almost feverish intensity in their
reactions.

"Come out!" I called to him.

There was suddenly from one of the urts an angry, intense,
shrill, high-pitched, hideous squeal. In an instant, almost like an
electric shock, a movement seemed to course through the animals in the circle. Indeed, this tremorlike reaction, like a shock,
seemed to move through the entire pack. Its passage's swift
route was actually visible in the animals, like a wave spreading
along, and registered in, their backs and fur, in their sudden
stillness, then in the sudden alertness of them, then in the
quivering agitation which seemed to transform the entire pack,
hitherto seemingly so tranquil, suddenly into a restless, roiling
lake of ugly energy.

"Come out!" I screamed at him.

Another animal in the circle ringing Nim Nim now took up
that angry, hideous, ear-splitting squeal, then another, and another.
They began to quiver uncontrollably; their eyes bulged in their
sockets; their fur erected, with a crackle of static electricity; their

ears laid back, flattened, against the sides of their heads. Every animal in that vast pack was now oriented toward that location, that sound. Several of the other animals began to press eagerly toward the sound, some even crawling and scrambling over the backs of others. Every animal in that circle about Nim Nim had now taken up that horrifying squeal. It, too, was now being taken up by the entire pack. It reverberated in the area, striking against the nearby cliffs, the stones and outcroppings, rebounding, resounding, again and again in that natural bowl, torturing the ear, tearing and shocking the air, seeming as though it must afright and terrify even the clouds themselves, which seemed to flee before it, perhaps even the sky, and a world. I suspected it could be heard in distant Brundisium.

I cupped my hands to my mouth. "Come out!" I screamed.

"I cannot!" he screamed.

The animals then charged, swarming in upon him. He tried to run between them, to reach the edge of the pack. I saw him fall twice, and each time get up. By the time he came near the edge of the pack he had lost a foot and a hand. He could not now fall, however, because of the animals pressing about him. Several had their teeth fastened in his body, tearing at him, eating. By the time he was within a few feet of me he had lost half of his face. His head rolled wildly on his shoulders. I was not even sure he was still alive then until I saw his eyes. In fury I sprang towards him, tearing urts back and away from him. I caught some by the scruff of the neck and others by the hind legs and hurled them back into the pack. Tearing at him they seemed oblivious of me. I was among them. I caught one and thrusting my arms under its forelegs and clasping my hands together behind its neck, broke its neck. I threw it behind me. Other urts pressed forward, many of them squealing and trying to clamber over their fellows, in order to reach what was now left of Nim Nim. I then, my legs brushing against urts, backed from the pack. I saw, between pressing tawny bodies, parts of Nim Nim being dragged backwards, back into the pack. I now stood, breathing heavily, at the edge of the pack. I trembled. I threw up into the grass.

Clearly, as I now understood, the recognition and acceptance disposition of the pack was connected with smell. There must be, in effect, a pack odor. If something had this it would be accepted. If it lacked it, it would not be accepted. Indeed, the lack of the pack odor apparently triggered the attack response. The hideous squeal which was so terrifying, so shrill and piercing, which had such an effect on the other animals, was presumably something like a stranger-in-our-midst signal, a stranger-recognition signal, so to speak. It, too, presumably, was intimately involved in the pack's general response, its defense response, or stranger-rejection response, so to speak. Clearly, it played a role in calling forth the attack response, or in transmitting its message to the other members of the pack.

I looked at the pack. It was now relatively calm. There was no sign of Nim Nim.

I looked back to the men at the crest of the hill. They had not yet released the sleen. Perhaps they wanted me to have a bit more time to think about things, a bit more time to anticipate what might occur to me, before they released the animals.

I looked back at the pack. The matter had to do with odor, I was sure. That would explain why a strange urt, though even of the pack's own species, would be fallen upon and killed if it attempted to join the pack. That explained, too, why Nim Nim had no longer been accepted. In his time in prison, some six months or so, he would have lost the pack odor. The Priest-Kings, I recalled, had recognized who was "of the Nest," and who was not, by means of the Nest odor. This odor is acquired, of course, after time is spent in the nest. Similarly, I supposed, the pack odor would be acquired after some time in the pack. How, I wondered, did the first of the urt people gain admittance to their packs. I suspected it had occurred hundreds of years ago. Some very clever individual, or individuals, must have suspected the mechanisms involved. They might then have considered how they might be circumvented. This secret, in the successive generations, might have been lost to the urt people, or, perhaps, it had been deliberately allowed to vanish in time by the discoverers of the secret, that others could not reveal it, or take advantage of it, to their detriment. Now, I supposed, the urt people, their children and such, would simply grow up with the packs, thinking perhaps that this was just the way things had been, inexplicably, or naturally, from time immemorial. Yet is it not likely, I pondered, there would once have been a reason, or reasons. Surely it is not always to be assumed that it is a mere inexplicable fact, a simple, brute given, something not to be inquired into, that things are as they now are. Might there not be a reason why grass is green, and the sky blue? Might there not be a reason for the movement of the winds and the rotation of the night sky, and a reason, say, why men are as they are, and women as they are?

I suddenly leapt to the beast whose neck I had broken. I looked to the men on the hill. They had not yet released the sleen. I tore away a tusk, breaking it loose, from the side of the jaw of the dead animal. Then, feverishly, with a will, I thrust it through its pelt and, pulling and tearing, using my hands, and teeth, as well, I began to remove its skin. Perhaps they would think I had gone mad. Yet I did not think it would take Flaminius long to grasp my intent.

I looked wildly back to the crest of the hill. Already the sleen, unleashed, were racing down the grassy slope.

I continued my work.

I tore loose part of the skin. I ran the side of my hand, like a knife, between it and organs and hot fat. I put my foot on the rib cage and, pressing down, then releasing the pressure, then pressing down, and releasing again, I turned the rib cage, drawing the pelt, rip by rip, away from it. I turned again to see the progress of the sleen. They could be upon me now in but Ihn. I could see their eagerness, their eyes. I tore the pelt mostly away from the animal. I had no time to remove the lolling, dangling head. With my foot, thrusting, I removed most of the remaining body and entrails from the hide, and clutching it, with both hands, wrapping it about my hips, I entered the pack.

Part of the hide was still warm on my skin. It was wet and sticky about me. My legs and thighs were bloody from it. I wedged between urts. Their fur was warm and oily. I felt their ribs through it, the movement of muscles beneath it. Noses pushed toward me. I pushed on, fighting to make my way through the bodies. Almost at the same instant the sleen reached the pack and plunged toward me. One climbed over the bodies of the closely packed urts, snapping and snarling. Its jaws came within a foot of me, and then it fell between the startled urts, it spinning about then, confused. I kept pushing through the urts, toward the other side of the pack, more than a hundred and fifty yards away. Behind me I suddenly heard again that hideous squeal of an urt, once more the stranger-recognition signal.

The sleen is a tenacious tracker, I told myself. It is a tireless, determined, tenacious tracker. Such thoughts had run through my mind earlier, when I had first come to the edge of the pack. They had then seemed provocatively, somehow significantly, but with no full significance which I had then grasped, lurking, prowling, at the borders of my understanding. Now I realized the thought with which my mind must have then been toying, the marvelous, astounding possibility which at that time I had not fully grasped, that possibility which would have seemed then, had I been fully aware of it, so disappointingly remote, yet so intriguing. But had I not acted upon this understanding, immediately, almost instinctively, whose earlier significance only

now came fully home to me? I had. What had once been only a
hint, a puzzling, intriguing thought which I had scarcely
understood, had, in the thicket of circumstances, in the crisis of
an instant, become a coercive modality of action, that path upon
which one must boldly and irrevocably embark. I had required
only the mechanism of my passage. Given that, everything,
luminously, like the pieces of a puzzle, had fallen into place.
Nothing could follow me through the urts. Nothing, not even
sleen.

I pressed on. Behind me I heard the intensification and multi-
plication of the squeals. The sleen is a tenacious tracker. In its
way it is an admirable animal. It does not give up; it will not
retreat. I turned about to look back. I could see three swarming
locations in the pack, almost as though gigantic tawny insects
infested the area, clambering about atop each other. I saw a sleen
rearing up on its hind legs, its shoulders and head emergent from
the hill of swarming, clambering urts. An urt was clutched
lifeless in its jaws. It shook it savagely. Then it fell back under
the urts, and I could no longer see it. I pushed on. Then I could
not move farther. Too many urts, seemingly intent upon me,
crowded about me. I was ringed. Then it seemed I stood in a
clear place, an open place, an empty place, a central place,
almost like a dry, lonely pool, separated out from, isolated in the
midst of, those tawny bodies. I did not move. Necks craned
towards me, noses twitching and sniffing. I did not move.

Through the bodies an urt came pressing towards me. It was a
large urt, darkly furred. It had one tusk broken at the side of its
jaw. It was about four feet high at the shoulder, extremely large
for this type of animal. It had a silvered snout. I recognized it. It
was the urt Nim Nim had earlier identified as the leader of the
pack. It began to sniff me, its nose moving and twitching.

"Tal, ugly brute," I said softly.

I turned, keeping it in sight as it circled me, sniffing. Then it
had completed its circuit. Those small, myopic eyes peered up at
me.

"You are a stinking, ugly brute," I whispered.

It sniffed me again, beginning at my feet and then lifting its
head until it seemed, again, to look me in the eyes. When it had
lowered its head I had lowered the pelt I grasped, holding it
about me, that it might be near its nose. When it had lifted its
head I had raised the pelt, too, keeping it safely between us. It
did not seem much concerned with the head of the urt, which
was still, by the skin, attached to the pelt. Its responses in this
situation I assumed, I trusted, I hoped, would be activated almost

exclusively by smell, and not by the smell of blood, or human, but by the smell of the pelt, by the pack odor.

I breathed a sigh of relief. It had turned away. The animals now returned to their business. Again was the pack tranquil, save where some animals, here and there, fed on sleen.

"Farewell, ugly brute," I said.

I then began, again, to press through the urts, wading through the pack. Once, a few yards before me and to my right, I saw a small, elongated head rise up suddenly, peering at me. Then, as suddenly as it had appeared, it disappeared. Again, then, I could see only the animals. This was the only concrete sign I had to suggest that there might be urt people traveling with the pack.

In a moment or two, now, I had emerged on the other side of the pack. I could see Flaminius, and his men, on the other side of the pack, quite near, now, to its edge. I observed them for a time. I watched while two or three crossbow quarrels, their energy spent in the distance, looped over the pack and fell short of me. Then they turned about, hurrying back the way they had come. They perhaps had tharlarion somewhere. I then turned, and climbed through the broken, cerrated edges of this natural stone bowl, found myself in the open fields, and began to run, with the long, slow warrior's pace, that pace in which warriors are trained, that pace which may be maintained, even under the weight of weapons, accouterments and a shield, for pasangs.

15

WHAT OCCURRED IN THE CAMP OF BOOTS TARSK-BIT

"Here he is!" cried Boots. "We have caught him for you!"

Lecchio and Chino held my arms.

In a moment, led by Boots, running, puffing, at the side of them, with a swirl of dust from the paws of the tharlarion, they were in the camp, the riders.

"Sleen! Sleen!" I cried to those of the troupe of Boots Tarsk-Bit.

The tharlarion now swirled about me.

I shook Chino and Lecchio violently in the swirling dust, my head down, almost dislodging them from me. But they retained their grip.

"Hold him! Hold him!" cried the Lady Yanina. "Do not let him escape!"

"Have no fear! He is in the keeping of Boots Tarsk-Bit," called Boots, "actor, promoter, entrepreneur and friend to the noble citizens of Brundisium!" He then approached me, carrying manacles. "It is you who are the sleen," he cried. Then he said to Chino and Lecchio, "Pull the sleen's hands behind him!" This was done, and the manacles were snapped on me. Chino and Lecchio, however, continued to hold my arms. Petrucchio, with the great wooden sword he used in playing the parts of the "Captain," stood resolutely by. Publius Andronicus stood near, a look of great satisfaction on his face. The player stood a bit away, his arms folded, dispassionately observing the proceedings.

Rowena, Lady Telitsia and Bina knelt in terror to one side, slaves, fearful in the presence of free persons, trembling in the face of this sudden invasion of the camp. Besides her collar, which was Boots's, to whom she belonged, Bina wore a slave bracelet. It had been put on her wrist by the player, whose bracelet it was, signifying that her use was his.

I pulled at the manacles. "Do not attempt to free yourself, fool," said Boots. "You have been manacled by Boots Tarsk-Bit!"

"Well done, friend to Brundisium!" cried Lady Yanina.

Boots bowed low to the Lady Yanina and then, beaming, handed her the key to the manacles. She seized it, laughing, and lifted it, in triumph, showing it to her men.

"I thought you might return here!" she said to me, in triumph, brandishing the key at me. "Flaminius did not think so! He is looking elsewhere! He is scouring the countryside! 'He would not be so much a fool as to return there,' he laughed at me. But I am more clever than he, a thousand times more clever! I thought that just for such a reason you would dare to return here, the one place most would be sure you would not go! I was right! I begged men and tharlarion from Belnar! Almost against his better judgment he granted them to me. We rode here, in all haste. My judgment is vindicated! Let Flaminius writhe in envy! It is I who was right! It is I who am triumphant! You are my prisoner, my prisoner alone, Bosk of Port Kar, the prisoner of the Lady Yanina!" Again she brandished the key at me, I looking up at her, she on the tharlarion. Then, laughing, she dropped the key triumphantly into the bosom of her garment.

"Your face is naked," I said.

"Stand away from him!" she cried. Then she drew forth a coiled whip from beside her saddle and struck me with it twice.

"Your legs look well," I said.

Again she struck me, and then again.

"I note that you have not yet been permitted footwear," I said. Her feet, bare in the stirrups of the saddle, were dark with dirt, as were her lower legs, from her ride. Her legs did indeed look well, covered with dust though they might be, shapely against the leather of the saddle, and the thick, scaled hide of the tharlarion. The skirt she had been permitted was almost slave short and was cut at the sides. She had not been permitted sleeves in the garment. She was attractive. Probably most men would have wanted to clean her up a bit before using her. It was interesting to conjecture what she might look like washed and combed, and perfumed, and put in a bit of slave silk, and appropriately collared, of course. The skirt she wore, though it

came high on her thighs, and was cut at the sides, had a very
high waist, its belting cord cinched just under her breasts. Yes,
altogether it was a fetching ensemble. Men who had an eye for
women must have designed it and she, doubtless, had been given
no choice but to wear it. It was opaque, of course. That was
surely a concession to her status, that of the free woman. If I
came to own her I thought I might give her a similar garment,
but one of diaphanous silk. Too, I might shorten it a bit. The
inmates of such garments, incidentally, suitably collared, of
course, also look well bedecked with barbaric Gorean slave
jewelry, but soon they are begging, object strenuously to
such jewelry, but they are begging for it. Her hair, I noted,
was loose. This was also doubtless meaningful. Slaves must
often wear their hair in such a fashion.

She struck me twice more with the whip, wheeling about on
the tharlarion.

"Your hair is loose," I observed.

"Sleen! Sleen!" she screamed.

Again and again the whip fell. I closed my eyes, that I not be
blinded. I was pleased she did not have a man's strength. Then,
sweating, angrily, she replaced the whip at the side of her
saddle.

I grinned up at her. Yes, she would look well, properly
attired, or properly unattired, cringing at my feet in a collar,
knowing that her least discrepancy from the absolute perfections
of slave service would instantly bring down upon her the stroke
of the five-stranded slave lash, or worse.

"Laugh, fool!" she cried. "It is you who are in manacles! It
is you who are my prisoner!"

I looked up at her, not speaking.

"You were the cause of my reduction in rank," she cried.
"You were the cause of my loss of status in Brundisium, my
descent from favor in the eyes of my Ubar, Belnar, the reason I
have been denied the right to conceal my features, my right as a
free female, the reason I have been placed in brief, shameful
garments, forcing me to make clear to men my femaleness, the
reason I may not bind my hair, but must wear it as though it
might be that of a slave, but that is all finished now. Now all
changes! Now, fool, you will be the reason not only for my
restoration to privilege and station in Brundisium, the reason for
my new rise to favor in the court, in the eyes of Belnar, my
Ubar, but the cause, as well, of my attaining there, in the palace
and in the service of my Ubar, and the state, new heights of

prestige, status and power! Let Flaminius weep with envy! I shall be a thousand times higher than he!''

"How is it that you follow a woman?" I asked one of the men with her, he who seemed probably the second in command.

"We follow the orders of Belnar," he said.

"I see," I said. Women, although they may occasionally function as artifacts, or symbols, or mystical objects, or something along these lines, seldom release the following instinct in men. Men, accordingly, do not on the whole, care to follow them. In doing so they generally feel uncomfortable. It makes them uneasy. They sense the absurdity, the unnaturalness, of the relationship. It is thus that normal men commonly follow women only unwillingly, and only with reservations, usually also only within an artificial context or within the confines of a misguided, choiceless or naive institution, where their discipline may be relied upon. Their compliance with orders in such a situation cannot help but be more critical, more skeptical. Their activities tend then to be performed with less confidence, and more hesitantly. This often produces serious consequences to the efficiency of their actions. It is interesting to note that even women seldom care to follow women, particularly in critical situations. The male, biologically, for better or for worse, appears to be the natural leader. In the perversion of nature, of course, anything may occur. It is ironic that certain leaders will place women over subordinates, for one reason or another, whom they would never accept as their own leaders. Most men, of course, find it easier to inflict inconvenience and pain on others than on themselves.

I looked up at the Lady Yanina. How small and soft, and luscious, she was. How absurd then, and how unnatural, seemed her position of power, temporary though it might be, over these men. How envious she seemed of men, particularly of her rival, Flaminius. How she was straining to seem a leader, how she must have studied what she took to be its lessons well, how she must have firmly resolved to act that role with determination. Perhaps if she did it well she could fool men; perhaps, if she did it well, she could boldly carry off the pretence; perhaps, if she did it well, she would be accepted almost as though she were a real leader, a true leader. Perhaps, if she did it well, no one would notice that she was really only a small, soft, shapely, lovely creature, one whose natural destiny would be found quite elsewhere than in the saddle of a tharlarion, at the head of troops.

"You are a despicable sleen," she said to me.

"Doubtless," I said. There was probably much in what she

said. I regarded her. How absurd that she could be in power over these men. They were soldiers. She should be put in her place, the place of the female, kneeling and serving. Perhaps one day someone would put her there, and she would then come to understand finally and profoundly what she was, a female.

"Smile, if you will, for whatever secret reason, fool," she said, "but it is you who wear the manacles, you who are held in irons at my stirrup."

"It would seem so," I said.

"You are my key to power," she said.

How insolent she was, how arrogant.

"Because of you," she said, "my fortunes will be made in Brundisium! Because of you I will climb there to hitherto undreamed of heights!"

"Perhaps," I said.

"It is I who am victorious," she said. "It is I who am triumphant!"

I recalled she had whipped me.

She turned to one of her men, he whom I had taken, apparently rightly, to be her immediate subordinate. "Put a chain on his neck," she said.

"We anticipated that one of your astuteness might not be deceived by the trickery of the fugitive," said Boots, "that you might suspect his bold return to this camp. Accordingly, we seized him and held him for you."

"Our thanks, actor," she said. "Have no fear. You will be rewarded."

Her man unlooped a chain.

"But moreover," said Boots, "we have arranged things in such a way as to enhance your triumph."

"How is that?" she asked, curious.

"That your prisoner, whom I gather is important to you, may be presented with drama, with flair, nothing so common, so mundane and predictable, as being led in like a pet tarsk."

"What do you have in mind?" she asked, interested.

"I envisage a feast," said Boots, "a triumphal feast."

"No," I said, "no!"

"Hold him," suggested Boots, apprehensively, to Chino and Lecchio. They again seized my arms.

"Anyone," said Boots, "could lead him in on a chain. That fellow Flaminius did it that way, as I recall."

"Yes," said the Lady Yanina. Indeed, she had been brought in on a chain by Flaminius at the same time, marched at the stirrup of one of his men, barefoot, her wrists bound behind her, wearing only a sack, that which had been her common garment in the camp, that in which I had put her long ago for my amusement, that which had once contained Sa-Tarna flour. It must have been a difficult moment for the proud Lady Yanina, to have been so returned to her city.

"Imagine this," cried Boots, expansively, with a great gesture, his eyes lighting up, "an incredible banquet, a glorious feast, a feast of victory, a triumphal feast, the most abundant and delicate viands, the finest of entertainment, and then, at the climax of this great feast, you bring forth a great locked trunk! You open it! Within it there is a slave sack! You untie this slave sack! You have its occupant drawn forth. He is helpless and in chains. You display him to the crowd! He is your prisoner! He is your prize! You give him then to your Ubar! It is your moment of triumph!"

"Yes," she cried. "Yes!"

"No!" I cried. "Never! Never! No such triumph for you! No such humiliation for me!" I shook Chino and Lecchio about, fiercely, throwing them even from their feet, but they clung, tenaciously, desperately, like sleen, to my arms. Then, in their grip, still in place, held now again below her, she in the high saddle of the tharlarion, I looked up at the Lady Yanina. She was smiling.

"Never!" I cried.

She did not respond.

"Do not subject me to such humiliation," I said.

She did not respond.

"How can you even think of such a thing," I asked.

She smiled.

"Please, no," I said.

"Bring the slave sack," she said.

16

WHAT OCCURRED IN THE FEASTING HALL

"Here," I said, snapping my fingers. The naked blond slave ran swiftly to me and knelt before me. "My fingers are greasy," I said. "Yes, Master," she said, and, putting down her head, she began to lick the palms of my hands, as I held them out to her, and then about my hands, and then to run her tongue down between my fingers and the hands, and then, not touching them with her own hands or fingers, carefully and delicately, to kiss and suck my fingers individually. She then extended her head towards me and I dried my hands and fingers on her long blond hair. She looked at me. The collar looked well on ner throat. I pulled her across the low table on her stomach, scattering vessels and plates, and then, turning her, threw her to her back on the tiles behind the table. Swiftly then I had her. Those near me took no note of this. I stood then over her. She looked up at me, gasping, fearful, one knee raised, the palms her hands facing down. Her fingernails had scratched at the tiles. I kicked her. "Return to your work," I told her. "Yes, Master," she said, hastening to rise, then hurrying away.

"More food," I said, returning to my place, "and clear this mess!" "Yes, Master," said a naked brunet. "Yes, Master!" said a naked redhead. They hurried to serve, kneeling. They looked well in their collars. The collar accentuates the nudity and beauty of a slave, and, too, of course, it proclaims her bondage. I retrieved a large grape, about the size of a small plum, from the table, before they could clear it away. It lay near an overturned wine goblet, in a wine stain. It had rolled there, across the sparkling cloth, when it had been dislodged from its position in its shallow, golden bowl in the blonde's transit. It was peeled and pitted, doubtless laboriously by female slaves. It was a Ta grape. One often associates them with the terraces of Cos, but they are grown, of course, in many other places, as well. I thrust it in my mouth. Then I gave my attention to the performance in progress between the tables, on a small, raised platform.

"Ho, varlets, craven churls, away!" cried lanky Petrucchio, drawing his great wooden sword from the preposterous sheath which dragged behind him. This took some time. "Away, away!" I say, he kept repeating, and at last had managed, bit by bit, yank by yank, to free the sword. He now waved it about, menacingly, seemingly almost as though it might decapitate anyone within a range of several feet. The three women seeming to cower behind him, covered from head to toe in robes of concealment, huddled together, ducking its great swings. Before Petrucchio, as though just having entered into the same area, the object of his attention, were Chino and Lecchio, in the garb of cloth workers, and with packs on their backs. "Back, even in your vast numbers, you warriors and foes," cried Petrucchio, grimly, "lest I slice you like roast tarsk, lest I shred you like tur-pah and peel you like suls!"

Chino and Lecchio, understood as two simple travelers on the road, come unexpectedly on Petrucchio and his companions, looked at one another, wonderingly.

"Avaunt, speedily!" cried Petrucchio, swinging the great sword again, the girls behind him ducking once more.

"But, good sir," called Chino, keeping his distance, "we are but two humble cloth workers!"

"Do not seek to deceive Petrucchio, captain of Turia!" cried Petrucchio. "To him your disguises, as brilliantly contrived as they may be to deceive others, are as flimsy and transparent as a veil of Anango!" The Petrucchio character, it might be noted, is commonly, in the northern hemisphere, portrayed as a captain from Turia, a city securely far away, off in the southern hemisphere. In the southern hemisphere, I have heard, he is usually presented as a captain from Ar. The important thing, apparently, is that he comes from a city which is large and impressive, and which tends to evoke a certain apprehension, or envy, and is far away. It is always easier to believe that folks far away are pretentious cowards. One has seldom met them in battle. Another advantage of choosing a distant city is that there

are not likely to be citizens of that city in the audience, who
might take exception to the performance, though, to be sure,
most Goreans understand what is going on and tend to enjoy the
farce immensely, even if the captain is supposed to be one of
their own.

My own identity, incidentally, at least if one could believe my
credentials, which had brought me into the feasting hall, was
supposed to be of Turia. These credentials had been loaned to
me by a fellow down whose throat I had stuffed enough Tassa
powder to put a kailiauk under for several Ahn. To make sure I
had also thrust him, tightly bound and effectively gagged, almost
as perfectly as though he might have been a female slave, into a
closet. He would presumably be found there tomorrow, or the
day after, by a cleaning slave. The reference to a "veil of
Anango," of course, was a reference to the veil in a well-known
farce, "The Veil of Anango," performed by many companies.
Indeed, it was one of the more frequently played items in the
repertory of Boots's company. The leading character in it, or the
female lead, is played by the Brigella character. That role now,
of course, was played by Boots's slave, "Lady Telitsia." It was
a reference which would be understood by Gorean audiences.
Too, of course, in this context, it was supposed to convey that
Petrucchio regarded himself as a very clever fellow, certainly not
one to be easily fooled.

"You see our garb," protested Chino. "It is that of the cloth
workers."

"Yes," insisted Lecchio.

"Hah!" cried Petrucchio, skeptically, but he rested the point
of the great wooden sword on the platform, and, with one hand,
beneath that long-nosed halfmask, he characteristically began to
twirl one half of that huge, fearsome mustache.

"And here are our packs!" cried Chino, exhibiting the packs.

"Doubtless filled with weapons," surmised Petrucchio, twirling the fearsome mustache.

The girls in the robes of concealment, cowering behind
Petrucchio, cried out in fear.

"Quiver not in such abject terror, my dears," said Petrucchio,
reassuringly. "Indeed, it is not even necessary to shudder, unless
it should please you to do so. Indeed, you may even breathe
calmly, if that should be your wish, for as much as though you
were safe in your beds within your stone keeps, protected each
by the vigilance of a thousand valiant guards, you are safe here,
nay, safer, though even on a public road, for here you stand
within the walls of my steel."

"My hero!" cried the first girl.

"My hero!" cried the second.

"My hero!" cried the third.

Chino and Lecchio looked at one another.

Petrucchio, then, twirling his mustache, turned confidentially to the audience. "In case it is not altogether clear what is going on here," he said, "I am Petrucchio, a captain from Turia, and have here, under my protection, three noble ladies, each of gentle birth and high station."

There was much laughter here. The girls, of course, as the audience well knew, would all be slaves. They were, after all, upon a stage. They were, of course, Rowena, Lady Telitsia and Bina. There were only men in the audience. To be sure, there was an empty place at the right hand of Belnar, the ubar of Brundisium. I had seen him only once before, in a royal box, set among the tiers at the baiting pit. He was a corpulent, greasy-looking fellow. On his left hand sat Flaminius, who seemed in a glum mood this evening. Also about them were various officers and officials. Two or three cushions down, on Belnar's left, was a fellow in the robes of the caste of players, Temenides, of Cos. It was interesting to me that a member of the caste of players should be seated at the first table, and particularly, in this city, one allied with Ar, one of Cos. To be sure, there tend to be few restrictions on the movements of players on Gor. They tend to travel about, on the whole, pretty much as they please. They tend to have free access almost everywhere, being welcomed, unquestioned, in most Gorean camps, villages, towns and cities. In this respect, they tend to resemble musicians, who generally enjoy similar privileges. There is a saying on Gor, "No musician can be a stranger." This saying is sometimes, too, applied to members of the caste of players. The saying is somewhat difficult to translate into English, for in Gorean, as not in English, the same word is commonly used for both "stranger" and "enemy." When one understands that, of course, it is easier to understand the saying in its full meaning.

"Is it true that you are," inquired Chino, "as you suggested when first you called our attention to your perspicacity in penetrating disguises, Petrucchio?"

"Yes," said Petrucchio.

"Who is Petrucchio?" asked Lecchio. "I have never heard of him. Surely you have not either."

"The noble Petrucchio, the famed Petrucchio?" asked Chino.

"Chino," protested Lecchio.

"Shhh," said Chino, admonishing his companion.

"Yes," said Petrucchio.

"The courageous Petrucchio?"

"Chino!" said Lecchio.

"Shhh," said Chino, again admonishing his companion to silence.

"Yes," said Petrucchio.

"The glorious and clever Petrucchio?"

"Yes," said Petrucchio.

"He of Turia?" inquired Chino.

"Yes," said Petrucchio. "Quake, if you must. Quail, if you would rather."

"Surely you have heard of this fellow, Lecchio," said Chino to his companion.

"No," admitted Lecchio, which response brought a swift kick in the shins. "Yes, yes!" cried Lecchio. "Of course, the great Petrucchio!"

"Was it not he who single-handedly carved broad swaths through the legions of ten cities in the seven meadows of Saleria?" asked Chino of Lecchio.

"I see that my reputation has preceded me," said Petrucchio, twirling his mustache.

"And lifted the sieges of eleven cities?"

"Maybe," said Lecchio.

"And breached the gates of fifteen?"

"Maybe," said Lecchio.

"And alone stormed the ramparts of twenty cities, reducing them to rubble?" asked Chino.

"I think so," said Lecchio, uncertainly.

"And when set upon by ten thousand Tuchuks in their own country routed them all?"

"Eleven thousand," said Petrucchio.

"Yes," cried Lecchio. "It was he!"

"None other," said Petrucchio.

"What brings you to these lands, noble captain?" inquired Chino. "Is it your intention to bring them to devastation, perhaps for some fancied slight to your honor?"

"No, no," said Petrucchio, modestly.

"Is it then the sacking of a few cities you are up to?"

"No," admitted Petrucchio.

"Not even the defeating of a small army?"

"No," he said.

"Not even the burning of a few fields, the seizure of a piddling harvest or two?"

"No," said Petrucchio.

"What then, possibly, could you be doing here?" inquired Chino.

"I am, as you may have by now surmised, Petrucchio," said Petrucchio, "a captain of Turia, and have here," and here he indicated the women behind him, "under my protection, for which services I have taken fee, three noble ladies, each of gentle birth and high station."

"They are, then, all free women?" asked Chino.

"Of course!" responded Petrucchio, somewhat huffily, seemingly prepared, at the drop of an innuendo, to take umbrage, with all the fearsome consequences which that might entail for a hapless offender.

"How fortunate they are to be under the care of one so skilled and courageous, as well as wise," said Chino, adding, seemingly *sotto voce*, to Lecchio, "or so it would seem."

"What, ho!" cried Petrucchio. "What means this 'or so it would seem'?"

"His hearing," said Chino to Leechio, who was sticking his finger in his ear and shaking his head, as though to restore his sense of hearing after having been partially deafened, "is more acute than that of the prowling sleen!" Then he said to Petrucchio, "Oh, it is nothing, I suppose."

"And what, good sir," demanded Petrucchio, "might be the meaning of this guarded 'I suppose'?"

"Why, it, too, is nothing," said Chino, adding, "—I suppose."

"Do you doubt my capacity to defend these damsels to the death, against even armies?" asked Petrucchio.

"Not at all," said Chino, hastily. "I was merely wondering if such extreme exertions on their behalf might, under the possible circumstances, be fully justified."

"I do not take your meaning, sir," said Petrucchio, warily.

"They are, of course, free women," said Chino, reassuring himself of the point.

"Of course," said Petrucchio.

"Then my fears are groundless," said Chino, relieved.

"What fears?" asked Petrucchio.

"From what rich, high city might you be coming?" he asked, as though it mattered naught, but, obviously, secretly, as though it might matter a great deal.

"Why from the high towers of Pseudopolis," said Petrucchio. There is no such city or town, of course. It was invented for the purposes of the play. Too, there is no really good translation into English for the town. Similar English inventions might be such things as "Phoneyville" or "Bamboozleberg."

"It is as I feared," groaned Chino, supposedly merely to Lecchio.

"It is?" asked Lecchio.

"Yes," said Chino, dismally.

"Here, here," called Petrucchio. "What is going on there?"

"No," said Chino, firmly. "It is impossible. The very thought is absurd."

"What are you talking about?" pressed Petrucchio.

"It is nothing, Captain," said Chino. "Though, to be sure, if it were not for my confidence in your acuity and unerring judgment, I would suspect there might be cause for serious alarm."

"Speak clearly, fellow," demanded Petrucchio.

"You have, of course, been paid in advance for your troubles?" asked Chino.

"Of course," said Petrucchio.

"In authenticated gold, naturally," added Chino.

"Authenticated gold?" asked Petrucchio.

"Of course," said Chino. "If you have not had the coins authenticated, my friend, Lecchio, here, is certified by the caste of Builders to perform the relevant tests."

"We assure you, good sir," said one of the women, Rowena, "that our gold is good!"

"It might not hurt to check on the matter, I think," speculated Petrucchio, suspiciously, "especially as we have here at our disposal one qualified to conduct the assays."

"Unnecessary!" cried Rowena.

"Insulting!" cried Lady Telitsia.

"Absurd!" cried Bina.

"It seems they are not eager for the coins to be tested," observed Chino, meaningfully, adding, "even though there would be no charge for the service. I wonder why?"

"No charge, you say?" asked Petrucchio.

"Not between friends, such as we," said Chino.

"By all means, then," cried Petrucchio, and, with difficulty, he sheathed his great sword, and drew three pieces of gold-colored metal from his wallet, stage coins, handing them to Lecchio.

Lecchio held the coins up, one by one, holding up also, behind them, one or two fingers, as though he would see if he could peer through them.

"How are they?" asked Chino.

"So far, they seem good," Lecchio muttered, "but many forgeries pass the first test." He then drew from his pack a glass of the Builders, used for identifying distant objects. "Oh, oh," he muttered, darkly.

"What is it?" asked Petrucchio, eagerly.

"It is too early to tell," said Lecchio, replacing the glass of the Builders in his pack. "I must be sure."

"Surely things are all right," said Chino, optimistically.

"Doubtless," said Lecchio. "Doubtless." But he seemed a bit uncertain about it.

✱ In a moment now he was clinking the coins carefully together. He listened to these small sounds intently, professionally. Then he spit on each coin and, with his index finger, carefully rubbed the moisture into small, exact circles, observing their appearance. He then lifted his index finger up, his eyes closed, holding it first turned to the wind, and then away from the wind, and then, his eyes opened, repeated the test, studying his finger intently. He then commenced his final doubtless decisive round of tests. He bit into one of the coins. Then he drew forth from his pack a small vial filled with white crystals which he sprinkled on the coins. "What is that?" asked Petrucchio. "They are best with salt," said Lecchio. He then repeated the test, and bit each of the coins carefully, thoughtfully, expertly, not hurrying, as a connoisseur might sample varieties of Bazi tea or fine wines.

"Yes, yes?" asked Chino.

Lecchio's face was drawn and grim.

"Yes, yes!" pressed Petrucchio.

"False," announced Lecchio, grimly.

"No!" cried Rowena.

"What is the meaning of this?" said Petrucchio to the women, sternly.

Lecchio dropped the coins into his wallet.

"If there should be anything wrong with the coins," said Rowena, "I assure you we have no knowledge of it. Further, if anything, in spite of our intentions and care in these matters, should prove to be truly amiss, perhaps because of some oversight or subtle inadvertence, have no fear but what it will be promptly corrected."

"Let us see your other coins," said Lecchio.

"Sir!" cried Rowena.

"That we may see if they be genuine," he said, menacingly.

"I assure you that they are," said Rowena.

"Let them be examined," said Lecchio, "that a determination on the matter may be made."

"He is certified by the Builders," Chino reminded them.

"Will it be necessary to remove them from you by force, for the tests?" asked Lecchio.

"No," said Rowena. She, then, and the others, handed over their purses to Lecchio, under the watchful eye of the suspicious Petrucchio.

"Now then, too," said Lecchio, grimly, "your secret purses, those concealed in your clothes, those strapped to your left thighs."

The girls, protesting, squeaking with outrage, turned away from the men, bending over and thrusting about under their cumbersome robes of concealment. More purses and packets were delivered to Lecchio.

"And now, ladies," said he, "your most secret purses."

"No!" they cried, outraged.

"Or we must make our own probes," he said.

"Oh, oh!" they cried in misery, and turned away again. Three more coins were produced for Lecchio. The women then, angrily, smoothed down their garments.

"Do you have any more?" asked Chino, in assistance to Lecchio.

"No!" said Rowena.

"Are you sure?" asked Chino.

"Yes!" cried Rowena. "We are now as coinless as slaves!"

"Excellent," said Chino.

"Excellent!" cried Rowena.

"Yes," said Chino. "And it is interesting that you should put it just that way."

"What mean you, Sir?" demanded Rowena.

"Oh, nothing," said Chino.

Lecchio, this time, it seemed, could make his determinations with little more than a cursory glance. "These coins are genuine," he said.

"Certainly they are!" cried Rowena.

"But they are doubtless stolen," said Lecchio, gravely.

"What!" cried Rowena.

"What is the amount?" inquired Chino.

"Three double tarns, fifteen tarns, eighteen silver tarsks, twenty-seven copper tarsks, and one hundred and five tarsk-bits," said Lecchio.

"It is as I feared!" cried Chino.

"Precisely," said Lecchio.

"I do not understand," said Petrucchio.

"That is the exact amount of money stolen from the vintner, Grop‾ ‾s, of Pseudopolis."

"Ah!" cried Petrucchio, scandalized.

"It could, of course, be a coincidence," said Chino. "When did you leave Pseudopolis?"

"Two days ago, in the afternoon," said Petrucchio.

"It was just two days ago, in the morning, that the theft took place," said Lecchio.

"It could be a coincidence," suggested Chino.

"Of course," agreed Lecchio.

"This is absurd!" cried Rowena.

"It is our money!" cried Lady Telitsia.

"Give it back to us!" cried Bina.

"Be patient, ladies," said Chino, "—if ladies you truly be."

"What means this 'if ladies you truly be'?" asked Petrucchio.

"It has to do with our suspicions," said Chino.

"What suspicions?" inquired Petrucchio, anxiously.

"Oh, nothing," said Chino, evasively.

"Speak, fellow!" cried Petrucchio, yanking at his sword. Then he gave up the attempt, it apparently being stuck in the sheath.

"You have known these women personally, of course, for several years?" said Chino.

"No," said Petrucchio. "I am actually from Turia."

"It is probably nothing," said Chino, reassuringly.

"Give us back our money!" cried Rowena.

"Speak!" demanded Petrucchio.

"It is only that two days ago, in the morning," said Chino, "in Pseudopolis, a sum of three double tarns, fifteen tarns, eighteen silver tarsks, twenty-seven copper tarsks, and one hundred and five tarsk-bits was stolen from the vintner, Groppus, by three female slaves masquerading as free women, reported to be heading in this direction, clad in garments precisely like those, on this road."

"That is the exact sum discovered on these women, it is not?" asked Petrucchio.

"Why, yes, it is," said Lecchio, apparently quickly checking the matter.

"And many other things, too, seem to tally," said Petrucchio, alarmed.

"It could all be a coincidence," said Lecchio.

"Of course," hastily agreed Chino.

"Perhaps to you it might all seem a coincidence," said Petrucchio, "but to one such as I, one of the caste of warriors, one trained in wariness and discernment, it seems there might be more to it."

"Oh?" asked Chino, interested.

"Yes," said Petrucchio.

"There is no vintner, Groppus, in Pseudopolis!" said Rowena.

"They are also reputed to be splendid liars," said Chino.

"I suspect that these three women with me might not be precisely what they seem," hinted Petrucchio, darkly.

"What!" cried Chino.

"What!" cried Lecchio.

"I think it is possible," said Petrucchio, confidentially, to Chino and Lecchio, "that these very women with me may be the escaped slaves of whom you speak."

"No!" cried Chino.

"No!" cried Lecchio.

"Think," said Petrucchio to them. "It was false coins they offered me in return for my services. Surely that is suspicious, if nothing else. Similarly the resources pooled among them, as we have ascertained, total the exact amount purloined from the wronged Groppus of Pseudopolis. Too, the theft took place just shortly before we left the city, thus permitting them to be in the place of the crime itself, and then giving them time to flee the city. Too, there are three of them, and they are heading on this road, in this direction, in exactly those garments."

Chino and Lecchio looked at one another, frightened, impressed.

Petrucchio then stood upright, and twirled his mustaches, meaningfully.

"What should we do?" asked Chino, looking to Petrucchio, naturally enough, in the situation, for guidance.

"Surely, for one thing," said Lecchio, "we must keep this money, until it can be determined who its proper owner, or owners, may be."

"That is for certain," agreed Petrucchio.

"What are you talking about there?" asked Rowena.

"Give us back our money," said Lady Telitsia.

Petrucchio turned about and looked sternly upon the women. They huddled together under this fierce gaze, drawing back.

Lecchio and Chino hastily poured the coins into their wallets.

"Are you all free women?" asked Petrucchio.

"Certainly!" said Rowena.

"Certainly!" said Lady Telitsia.

"Certainly!" cried Bina.

"What were the names of the escaped slaves?" asked Petrucchio of Chino and Lecchio.

"Lana, Tana and Bana," said Chino, quickly.

"Yes, that is right," said Lecchio.

"Are you Lana, Tana and Bana?" asked Petrucchio.

"No," cried Rowena. "I am the Lady Rowena of Pseudopolis!"

"And I am the Lady Telitsia of Pseudopolis!" said Lady Telitsia.

"And I the Lady Bina of Pseudopolis!" said Bina.

There was some laughter at this from the audience, for "Bina" is a not uncommon slave name. The word "bina" is generally used to designate very pretty beads, but beads which, nonetheless, are cheap, common, and simple. They are usually of painted wood or glass. With such beads common slaves, if they are sufficiently pleasing, might hope to be permitted to adorn themselves. Sometimes slave girls fight fiercely over such beads. The best simple translation of "bina" is "slave beads." In the context of the play, of course, the audience took her, like the others, for the free woman she was supposed to be.

"It seems our suspicions are unfounded," said Petrucchio, relieved, "for these are not Lana, Tana and Bana, miserable escaped slaves, but the ladies Rowena, Telitsia and Bina, of Pseudopolis."

Chino and Lecchio looked at one another, disbelievingly. Then Chino said, "Unless, of course, they are lying."

"Ah!" said Petrucchio, thoughtfully, twirling a mustache.

"Give us back our money!" said Rowena.

"Let us make a determination on the matter," said Chino.

"How shall we do that?" asked Petrucchio.

"Give us our money" cried Rowena.

"Be silent, female," said Chino.

" 'Female'?" she said, startled.

"Yes, 'female'," he said.

"What do you suggest?" asked Petrucchio.

"Tests," said Chino, grimly.

"What do you have in mind?" asked Petrucchio, alarmed.

"Put back your hood, take off your veil, you," said Chino to Rowena.

"My hood! My veil!" she cried.

"Yes," said Chino.

"Never!" she cried.

Chino regarded her, grimly.

"Why?" she asked.

"We wish to determine whether you are a free woman, or a slave," he said.

"A slave!" she cried, outraged. "I shall have you taken before the law for slander!"

"Do you wish to have it done for you?" inquired Chino, meaningfully.

"No!" she cried.

"Then, comply," said Chino.

" 'Comply'!" she cried.

"Yes," said Chino, "and quickly."

"This is an outrage!" she cried. "It is an unspeakable insult! I shall have the magistrates on you for this!"

Chino took a quick step toward her, and she stepped back hastily, fumbling with the hood and veil.

"We shall now quickly see if you are a free woman or a slave," he said.

"How dare you even suggest such a thing!" she cried. "You are a slandering sleen!" But she removed her hood and veil, quickly, frightened, complying.

"There!" cried Chino, triumphantly.

"There!" cried Lecchio, triumphantly.

"That is the face of a slave, if I ever saw one!" cried Chino.

"Yes!" cried Lecchio.

"No!" cried Rowena, but, to be sure, she put down her head and almost began to laugh. Men in the audience, too, laughed. Too, there was genuine applause in the audience for her beauty. She kept her head down for a moment, appreciatively basking in this, radiantly. Only too obviously she was that beautiful, beautiful enough to be a slave. Then she lifted her head again, struggling to return to character. "No! No!" she said, half laughing.

"Oh, but yes!" called a man from the audience.

"Yes, Master," she whispered, her lips forming the words. "Thank you, Master." Then her lips pursed a moment and sped him a kiss. I had little doubt he would call for her after the performance.

"You, there, too!" called Chino to Lady Telitsia. "And you, as well, little female," he said to Bina.

In a moment they, too, had thrust back their hoods and removed their veils.

"There!" cried Chino, triumphantly. "And, there! Those, too, are the faces of slaves!"

There was agreement shouted from the audience. They were pleased, of course, to see the girls, at last.

"No!" cried Lady Telitsia.

"No!" cried Bina, dutifully.

There was more laughter from the audience.

"You see," said Chino to Petrucchio, "they have the faces of slaves."

"Clearly," agreed Petrucchio.

The girls cried out in protest.

"It remains, of course," said Chino, "to see if they have the bodies of slaves."

"Of course," granted Petrucchio, twirling a mustache.

"No!" cried the girls.

"Strip," commanded Chino, "now, totally!"

"No!" cried the girls, but, at a menacing gesture from Chino, the meaningful lifting of his open right hand, suggesting that the least dilatoriness might be rewarded with cuffings, or worse, as though they might be mere slaves, they hastened to comply. The audience shouted its encouragement. The girls were quite lovely. Their disrobing, leaving only scarves about their necks, concealing their collars, and round, adhesive patches on their thighs, concealing their brands, was done mostly in character, but Bina, once, with a final wrap-around, sliplike garment, drew it away from her with a sensuousness, a pride and insolence, that clearly proclaimed her slave. I did not think she would have done this before having been given into the use of the player. Indeed, she was facing the player when she did it, and I suspected that it was primarily for him that she had so slave-bared herself. He, in the audience, joined in the applause. She smiled. His slave bracelet was on her wrist. Her use was his.

Chino seized Rowena by the hair, and, lifting his arm up, held her up straight, before Petrucchio, and Lecchio took Lady Telitsia and Bina into custody, one in each hand, in exactly the same fashion, making them stand up straight, displaying them identically. "Do they have the bodies of slaves?" Chino asked the audience.

"Yes!" shouted several of the men in the audience. It was true. Their bodies had been designed by nature to be incredibly exciting and attractive to men, and to provide men with incomparable pleasures and services.

"Note the slave bodies," said Chino to Petrucchio.

"Yes," said Petrucchio, noting them well.

"And their delicious slave curves," said Chino, bending Rowena back a bit.

"Yes!" said Petrucchio.

"No! No!" cried the girls.

"But can they move as slaves?" inquired Chino.

"Never!" cried Rowena.

"Wiggle, Lana," said Chino.

"I am the Lady Rowena of Pseudopolis!" cried Rowena.

"Now," said Chino.

"Never!" she cried. "Oh!" she cried, wincing, Chino's hand in her hair, tightening and twisting, instructing her in obedience.

"See?" asked Chino of Petrucchio.

"Yes," said Petrucchio.

"Very good, Lana," said Chino. "That is enough for now, thank you. You, now, Tana. You, now, Bana." At his words, of course, Lady Telitsia and Bina, too, wiggled, and, in Lecchio's grip, having little choice, wiggled well. The girls were not dancers, of course, but they were slaves. A woman who has been in a collar and helplessly in the hands of men does this sort of thing rather differently, of course, then would a virgin or an inert free woman. They cannot help it. Still, in the comedic situation, given their characterizations, they strove, successfully, I think, to give the impression of free women being forced to move in this fashion and yet, at the same time, marvelously, managed to be sexually attractive. The movements, of course, were not, nor were they intended to be, those of an actually displayed slave in such a predicamant, say, in a market or capture camp, being commanded, say, to "move" before men. On the other hand, at one point, Bina did twist toward the player and, somewhat out of character, moved in such a way that there was no doubt that it was to him, he who had her current use, that she was presenting herself. He raised his hand a small way above the table, hardly more than a movement of fingers, acknowledging this. She then returned to character, still helpless, of course, in Lecchio's grip.

"Very good, girls," said Chino. "What do you think?" he asked.

"Clearly they are slaves," said Petrucchio.

"No!" protested the girls.

"Down on your hands and knees, facing that direction," said Chino to Rowena. "You, Tana, behind her, identically postured, and you, Bana, behind her, same position!"

"I assure you," said Rowena, "you are making a terrible mistake. I am the Lady Rowena of Pseudopolis!"

"And I am the Lady Telitsia of Pseudopolis," said Lady Telitsia.

"And I," cried Bina, "am the Lady Bina of Pseudopolis!"

"You see?" asked Chino. "They position exactly like slaves."

"Yes," said Petrucchio, considering this additional evidence.

"I assure you," protested Rowena, "our identities are exactly as we claim. Examine our documents!"

"It is a simple matter to produce forgeries," said Lecchio.

"Oh!" cried Rowena, in frustration.

"You are clever slaves, to be sure," said Chino, "but now it is all over for you. You have been caught."

"We are not slaves!" cried Rowena.

"They look well, positioned, do they not?" asked Chino.

"Yes," admitted Petrucchio.

"We are not slaves!" cried Rowena. "Look! Look! We are not collared! We are not branded!" These lines were quite acceptable in the context of the play. In the play, as I have indicated, the collars were covered by light scarves and the brands by circular, adhesive patches. Thus in virtue of these simple theatrical conventions, the slaves were understood as, and unhesitantly accepted as, free women.

"That was doubtless much the trouble," said Chino, disapprovingly. "Their former masters were too indulgent with them."

"I shall have the law on you for this!" cried Rowena.

"Slaves have no standing before the law," said Chino. "Surely you know that, Lana."

"I am not Lana," she cried. "I am a free woman! I am not a slave!"

"Perhaps you should consider being silent," suggested Chino, "lest you be whipped for lying."

"Perhaps we should proceed with caution," said Petrucchio.

"They are clever slaves," mused Lecchio.

"I doubt that they are clever enough to fool one such as the great Petrucchio," said Chino.

"I do not know," said Lecchio, worryingly. Then he turned to Petrucchio. "Can such slaves fool you?" he asked.

"No," said Petrucchio. "Of course not!"

"See?" Chino said to Lecchio.

"Yes," said Lecchio.

"We are not slaves!" cried Rowena.

"Let us see if they chain as slaves," said Chino. "Do you have some chains in your things?" he asked Petrucchio.

"Yes," said Petrucchio.

"What are you talking about?" demanded Rowena.

Chains, with collars, were brought out. "Oh!" said Bina, a collar, with its looped chain in the hands of Chino, closed about her neck.

"What is going on?" asked Rowena, at the head of the line.

The chain, with two more collars, was passed between the legs, under the body, and between the arms of Lady Telitsia. "Oh!" she said. She now wore the chain's middle collar.

"I hear the clink of chain!" cried Rowena. "What is going on?"

"Oh!" she cried, now in the first collar, its chain looping back beneath her body, and then looping up to Lady Telitsia's collar, from whose collar, of course, her own chain, passing beneath her body, swung back to keep its own sturdy, linked-steel rendezvous with the ring on the third collar, that locked on Bina's neck.

"You see," said Chino. "They chain as slaves."

"Yes," said Petrucchio, twirling a mustache. "The evidence mounts moment by moment. They have the faces of slaves. They have the bodies of slaves. They wiggle like slaves. They position like slaves. They chain like slaves. Clearly they are slaves. The matter is beyond all doubt."

"Not quite," said Lecchio, musingly.

"Oh?" asked Petrucchio.

"He is right," granted Chino. "We must see if they switch as slaves."

"Do not you dare!" cried Rowena.

Lecchio produced a switch, presumably from somewhere at the roadside.

"Oh!" cried Bina. An elongated, bright red mark was now upon her pretty white fundament, and now her entire cheek flared scarlet.

Again there was a hiss of the switch.

"Oh!" cried Lady Telitsia, similarly marked and colored.

"Do not you dare!" cried Rowena. "Do not you dare!" But her cries went unheeded. "Oh!" she cried. "Oh!" she cried again. "Oh!" she cried, yet again. Lecchio, incidentally, although he did not strike the girls as hard as he might have, was, nonetheless, in many ways, all things considered, a stickler for theatrical verisimilitude. He did give the girls actual, sharp, smart blows. This was called for in the characterization, and in the dramatic situation, of course. To be sure, had the actresses actually been free women, in real life, it would have been unthinkable.

"The evidence is complete," said Lecchio.

"You have now captured Lana, Tana and Bana," said Chino to Petrucchio. "Well done, Captain."

"It is nothing," said Petrucchio, modestly.

"We are free women!" cried Rowena. "Let us go!"

"When you slaves are properly branded and collared," said Chino to Rowena, "that will be the end of your silliness. Your days of pretending to be free females will then be over."

"Let us go!" she cried. "Oh! Oh!" she cried, again striped, and twice.

"Did you have anything more to say?" asked Chino.

"No!" she said.

"No, what?" he asked.

"Never!" she said.

Again the switch fell.

"No—Master!" she said.

Lecchio now raised the switch near Lady Telitsia, and Bina.

"Master!" cried Lady Telitsia. "Master!" cried Bina.

"Well," said Petrucchio. "I shall now return these captured slaves to Pseudopolis, where, doubtless, I shall receive a fine reward."

"A fine reward indeed he would be likely to receive," said Chino, confidentially, to the audience. "He would be fortunate, indeed, if he were not subjected to a thousand tortures, and then, if time permitted, impaled on the walls by sundown."

"If we let good Petrucchio return to Pseudopolis," said Lecchio, also addressing the audience, "that might well be the end of him and then our troupe, and hundreds of other troupes, inferior to ours, would be forced to do without him."

"I do not think the theater could sustain such a blow," said Chino to the crowd.

"Nor I," agreed Lecchio.

"Too, of course," confided Chino to the crowd, "we have had our eyes on these wenches from the beginning. It is our intention to make a profit not only on their coins and clothing, but on them, as well. I think they should bring us a few coins. What do you think?"

There were shouts of agreement from the audience.

"What are you babbling about?" inquired Petrucchio. "And to whom are you talking?"

"Oh, to no one," said Chino, innocently.

Petrucchio himself then turned to the audience. "I must be wary of these rascals," he said. "They seem like good fellows, but on the road one can never be too sure."

"To whom are you talking?" asked Chino.

"Oh, to no one," said Petrucchio, innocently.

"Give us these wenches," said Chino. "In some towns that way," he said, gesturing behind him with a jerk of his thumb, "we know some shops where these little puddings should bring a good price. Let us sell them for you."

"I grow instantly suspicious," said Petrucchio to the crowd. "But," said he to Chino, "what of returning them to their masters for rewards?"

"But what if there are no rewards?" said Chino.

"That is a sobering thought," said Petrucchio to the audience. "Well, then," said he to Chino, "let me take them down the road and see how at these shops of which you speak go this day's pudding prices."

"Return us to Pseudopolis!" begged Rowena.

"To weak masters who did not even have you collared and branded!" scoffed Chino. "No! You will be sold to strong men who will well teach you your womanhood."

Rowena groaned.

"Did you ask permission to speak?" inquired Lecchio.

"No," she said, "—Master."

She was then, to the amusement of the crowd, given another stripe.

"May I speak, Master!" begged Rowena.

"No," said Lecchio.

"I thought," said Petrucchio, "that you two were going toward Pseudopolis, not back the other way."

"We were," said Chino, "but Lecchio here forgot a ball of yarn, having left it in a Cal-da shop."

"I did?" asked Lecchio.

"Surely you remember?" asked Chino.

"No," said Lecchio.

"I remember it quite clearly," said Chino.

"That is good enough for me," said Lecchio. "It was probably not an important ball of yarn."

"And we are going back for it, anyway," said Chino.

"All that way," asked Lecchio, "for only a ball of yarn?"

"Yes," said Chino, irritably.

"It must have been an important ball of yarn," said Lecchio.

"It was," said Chino, angrily.

"Then it seems I should remember it," said Lecchio.

At this point Chino delivered to Lecchio one of the numerous kicks in the shins, and such, which the crowds had come to expect in these diversions.

"That ball of yarn!" cried Lecchio.

"Yes, that one," said Chino.

"I remember it clearly," said Lecchio. "It was red."

"Yellow," said Chino.

"Well, I remembered it fairly clearly," said Lecchio.

"Very well, my friends," said Petrucchio, indicating the direction from whence Chino and Lecchio had come, "we shall all go this way. We can travel together."

"We welcome your company," said Chino. "There is little to

fear in that direction, as long as one is not from Turia. By the way, where did you say you were from?''

"Turia," said Petrucchio, puzzled.

"That could be very unfortunate," said Chino, apprehensively.

"How is that?" sasked Petrucchio.

"But it probably does not matter," speculated Chino, "given your prowess in combat."

"I do not understand," said Petrucchio.

"It is only that we have recently come from that way," he said, gesturing with his head back down the road.

"Yes?" said Petrucchio.

"You have probably not yet heard the news," said Chino. "Yet perhaps you have. It is spreading like wildfire."

"What news?" asked Petrucchio.

"The war," said Chino.

"What war?" asked Petrucchio.

"The war with Turia," said Chino.

"What war with Turia?" inquired Petrucchio.

"Ten towns down the road," he said, "have just declared war on Turia. A great hunt is on. They are looking for fellows from Turia."

"What for?" asked Petrucchio, alarmed.

"I am not sure," said Chino. "It was hard to make out, for all the shouting and the clashing of weapons. I think it was something about frying them in tarsk grease or boiling them alive in tharlarion oil, I am not really sure."

Petrucchio began to quake in terror.

"I see that you are trembling with military ardor," said Chino.

"Yes," Petrucchio assured him.

"You are welcome to come with us, of course," said Chino. "The warding off of bloodthirsty troops and maddened, hostile mobs, with bulging eyes, would be nothing for you."

"True," asserted Petrucchio, "but I am in spite of my fierce appearance sometimes a gentle fellow, one who is often hesitant to wreak broadcast massacre too impulsively, particularly on so balmy a day. Too, only this morning, as luck would have it, I cleansed my sword from my most recent slaughters and I am accordingly loath to immerse it so soon once more in baths of blood."

"You may actually spare, then, the maddened mobs and the town militias, the assembled soldiery of the district?"

"Perhaps," said Petrucchio.

"It is a lucky day for these lands then," said Chino.

"Dispose of the puddings," said Petrucchio. "I shall wait here."

"It may be difficult to make it back through the war zone," said Chino. "Too, it may be dangerous to remain here."

"Dangerous?" asked Petrucchio.

"Yes, for the mobs and soldiers," said Chino. "They are scouring the countryside, looking for Turians. If they should find you here, it would be too bad for them, even in all their numbers."

"Certainly, certainly," said Petrucchio, looking anxiously about himself. "What do you suggest?"

"I wonder what all that dust is over there," said Chino, looking off in one direction.

"I do not see any dust," said Petrucchio, anxiously.

"It was probably just my imagination," said Chino.

"Perhaps you could give me something now," said Petrucchio.

"We are very short on cash," said Chino.

"But you have the gold," said Petrucchio.

"You do not wish to be paid in false gold, or stolen gold, do you?" asked Chino, disbelievingly.

"No, of course not," said Petrucchio.

"Perhaps we could have a wager," said Chino, drawing out a coin. "Do you wish top or bottom?"

"Top," said Petrucchio.

Chino flipped the coin, looked at it, and tucked it back in his wallet. "Bottom," he said.

"I did not see the coin!" said Petrucchio.

"There," said Chino, fishing out the coin, and pointing to it. "Bottom," he said, indicating the coin's reverse.

"You're right," said Petrucchio, dismayed.

"Would you care for another wager?" asked Chino.

"Yes," said Petrucchio.

"I am thinking of a number between one and three," said Chino.

"Two!" cried Petrucchio.

"Sorry," said Chino. "I was thinking of two and seven eighths."

"Captain Petrucchio," cried Rowena. "May I speak!"

"Of course," said Petrucchio.

"Do not let these rascals trick you!" she cried. "I assure you we are truly free women."

"Are you?" asked Petrucchio, now that he had lost the wagers apparently being willing to reconsider that matter.

"Yes," she cried. "Do not be beguiled by our brazenly bared

flesh, our degrading positions, our neck chains, forced upon us by men!''

"I wonder," mused Petrucchio.

"You know the nature of Gorean masters," she said. "Do you think that if we were truly slaves, we would not be branded and collared? Gorean masters are not that permissive, not that indulgent, with their women!''

"You will soon learn, Lana," said Chino, "and more clearly and vividly than you can even now begin to imagine just how true that is."

She groaned.

"I am perplexed," Petrucchio informed the crowd. "Yet I think that I, as a soldier, must be prepared to take prompt and decisive action." He then turned to Chino and Lecchio. "Hold, rogues!" he cried. "I suspect chicanery here, for which I intend you shall sorely answer. Tremble! Shudder! Quake in terror, for I, Petrucchio, draw upon you!'' He then began to try to pull his great wooden sword from its lengthy sheath, dragging behind him. As was not unoften the case it seemed to be stuck. Chino, and then Lecchio, too, helped Petrucchio, bit by bit, to free that mighty wooden blade. "Thank you," said Petrucchio. "You are welcome," said Chino and Lecchio.

"Now, craven sleen," cried Petrucchio, flourishing that great blade, freed at last of its housing, "be off!"

"Very well," said Chino. "Come along, girls."

"Hold!" cried Petrucchio.

"Yes?" asked Chino.

"Surrender to me these poor wronged women!"

"Wronged women?" asked Chino.

"These are not slaves," cried Petrucchio. "They are free women!''

"But all women are slaves," said Chino. "It is only that some lack the collar and brand."

"Save us!" cried Rowena.

"They are not yet legal slaves!" said Petrucchio.

"Even if they are not yet legal slaves, for the sake of argument," said Chino, "that detail can be rectified by sundown."

"Surrender them to me," demanded Petrucchio, grimly, resting the point of that sword on the platform, its hilt now, in his hand, over his head. With his other hand he characteristically twirled a mustache. "If you surrender them promptly, without a fight, I may be tempted to spare your miserable lives."

"That sounds fair," said Lecchio.

"We would be happy to surrender them," said Chino, paying his partner no attention.

"Good," said Petrucchio, transferring his sword to his left hand, that he might now twirl his mustache with his right hand.

"But unfortunately," continued Chino, "we cannot, according to our caste codes, do so without a fight."

"What?" asked Petrucchio, paling.

"I am very sorry," said Chino, "but the codes of the cloth workers are very strict on such matters."

"Oh?" asked Petrucchio, quavering.

"Yes," said Chino. "I am very sorry, but we must engage now, it seems, in a blood melee."

"Are you sure?" asked Petrucchio.

"Yes," said Chino. "But do not blame me. It is not my fault. You know how uncompromising the codes are."

"Do we have enough combatants on hand for a melee?" asked Petrucchio.

"Doubtless much depends upon definitions," said Chino, "but we must make do as best we can."

"I really do not think we can muster the numbers necessary for a genuine melee," insisted Petrucchio.

"Then," said Chino, "we must substitute a duel to the death."

"To the—death?" inquired Petrucchio.

"Yes, I am afraid so," said Chino. "It seems that only one of us can leave the field alive."

"Only one?" asked Petrucchio.

"Yes," said Chino.

"That is not very many," said Petrucchio.

"True," granted Chino.

"But you have no weapons," said Petrucchio.

"There you are mistaken," said Chino.

"I am?" inquired Petrucchio, anxiously.

"Yes," said Chino, drawing forth from his pack a large pair of cloth-worker's shears.

"What are those?" asked Petrucchio, alarmed.

"Fearsome engines of destruction," said Chino, "the dreaded paired blades of Anango. I have never yet lost a fight to the death with them." At this point he snipped the air in his vicinity twice, neatly. "Though to be sure," he said moodily, "I suppose there could always be a first time. There is seldom a second in such matters."

"The sun glints hideously from their flashing surfaces," said Petrucchio.

"I shall do my best," said Chino, "not to reflect the sun into your eyes with them, thereby blinding you, making you helpless, and thereby distracting you from your charge."

"Are they efficient weapons?" inquired Petrucchio, shuddering.

"Against one such as you, doubtless they will be of small avail," said Chino, meditatively, "but against lesser warriors, war generals, high captains, pride leaders, battle chieftains, instructors in swordsmanship, and such, they have proven more than adequate. Let me say simply that they, in their time, have divided the tunics, so to speak, of hundreds of warriors."

"Perhaps the women are not all that beautiful," said Petrucchio.

"What!" cried Rowena.

"Stay on all fours, Lana," warned Chino.

"Yes," said Rowena, quickly adding, as Lecchio lifted the switch menacingly, "—Master!"

"They do seem to be slaves," said Petrucchio.

"Clearly," said Chino.

"We are free!" cried Rowena. "Ai!" she cried, in misery. Her outburst had earned her a smart stroke from Lecchio's switch. She was then silent, the chain clinking, dangling from her collar.

"Perhaps it would be churlish of me," said Petrucchio, "to slay you here upon the road, after we had become such fast friends."

"I would really think so, honestly," said Chino.

"I spare you your lives," said Petrucchio, generously.

"Thank you," said Chino, warmly.

"That is a relief," said Lecchio. "I was preparing to return a tarsk-bit to Chino from whom I borrowed it last year. Now I need not be in a hurry to do so."

"Furthermore," said Petrucchio, grandly, "I give you the slaves!"

"Slaves!" cried Rowena. Then she again cried out sharply, in pain and protest, and then again, Lecchio having seen to it that a certain portion of her anatomy had renewed its unwilling acquaintance with his fierce switch, was quite docile, and quite silent.

"That is an act of incredible nobility!" cried Chino, overwhelmed.

"Do not even consider it," said Petrucchio, as though the astounding magnanimity of such a gesture could possibly be dismissed lightly.

"I cannot praise your generosity too highly," said Chino,

leaving it to the audience to interpret this perhaps somewhat ambiguous remark.

"It is nothing, my friend," said Petrucchio, modestly.

"Surely the glory of such an act must be long remembered in the songs of Petrucchio, Captain of Turia," exclaimed Chino.

"Have you heard such songs?" inquired Petrucchio.

"In a hundred halls," said Chino, "about a thousand campfires."

"Really?" asked Petrucchio.

"Surely you know them well?" asked Chino.

"Well, some of them," said Petrucchio.

"Your modesty, then, and our time, they being so numerous and lengthy, forbid me recounting them to you."

"Naturally," said Petrucchio.

"We wish you well, noble captain," said Chino, shaking Petrucchio's hand, warmly. "I do not think we shall soon forget our chance encounter with the great Captain Petrucchio."

"That is for certain," said Lecchio.

"Few do," Petrucchio admitted.

"May we have your permission to tell our children and our grandchildren about this?" inquired Chino.

"Yes," said Petrucchio.

"Thank you," said Chino.

"It is nothing," said Petrucchio, as though it might really have been nothing, the bestowal of so priceless a right.

Chino took the switch from Lecchio, and lightly tapped Rowena on the shoulder with it. "Lana," he said, instructing her as to her new name. "Yes, Master," she said, trembling at the touch of the switch, accepting the name. "Tana," he said, tapping Lady Telitsia on the shoulder with the switch. "Yes, Master," she said, accepting the name. "Bana," he said, tapping Bina on the shoulder. "Yes, Master," she said, accepting the name.

Chino handed the switch back to Lecchio who used it, tapping the girls here and there, and brushing it against them for delicate adjustments, to line them up in an exact and careful order.

"Well," said Chino to Petrucchio, after having satisfied himself with the quality of Lecchio's work, "it is time to be on our way. It is time to herd these pretty little she-tarsks to market."

"I hope you get good prices for them," said Petrucchio.

"I am sure we will," said Chino.

The girls, together, aghast, reproachfully, regarded Petrucchio.

"Come now, girls," said Chino, "we must be on our way."

"Move, Lana!" said Lecchio, speeding her into motion with a

swift stroke of the fierce, supple switch. "Move, Tana!" said Lecchio, adding another stripe to her, as she, in her place, hastened to move past him. "You, too, Bana!" said Lecchio, adding a swift, smart stripe to her, as well, as she, moaning, at the end of the chain, tried to hurry past him.

Chino and Lecchio, then, following the neck-chained girls, left the stage.

"I wish you well!" Petrucchio called cheerily after them. He then turned to the audience, twirling a mustache. "And thus," he said, "concludes another of the adventures of Petrucchio, Captain of Turia. This has been the story of how Petrucchio penetrated the disguises of three clever female slaves, masquerading as free women, captured them, and returned them to their rightful bondage. In it has also been told how he generously bestowed the slaves, asking nothing for himself, upon two needy wayfarers."

Petrucchio then apparently looked into the distance. "Oh! Oh!" he cried. "Is that dust upon the horizon? Or is it perhaps my imagination? It could be a group of verr, browsing in the fields. But, too, perhaps, it is nothing. But, too, perhaps it is men from the warring towns, as reported by the cloth workers, intensely combing the hills and fields for harmless Turians. Perhaps I should teach them a lesson. But then again, perhaps it is nothing, a stirring of wind, or even only my imagination. I wonder in what direction I should go? I shall let my sword decide!" Here he seemingly closed his eyes and swung his sword about in vast, eccentric circles. "Very well, sword," he said, opening his eyes. "You have made the choice. I must abide by it, however reluctantly. It is in this direction that we will seek new adventures, lands to be devastated, armies to be defeated, cities to subdue, noble free women to be protected and guarded on dangerous roads." He then set out in the direction in which the sword had pointed. It was, of course, the direction exactly opposite that in which he had, but a moment ago, fearfully, thought he might have discerned a movement of dust in the distance.

In a moment, smiling and bowing, all the actors had returned to the stage. Rowena, Lady Telitsia and Bina, freed of their chains, now had their collars bared. The scarves which they had worn about them were now knotted about their hips. They were knotted at the left hips, so that the opening was at their left thighs, where, on the thighs, could be seen the circular, adhesive patches they had worn during the play, those patches which, in the conventions of the theater, informed the audience that they were to be taken, for the purposes of the play, as free women, and not the slaves they really were. Boots Tarsk-Bit leaped, too, to the stage, bowing to the audience, and, with expansive gestures, proudly displayed his actors. Petrucchio, stepping forward, received the most applause. Boots removed, one by one, the circular adhesive patches from the thighs of the girls, this baring their brands. The theatrical convention was now terminated. Once again the girls were revealed to be what they had actually been all the time, only female slaves.

"Thank you, generous folks, noble patrons, citizens of Brundisium, guests and friends of Brundisium!" called Boots. No copper bowls were passed. No coins rattled to the stage. The troupe had already received a purse of gold from Belnar, Ubar of Brundisium. As a reward for their part in my capture the Lady Yanina, as Boots had hoped, had arranged for their performances at the banquet. Boots had spoken to her of such a banquet, and of the "finest entertainment." He, of course, had had in mind his own troupe. "Thank you! Thank you!" called Boots, blowing kisses to the crowd in the Gorean fashion, brushing them from the side with an open hand to the audience.

I looked to the table where reposed Belnar, Ubar of Brundisium. On his left hand sat Flaminius, who, it seemed, had not joined in the applause. Flaminius, as I had earlier noted, did not seem too pleased with the nature and progress of the evening. It was at this table, too, where sat Temenides, a member of the caste of players, one who stood among the high boards of Cos. At the right side of Belnar there was a vacant place. Since this evening was to be a great triumph for the Lady Yanina, celebrating her capture of me and her restoration to favor in Brundisium, I supposed that that place had been reserved for her.

"Present yourselves," said Boots to Rowena and Lady Telitsia, thrusting them forward on the stage.

Rowena stood at the front of the low stage. She put her head back, her hands clasped behind the back of her head, and arched her back, her legs bent. Then she put her arms down and back to the sides, her shoulders back, her breasts thrust forward. "Who wants me?" she called. There was then much shouting and clashing of silverware on goblets. Men rushed forward and seized her bodily and carried her, lifted high among them, back to the tables. Then Lady Telitsia stepped to the front of the stage. She thrust her hip out to the left and put her hands high over her head and to the right. She looked down and to the right. "I am not such a beauty," she said to the crowd, plaintively. "I am sure no one will want me."

"Ask! Ask!" demanded dozens of men, laughing, pounding on the goblets and tables with utensils.

"Who wants me?" called out Lady Telitsia, laughing, vibrant and alive in her collar, a slave, the property of Boots Tarsk-Bit, her master.

"I do! I do!" cried more than a dozen men. There was a rush to the stage. Then Lady Telitsia, too, was seized from the stage and carried helplessly, held high above the heads of several men, others crowding about them, back to the tables. Rowena, gasping and writhing, crying out, the scarf torn from her, flung down among the tables, pressed back helplessly to the tiles, held down by the arms, kept in place, by two men, was already serving.

Bina, smiling, hung back, standing between Petrucchio and Chino. On her left wrist she wore a slave bracelet. It had been put on her by the player. It signified that her use was his. I saw the player from Cos, Temenides, lean toward Belnar, and speak to him. He nodded. Temenides, then, rose behind the table. It was the table of the Ubar.

"Actor!" called Temenides to Boots, contemptuously, loftily.

"Yes, Master?" inquired Boots, pleasantly.

"What of her?" inquired Temenides, pointing to Bina.

"That is our Bina," said Boots. Bina, finding herself the subject of the conversation of free men, instantly knelt. Her time with the player had clearly honed her slave responses. He had not had her use more than a day or two before she had learned, incontrovertibly, what she was.

"Are you her owner?" asked Temenides.

"Yes, Master," said Boots.

"Send her to my table," said Temenides.

"That is not so easy," said Boots.

"Now," said Temenides.

"Though she is my slave," said Boots, in explanation, "yet her use has been given to our player, he who travels with my small and humble troupe."

At this point Bina, alarmed, suddenly put her head down and lifted and extended her left arm, the wrist hanging down. In this fashion she prominently displayed the slave bracelet on her left wrist.

"I want her," said Temenides.

"Please, Master," suggested Boots. "Take our Rowena or Telitsia. Both have learned passion in the collar, and the total pleasing of men."

"It is she whom I want," said Temenides, pointing at Bina. She kept her head down, trembling.

"I have given her use to another," said Boots, desperately.

"It is now time to revoke your misguided and meaningless courtesy," said Temenides. "I instruct you to do so."

"Please, Master," said Boots. "Consider my honor."

"Consider something yourself," said Temenides, player of Cos, "your life."

"Sir?" asked Boots, turning pale.

It interested me that the player should be so bold. He was not in Cos. Indeed, it was somewhat strange that he was here, and certainly strange that he was seated at the table of Belnar. Brundisium was not even an ally of Cos. She was an ally of Ar.

"Reclaim her use rights, now," said Temenides. "You are her master. The ultimate say in this matter is yours. Be quick about it."

Belnar, I noted, rather than suggesting civility in his hall, quaffed paga, noncommittally.

"I am waiting," said Temenides.

Suddenly the player, the hooded player, he called the "monster," he who now had Bina's use, rose from his place at a table and climbed the stairs to the stage. He looked about himself scornfully, regally, an attitude that seemed sorely at odds with his station in a lowly, intinerant troupe. He placed a coin, a golden tarn disk, in the palm of Boots Tarsk-Bit. Boots looked at it, disbelievingly. He had probably not seen too many coins of that sort in his life. He had particularly, doubtless, never expected to receive one from the player.

"I do not own her!" cried Boots suddenly to Temenides, in relief. He pointed at the player. "He owns her," he said. "He just bought her!"

The girl cried out in astonishment, looking up at the player from her knees.

The hall was now muchly silent. That something of interest might be transpiring on the stage seemed somehow, suddenly, almost as if by secret communication, to be understood by all in that hall. Rowena and Lady Telitsia, breathing heavily, their nipples erected, their bodies red with usage, bruises on their arms where they had been held down and roughly handled, turned to their sides and, palms on the tiles, looked up to the stage. Even the numerous naked slaves who were serving the tables and, as men wished them, the banqueters, stopped serving, and, carrying their vessels and trays, stood still, looking, too, to the stage.

Slowly, beautifully, kneeling before him, looking up at him, Bina opened her thighs before the player.

"You own me," she said to the player.

"Yes," he said.

"You are the first man before whom," she said, "I have ever willingly opened my thighs."

He looked down at her, not speaking.

"I love you," she said.

He did not respond to the slave.

"I love your strength, and your manhood," she said. "And that you have taught me my slavery."

"Kiss my feet," he said.

"Yes, Master," she said.

"So, player," said Temenides, "you now own her. You are a fool to have paid a golden tarn disk for such a woman. But it changes nothing. Send her to my table."

Bina lifted her head from the player's feet. She knelt before him, tears in her eyes, looking up at him. "I love you," she said.

"How can you love a monster," he asked.

"I have secretly loved you for months," she said. "I loved you even when I despised you and hated you, and thought you weak. Now I love you a thousand times more, that you are strong."

"But I am a 'monster,' " he said.

"I do not care what you are, or think you are," she said.

"But what of my hideousness?" he asked.

"Your appearance does not matter to me," she said. "I do not care what you look like. It is you, the man, the master, I love."

"I have never been loved," he said.

"I can give you only a slave's love," she said, "but there is no greater, deeper love."

He looked down upon her.

"Do not be weak with me," she begged.

"I will not," he said. "You will when necessary, or when it pleases me, know the whip."

"Yes, Master," she said, happily.

"Perhaps you did not hear me," said Temenides, angrily. "I told you to send her to my table!"

"Send me to his table, Master," she begged. "I will try to serve him well."

"Oh!" she cried, in pain, cuffed to her side on the stage. She looked up at the player, startled, blood at the side of her mouth.

"Were you given permission to speak?" inquired the player.

"No, Master," she said.

"Then be silent," he said.

"Yes, Master," she said.

The player then turned toward Temenides. "Did you say something?" he asked.

"Send the female slave to my table," said Temenides, angrily, pointing at Bina.

"No," said the player.

"Ubar!" cried Temenides, turning to corpulent Belnar, lounging behind the low table, rolling in his fat, eating grapes.

"Perhaps you could buy her," suggested Belnar, dropping a grape into his mouth.

"He just paid a golden tarn disk for her," protested Temenides.

Belnar, not speaking, slowly put two such disks on the table.

"Thank you, Ubar!" said Temenides. He snatched up the two coins. "Here, fool," he said to the player, lifting up the coins. "Here is a hundred times what she is worth, and twice what you paid for her! She is now mine!"

"No," said the player.

Temenides cast a startled glance at Belnar. Belnar, saying nothing, put three more coins on the table. There were gasps about the hall. Then five coins altogether, five golden tarn disks, and of Ar herself, as it was pointed out, were offered to the player for his Bina, lifted in the furious, clenched fist of Temenides, of Cos, one of the masters of the high boards of Kaissa in that powerful island ubarate.

"No," said the player.

"Take her from him," said Temenides to Belnar. "Use your soldiers."

Belnar glanced about himself, to some of the guardsmen at the side of the hall.

"I am a citizen of Ar," said the player. "It is my understanding that the cities of Brundisium and Ar stand leagued firmly in friendship, that the wine has been drunk between them, and the salt and fire shared, that they are pledged both in comity and alliance, military and political. If this is not true, I should like to be informed, that word may be carried to Ar of this change in matters. Similarly, I am curious to know why a player of Cos, no understood ambassador or herald, sits at a high table, at the table even of Belnar, Ubar of this city. Similarly, how is it that Temenides, only a player, and one of Cos, as well, to whom both Brundisium and Ar stand opposed, to whom both accord their common defiance, dares to speak so boldly? Perhaps something has occurred of which I was not informed, that ubars now take their orders from enemies, and those not even of high caste?"

Belnar turned away from the soldiers. He did not summon them.

"I have soldiers of my own," said Temenides. "With your permission, Ubar, I shall summon them."

I found this of interest. Surely members of the caste of players do not commonly travel about with a military escort.

Belnar shrugged.

Temenides, triumphantly, turned about, looking about the hall.

"I cannot believe the great Belnar is serious," said the player. "Are soldiers of Cos within the walls of Brundisium to receive an official sanction to steal from citizens of Ar? Is that the meaning of our alliance?"

Belnar put another grape in his mouth.

"Ubar?" asked Temenides.

"I have a much better idea," said Belnar, smiling. "He is a player. You will play for her."

The player folded his arms and regarded Temenides.

"Ubar!" protested Temenides. "Consider my honor! I play among the high boards of Cos. This is a mountebank, a player at carnivals, no member even of the caste of players!"

Belnar shrugged.

"Do not think to suggest that I should dishonor my caste by stooping to shame this arrogant cripple. Far nobler it would be to set your finest swordsmen upon some dimwitted bumpkin brandishing a spoon. Let him rather be driven from the hall with the blows of belts like a naked slave for his presumption!"

"Would the court not find such a contest amusing?" inquired Belnar.

Several of the men slapped their shoulders in encouragement. Others called out for a game. I gathered that among those present this discomfiture of Temenides, matching him with so unworthy and preposterous an opponent, might not be unwelcome. In its nature it would be a prank, a practical joke, perhaps a somewhat cruel one, at the least a broad Gorean jest.

"Ubar," said Temenides, "do not call for this match. I have no desire to humiliate this deformed freak more than I have already done. Order the female suppliantly to me."

Bina, terrified, threw herself to her stomach before the player on the platform. She kissed the wood twice before his feet. Then, lifting herself on the palms of her hands, she looked piteously up at him. "Risk not so much in this hall, I beg of you, Master," she wept. "Permit me to crawl suppliantly to him, proposing myself for his pleasures."

"Strip," snarled the player.

Instantly Bina tore away the scarf knotted about her hips, that which had formerly been tied about her throat, concealing her collar.

The player continued to regard her.

She now knelt weeping, trembling, before him, at his mercy, owned, slave naked.

"Now," said the player, "what did you say?"

"Permit me to crawl suppliantly to him, proposing myself for his pleasures," she whispered, frightened.

The player suddenly, angrily, kicked her to her side. She cried out with pain and twisting, frightened, a spurned and disciplined slave, turned to look at him. On her left wrist there was a use bracelet. On her neck there was a collar. On her thigh was a brand.

"You belong to me," he said.

"Yes, Master," she said.

"It seems," said Belnar to Temenides, amused, "that the player is disinclined to extend to you the female's use."

"Do not seek to force a match between us, Ubar," said Temenides. "I will not consider a match with such a fellow, not with a creature of such outrageous deformity, not with one such as he, one who is, by all reports, at best naught but a harrowingly disfigured monster."

"The slave is exquisite," said Belnar. "Apparently you do not wish to have her yielding helplessly, passionately, obediently in her collar, in your arms."

"Ubar," said Temenides, in protest.

"Play," said Belnar.

"Forcing me to such an extremity," said Temenides, "could well be construed as a state insult in the lofty chambers of Cos."

This remark surprised me. How could such a trivial thing as a joke in Brundisium, one having to do with a mere member of the caste of players, the fellow, Temenides, involve relations among thrones?

"Very well," said Belnar, agreeably, "but forgo then the woman."

Temenides' fists clenched. He regarded Bina, who shrank back from his gaze.

"Play, play!" urged more than one man.

Temenides looked about himself, angrily. Then he regarded the player.

"Perhaps the great Temenides, who holds a high board in Cos, fears to enter into a banquet's friendly game, or, say, an evening's casual tourney, with one who is a mere mountebank, a monster," suggested the player.

There was laughter at this suggestion. Temenides turned red.

"Could it be?" asked the player.

"I do not play bumpkins," said Temenides.

"I, on the other hand," said the player, "am obviously willing to do so."

This remark brought a roar of laughter from the crowd. Even Belnar chuckled. Temenides turned even more red, and clenched his fists savagely. His mood was turning ugly.

Near the feet of the player, Bina trembled, head down.

Temenides rose to his feet. In his movement, studied and unprecipitate, there was resolution and menace. "Very well," said he. "I shall play you, but it shall be but one game, and upon one condition, that the game may be worth my while." The hall was suddenly quiet. Temenides spoke softly and clearly. In his words there was an exactness, and a chill. His anger now was like the stirring of a beast beneath ice, whose shape may be vaguely seen below, giving some hint of the force and danger lurking in the depths. "We shall play," said he, "not for the mere use of the female, but for her ownership, to see whose collar it will be that shall be locked upon her throat. Further, the life of he who loses shall be forfeit to the victor, to be done with as he pleases."

Several of those in the hall gasped. "But he is a free man," protested one. It is one thing to play for a female, of course, for Goreans tend to regard such as fit for spoils and loot, particularly if they should be, to begin with, naught but properties, mere chattels, but it is quite another to set free males at stake.

Temenides did not respond to this protest.

"And," asked the player, "if you should win, and claim, this forfeit, what might I expect to be your pleasure?"

"That you be boiled alive in the oil of tharlarion," said Temenides.

"I see," said the player. Bina moaned.

"There will now be no game," said one of the fellows at the Ubar's table.

"Well, fellow?" inquired Temenides.

"Agreed," said the player.

Several of those in the hall, free men and naked slaves alike, gasped. "No, no, Master, please!" cried Bina.

"Be silent," said the player.

"Yes, Master," she wept.

"Secure the female," said Belnar. "Let a board and pieces be brought."

Bina's hands were thonged tightly together before her body. A ring, on a rope, one of several, was lowered from the ceiling. These rings, when lowered, hung a few feet above the floor, some six or seven feet above it, in the open space between the tables. These rings may serve various purposes, such as the display of disgraced females destined for slavery, most likely debtors, or the public punishment of errant slaves, but their number is largely dictated by the occasional use of displaying captured, stripped free women of enemy cities. These women, during the course of a victory feast, are caressed by whips, or beaten by them, until they beg, though free, to serve the tables as slaves. After they have so served, Ahn later, they are taken below. There they will be properly branded and collared, and will begin to be taught the lessons, intimate and otherwise, appropriate to their new condition in life. The lowered ring dangled near the center of the hall, in the space between the tables. Bina was dragged to the ring and her bound wrists tied over her head to it. She was tied in such a way that her heels were slightly off the floor. She was beautiful then, her legs extended, her heels slightly lifted from the floor, her back straight, her stomach flat, her small breasts arched, the entire line of her slim, lovely body lifted by her upraised wrists, helpless under the duress of the thongs and ring, tied in place, displayed as stake.

A table was brought and placed near the ring. Too, a board and pieces were brought. Bina looked down upon it with a lack of understanding. Once or twice, long ago when she had been haughty and cruel, before she had come to learn her slavery properly, the player would have been willing to teach her the moves of the game but after she had come into his use, his attitude towards her had significantly changed. He was then no longer interested in trying to please her. It had then been up to her to try and please him, and perfectly. Their relationship had completely changed. She was then to him only as slave to master. It was perhaps just as well. Bina did not have the sort of intellect that lent itself naturally to the game, nor the patience for it.

Her intelligence, which was considerable, tended to find its most natural expression in a different domain, in the modalities of the sensuous. Indeed, she had proved herself extremely gifted in matters of sexuality and love. Clearly the collar belonged on her neck. Perhaps it was just as well that the player had not tried to force her to become a player, an activity for which she was not naturally suited, and in which she would have, at best, after years of work, achieved only a hard-won and mediocre success, but had instead forced her to become that for which she was most deeply suited and that which, ultimately, she was and wished to be, a profoundly marvelous female. At any rate, whatever might be the truth and falsity in such matters, poor Bina would not now be permitted to so much as touch the pieces of the game. She was a slave. She looked down at the board without understanding, but with misery. On it her ownership would be decided.

Her placement, standing, near the board, of course, was not a mistake. It is thought amusing to place the slave in this position. The informed slave, perhaps once a free woman who has some comprehension of the game, may thus observe fearfully the careful processes that will determine her disposition; and even the uninformed slave, such as Bina, who in her fearful, agonized observation of the board may understand next to nothing, not even being certain often who is winning, may sense such things as the shifting tides of battle and the removals of pieces from the board; in both cases, of course, the reactions of the slaves, tied as they are, are available for the delectation of the crowd. The major reason, however, for tying the slaves in this position is doubtless that the game's stakes and their value, so prominently displayed, may be properly considered and appreciated.

The player, and Temenides, of Cos, came to the board. "You may surrender the woman, and withdraw," said Temenides.

"Temenides is generous," said the player.

Temenides nodded, and then he said, "Cut down the woman, and take her to my place at the table."

"No," said the player.

"No?" asked Temenides, startled.

"Let the pieces be put in place," said the player.

"You are a fool," said Temenides. "You will pay dearly for your folly."

The pieces, with the exception of the Home Stones, were marshaled on the board. They were tall, and of weighted, painted wood. The two Home Stones cannot be placed on the board before the second move nor later than the tenth.

"Who will move first?" asked the player.

"You may move first," said Temenides.

"No," said Belnar, Ubar of Brundisium.

"Come now, Ubar," said Temenides. "Let the fool extend the game, if he can, by two or three moves."

"He of Cos is our guest," said Belnar. "He will move first."

"Spearmen might be chosen," said a man.

"Yes," said another.

There are many ways in which this can be done. If the pieces are small enough a red spearman can be held in one hand and a yellow spearman in the other. He not holding the spearmen then guesses a hand. If the guesser guesses the hand in which the yellow spearman is held, he moves first. If he guesses the hand in which the red spearman is held he moves second. Yellow, of course, moves first, red, second. Another common way of doing this is to place the two pieces behind a cloth or board, or to wrap them in two opaque clothes, the guessing proceeding similarly.

"I will conceal the pieces," volunteered Boots Tarsk-Bit, helpfully.

"No," said the player.

"I will hold them," said Belnar.

"Ubar," acceded Temenides.

Belnar then, disdaining subterfuge, picked up two yellow spearmen. There were gasps in the audience. Bina moaned, in her ropes. Even she knew this much, that her champion was to be categorically denied the privilege of the initial move, with its weight and influence in determining the nature of the game. "Choose," said Belnar, to Temenides. Temenides shrugged. "Choose," said Belnar. Temenides, angrily, pointed to Belnar's right hand.

Belnar, grinning, lifted up the yellow spearman in his right hand, showing it to the crowd. Then he put the pieces down.

"You have won the guess," observed the player. "Congratulations."

"I was willing to show you mercy, if only to protect my honor," said Temenides. "But now I shall destroy you, swiftly and brutally."

"I, on the other hand, will take my time with you," said the player.

"Arrogant sleen!" cried Temenides. "Recall my conditions, and intentions!"

"I do," said the player.

"The mountebank grows tiresome," said Belnar. "Let a vat of tharlarion oil, suitable for the immersion of a human being, be prepared."

"Yes, Ubar," said a soldier.

"With stout neck ropes," said Belnar.

"Yes, Ubar," said the man, turning about, to leave the hall. The purpose of the neck ropes, stretched from holes drilled near the top of the vat, is to hold the victim, whose hands are usually bound behind him, in place, preventing him not only from attempting to leave the vat but also from trying to drown himself. The oil is heated slowly.

"Play," said Belnar, turning to the player and Temenides.

"I beg you once more, Ubar," said Temenides, "not to perpetrate this farce."

"Play," called men, standing about. Bina moaned.

"Play," said Belnar.

"Ubar's Spearman to Ubar Five," said Temenides, angrily.

A man made the move.

"Ubara's Rider of the High Tharlarion to Ubara's Builder Three," said the player.

"Have you ever played before?" asked Temenides.

"Occasionally," said the player.

"Do you understand the moves of the pieces?" asked Temenides.

"Somewhat," said the player.

"That is an absurd move," said Temenides.

"I believe it is a legal move," said the player.

"I have never seen anything like it," said Temenides. "It violates all the orthodox principles of opening play."

"Orthodoxy is not invariably equivalent to soundness," said the player. "Your great master, Centius of Cos, should have taught you that. Besides, from whence do you think orthodoxy derives? Does it not blossom from the root of heresy? Is it not true that today's orthodoxy is commonly little more than yesterday's heresy triumphant?"

"You are mad," said Temenides.

"Similarly," said the player, "the more orthodox your play the more predictable it will be, and thus the more easily exploited."

"Sleen!" hissed Temenides.

The player's move brought Temenides' Ubar's Spearman under immediate attack by the player's Ubara's Initiate. This might lure Temenides into wasting a move, advancing the Spearman again, perhaps overextending his position, or even, perhaps, defending prematurely. Still, I did not think I would have made the move.

"To be sure, if I respected you more highly," said the player, "I might have selected a different opening move."

"Sleen! Urt!" said Temenides.

"It is your move?" asked a man of the player.

"Yes," said the player.

The man moved the piece.

"Thank you," said the player.

"I think this fellow may not be such a fool as we thought," said Belnar.

"Nonsense," said Temenides, angrily. "He is a mountebank, a bumpkin!"

"It is warm in here," said the player. He casually opened the light, dark robe he wore. Beneath it, as I had suspected, was the robe of the players, the red-and-yellow-checked robe that marked those of that caste. I think it must have been years since he had worn it openly. There were cries of astonishment. Bina looked at him, startled, her hands twisting in the cruel thongs that confined them.

"He is of the players," gasped a man.

"I had suspected it," said Belnar. "He did not seem truly insane."

"It matters not," said Temenides. "I hold a high board in Cos. I shall destroy him. It means only that the game may be somewhat more interesting than I had originally anticipated."

"Are you truly of the players?" asked the man.

"It is my caste," said the player. The hair on the back of my neck rose up. I think in that moment the player had come home to himself.

"And in what minor ranks of the players do you locate yourself?" asked Temenides, scornfully. Rankings among players, incidentally, resulting from play in selected tournaments and official matches, are kept with great exactness.

"I was a champion," said the player.

"And of what small town, or village?" inquired Temenides, scornfully.

"Of Ar," said the player.

"Ar!" cried Temenides. "Ar!" cried others.

"Perhaps you have heard of it," said the player.

"Who are you?" whispered Temenides, fearfully.

The player reached to the mask, that dark hood, which he wore. He suddenly tore it from his head. Bina closed her eyes, wincing. Many were the cries of astonishment in the hall, from free men and slaves alike. Bina opened her eyes. She cried out, startled, wonderingly. No longer did the player wear that dark concealing hood. He looked about himself, regally. His visage bore no ravages, either of the terrors of flames or of the instruments of men. On it there was not one mark. It was a proud face, and a severe one, at this moment, and one expressive of intellect, and power and will, and incredibly handsome. "I am Scormus of Ar," he said.

"Scormus of Ar no longer exists!" cried Temenides.

"He has returned," he said.

"I cannot play this man," cried Temenides. "He is one of the finest players on Gor!"

"But the game has begun," Scormus reminded him.

"Master!" cried Bina. "Master! I love you, Master!"

"For speaking without my permission," said Scormus of Ar to the slave, "you will in the morning beg for ten lashes. If this matter should slip your mind, you will receive fifty."

"Yes, Master," she said, joyfully.

"Too, if you should speak again, before the conclusion of the game," said Scormus of Ar to her, "your throat will be cut." She looked at him, frightened, lovingly. "See to it," said Scormus to a man. "Yes, Player," said he. He drew forth a knife and went to stand near Bina, a bit behind her. He drew her head back by the hair, gently, and lifting up her collar slightly with the edge of the knife, with a tiny scraping sound, let her feel the blade lightly, but unmistakably, against her throat, just under the steel edge of the collar. The man then removed the knife from the vicinity of her throat. He thrust it in his belt. He remained standing near her. Bina trembled. Bina was silent. If Bina spoke again before the conclusion of the game, she would be slain.

"The first move was yours," said Scormus to Temenides. "The last move will be mine."

Temenides looked in agony to Belnar for succor. "I cannot play with one such as he," he said.

"Play," said Belnar.

"Ubar!" begged Temenides.

"It is amusing," said Belnar.

"Please, Ubar," said Temenides.

Some men then, near the back of the hall, using poles, brought in a giant vat of tharlarion oil, mounted over a large, flattish, curved-edge iron plate. Fuel in this plate was then kindled.

"Ubar!" protested Temenides.

"Play," said Belnar.

I then took my way quietly from the hall. I had business elsewhere. I would have time. The player would not hurry with Temenides.

17

WHAT OCCURRED IN THE PRISON COURTYARD

In the light of the three moons I made my way across the prison yard, through the sand of the baiting pit.

"Who goes there!" called a voice.

"I did not see you in the hall," I said. "I thought you might be here."

"Who are you?" he called. "Stand back. Do not approach!"

I slipped the robes from my arm where I had been carrying them. "Do you not remember me?" I asked.

"Step from the shadows," he said, backing away. "What is the password?"

"Steel," I said.

He stepped back further.

My sword slipped from the sheath. The sound of such a draw is unmistakable.

He backed further away. "Do you truly think you can reach the alarm bar before I can overtake you?" I asked. His own steel then left its sheath. I stepped from the shadows, toward the center of the sand.

"You!" he cried.

"Yes," I said.

He lunged towards me. The exchange was swift. He was not unskillful. Once he fell, tangled in the chains that had linked the beast to the baiting pole. I permitted him to rise. Then I finished him. I took the keys from his belt.

18

WHAT OCCURRED LATER IN THE FEASTING HALL; I LEAVE THE FEASTING HALL

I reentered the hall.

The game, as I entered, moving past the simmering vat of tharlarion oil, was no more than a move from its conclusion. I made my way near the board.

"Never have I seen such play," marveled a man.

"It was not a mere slaughter," said a man, "but a profound humiliation."

"Piece by piece was stripped from Temenides," said a man. "He now has only his Home Stone, isolated in a gauntlet of enemies."

I looked down at the board. The player need not have done that. Doubtless at a hundred points he could have brought the game to its conclusion, but he had preferred to dally with his opponent, divesting him of material, herding him like a nose-ringed tarsk helplessly about the board.

"Build up the fire beneath the oil," said Belnar.

"Yes, Ubar," said a man.

Temenides was white-faced, sitting before the board.

"Capture of Home Stone," announced the player.

"An excellent game," said Belnar.

"Thank you, Ubar," said Scormus of Ar. He rose to his feet. Temenides did not move. He continued to sit before the board. He seemed transfixed with terror.

I had known, or at least suspected, the identity of the player, incidentally, even from Port Kar, when I had first seen him. His limp was distinctive, as well as his demeanor and manner of speech. I had seen him, too, at close hand, long ago, in the hall of Cernus of Ar. His touchiness on the matters of Scormus of Ar and Centius of Cos, and the great match of 10,125 C.A., had also been revealing. Too, of course, his play had been brilliant. Too, how many poor players would have had in their possession a Champion's Cup, and that of Ar, that cup which the brigands had found when they had raided the camp of Boots Tarsk-Bit, that which had so fascinated them and which the player had been so anxious to conceal? Yet he had not sold it nor had he cast it from him. Under his dark robes and grim hood, it seemed, in his heart, he had remained always, and as I had suspected, Scormus, of Ar, and a loyal citizen of that municipality.

"Free the slave," said Belnar. "She belongs to Scormus of Ar. He has well earned her."

"Yes," said a man. "Yes," said another.

The fellow who had stood near to Bina during the match, he who would have cut her throat if she had erred in her behavior, speaking before the conclusion of the game, now cut her wrists free of the thongs. She threw herself to her belly before Scormus of Ar, weeping with joy, covering his feet with kisses. "I am yours!" she cried. "I am yours!"

"That is known to me," said Scormus of Ar.

"I love you!" she wept.

"That, too, is known to me," said Scormus.

She scrambled to her knees, clutching him about the legs, looking up at him, weeping. "You paid a golden tarn disk for me," she said. "I am not worth so much!"

"I will let you know in the morning," said Scormus.

"Take Temenides into custody," said Belnar. "Strip him. Bind him. Put ropes on his neck."

Men seized the moaning Temenides and tore away his robes and tied his hands behind his back. Then heavy ropes, suitable for confining him in the vat of oil, were put on his neck. He looked wildly about himself in terror. "Ubar!" he wept.

"I have had the oil heated," said Belnar. "Doubtless it is now, or soon will be, boiling. In this fashion the end will come swiftly. We have not forgotten, in the hospitality of Brundisium, that Temenides is our guest."

"Ubar!" wept Temenides.

"Ubar," said Scormus.

"Yes, Player?" said Belnar. Obviously the player had earned his respect. There are few on Gor who do not stand in awe of the skills of high players.

"As I recall," said Scormus of Ar, "the life of Temenides, my worthy opponent, whom perhaps I treated a bit harshly, being carried somewhat away in the heat of the moment, is forfeit not to you, but to me."

"So it is," said Belnar. "Forgive me, Player. I was thoughtless. I shall have the temperature of the oil reduced, that it may then again be built slowly to boiling. Thus the gradually increasing intensity of your opponent's torments, and their prolonged nature, will be all the more amusing."

"That will not be necessary," said Scormus.

"Player?" asked Belnar.

"Temenides," said Scormus to Temenides, "your life, which was forfeit to me, I return to you, and gladly. Once more it is yours. Take it, and those soldiers with you, mysteriously here from Cos, and depart this night from Brundisium's walls."

"Caste brother!" cried Temenides, gratefully. Some of the men with him then freed him and put his robes about him. He hurried with them from the hall. Belnar looked after them. He spoke words to a menial. The man, too, then left the hall.

"Scormus of Ar is generous," said Belnar.

Scormus inclined his head, briefly. Though Belnar smiled, I do not think he was much pleased with the evening's outcome. He once more looked towards the great exit from the hall, through which, moments before, hurrying, Temenides and some soldiers from Cos had vanished. Clearly Belnar, the ubar of Brundisium, had expected Temenides to best the player, taken then to be a mere low player, a troupe's player, and this had not turned out as he had anticipated. He was not too pleased with Temenides, I was certain, and, for some reason, he also seemed to find himself uncomfortable, at least at this time, with the presence of Scormus of Ar in his palace. Belnar turned graciously to Scormus. "Player," said he, "honor us by sitting at the table of Brundisium's Ubar."

"I thank you, Ubar, but, with your permission, if you see fit graciously to grant it, I would prefer to return to my quarters." He looked down at Bina, at his feet. "There, with chains and a whip, I would like to continue the education of a slave."

"Master," whispered Bina, licking softly at his ankle.

"Of course," said Belnar.

"Ubar, too," said Boots Tarsk-Bit, "we have traveled far to
entertain you, and we are now weary. Please permit us also,
myself, my fellows, and our girls, our troupe, to withdraw. We
have enjoyed performing for you."

"For a sack of gold, I should think so," said Belnar. There
was laughter from the courtiers and guests about. Belnar smiled,
pleased at this response to his jest. "You may withdraw," he
said.

"Thank you, Ubar," said Boots, bowing low. He then, following Scormus and Bina, followed by his troupe, and the troupe's
girls, left the hall. They would not be going to their quarters, of
course. They, with their documents of departure, earlier prepared,
seen to routinely, and unsuspectingly, by the Lady Yanina, upon
the request of Boots Tarsk-Bit, who had a knack for such details,
would flee the city. I slipped back among the other guests in the
hall. I did not think it would be too long before the alarms were
sounded.

"Come now, my guests," called Belnar, cheerily, "return to
your places. The best of the evening's entertainment is yet to
come!" There was then a returning to places among the banqueters.
Naked slaves again scurried about, hurrying in their perfume and
steel collars, bringing wine, delicacies and assorted exquisite
viands, zealous to please masters.

"Where is the Lady Yanina?" inquired Belnar of Flaminius,
irritatedly.

"I know not, Ubar," admitted Flaminius.

"She is late, quite late," said Belnar.

"Yes, Ubar," said Flaminius.

"She should have been here by now," said Belnar. "She
should have been here long ago."

"Yes, Ubar," granted Flaminius.

"I know you have an eye for her beauty," said Belnar to
Flaminius. "I trust you have not had her taken to a villa outside
the walls, where she awaits you now in chains and a collar?"

"No, Ubar," said Flaminius.

"She might be quite attractive in such," said Belnar.

"Yes, Ubar," said Flaminius.

"Like any woman," said Belnar.

"Yes, Ubar," said Flaminius.

"You have not had her enslaved on the evening of her triumph,
have you?"

"No, Ubar!" said Flaminius.

"I am joking," said Belnar.

"Yes, Ubar," said Flaminius, uneasily, wiping his brow.

"Citizens of Brundisium, and guests," called Belnar, rising to his feet, "I would have preferred for the Lady Yanina, that distinguished citizeness of Brundisium, known to you all, that true servant of our palace and state, that lovely courtier, my trusted agent, my beautiful operative, to conduct the next portion of the evening's entertainment, for the triumph implicit in this moment is in a special sense hers. Yet, alas, she is detained! Unfortunately, as the evening now arrives at its climax, we must proceed without her."

There were some cries of disappointment, of protest.

"Shall we wait longer?" asked Belnar.

"No," called several men. "Proceed," called others.

"Let the trunk be brought forth, and placed upon the platform," said Belnar.

Some men, from a room to one side, carried out the large trunk which had once reposed in the storage wagon of Boots Tarsk-Bit. In that wagon Boots kept many things, such as souvenirs, costumes, and props. In it he also kept much of the paraphernalia associated with his illusion and magic. It seemed like an ordinary trunk and, indeed, if desired, could serve as one. It was, of course, the trunk in which I had been placed earlier, that in which I had been transported to Brundisium, that from which I was to be produced, that from which I was to be presented, a completely helpless, chained prisoner, by the Lady Yanina to her ubar, Belnar of Brundisium.

"In this trunk, sacked and shackled, at our mercy, lies an enemy of Brundisium, an arrogant fellow who dared to displease our throne, a captain and slaver of Port Kar, one of whom you may have heard, the supposedly mighty and redoubtable Bosk of Port Kar!" called out Belnar.

At this point there were applause and shouts of encouragement.

"Taken by the Lady Yanina!" cried out Belnar.

Here there was laughter, and more applause.

"After, it might be mentioned," added Belnar, "he managed somehow to escape from others." At this point Belnar cast a good-humored glance at Flaminius. Flaminius smiled wryly, accommodatingly. There was laughter. His right fist clenched. To be sure, this was to be an evening of triumph for the Lady Yanina. Her conquest this night was not to be merely over me, a fellow named Bosk, merely a fellow from another city, but more importantly, I gathered, over Flaminius, her rival, as well. I recalled her words to me earlier, in the camp of Boots Tarsk-Bit. "Because of you," she had said, "my fortunes will be made in Brundisium. Because of you I will climb there to hitherto

undreamed of heights." I still could not understand my importance to those in Brundisium.

"I am pleased with the Lady Yanina," called Belnar to the
crowd.

There was applause.

"It is my intention to reward her richly," said Belnar. "She
will know my generosity. She will be rewarded in gold, in
power, in privilege and position!"

"Belnar the Generous!" called out courtiers. "Belnar the
Great!" cried others. Belnar lowered his head modestly, waving
his hand in a half-hearted plea for order. Much applause, too,
greeted his assertions. Many of those present stood, applauding
and calling out their congratulatory remarks. Courtiers, I gathered,
might be quick to commend generosity on the part of their
superiors. Flaminius, I noted, did not join in this acclaim. As
generous as Belnar might be with those who served him well, I
did not doubt but what he might be correspondingly merciless
with those who did not succeed in pleasing him.

"I wish only," said Belnar, "that the Lady Yanina was here,
that she might be present on this night of her triumph."

There were again sympathetic noises from the crowd. Most of
those present, however, I think, were probably just as well
pleased that the Lady Yanina was not in evidence. She was, after
all, in a sense, one courtier among others, and thus, in a sense,
was doubtless in rivalry with many of them, not just Flaminius.
It is one thing to praise the generosity of a ubar and quite another
to be genuinely enthusiastic over the exaltation and promotion of
a possible competitor. Too, Belnar was obviously enjoying himself.
Had the Lady Yanina been at his table, he would have had to
share this moment of triumph, the absence of which eventuality,
despite his apparent desires and protestatons, it might be suspected he did not regret.

"Let the trunk be opened!" called out Belnar. "Let Bosk of
Port Kar, helpless and a fool, taken by the Lady Yanina, be
displayed for our amusement!"

Two soldiers went to the trunk. Its key hung on the outside of
it. One of them thrust the key into the first lock. "Hurry, Lads!"
called Belnar. Then the key went into the second lock. In a
moment the heavy lid was freed and lifted. Men stood up, to see
better. Within the trunk there was a sack. It was a large sack. It
was of stout, heavy leather. Something was in it. It was tied shut
at the top. "Make haste, Lads!" called Belnar. "We are waiting!"
The soldiers lifted the sack. It now stood upright within the
trunk. Something was within the sack. There was no doubt about

that. But it did not seem large enough to be a man, let alone one such as Bosk of Port Kar. It was much too small, much too slight. Too, the captive's body, even concealed within the confines of the sack, did not suggest the form of the male. There was clearly the hint of delicious curves. The soldiers looked at one another. Men exchanged glances. The hall was silent.

"Open the sack," said Belnar.

Swiftly one of the soldiers tore away the knotting at the opening of the sack. This was not the same sack in which I had originally been placed, of course, but another, left in the trunk, which had been hidden beneath the first. The first sack had had a cunning opening concealed beneath a double seam, an opening through which a performer might exit or enter, as he pleased. The second sack, on the other hand, was a common slave sack, of a sort commonly used on Gor for the transport, security and punishment of slaves. It was stout enough to hold a strong male. The tenant's occupancy in such a device, incidentally, as the tenant, bound and gagged, soon comes to realize, is going to be determined not by his own efforts, but rather, purely, by the convenience, and pleasure, of others.

"Hurry!" cried Belnar.

The soldiers tore open the sack and pulled it down from the head and shoulders of its occupant. The occupant was hooded. "It is a female," said a man. The sack was then trust down about her hips. She was naked. She threw her head back in the hood. Her hands jerked wildly at the slave bracelets that confined her wrists behind her back. She did not wear the heavy trick manacles, seemingly suitable for men, in which I had been placed earlier in Boots's camp. I had shed them moments after being placed in the first sack. Rather she wore ordinary slave bracelets, which would serve their purpose well, that of confining females. They were, however, I thought, rather attractive. I had picked them out before leaving Boots's camp. She also wore, though they could not now be seen, as she stood in the trunk, a set of linked ankle rings. These, too, were not portions of Boots's props but practical custodial hardware, rings of a sort common on Gor for the chaining of women, generally slaves.

"Who has put a slave in this trunk?" cried Belnar, in fury. "What joke is this!"

"Where is Bosk of Port Kar?' asked a man.

"Unhood the slave!" cried Belnar.

"I see no brand on her," called one of the soldiers to Belnar. He had just thrust the sack down from her hips, and turned her roughly from side to side, examining her thighs for brands.

"Unhood her!" screamed Belnar.

The sack was now down about her knees. She was held upright by one of the soldiers. The other fumbled with the straps to her hood, loosening the buckles under her chin.

"Hurry!" screamed Belnar.

The trunk on the stage was the same one in which I had been placed originally in Boots's camp. However, I had made certain adjustments in it. The back and bottom, either of which may open from the inside or outside, depending on whether a wall panel or a floor trap is to be utilized in the escape, I had closed with bolts. In this fashion the trunk becomes, for most practical purposes, a normal trunk. This is useful not only when it serves normal purposes of storage and transport, but also, of course, when it is submitted for the inspection of members of an audience. After the inspection it is easy enough, in seeming to do other things, to fix the bolts as one wishes. The bolts, of course, are on the outside of the trunk, so that they may be released by the outside performer. A consequence of this is that the inside performer, if his external confederate should neglect to free the bolts, would find himself kept in the trunk. Naturally, for my purposes, I had neglected exactly this detail. The result, accordingly, was that the trunk's occupant, even had it not been for her other bonds and the sack, would have been confined within it as perfectly as though she might have been a stripped kajira in a slave box.

"Hurry!" screamed Belnar. "Hurry!"

The hood, unbuckled, was thrust up over her head. Her eyes were wild. Her face was red, and broken out. She flung back her head, freeing the damp wet hair about her face.

"Lady Yanina!" cried many voices.

She could not speak. She whimpered. The packing was still well fixed in her mouth. The gag scarf was still tight.

"Ungag the slut!" cried Belnar. Lady Yanina put back her head while one of the soldiers fought with the scarf knots. On her body there were stripes, ten of them. I had decided earlier, in the camp of Boots Tarsk-Bit, that she would be whipped. I had not found her entirely pleasing. After I had left the trunk, which I had done late after being brought into the palace, this ruse having accomplished my entry into these precincts, I had donned the uniform seemingly of an officer of Brundisium. This had been fashioned from costumes in Boots's stores. I had then, late at night, carrying suitable articles in a folded slave sack, located the quarters of the Lady Yanina in the palace. Her door was pounded on. What could it be? There was some message, it seemed, come from Belnar, for her ears alone, something having to do with some emergency, something perhaps requiring immediate consultation, perhaps even a conference of the high council. She hastened to the door to open it, clad only in a light gown. I entered, stripped her and put her at my mercy. In a few moments I was then again making my way through the halls of the palace, dragging a slave sack by its cords behind me. I took her far below, to the pens beneath the palace. There I put the stripes upon her. Her cries, muffled by the damp, thick walls, as she twisted at the ring, carried in no clear fashion to the guards. They assumed only that another wench was being disciplined, not an unusual occurrence in such a place. I then conducted her, gagged and hooded, leashed and braceleted, back to the main levels of the palace. In a short while then I had returned to the room off the great hall where the trunk had been left. There I put the ankle rings on her, put her in the slave sack, tied it shut and placed it the trunk, through the rear panel. I then secured the bolts, locking the trunk. Its ostensible locks, with the key hanging in front of the trunk, had not been disturbed. Things looked the same as they had. To be sure, the trunk now had a new occupant, and one that was now truly its prisoner. I had then, using my assumed identity as an officer, located the room of a fellow from Turia. He also opened the door to me. He was then kind enough to loan me his credentials, by means of which I had obtained entrance this evening to the banquet. He would doubtless be found in the morning by some startled cleaning slave.

"Ubar!" cried the Lady Yanina, the scarf torn away, the heavy, wet packing of the gag pulled with a finger from her mouth.

"Who did this to you!" cried Belnar.

"Bosk of Port Kar!" she cried, pulling helplessly at the bracelets that confined her.

"Where is he!" cried Belnar.

"I do not know!" she cried.

"Fool! Fool!" cried Belnar in rage.

"He must still be within the palace!" cried Flaminius, leaping to his feet. There was consternation in the hall.

"Go to the quarters of the players!" said Belnar. "Arrest them. They must be involved in this!"

"They did not go toward their quarters," called out a man, near the door.

"They will be fleeing the city!" said a man.

"Stop them!" cried Belnar.

"Wait!" cried a man. "I hear alarm bars."

He was right. Faintly now, but clearly, now that there was a brief silence in the hall, one could hear the ringing of alarm bars.

"What is wrong?" said Belnar. "What is going on?"

At that moment a soldier hurriedly, distraught, entered the room. "There has been an escape from the prison!" he cried. "Gatch has been slain. The cells have been emptied. Prisoners have poured into the streets."

This, I had hoped, would provide an emergency of such gravity that Belnar might be moved to see to the safekeeping of significant valuables.

"Martial law exists," said Belnar. "Summon all guardsmen. Secure the palace!"

If the escape of the prisoners did not seem sufficient for that purpose the sudden knowledge that I was still free in the palace, and mysteriously so, should prove more than adequate to accomplish that end. I trusted that Boots had set up the mirrors outside the hall in the location we had agreed upon. To be sure, if he had not done so, it did not seem likely, all things considered, that he would ever have to fear being reprimanded on the point.

"Ubar!" cried the Lady Yanina.

"Seize her!" cried Belnar to the soldiers near the Lady Yanina. "Take her to the oil! Boil her alive!"

"No, Master!" she cried, terrified.

There was a sudden, shocked silence in the hall. The Lady Yanina, from the depths of her, in her terror, had cried out the word "Master." She shuddered, and shrank back. The word "Master," in her terror, had come from the depths of her. All had heard it.

"In her heart she is a slave," said a man.

"She is a slave," agreed another.

"No, no," whimpered the Lady Yanina, lamely.

"Put her in the oil for having denied her slavery," said a man.

"No, please," said the Lady Yanina.

"No," said another. "Let it rather be manifested upon her."

"Please, no, no," said the Lady Yanina.

"The oil is too good for her," said Belnar. "Take her below. Put her in a collar. Brand her!"

"No, No, Ubar, please!" cried the Lady Yanina.

"Ubar?" asked Belnar.

"Master! Master!" cried the Lady Yanina.

"Take her below!" screamed Belnar.

A soldier lifted the shuddering Lady Yanina lightly and threw her over his shoulder, her head to the rear. She was to be taken below, there to be enslaved. After that Belnar, at his leisure, in his mercy, could always decide what might further be done with her.

"Ho, greetings!" I called.

"What?" cried men.

I had now slipped toward the back of the room, near the great vat of scalding, bubbling oil. I had my hands on one of the long poles, wherewith the giant vat, on its lifting rings, had been brought into the hall.

"It is he!" cried a fellow. "It is he, Bosk, of Port Kar!"

"Seize him!" cried Belnar.

"Beware!" cried a man. "Look out!" cried others. Slave girls screamed and fled back.

"No!" cried men.

With the pole, using it as a lever, thrusting it beneath the vat and its large, raised fuel plate, I tipped, and then turned, the vat and plate. A sudden vast hissing flow of boiling oil spread eagerly, deeply, outward, away from the tilted rim. Men leaped to the tables. I heard men scream in pain. The vat was now overturned. I kicked a flaming brand toward the oil, spread now and slick, hot, about the floor. Instantly, as men and slaves screamed and fled, a frightening torrent of sheetlike flames, like narrow, roaring, successive walls of fire, leapt upward and outward, surging, racing away from me, seeming for a moment to engulf the room. I struck a guard away from me with the pole. I saw a man screaming, trying to put out flames at the foot of his robe. Others were fleeing back about the walls. I struck another guard, sweeping the pole at him. He staggered back against the wall. The temperature of the room had dramatically increased. It was difficult to breathe from the fumes. I saw Belnar through the flames and smoke. Men were choking. Slaves pressed back against the walls. Weapons were drawn. "Have at you!" cried a fellow, boldly racing towards me through the flames and smoke. He took the pole unpleasantly in his stomach. I looked about. In a moment the flames would subside to the point where they might be waded through, becoming little more than more than flickering puddles.

"Seize him!" cried Belnar, coughing, the sleeve of his robe up about his nose and mouth. I flung the pole into a pair of aggressive guests, knocking them back. I must now take my leave. I resisted an impulse to wave cheerily to the crowd. Such gestures have their value, but too many fellows have been pierced by crossbow bolts while doing so. I hastened from the hall.

"Save your Ubar!" I called to two confused, startled guards outside, still loyally at their posts, sweeping my arm toward the hall. They could not resist this plea and vanished within, into the smoke and tumult. I swung shut the door after them and tied shut the handles with the silken belt of my robes. Almost instantly the door was being forced from the other side, and I saw a sword flash through the crack, hacking at the silk. The corridor was long and seemingly empty, on both sides of the door, save for such things as closed doors, presumably locked, slave rings, niches here and there, vases, and decorative plantings. In a moment the crowd, soldiers in advance, would come plunging through the door.

I looked wildly up and down the corridor. It stretched far in either direction. I could see no one. At its turnings I supposed there might be guards.

The door to the great hall burst open, its sides flung back, cracking into the walls. I heard shouting, the grunting of men, the rushing of feet. Then there was suddenly silence.

"Where is he?" asked a man, startled.

"He must be here," said someone.

"The hall is empty," said another.

"It cannot be," said a man. "He was only Ihn before us."

"He is gone," said another.

"The corridor doors," cried Belnar. "He has slipped through one of them! Hurry! Find him!"

I heard men running down the corridor, in both directions. One passed within a few feet of me. The reports were soon being passed back. "The doors are locked!" I heard. "They are locked!" Then from the other direction I heard, "They are locked! None are forced!"

"Perhaps he had a key," said someone.

"He would not have had time to use it," said a fellow, fearfully.

"The keys to these doors are kept in the quarters of the captain of the guards," said another fellow, hesitantly.

"See that a key check is conducted, immediately," said Belnar. "We shall see what key is missing. He will then have fled through that door."

"We were out of the hall in an instant," said a man, uneasily.

"I do not think he would have had time to reach one of those doors," said a fellow.

"Surely," said another, uneasily, he who had spoken fearfully earlier, "if he had been able to reach one of the doors, he would not have had the time to pause and let himself in."

"The door could have been open, left open," said another fellow. "It would only be necessary that he had managed to have a key earlier."

"It could then have been locked from the inside," said a fellow.

"That is it," said another.

"I do not think he would have had time to reach one of the doors," said a fellow, one who had spoken earlier.

"What are you suggesting?" asked another, impatiently.

"I do not know," said the fellow, uneasily.

"Fools!" cried Belnar. "Take reports from the guards at the ends of the corridor. They probably have him in custody already!"

I heard running footsteps, fading down the corridor in both directions.

"Here comes the officer of the guard," said a man. "Borto is with him."

"Ubar!" I heard.

"What keys are missing, from this corridor, quick!" said Belnar.

"None, Ubar!" said the man. "No keys are missing, not from anywhere!"

"From this corridor!" screamed Belnar.

"No keys are missing, Ubar," said the man, "not from this corridor, nor from elsewhere."

This announcement was greeted with silence.

"Ubar," called a man. "We have the report from the west guards. No one has left the corridor in the vicinity of their post."

"Very well," said Belnar. "The matter is done. He will now be in the custody of the east guards."

"The eastern post," said a man. "We were just behind him. How could he have reached it so quickly?"

"There is no other explanation," said Belnar. "He is there."

"Here comes Elron," said a fellow. "He will have the report from the east guards."

"He is in their custody," said Belnar.

"Ubar," said a voice.

"Speak," said Belnar. "Was the fellow taken easily, or with difficulty?"

"Ubar?" asked the man.

"You come from the east guards, do you not?" demanded Belnar.

"Yes, Ubar!" said the man.

"Render to us then the report of the east guards, man!" said
Belnar. "They have taken him, have they not?"

"They have not seen him, Ubar," said the man.

"What!" cried Belnar.

"He did not pass their post," said the man.

"Impossible!" said Belnar.

"It is true, Ubar," said the man.

"He must have passed them," said a man.

"No," said the man.

"He must have," insisted the man.

"That is highly unlikely," said the man. "The corridor is
narrow. There are five guards there."

"He would not have had time to reach that area anyway,"
said another man. "We were almost upon him."

There was then another silence.

"He must be here, somewhere," said a fellow.

"He is not in the corridor," said a man. "We have examined
it. You can see that it is empty."

"Where can he be?" asked a man.

"Where is he?" asked another fellow.

"I do not like it," said a man.

"He is gone," said a man. "He is just gone."

"He has disappeared," whispered a man.

"Ubar," said a voice, the voice of Flaminius. "The alarm
bars still sound. I submit that attention be given to more serious
matters than the apprehension of an elusive brigand."

"I want him found!" screamed Belnar.

"He was wearing robes of white and gold, merchants' robes,"
said a man to another.

"They were sewn with silver," said another man.

"They were of a Turian cut," said another.

"Ubar," said Flaminius.

"Search the palace!" screamed Belnar. "Find him!"

"Yes, Ubar!" cried men, running from the place.

"Ubar," protested Flaminius.

"Contact the appropriate officers, civic and military!" screamed
Belnar. "Issue orders! Are you a fool? Have them see to the
safety of the streets, the security of the gates, the search for
escaped prisoners!"

"Surely you will take command personally," said Flaminius.

"I have other matters to attend to," said Belnar.

"I will take command then, with your permission," said
Flaminius. "Have no fear. I will restore order shortly."

"You will do precisely what I have commanded," said Belnar, "and only that."

"Ubar?" asked Flaminius.

"You will organize matters expeditiously," snarled Belnar. "You will then surrender the supervision of these operations to the city captain. You will then join with men in the search for this Bosk of Port Kar. I want everyone who can recognize him, who knows him, guardsman or not, male or female, free or slave, involved in the search!"

"Is he so important, Ubar?" asked Flaminius. "Ubar?" he called. But I gathered that Belnar had strode from the place already, followed by others.

In a moment, too, Flaminius, his voice fading down the hall, calling to subordinates, had hurried away.

"Where could Bosk of Port Kar have gone?" asked a man.

"I do not like it, at all," said another.

"He is just gone," said another.

"Disappeared," whispered another, frightened. I could have reached out and touched him. To be sure, it would have given him quite a start.

"Let us to our quarters," said one of the fellows.

"Are you not going to join the search?" asked another.

"There are many others who may do that," said the man.

"You are right," said another. They then left.

The illusion, of course, must be carefully constructed. The mirrors must be most judiciously placed. The principle involved is that certain surfaces are reflected in such a way that the observer is led to misinterpret his visual data; for example, he is led to take a reflected surface, a mirrored surface, in a given location, for an actual or real surface in a different location; he normally does not expect mirrors, and does not think in terms of them; and even if he does expect mirrors and understands, in general, the principles involved, he will still "see," so to speak, or seem to see, precisely what the illusionist desires. In this fashion, such illusions can be delights not only to uninformed observers but even to more critical, more informed observers, even, it seems, if carried off with showmanship and flair, to fellow illusionists. To be sure, and I had counted on this, no one was even suspecting such a trick in the hall at Brundisium. If they had been, it could have been found out very quickly by a close, detailed examination of surfaces. But by the time it might occur to someone, recollecting my connections with the troupe of Boots Tarsk-Bit, that a trick of so devious a nature might be not only practical but, given the peculiar circumstances of my escape, likely, I did not expect to require the eccentric premises of my unusual hiding place.

I was, of course, behind mirrored surfaces, indeed, within an intersection of such surfaces, in one of the niches. The joining of the mirrors, facing outwards, was concealed by a narrow free-standing decorative pole, from which plantings might be hung, which pole, thanks to Boots, was now somewhat recessed in the niche. The casual observer would take the mirrored surfaces of the two opposite walls for a single, solid surface, that well behind the pole, at the back of the niche. The recessing of the pole, with the joining of the mirrors behind it, made it impossible, because of the angles involved, for an observer to see his own reflection in the mirrors unless, of course, he were to come into the niche himself.

The hallway now seemed quiet. I could hear shouting in the distance. I slipped from the robes I wore. Those in the search parties would presumably be looking for a fellow in merchants' robes, yellow and white, perhaps even of a Turian cut or fashion, and sewn with silver. Beneath the merchants' robes I wore that uniform seemingly of an officer of Brundisium. In a city the size of Brundisium, in an hour of confusion and tumult, with soldiers rushing about, coming and going with orders and reports, with agents sometimes in uniform and sometimes not, I did not expect to be easily recognized. Too, I had gathered that many of the courtiers, scions of an ilk not signally noted for its valor, those who had seen me in the hall, had perhaps managed to resist the temptation to join heartily in a search which might be not without its dangers. Better, perhaps, they might reason, to hold themselves boldly in reserve, in their own quarters, sternly readying themselves to sally forth if needed, immediately upon the behest of their ubar. In the meantime, of course, they could keep themselves abreast of the latest news. I prepared to step forth into the hall. With luck I might even be able to commandeer a few soldiers, to form my own search party. That seemed a good way to go almost anywhere. Who knew where that rascal, Bosk, of Port Kar, might be?

I poked my head warily out of my hiding place. The corridor was empty. I stepped boldly forth. I did pause long enough to move the mirrors about a bit, setting them apart from one another. In this fashion a supervisor of cleaning slaves tidying the hall, his whip on his wrist, puzzled by them, by their presence in this place, might have them removed to various individuals' quarters or have them stored somewhere. In a moment or two I was striding boldly along the hall. I could still hear the shouting in the distance. Too, from outside the palace, from the prison area, and from various parts of the city, I could hear the ringing of alarm bars.

19

A LATTICE HAS BEEN
FORCED IN,
FROM THE OUTSIDE

"Hold!" cried a guardsman, one of two, at his post on one of the long, arching, graceful, railless, narrow bridges interlaced among the towers of Brundisium. Such bridges are a feature of many Gorean cities. They are easy to defend and serve to link various towers at various levels, towers which in a time of attack or siege may serve on given levels or in isolation, if the defenders choose to block or destroy the bridges, as independent keeps, each an almost impregnable, well-stocked fortress in its own right. In Brundisium there were eleven such towers.

In many of the high cities there are many more. In Ar, for example, there are hundreds. Other than in their military significance, of course, such bridges tend to be quite beautiful and, functionally, serve to divide the cities into a number of convenient levels. Many Gorean cities, in effect, are tiered cities. Gorean urban architecture, in the high cities, tends to be not so much a matter of flat, spreading, concentric horizontal rings, as in many cities, as a matter of towers and tiered levels, linked by soaring, ascendant traceries. The security-mindedness of Brundisium, incidentally, was manifested also in the tarn wire strung among its towers, extending down in many cases to lower rooftops and even the walls. Such wire can be quite dangerous. It can cut the head or wings from a descending tarn. It is usually strung only in times of clear municipal peril, as when, for example, the city may be expecting an attack or is under siege. If all went well I hoped to be able to use it in my plans.

"Out of the way, fellow!" I said.

"You cannot pass," said he. "This is the bridge to the private apartments of Belnar!"

"We search for Bosk of Port Kar," I informed him.

"I have not seen him," said the man.

"Do not be too sure of that," I said.

"You cannot pass," he said.

"Surely you are aware of the urgency of this search?" I said.

"Of course," said he.

"Step aside," I said.

"I may not do so," he protested.

"Surely you have heard of the fellow's mysterious escape from the palace below?"

"Yes," he said.

"Who knows where he might be?" I asked.

"He is right," volunteered the fellow's companion.

"But this bridge leads to the private apartments of Belnar," said the man.

"And is not that the last place one would expect to find Bosk of Port Kar?" I inquired.

"Perhaps," said the man.

"What better place then for such a cunning rascal to take refuge?" I asked.

"He is perhaps right," said the fellow's companion.

The man's face turned white.

"It is there then that I intend to search," I said.

"Pass," he said. I then trod meaningfully past him, followed, single file, by some five foot soldiers I had ordered to accompany me, fellows I had found mustered within the palace walls, near the east gate, awaiting orders. I saw some fires below, off to the right in the city. I did not not know if these had been precipitated in the possible confusion attendant on the ringing of the alarm bars or if they might have been set by escaped prisoners, perhaps as a diversion, perhaps to cover their flight or to distract men from their pursuit, perhaps even turning them to more pressing tasks.

"Wait here," I said to my men, near the entrance to the balcony garden outside the apartments of Belnar. I then proceeded to the palings of the gate outside the garden. "I have information for the ubar," I said.

"He is not to be disturbed," said the man. "He is in seclusion."

"I know the location of Bosk of Port Kar," I said.

"Enter," he said, "swiftly!"

I was ushered through the garden now, the foliage black in the shadows, silvery in the moonlight. It occurred to me that in such a garden there would be many places to hide. It might be reached, too, I supposed, by climbing the ornate exterior of the tower. I myself, however, would not have cared to do so. The bridges served very well for me, and I had a simpler exit in mind. Also, of course, it would be patrolled. "Tidings of Bosk of Port Kar," said my guide to the fellows at the household door.

I waited there while these fellows consulted further guards within. Moonlight glinted on swaying tarn wire overhead. "You may return to your post," I told my guide. He withdrew. I then signaled to my men, a few yards beyond the gate, raising my arm. They entered the area. "Examine the garden," I said. It would not hurt, I speculated, to keep them busy. Too, it might make me seem a more efficient officer. Too, my men might expect this sort of thing. As far as they knew, not the fellow at the gate, they were supposed to be looking for Bosk of Port Kar, a fellow in the yellow and white robes of the merchants. The fellow at the gate was free to suppose that they might be scouting about for some other reason, doubtless escaped prisoners. Some, after all, might be about, though, to be sure, up here, it was not very likely.

"Enter," said a man within.

I stepped within. "I have tidings for Belnar," I said. "They pertain to the fellow, Bosk, of Port Kar."

"Belnar is not here," he said.

"That is impossible," I said. "He must be here, though perhaps in seclusion."

"It is to be thought that he is here," said the man, "that he is here in seclusion, but he is not. He was here, but he left. When you leave, pretend that you have seen him here. All are to believe that he is here, in his compartments."

"He could not have left," I said. "Surely, had he done so, he would have passed me on the bridges."

"Do not be naive," said the man.

"I understand," I said. I had clearly underestimated this Belnar. How naive, in particular, I had been, to suppose that I might locate him this simply. Probably even the men outside thought him within. How could I find him, if even the majority of his men did not know where he was? He might be anywhere in the city. I was furious. But he had come here earlier, it seemed. I had a good idea why. He had thought to guarantee the safekeeping of something of great importance. Doubtless he had taken it with him. He had not passed me, with a retinue, on the bridges. There was, of course, another exit, another way out.

"Where is Belnar?" I asked.

"I do not know," said the man.

I suppose he might be telling the truth. Doubtless few knew the location of the Ubar.

"What of my report?" I asked.

"Deliver it to Flaminius, the confidant of the ubar," suggested the man.

"Of course," I said, preparing to withdraw. I was extremely angry. That would be all I needed, I thought, to report myself in to Flaminius. There was suddenly a shouting outside. One of the door guards, accompanied by two of the men I had brought with me, were at the door.

"What is wrong?" demanded the fellow with me.

The men were shuddering. Others were behind them. One of those in the background turned aside and threw up into the grass. "Lysimachus is dead," said the door guard.

The fellow from within, who seemed to be chief among those on the premises, and myself, followed men through the garden. In a moment we had come to an open space. "I found it there," said one of the men who had come with me, indicating a place in some bushes. "I pulled it out here."

"Aiii," said a man, looking down.

"It is Lysimachus," confirmed a man.

"It was Lysimachus," said a man.

"It was part of him," said another.

Most of the throat was gone.

I crouched beside the body. I touched the tissues, the stained darknesses on the body. "This was done perhaps an Ahn ago," I said.

"What could have done this?" whispered the officer with me.

"Can you not guess?" I asked.

"I dare not," he whispered.

"Such a thing is loose in the city?" asked a man.

"Obviously," I said.

"Why should it come here?" asked a man.

"Because," I said, "like a man, it is more than a beast."

"I do not understand," said the man.

"It is looking for something," I said.

I looked down grimly at the body.

"Poor Lysimachus," said a man.

"Horrible," said a man.

The kill, as these fellows would have had difficulty realizing, had actually, given the usual manner of such attacks, been rather neatly done. Its manner, considering the sort of entity which had been involved, had almost suggested refinement. It had wanted to do little more than silence a man. Indeed, only part of an arm had been fed upon and that, I suspected, had been only to generate the strength to pursue a less material objective. The whole business, in its manner of accomplishment, suggested an almost terrifying patience and restraint, given the size and needs, the ferocity and energy, of the entity involved. The thing had not been after Lysimachus. It had been after something else. I sensed incredible menace and purpose. I shuddered.

The officer beside me stood up. "What did this may still be about," he said. "Search the garden. Search the house. Find it! Kill it!"

Men hurried about, frightened. Torches were lit. I stood up, beside the body. I did not hasten to join the search. They would not find the assailant. It would no longer be here.

"Shall we join the search, Sir?" asked one of the men who had come with me.

"Yes," I said, wearily.

I, too, after a time, entered the house, making my way through the rooms. In one place, in a far room, I found an iron gate, of heavy bars, in my path. It had apparently, some time ago, been lowered from the ceiling. Apparently it could be dropped suddenly. It sealed off the room behind it. I smiled. Such a gate might have dropped between Belnar and myself, doubtless, at a moment's notice. It would have served to protect him from anything, from almost anything. In the light of a torch lifted behind me, I could see a coffer, apparently, from the lock thrown beside it, hastily opened. That for which I searched had probably been extracted from that coffer even before I had begun to climb the high bridges. He had then apparently taken his swift leave. That, as it had turned out, had been very fortunate for him. In this fashion, he had not been on hand to welcome his dark guest. In this fashion, he had doubtless managed to save his life. Somewhere now, he was doubtless safe.

"What is that?" I asked the officer, pointing to a dark aperture at one side of the room.

"It is nothing," he said, evasively.

It would be, of course, the opened trap through which Belnar had taken his leave, a passage leading down through the tower.

"Lift the torch higher," I said to my man nearby. I looked about the room, from the other side of the gate.

"The search is complete," said a guardsman, reporting to the officer. "We have made a thorough examination of the premises, both inside and outside. They are clear. There is no sign of a beast."

"There is at least one sign," I said.

"What?" asked the officer.

"Look," I said. I pointed to a defensive, opened iron lattice on one of the windows in the room behind the barred gate.

"It is opened, of course," said the officer, puzzled.

"Examine, as you can, at the distance, in the light, the latch clasps," I said.

"They appear to be broken," he said.

"They are broken," I said.

"The lattice seems to have been forced open," he said.

"From the outside," I said.

"Impossible," he said.

"Does it not seem so to you?" I asked.

"Yes," he whispered.

"Search out Belnar," I said. "He is in grave danger."

Men hurried away, those with them, by my leave, who had come with me. Again I was alone. I remained there, for a time, looking through the bars. I strained to test the air. Then, after a time, I detected it, a lingering, residual, faint odor. I was not unfamiliar with the odor. I had smelled such an odor before, and knew it well. I was bitter. I was not the first to have come to the compartments of Belnar. I myself would have had great difficulty locating him in Brundisium, but I, on the other hand, could not follow him softly, swiftly, silently, through numerous passages, with the tenacity of a sleen, with the menace of a larl, intent upon his tracks.

I shook the bars violently, in fury. I had no idea where Belnar might have gone. Then suddenly it seemed I felt chilled, grasping the bars.

I turned about and sped from the room.

20

THE BAITING PIT;
I MAKE THE ACQUAINTANCE
OF A GENTLEMAN;
I WILL RETURN TO THE
APARTMENTS OF BELNAR

"Stop!" I cried, from the height of the tiers surrounding the baiting pit. "Stop!" But I was too late. Already was the chained ubar screaming under the teeth of sleen. I looked to the ubar's box. There, in the moonlight, sitting back on its haunches, was the Kur.

I descended swiftly to the level of the sand. The Kur, with that agility seemingly so unnatural and surprising in a beast of its size, descended from the ubar's box and interposed itself between me and the pathetic figure, now staring wildly upward, fallen, twisting and shuddering, moved this way and that, being pulled and shaken, being torn by the sleen. The Kur bared its fangs at me. I did not think it would attack. It was I who had earlier released it, with the other prisoners. I sheathed my sword. I was not sure if Belnar was dead or not. Five sleen were gnawing at the body. Its eyes were still open. Belnar, I thought, in spite of his size, and his ponderous bulk, had fought well. Two sleen, their blood dark in the silverish moonlit sand, lay dead near him. The Kur had given him an ax. That was more than it had had to defend itself in its own ordeals. Still one would have bet upon the sleen.

Belnar had been fastened some five feet from the post by a stout chain. It had been jerked tight about his gut, then locked there. It made him seem slim. It was the same chain, differently employed, that had fastened the Kur in the same place. It would have held a kailiauk. The chain clinked as the body was pulled this way and that. The sleen had then been released, the iron grating slid upward which had opened the way for them into the pit. The ax lay nearby. One of Belnar's hands, his right, lay near it. Seeing that I did not challenge it, the Kur turned away from me, and went, on all fours, to where the sleen were feeding. To my horror, it thrust itself in among them, its shaggy shoulders rubbing against theirs. I saw it put its head down.

To one side in the pit, safely away from flammable materials, was the huge vat, or cauldron, which had been in the great hall earlier. It was again filled with oil, and, heated by new fuel on its plate, boiling. Near it, one a few feet from it, the other a little further from it, the backs of their necks bitten through, lay two dead servitors of the ubar. I had little doubt but what Belnar had ordered the oil once more prepared. Too, it was not difficult to speculate as to why he had done so. I shuddered. These preparations now, however, it seemed, would go to waste. I did not think that Flaminius, or a city captain, or a captain of the guard, would care to impose such niceties on a victim.

I then pushed in between the sleen and the Kur. Belnar was inert, moved only by the beasts. His eyes were still open, staring upward. One of the sleen snarled, but it did not so much as look at me. Sleen are extremely single-minded beasts, even in feeding, and, as long as I did not attempt to interfere with it, or counter its will, I did not fear the Kur. Interestingly, though its jaws were red, it did not seem to have been feeding. It had, however, it seemed, tasted, or tested, the meat. I moved my hands about, as I could, examining the body and torn clothing of Belnar. I took the pouch and pulling it back from the body, ransacked it. I stood up and moved about the post. I examined the sand. Nowhere did I find that which I sought. If he had brought it with him it was now gone.

I heard a key turn in a heavy lock. The Kur then, snarling, scattered the reluctant sleen away with blows. It pulled Belnar free of the chain and dragged Belnar through the sand, behind him, toward the vat.

"Can you understand me?" I asked it. Some Kurii can follow human languages. Some can make semihuman sounds.

It regarded me, Belnar in his grasp.

"What are you going to do?" I asked.

"I was put in the pit like an animal," it said.

"Those of Brundisium did not understand," I said. "I am certain of that."

"I was caught," it said. "I was treated like an animal."

"Yes," I said.

"I am a civilized being," it said. "I am what you might call a gentleman. I am different even from most of my kind."

"I am sure of it," I said. "What are you going to do?"

"In the prison," it said, "we were not well fed."

"Stop!" I said.

Belnar's eyes suddenly, wildly, to my horror, opened further. On his face there was suddenly an instant of terrified consciousness, of comprehension. A weird scream, prolonged, and almost silent, escaped from his lips, as he was plunged into the oil. Then, in a moment, the torn, half-eaten body, shuddered wildly, and was limp. I had thought he had been dead, but he had not been, until then.

I regarded the beast with horror. A moment or two later he had drawn forth the body of the ubar from the oil. "Why do you look at me like that?" it asked.

"It is nothing," I said.

"I am a civilized being," it said. "I am different even from many of my own kind. They are barbarians."

"Yes," I said.

"As you can see," it said, feeding, "I even cook my food."

"Yes," I whispered.

I was in dismay. I was certain that Belnar would have been carrying that which I sought. I had even seen the opened coffer in his apartments. "He," I said, slowly, pointing at the meat in the beast's grasp.

It lifted its eyes, regarding me, its jaws bloody.

"He carried papers, something?" I asked.

It shrugged, a movement which in the Kur carries throughout most of its upper body, and, chewing, returned its attention to its feast.

I think it understood me, and just did not understand how it might respond. If it had seen something of interest in the ubar's possession, a packet, a sheaf of papers, something, I think it might have given me some affirmative response. I do not think it would have tried to hide anything from me. It was, in its way, I believe, well disposed toward me. Too, it now had another way of satisfying its hunger.

Belnar, of course, might have removed the materials from the room and secreted them somewhere, perhaps in the passages between his apartments and the location where he had first felt the paw of the beast upon his shoulder. That would seem to make some sense. But where in such passages, presumably unguarded, lonely and seldom used, would a suitable place be found for such a deposit? No, it seemed more likely he would have carried them with him, away from the room, on his person. That is what one would expect. Yes, I thought, that is exactly what some would expect. The hair, then, on the back of my neck rose up. I considered the cleverness of Belnar, and the probable audacity and daring of such a man, one deviously implicated, I suspected, in the intricate and dangerous games of Gorean high politics, and how easily I had been earlier outwitted in my first attempt to close with him, in my first attempt to gain my elusive objective. Belnar was brilliant! That is what I must remember! That is what I must not permit myself to forget!

The Kur looked up at me, startled. I had cried out with pleasure. "I know where they are!" I cried.

It blinked.

"I do," I cried, happily. "I know!"

"Look!" I heard, a cry from near the top of the tiers. "Who are you? What are you doing down there! Stand!"

"It is the beast!" we heard a man cry.

"Stand!" cried a man from the other side.

I looked wildly about. The rim at the top of the tiers seemed suddenly alive with helmets, with spear points and plumes. "We are surrounded!" I cried.

The animal continued to feed. I drew my blade. I prepared to make a stand. The sleen were still lurking about, prowling in a circle about us. It seemed they feared to approach what crouched near me, in the vicinity of the vat, eating. I think not only, however, did they respect its size and ferocity but, too, trained sleen, that they were confused, that they did not really understand it, or how they were to relate to it. It had not been tethered at the post. It had released them. It had given them feeding.

"Stand!" cried a fellow, stepping down the tiers towards us. Behind him were others.

The Kur then rose to its hind legs. It must have been about eight feet tall, tall even for such a beast.

"By the Priest-Kings," cried a man. "Look at the size of it."

"I did not recall it was so large," said another.

"Approach warily," said a man. "There are sleen there, too."

"That was good," said the Kur. Its long, dark tongue moved about its jaws, licking its lips. It then threw the remains of Belnar to the sleen, who pounced eagerly upon them. "I smell glory," said the beast, looking about. "It is a smell more exhilarating even than that of meat." At the time I did not fully understand what it had said. Indeed, I had thought that I had perhaps heard it incorrectly. In retrospect, now, however, particularly in the light of those events which later evidenced its intentions, I think that I do understand it. At any rate, I have reported it as I am certain it was said. Many and mixed can be the motivations of men and beasts, and the motivations of some beasts, and some men, will be forever beyond the ken of others. To beasts moved only by meat, and the pressure of blows, the hungers of higher and more terrible organisms will remain always exceedingly mysterious. I know of no way to prove the existence of glory to those who lack the senses for its apprehension. By what yardsticks can its magnitude be measured?

"You are unarmed," I said. "Flee. Do not die here, in this empty place, in this moonlight, on this foreign sand. Who will know, or care?"

"It does not matter," it said.

"Flee," I said. "There is no one here to recognize your glory."

"You are mistaken," it said.

"Who is here, then?" I asked.

"I am here," it said.

"Approach warily, men," said a man, one on the tiers, descending with others.

"I never thought to perish, back to back, with one such as you," I said.

"I was cast out of my own country, a steel country, faraway," it said, "as a weakling."

"I find that hard to believe," I said.

"Nonetheless, it is true," it said. "Many of my compeers, many of whom are honestly little better than barbarians, found it difficult to appreciate my taste for the niceties of life, for the tiny refinements that can so redeem the drabness of existence."

"Such as cooking your meat?" I asked.

"Precisely," it said. "Accordingly I was put into exile, cast weaponless, not even with combs and brushes, without even adornments, upon this world. How could I be expected to groom myself? How could I be expected to keep up my appearance?"

"I do not know," I admitted.

"It was dreadful," it said.

"I suppose so," I said.

"Surely one can be both brave and a gentleman," it said.

"I suppose so," I said. I thought of many of the Goreans I knew, with their chains and whips, and their naked, collared slaves kneeling apprehensively before them. Those fellows, I thought, would probably not count as gentlemen. On the other hand, I knew Goreans, too, who would surely count as gentlemen and their slaves were treated in much the same way, if not more so. Their gentlemanliness tended to be manifested in the exquisite and exacting refinements expected of their females, for example, in costume, appearance, behavior, deportment and service, not in any weakness exhibited towards them. Indeed, many Gorean slave girls fear terribly that they might be purchased by a "gentleman." Such can be very difficult to please.

"Do you think I am a weakling?" it asked.

"No," I said.

"Good," it said.

"Indeed," I said. "I would deem it an honor to die in your company."

"I hope you will not be offended," it said, "but I would not deem it an honor to die in yours."

"What?" I asked.

"To some extent your presense here diminishes the splendor of the occasion," it said. "Too, you are not of the people. You are a human being."

"I was born that way," I said.

"Do not misunderstand me," it said. "Similarly, do not be offended. I am not blaming you. I know it is nothing you can help."

"But still—" I said.

"Precisely," it said.

"You are unduly fastidious," I said.

"Do not be angry," it said. "Also, I am sorry. It is just that there are standards."

"I see," I said.

"Besides," it said, "being fastidious is a necessary condition for being a gentleman."

"What do you suggest?" I asked. "Should I walk over there, perhaps to some inconspicuous corner, and there engage in desperate swordplay, in order not to obviously share the field with you?"

"That will not be necessary," it said.

"I thought you might like me," I said.

"I do," it said. "Surely you have noted that you have not been eaten."

"That is true," I granted him, noting it. I had not really thought of that before.

The fellows who had been descending the tiers were now on the sand, ringing us.

"Be ready, men," said an officer. "Level your spears. Take them within the points."

"Just behind the ubar's box," said the creature to me, "there is a partly opened trap. I emerged through it with dinner. It is apparently a private passage to the ubar's box, through which he could arrive here without passing through crowds. Once closed it is difficult to detect."

"What are you telling me?" I asked.

"I doubt that I could easily pass myself off as a human," it said, "even if I could accept the indignity of the pretense. You, on the other hand, an actual human being, would presumably have little difficulty in doing so. Similarly, if I am not mistaken, you are wearing a uniform of Brundisium."

"I cannot reach it," I said.

"In a moment," it said, "there is going to be a great deal of confusion."

"Come with me," I said.

"I dreamed for years on the cliffs of such a moment," it said. "I shall not forfeit it now, nor, I assure you, shall I share it."

"Look," said one of the men. "Is that not the fellow in the hall, Bosk of Port Kar, he who disappeared so mysteriously?"

"You are correct," I told him.

"Watch him! Watch him carefully!" said a man.

"He cannot just vanish here," said another.

"Sleen are variously trained," said the beast to me. "These in the pit respond to verbal signals, regardless of their source. They were of little use to me when I was chained at the stake, as they were set upon me, as upon a target. On the other hand, I am not now in the position of the target, or prey, but in that of the trainer."

"Such signals are secret," I said. "They are carefully guarded. You could not know them. How could you know them?"

"I heard them whispered to the sleen," it said. "Just because you cannot hear such sounds at such distances, does not mean that the sleen cannot, or that I cannot."

Once again the hair lifted on the back of my neck.

"Be ready," it said.

"Now," said the officer. The men began to move forward, slowly, step by step.

The beast beside me then, almost inaudibly, but intensely, uttered an approximation of human vocables.

The sleen, startling me, suddenly spun about, the five of them, six-legged, agile, sinuous and muscular, some nine or ten feet in length, and crowded about our legs, hissing, snarling, looking upward.

"By the Priest-Kings!" cried a man, in horror.

Suddenly, at the utterance of a hissed syllable, coupled with a fierce, directed gesture from the beast, a movement almost like throwing a weapon violently underhanded, one of the animals, fangs bared, lunged fiercely toward the men. In an instant it was under, and among, the spears, tearing and slashing. There were wild screams and a sudden breaking of ranks. The men had not expected this charge, and were not ready for it. Even if they had been regrouped and set, the distance was so short and the attack of the beast so precipitous and swift that there had been no time to align their weapons in a practical, properly angled, defensive perimeter. The beast, accordingly, had simply darted into what, from its point of view, was an obvious opening. Another sleen then, another living weapon, with another fierce syllable and gesture, was launched by the beast. Then another, and another, to scattering men, to wildly striking weapons, and then the last!

"Behind the ubar's box!" said the beast to me.

I regarded it, reluctant to leave it.

"Go," it said. "They will learn that even a gentleman knows how to fight."

"Are there many like you in your country?" I asked.

"Countries," it said.

"Countries," I said.

"Some," it said.

"I see," I said.

"Go," it said.

"What is your name?" I asked.

It made a noise. "That is my name," it said.

"I cannot pronounce it," I said.

"That is not my fault," it said.

"I suppose not," I said.

"I would really appreciate it, if you would leave," it said.

"Very well," I said.

I darted between two groups of men, each striking down at a twisting sleen. I heard screams. I saw that one of the sleen had its teeth fastened on the leg of a man. Several other men were about the periphery of the baiting pit. I hurried to one group of such men. "What are you doing here!" I cried. "Search for Bosk of Port Kar!"

"We do not know where he is!" protested a man. It was hard to see his features in the moonlight and shadows.

"There are sleen there!" cried another.

I struck the first fellow a rude blow with my fist, my sword in it. "Hurry!" I said. "Move!"

They rushed confusedly down to the sand.

"You, too!" I ordered another fellow.

"Yes, Sir!" he cried. I then ascended to some of the tiers before the ubar's box and stood there, as though directing the operation. With my sword, fiercely, I gestured to other fellows, that they, too, should hurry down to the sand. They did so.

"Who is in command?" called a minor officer, confused.

"I am," I said. "Look for Bosk of Port Kar!"

He, too, then hurried, taking two men with him, down to the sand. I looked about myself. The ubar's box was behind me. I returned my attention to the sand below. The beast must have uttered another command to the sleen. Suddenly, to my amazement, they relinquished their attack and, together, bristling and snarling, slunk back, one after the other, through the small, grated opening through which they had emerged. A man, limping, hurried to the tiny gate and flung it down.

"Aiii!" cried a man, striking with his foot against an object on the sand.

"What is it?" cried another.

"It is a head!" cried the man, stepping back.

"There is a pouch here, on the sand," said a man.

"Here is the medallion of the ubar," said a man, lifting a chain and medallion.

"The pouch bears the sign of Belnar," said the man who had found the pouch.

"There are parts of a body about," said a man. "The sleen had them."

"The head is the head of Belnar!" cried a man, crouching down near it.

"The ubar is dead!" cried a man.

"The beast has done this," said an officer, in horror. "Kill it! Kill it!"

The men turned to the Kur. It took a brand from the fire plate beneath the oil vat and hurled it into the vat. Instantly a torrent of flame blasted upward from the vat. The men drew back. The Kur then, with a prodigious strength, slowly lifted the flaming vat of bloodied oil over its head. "Look out!" cried a man. "It will be crushed!" cried another. "Back!" cried another fellow. The beast hurled the vat away from itself, toward the men. They fled back. Two, screaming, were caught under the cauldron. For one terrible moment it had seemed as though the air itself had burst into flame.

"Regroup!" cried an officer. "Regroup!"

The Kur, at this time, did not attempt to escape, though I believe it might have made its way then at least from the baiting pit. Rather, it took six brands, still flaming, from the sand, scattered from the fire plate, and set them upright, torchlike, in a circular pattern, about itself. It stood then within this ring, a ring with a diameter of some twenty feet. I wondered if such rings were occasionally erected on the steel worlds. I wondered if it had ever stood within such a ring before. The number six is a number of special significance to Kurii. This possibly has to do with the tentaclelike, multiply jointed, six-digited paw of the beast. This number, and its multiples and divisions, figures prominently in their organizations, their timekeeping and their chronology. They employ a base-twelve mathematics. The beast now stood within that circle, or ring. I did not understand the purpose of the ring, but I gathered that it was important to the beast. I recalled it had sent the sleen back to their lair. It would face the men alone, it seemed. I did not think it wanted their aid, nor mine.

Suddenly it began to leap about, turning in the ring. It even turned a backwards somersault, uttering what sounded like gibberish, and then, bounding up and down, struck at its knees and thighs. I think the men feared it had gone insane. These things, however, are signs of Kur pleasure. Then it stood upright and looked at me. I had no doubt its nocturnal vision saw me very well. Its lips curled back about its fangs. I smiled. The resultant expression, although perhaps somewhat fearsome in the abstract, was a Kur approximation of a human smile. It is very different, as would be clear if you saw it, from that baring of fangs which indicates true menace. Too, the ears were not laid back, which is an almost invariable sign among Kurri of readiness to attack, of intent to do harm. "Farewell," I whispered to it. I saw the smile spread more widely. I suddenly realized that it had heard me, though the men between us could not.

"Ready," said an officer. "Be ready."

I saw spear points lower. The beast in its own ring was ringed, too, with steel.

It snarled at the men, and they hesitated. Then it threw back its great shaggy head and howled its defiance to the three moons, to the men who threatened it, to the universe and stars, to the world. Men shuddered, but did not break their circle. I admired them. They were good soldiers. Then the beast again turned its attention to the men. I thought I detected a low, almost inaudible growl. I saw the lips draw back again about the fangs, but this was no smile. For an instant, as it turned its head, its eyes, reflecting the light of one of the torches, blazed like molten metal. I saw the ears lay back against the side of the head.

Suddenly, at a word of command, the men rushed forward. The beast seized at spears, slapping them away, seizing some, breaking them, taking others, perhaps a dozen, in its body. I saw it standing, fighting and tearing, in the midst of men. More than one man I saw lifted and thrown aside. Then I saw it go down beneath bodies. Men swarmed about it, thrusting with their spears, some hacking downward with their swords. "We have killed it!" cried one of the men. "I smell glory," it had said. "It is a smell more exhilarating even than that of meat." "It is dead!" cried one of the men. "It is dead!" cried another. Was there so much glory here, I wondered. It did not seem a likely place for glory, the sand of a baiting pit, in a torchlit moonlight, in a country far from its own. No monuments would be erected to this beast. There would be no odes composed. Surely it would never be revered among its people. It would not be remembered, nor, if they had them, would it be sung in their songs. Its glory, if it had it, would have been its own, perhaps the splendor of a lonely moment that only the beast itself truly understood, a moment that was its own justification, and that needed no other, a moment that was sufficient onto itself.

"It is moving!" cried a man in terror.

Suddenly, from the midst of those bodies, howling, the Kur, spears in its body, thrust upward clawing and raging like some force of nature. It stood knee deep in bodies.

"Kill it!" screamed the officer. Again men charged, with spears and swords. In the bloody tumult men struck even one another. I saw it reach out and tear a man from his fellows, disposing of him, half decapitating him with a slash of fangs to the throat, and seize another, tearing his head from his body. Then it went down, bloody and terrible, again, beneath the weight or iron, and men. That was the thing, I recalled, which had been cast out of its own world for its alleged weakness. "It is moving again!" screamed a man.

Once more I saw it rise up among bodies. I heard men weep, and continue to strike at it. How it prided itself on its refinements, on its sense of gentility. How vain it had been! How irritated I had even been with it, with its confounded supercilious arrogance. How jealous it was of being a gentleman. It went down again. "We can't kill it!" screamed a man. "We can't kill it!" It even cooked its meat. Once more it thrust its way up through bodies, now waist-deep about it. An arm hung from its jaws. Spears and swords struck at it, again and again. "They will learn," it had said, "that even a gentleman knows how to fight." Twice more it tore its way up among bodies, and then, at last, men stepped wearily back from it. Bodies were pulled away. It lay alone on the sand, dead. I could not even pronounce its name.

"Wait," said one of the officers. "Where is the other fellow, Bosk of Port Kar?"

I then stepped behind the ubar's box and lifted the partly opened trap and lowered myself into the passage below. I then closed and locked the trap, from the bottom. As it was designed, it was almost impossible to distinguish, from the surface, from the arrangements of tilings behind the box.

I, below, heard men walking about on the tilings, and on the wooden tiers.

"Where is Bosk of Port Kar?" I heard.

"He is gone," said another.

"He has disappeared," said another.

21

WHAT OCCURRED IN THE APARTMENTS OF BELNAR; LEATHER GLOVES

I spun about.

"I thought you might come here," said Flaminius. "No, do not draw."

My hand hesitated. He had not drawn his own weapon. Behind him, in a rag of silk, was a female slave.

"You may kneel, Yanina," he said.

"Yes, Master," she said, swiftly falling to her knees.

"You must forgive her," he said. "She is new to the collar. Only an Ahn or so ago was she branded."

She who had been the Lady Yanina looked at me, frightened. Then she put down her head, swiftly. I had seen in her eyes, in that brief moment that she had looked at me, that already she had learned that she was slave. This does not take long in the vicinity of Gorean men.

"Do not draw," he said.

"Is she yours?" I asked.

"Yes," he said.

"A pretty slave," I said.

"Yes," he said.

She trembled, scrutinized.

"I brought her along," he said. "She was with another search party. Almost anyone who could recognize you was with one party or another.''

"I gathered that that might be the case," I said.

"She was given to me by Belnar," he said.

"Belnar is now dead," I said.

"So I understand," he said.

"The slave seems frightened," I said.

"You have reason to be frightened, don't you, my dear?" asked Flaminius.

"Perhaps, Master," she whispered. "I do not know, Master."

"Put your head down to the floor," he said.

"Yes, Master," she said.

"She was put in a state collar," said Flaminius, "with no specifications or restrictions. Accordingly, even if she had not been given to me, I could have obtained her for myself, sending a silver tarsk to the exchequer. Who would gainsay me in that?" He looked down at the girl. "So in either case you would have come into my chains, wouldn't you, Yanina?" he asked.

"Yes, Master," she said, her head to the floor.

"Are you here for the same reason that I am?" I asked.

"Perhaps," he said.

I had returned by way of the passage behind the ubar's box in the baiting pit. Once here, I had begun my search, in various rooms, for obvious, unconcealed paraphernalia, of a sort that might be germane to kaissa, such things as boards and pieces, books, sheafs of papers, and records. I had, of course, in my return, lifted the dropped iron gate separating the private room, giving access to the passage, from the rest of the area. This was not difficult from the passage side. It had taken only a moment to locate the appropriate apparatus. I had then freed the lock bolts, which keep the gate in place once it has dropped, and, by means of a wheel, associated with chains and counterweights, raised the gate. The gate is freed, incidentally, by a small lever. Its fall is gravity controlled. The fall, though swift, is not destructive. The speed of its descent is controlled largely by the counterweights.

I had found what I had been looking for in a room apparently devoted to kaissa, in the midst of what were apparently merely the records of games, jotted on scraps of paper. Among those records, fitted in with them, were other papers. There was little doubt these were what I had sought. On one paper was a numbered list of names, names of well-known kaissa players. That, even, of Scormus was among them. On another paper there was what purported to be a list of tournament cities, and on another a list of names, of individuals supposedly noted for their craftsmanship in the skill and design of kaissa boards and pieces. There were also, on other papers, numbered, too, the representations of boards.

Arranged in various ways on these boards were letters, sometimes beginning from a word, sometimes from a random, or seemingly random alignment of letters. These were all, I took it, keys to kaissa ciphers of one level of complexity or another. In a very simple case, for example, a given word, say, "Cibron," the name of a wood worker of Tabor, might occur. This key, then, in a simple case, without variations, would presumably be used in the following manner: the deciphering individual would write "C-I-B-R-O-N" in the first six spaces at the top of a kaissa board, moving from left to right, then following with the other, unused letters of the alphabet, moving from right to left on the second line, and so on, as "the ox plows," as standard Gorean is written. In this fashion each square of the board, with its name, such as "Ubar Five," and so on, would correspond to a letter, and some spaces, of course, would correspond to the same letter, thus providing cipher multiples. When one comes to the end of the originally unused letters, one begins anew, of course, starting then with the first letter of the alphabet, writing the full alphabet in order, and then continuing in this fashion.

Some of the lists had small marks after some of the words, seemingly casual, meaningless marks. These, however, depending on the slants and hooks, indicating direction, would indicate variations in letter alignments, for example, "Begin diagonally in the upper-left-hand corner," and such. Those keys on which the entire board appeared usually possessed complex, or even random, alignments, of letters, and several nulls, as well as the expected multiples. A Gorean "zero" was apparently used to indicate nulls.

I had thrust these papers in my pouch. The hastily opened coffer, which had seemed so momentous, and inaccessible, before, of course, had been only a diversion. The true concealment of the papers, one assuredly calculated to deceive those individuals who might have some just notion of their value, one worthy of Belnar's brilliance, was to have them lying about, almost casually, mixed in, and seemingly belonging with, papers of no great importance. This subterfuge, was, so to speak, the disguise of unexpected obviousness. In this manner, too, of course, they would tend to be safe from common thieves, whose investigations presumably would be directed more toward the breaking open of strong boxes and the search for secret hiding places.

Given their relative accessibility and their apparent lack of value common thieves would not be likely to find them of interest.

If Belnar had erred here, I think it was in a very subtle matter. The pieces in the kaissa room, and the boards there, did not indicate frequent usage. The wood was not worn smooth and stained with the oil of fingers; the surface of the boards showed little sign of wear, or use, such as tiny scratches or even the subtle indications, the small rubbing marks, of polishings. Belnar, like most Goreans, was doubtless familiar with kaissa. On the other hand, it did not seem he often played. That being the case the abundance of hand-written notes and records about, seemingly related to the game, must, at least to some observers, appear something of an anomaly. It was at this point that I heard a subtle noise behind me. I had spun about.

"No," he said. Do not draw."

"Why not?" I asked. "Do you expect to leave this place alive?"

"Of course," he said. He made no move to remove his blade from its sheath.

"You will, of course," I said, "tell me that I am surrounded."

"I have men about, of course," he said. "Some are stationed in the vicinity of the ubar's box, and at other openings, known to me, of the passage from the tower. Do not think to escape that way. Other men I have outside, but at a distance, on the bridges, outside the gate to the garden."

"That," I said, "the distance involved, would seem to be a flaw in your plan." I moved my hand to the hilt of my sword.

"I do not really think so," he said. "We certainly would not want them present at just any conversation which we might choose to have, would we?"

"I suppose not," I said. "Have you also considered how you might save your life, before I can reach you?"

"Of course," he said.

"Oh?" I asked.

"Come with me, to the front threshold," he said. He turned about, exposing his back to me, to lead the way. I was intrigued. "You may come, too, Yanina," he said.

"Yes, Master," she said.

"Precede me, girl," I said.

"Yes, Master," she said.

I followed Flaminius and Yanina through the house. I wanted them both in front of me. I was wary as we passed through doors and archways. Yanina, I could not help noting, was quite lovely.

She walked well, doubtless conscious of being a slave before a free man. I felt a brief wave of gratitude to the fellows who wove, and designed, slave silk. It displays a female marvelously. It was tiny, and all she wore, except a close-fitting steel collar. She was barefoot. Whether or not she might have footwear was no longer her decision, but that of a master.

"See?" asked Flaminius, at the exterior threshold, that leading to the balcony garden.

"What?" I asked.

He raised his arm, signaling to some men on the other side of the garden gate, on the narrow bridge outside it.

"No," I moaned.

His men lifted up holding him by the arms, a tall, lanky figure, limp and bleeding, showing him to us.

"He is your fellow, Petrucchio, I believe," said Flaminius. "I encountered him on the bridge. Apparently, anticipating your interest in the quarters of the ubar, he had come here, to defend the bridge, to keep you safe. He had only his huge, silly sword. I felled him in an instant."

"He should have fled the city," I said.

"Apparently he turned back, hoping to be of assistance to you, or rescue you," said Flaminius.

I groaned. I could well imagine Petrucchio, poor noble, brave Petrucchio, Boots Tarsk-Bit's "Captain," on the bridge. What an absurd, frail, pathetic, splendid figure he must have cut there, with that silly sword and those fierce mustaches.

"What a preposterous fool," said Flaminius. "Can you imagine that? A mere player, a member of a troupe, daring to cross swords with me?

"You have done well against one untrained in arms," I said, "one who dared to face you with only courage and a wooden sword. Perpare now to try the skills of another member of the troupe of Boots Tarsk-Bit, but one whose sword is of steel."

"I have no intention of meeting you with steel," said Flaminius. "Do you think I do not know the reputation of Bosk of Port Kar? Do you think I am mad?"

"Kneel then," I said, "and bare your neck."

"I have your friend, Petrucchio," said Flaminius.

"I have you," I said.

"If I am slain," said Flaminius, "Petrucchio, of course, will die."

"If Petrucchio dies," I said, "you will be slain."

"Surely it is time to have a conversation," said Flaminius.

"Speak," I said.

"Let us step back inside, away from the door," he said.

"Very well," I said.

We withdrew into the room. He closed the door.

"You may kneel, Yanina," he said, "head to floor."

"Yes, Master," she said.

"Speak," I said.

"Belnar, and other members of the high council," he said, "have been conducting negotiations with individuals in various states, in particular, Cos and Ar. I do not fully understand all that is transpiring, but I have some idea. These negotiations, I gather, are generally in cipher. I would like to guarantee the security of those ciphers. One set of cipher keys, at least, is doubtless somewhere here. If you have found them, turn them over to me. Too, surrender yourself unto me, to be bound as a prisoner."

"What if I agree?" I asked.

"You must agree." He smiled. "You have really no choice, at least no honorable alternative."

"You would trap a man by his honor?" I asked.

"Or by his greed, or his ambition, or whatever proves itself useful," said Flaminius.

"I see," I said.

"Comply with my wishes," said Flaminius, "and Petrucchio goes free."

"And what of me?" I asked.

"Your disposition will be determined by others," said Flaminius. "Who knows? You might even be permitted to live, perhaps as a blinded, tongueless slave chained to the bench of a Cosian galley."

"Cosian?" I asked.

"Perhaps." He smiled.

I hesitated.

"Petrucchio bleeds," he said. "I have given orders that his wound not be bound. He does not appear overly strong. It is quite conjectural how long he can survive without care."

"I see," I said.

"Your sword, Captain?" he asked.

I reached to the sword, to surrender it.

There was, however, at that moment, a great, authoritative pounding on the door.

"I gave orders that we were not to be disturbed," said Flaminius angrily.

"Open in the name of Saphronicus, General of Ar!" I heard. "Open in the name of alliance!"

"A general of Ar, here?" said Flaminius.

I stepped back, my hand on the hilt of my sword.

There was then a repetition of that fierce pounding. It seemed any delay in opening that portal would not be lightly brooked.

Flaminius looked at me. I shrugged. "Perhaps you should open it," I said.

Flaminius hurried to the door and opened it. A tall, broadshouldered, imposing, caped figure stood there. "I am Saphronicus, general of Ar, envoy from the state of Ar," it said. "I have entered the city only within the Ahn, immediately ordering the city captain to report to me. Here I find slaughtered ubars, chaos and fire! I have assumed command in the city until the high council appoints a new ubar. I was told by the city captain that he received his orders from some fellow named Flaminius, and that he might be here. Who is this Flaminius?"

"I am Flaminius, who was confidant to Belnar," said Flaminius. "I was appointed to deal with the emergency, delegating secondary authority to the city captain, by Belnar. His authority is now done, of course. My sword is at your service."

"The city is in flames," said the fellow.

"They are difficult to control," said Flaminius. "We have been fighting them through the night."

"I have heard," said the figure, sternly, "that hundreds of men, who might better have been used in protecting the city, have been spent in fruitless searches for some fugitive!"

"Not fruitless, General!" cried Flaminius. "He is here! That is he! I have captured him!"

"I would not be too sure about that, if I were you," I said. I was curious to see how the arrival of this new fellow might alter matters, if at all.

"He does not appear to be bound," observed the new fellow. "He still carries his sword."

"I have him helpless, General," Flaminius assured him. "I have his friend in my power, whose life is forfeit, does he not surrender."

"That would not be that tall, thin fellow, the one with a wooden sword, would it?" asked the caped figure.

"Yes, General!" said Flaminius.

"I have had my men bring him to the garden," said the caped figure. "He was wounded, and his wound had not been attended to, an astounding evidence of inhumane barbarism. He is now being seen to by my men."

Flaminius turned white. "Where are my men, General?" he asked, uneasily.

"I ordered them to withdraw," said the caped figure. "I put them where they should be at this time, about their proper business, fighting fires in the city."

"Where then are your men?" asked Flaminius, fearfully.

"Do not fear," said the stern figure. "They are just outside." Flaminius relaxed, visibly.

"One is juggling larmas," said the caped figure. "The other is walking back and forth on the tarn wire strung between two bridges."

"What?" asked Flaminius, aghast.

The caped figure removed his helmet.

"Publius Andronicus!" I cried.

" 'The Imperious General,' " said Publius Andronicus, "is one of my best roles."

"You can act!" I cried.

"Of course," he said, "did not Boots Tarsk-Bit tell you that?"

"Yes," I admitted.

"To be sure," said Andronicus, "I choose my roles with care."

I seized Flaminius by the neck and pushed him back against a wall.

"Oh, no, my dear," said Andronicus, seizing the bolting Yanina by an arm and returning her to her knees, trembling, on the floor, "you are not going anywhere, at least not yet."

"Bring Petrucchio in," I said. "We must see to him."

"Alas," cried Petrucchio, "I die!"

"Nonsense," I said. "It is only a scratch."

"Let a great pyre be built of hundreds of logs," cried Petrucchio.

"You are not entitled to such a funeral," said Chino. "You are only a player."

"You will be lucky if people remember to throw you in a garbage dump," said Lecchio.

"I tell you it is only a scratch," I said.

"Oh?" asked Petrucchio.

"Yes," I said, replacing the bandages. "It would scarcely discomfort a neurotic urt."

"Was my sword recovered?" asked Petrucchio.

"Yes," said Chino. "We picked it up."

"There were hundreds of them," Petrucchio assured me. "I fought like a larl. On it, at one time, I spitted eleven men!"

"That is a large number," I admitted.

"The story of how Petrucchio held the bridge will be long remembered," said Petrucchio.

"I am sure it will," I said.

"And of how he fell at last, bloodied beneath the blades of frenzied, hostile brigades!"

"Yes," I said.

Petrucchio suddenly slumped in my arms.

"He is dead!" cried Chino.

"Petrucchio," I said.

"Yes?" he said, opening his eyes.

"Don't do that," I said.

"Did I play it well?" Petrucchio asked Andronicus, his mentor in such matters.

"Splendidly, old friend," said Andronicus.

"It was nice of you to come looking for me," said Petrucchio.

"It was nothing," Andronicus assured him.

"Not that I needed help," said Petrucchio.

"Of course not," said Andronicus.

"If the sheaf of notes on acting hints, those on the detailed deportment of the head and hands, prepared for you by Publius Andronicus, had not somewhat turned the blade of Flaminius, it might have been a difficult matter," I told Petrucchio.

"Perhaps," he admitted generously. "I had thought that perhaps such theory might one day prove its value."

"Petrucchio," said Andronicus, warningly.

"You must get him out of here," I told Andronicus. "I think you can manage it in your guise as a visiting general."

"I fear it will be more difficult for you to leave the city," said Andronicus. "It seems every guardsman in Brundisium is on the lookout for you. Some who can recognize you, slaves, courtiers, and such, will be, I suspect, at every gate."

"I will leave the city as originally planned," I said. "It seems the only practical way."

"Do you still have the device I gave you?" asked Lecchio.

"Yes," I said.

"And when it no longer suffices," he said, "you must make do otherwise."

"I know," I said.

"Remember not to look down at your feet," he said, "for you will not be able to react that quickly, but to look ahead of you, where you are going."

"Yes," I said.

"You must think, too, with your feet and body, with its slightest sensations."

"I remember your training," I said.

"So do I," he said. "Thus I urge you to be careful."

"Of course," I said.

"Do you have the other material, as well?" he asked.

"Yes," I said.

"Perhaps we should be on our way," said Andronicus, "before those of Brundisium begin to gather their wits about themselves."

"Take these papers," I said to Andronicus. "They are important. Give them to Scormus. He will know what to do with them. He has the other papers, too, that are pertinent to these matters."

"Where will we meet you?" asked Andronicus.

"At the prearranged place," I said, "if all goes well."

"I wish you well," said Andronicus.

"I wish you well, too, all of you," I said.

In a moment, then, Andronicus had again placed his helm over his features. He did so majestically. He straightened his body, regally. He was again a general.

"Come, men," said he, "and bring the prisoner, he who is wanted in Ar."

He was quite impressive.

"Not bad, eh?" asked Andronicus.

"No," I said.

"Do not forget my sword," said Petrucchio.

"We will pick it up on the way out," Lecchio assured him.

"Come, men!" said Andronicus, again the general. He then exited, somewhat grandly, followed by Chino and Lecchio, supporting Petrucchio between them.

"I did not know Petrucchio was wanted in Ar," Lecchio was saying, in character.

"Be quiet!" Chino was cautioning him, grunting, and not altogether amused.

I watched them, to make certain they did not get into any trouble, at least as far as I could follow them visually. Then I took my way back through the apartments to where we had secured the prisoners. We had tied them, stripped, standing, their backs to the bars, their arms lifted and spread, wrists tied back to the bars, ankles, too, to the barred gate, then again dropped, which had originally prevented me from immediately following Belnar. We had used it because it resembled a slaver's grid, to which slaves may be bound at a master's pleasure in an almost infinite variety of attitudes and positions, ranging from quite standard to exquisitely exotic. We had lowered the gate this time from the outside, from the apartment side, by means of a cord which we attached to the drop lever and then passed through the bars. In this fashion, it could be dropped from the front, rather than the rear. We had then only to fasten our prisoners, in whatever manner we chose, to it.

"Do not kill me!" cried Flaminius, twisting in the cords, seeing me approaching through the apartments, the steel of my sword bared. "Please, no, Master!" cried Yanina, pulling help- lessly at the restraints that held her back against the bars. "Please have mercy on a slave! Please do not kill me!" They had both hoped, doubtless, desperately, that we had all taken our leave. But I had come back.

I put the point of the sword to the throat of Flaminius. He began to sweat. "Don't kill me," he whispered. Then I lowered the sword. "No," he said, "please, no."

I then resheathed the blade. I then freed Yanina from the bars and threw her to the tiles before Flaminius, there having her. "Oh, oh," she wept.

I thrust her from me. She lay near me, shuddering, trying to comprehend what had been done to her. Being had as a collared slave is quite different, in all its modalities, and however it is done, to having polite love made to one as a respected free woman. I lay propped on my elbow. I regarded Flaminius. "Your slave is not much good," I said.

"Forgive me, Master," whispered the girl. "I was terrified."

"Terror, mixing in with the other feelings of a female, can be a powerful stimulant to passion," I said.

"Yes, Master," she whispered.

"Surely many girls have known terror at the very thought of not being fully pleasing to a master."

"Yes, Master," she said.

"Doubtless men will be coming soon," I said to Flaminius, "to look for you. Thus I should quickly have done with you and be on my way."

"There is no hurry," cried Flaminius. "It may not even be known we are here. Men may not come for Ahn!"

"Oh?" I asked.

"She can do better!" said Flaminius, hastily.

"Master!" protested Yanina.

I took her again into my arms, and looked into her eyes.

"Yes, yes!" said Flaminius. "Use her again! I freely grant her use to you."

"You are generous," I said. She struggled, naked, in my arms.

"Is she not beautiful?" asked Flaminius. "Do you not desire her?"

"She is lusciously soft," I admitted, "and is appealing, held helplessly. Too, she has a lovely face and figure."

"Use her!" urged Flaminius.

"Master!" wept Yanina.

"You dolt!" hissed Flaminius to Yanina. "Beguile him! Please him! Encourage him to dalliance! Buy time! Do you want us both to be killed?"

"What are you saying to her?" I inquired, getting up.

"Nothing," said Flaminius.

"I must be on my way," I said. I put my hand on the hilt of my sword. I noted, out of the corner of my eye, a look of terror transforming the lovely countenance of the slave, Yanina.

"Master," she cried, anxiously, frightened, grasping me about the knees, "do not yet go!"

"I must be on my way," I said.

"Dally," she begged. "Let Yanina please you!"

I looked at Flaminius.

"There is time," he assured me.

"Yanina begs to please Master!" she said. "Yanina will do anything!"

"Anything?" I asked.

"Yes, Master!" she said.

I smiled to myself. Her protestation evidenced her newness to the collar. Did she not yet know that any slave must do anything, and everything, at the merest suggestion of a master, at his merest word, even at his slightest gesture, or glance? That is something that most girls learn quite quickly.

I looked down at her.

"Yanina begs to please Master!" she whispered.

"Perhaps," I said.

I rose to my feet. It was late in the afternoon. There was only some smoke over Brundisium now, and I gathered that the fires were now mostly under control. No one had come to the apartments. I had not expected them to, or at least not quickly. In this my own anticipations had proved sounder than those of Flaminius. There had been much for them to do elsewhere. Too, I suspected that the city captain had now assumed authority in the city, now that Belnar had been killed. Flaminius's power, I suspected, had largely been a matter of his closeness to the ubar, and his control of special projects, under the direction of the ubar. He was not, as far as I knew, a member of the city

administration nor did he hold, as far as I could tell, any official
position or rank in the army, or the civic or merchant guard, of
Brundisium. He did have, presumably, through Belnar, connections with members of the high council of the city. Members of
that council had doubtless been closely associated with Belnar in
his various projects. No new ubar, as far as I could tell, had yet
been appointed by the council. There had been, at least, no
general ringing of bars such as might be expected to announce
such an appointment. Had men arrived at the apartments, of
course, they would have found them locked. They would then
presumably leave. If they chose to enter, they would have had to
break through doors. By that time, of course, I would have had
time to take my leave, in the manner originally planned.

I glanced down to Yanina. She lay on her stomach, on some
furs I had thrown before the barred gate. Her hands, palms
down, on the soft furs, were at the sides of her head. There was
now a chain on her neck. I had found it in the apartments. It was
some eight feet in length. It was padlocked about her neck, a
heavy lock under her chin, and when I wished, as now, not
wanting it for a leash or alternative tether, it was fastened by a
similar lock about the bars of the gate, near its foot.

She had served well on it, for Ahn. On it she had, at my
direction, assumed slave poses, and had been put various times
through intricate slave paces. On it she had even performed
placatory slave dances, dances of the sort in which the female
tries to convince the male that she might perhaps be worth
sparing, if only for the pleasure she might bring him. Too, of
course, as it had pleased me, and in a variety of fashions, I had
used her. Flaminius, however, it seemed, did not derive the
same pleasure from this that I did. I now glanced to Flaminius.
He was now sitting on the floor, back against the bars, his wrists
spread, where I could see them, tied back against them, at
junctures of vertical bars with a flat, supportive crossbar, some
six inches from the floor. In this fashion he could not get up nor
could he effectively use his feet. I had put him in this fashion,
thinking it might be more comfortable for the fellow.

Flaminius, my prisoner, looked away, not wantng to meet my
eyes.

I went to the side and removed a bowl from its padded,
insulating wrap. Its contents were still warm. It was a mash of
cooked vulo and rice. Earlier I had taken Yanina to the kitchen.
There, under my supervision, on her chain, kneeling, she had
cooked it. It was perhaps the first thing she had ever cooked. I
had, too, once, later in the afternoon, taken her into a couple of

rooms, where I had her tidy them up. It pleased me to see her, once the proud Lady Yanina, helplessly performing these small, domestic tasks. Being a slave is a whole way of life, involving a total modality of existence. There is a great deal more to it than simply serving a master in the furs.

"Eat," I said to Flaminius, spooning some vulo and rice into his mouth. Then, in a bit, I took the bowl, the spoon in it, to where the girl lay. "Kneel," I said to her.

"Yes, Master," she said.

I then took bits of vulo from the bowl and held them out to the girl. I also put some rice in the palm of my hand, from which she took it. I heard Flaminius gasp in anger. "Do you object?" I asked. His slave, before him, was eating from the hand of another man. To be sure, we had all eaten earlier, as well. Then, however, I had had Yanina eat from a pan on the floor.

"No," said Flaminius, hastily.

Yanina looked up at me. She had taken food from my hand.

"Are you sure you do not object?" I asked.

"No, no!" he said, quickly.

I then put the bowl aside. I also picked up my sword sheath, the belt wrapped about it, the blade housed in it.

I looked at Flaminius.

"Do not kill me!" he said, suddenly.

"By now," I said, "I believe the papers which I sought, those whose security you had hoped to guarantee, have left the city."

"It does not matter," he said, hastily.

"Once, long ago," I said, "when you sought to consign me to the mercies of urts, I questioned you as to certain matters. You informed me, as I recall, that you did not choose to answer my questions."

He regarded me, frightened.

I drew the blade.

"Perhaps now," I said, "you will choose to answer them."

"I know little about what transpires between Cos and Brundisium," he said. "It has to do with Ar. Too, negotiations have been conducted with secret parties in Ar, parties traitorous to that city."

"Such as yourself?" I asked.

"Perhaps," he said, fearfully. "But what is that to you? Are you of Ar?"

"No," I said. "But I respect the Home Stone of Ar, as that of other cities."

He shrugged.

"Your response," I said, "is unsatisfactory." My blade was at his throat.

"You must have the secret papers," he said. "Otherwise you would not have sought the keys so diligently. Examine them. The answers you seek, or some of them, must be there!"

"An attempt was made on my life, in Port Kar," I said. "Were you responsible for that?"

"No," he said. "We only followed orders, through Belnar."

"What interest would Belnar have had in such a thing?" I asked.

"None, really," he said, wincing, the blade at his throat. "He acted in obedience to the will of another, one more powerful than he."

"What other?" I asked.

"Lurius," he said, "Lurius of Jad, Ubar of Cos!"

"Lurius?" I said.

"Yes!" he cried. "Don't kill me!"

I withdrew the blade from his throat, and he shuddered in his bonds. I had not even thought of gross Lurius, he of Jad, he who was ubar of Cos. Once, long ago, I had sacked a treasure fleet bound from Tyros to Cos, intended for Lurius. Too, at that time, I had taken and chained naked at the prow of my flagship, as a trophy of my victory, the lovely young Vivina, who was being brought to Telnus, the capital of Cos, to be entered into companionship with him, then to be his royal consort. In Port Kar then, later, I had had her collared, and locked beneath the slaving iron. She was now the preferred slave of Henrius, a captain in Port Kar.

"Why has Lurius acted in this matter only now?" I inquired.

"I do not know," said Flaminius, frightened.

It had to do, I was sure, with new movements in the politics of cities. It had to do, I supposed, not only with me, personally, but with Port Kar, as well. To be sure, Lurius had a long memory.

"I am naked and bound," said Flaminius. "You cannot kill me in cold blood!"

"I can," I said.

He regarded me with horror.

"If the semantics of the matter trouble you," I said, "you may regard it as an execution."

"On what grounds!" he cried.

"For treason to Ar," I said.

"I am at your mercy," he said. "Spare me!"

"I may consider doing so," I said.

"Please him!" cried Flaminius to Yanina. "Please him!"

I felt Yanina's tongue, and lips, at my feet. "I desire to do so," she said.

"Slut!" cried Flaminius.

I looked down at the girl rendering her submission at my feet. I sheathed my sword.

I held Yanina in my arms, before Flaminius. I looked down into her eyes.

"You well tricked us," she said. "How you had me thinking myself so clever! What you had out of me, what you made me do! How shameless and wanton I had to be! How you let me think that I was beguiling you, that I in a desperate fashion was buying time for rescuers to appear. But you had all, all, and no rescuers appeared!"

"The slave owes such, and more, to any master who commands her," I said.

"Yes, Master," she said.

"Rescuers might have appeared," I said. "It was merely that I did not expect them to do so."

"What would you have done, if they had arrived?" she asked.

"I would have left," I said.

"So simply?" she said.

"Yes," I said. "Do you question me?"

"No," she said. "Yanina does not question Master."

I took the heavy padlock in my fingers, that under her chin, that which held the chain on her neck. I flipped it, and let it fall back. She could feel its weight drag against the chain. "It holds me well," she said.

I put my head down, and kissed her, and her lips met mine, yielding, in the unmistakable softness, and submission, and gratitude, of the owned slave.

"Slave!" snarled Flaminius.

"I began, Master, this morning," she whispered to me, "pretending, but somewhere, I am not sure where, surely by this afternoon, I realized that I was no longer pretending. I realized then that somehow I truly desired, from the bottom of my heart, more than anything, to love and serve men, and to please them wholly and selflessly, as a slave her masters."

I then, gently, to the fury of Flaminius, took her, as she gasped, and clutched, and thanked me.

"You yield well," I told her.

"Hateful slut!" cried Flaminius. "Despicable slave!"

"I am a girl on a chain," she smiled. "Is it not appropriate that I so yield?"

"It is," I said.

"And if I did not yield well," she asked, "would you whip me, or have your menials do so?"

"Under certain circumstances, and in certain contexts," I said, "of course."

"You have taught me much," she said.

"Perhaps," I said.

"You know you have spoiled me forever for freedom," she said.

"Oh?" I said.

"I now want my collar," she said. "I love it. I want to serve, and love. It is what I am."

"You are a female," I said.

"Yes, Master," she said. "But even did I not desire it, men would see to it that I now served choicelessly, and with perfection, would they not?"

"Yes," I said.

"That is what I desire," she said.

"It is late," I said. "I must now take my leave from the city."

She began to tremble in my arms.

"What is wrong?" I asked.

"Now that I have yielded to you, and now that I have learned my slavery, you will not kill me, will you?"

"Perhaps not," I said.

"But you have something else in mind for me, don't you," she asked, "something appropriate for what I now am, a slave?"

"Perhaps," I said.

"But Flaminius you might kill," she said.

"Yes," I said.

"No!" cried Flaminius, sitting naked before the bars, his back to them, his wrists tied back to them on either side of his body.

I rose to my feet and donned my garments, and retrieved the sheath, with the belt and sword. It was now late. The moons were out. I came back and stood before Flaminius.

"No!" he said. "Do not kill me, please!"

I glanced down at the girl. She was lying on her belly, on the furs, the heavy chain padlocked about her neck, over her collar, the other end of it fastening her to the foot of the bars. Moonlight, and a tracery of shadows, from the lattice of a window, was on her body.

"I give her to you!" cried Flaminius. "I do not want her! She is only a slut and a slave!"

"Do you do so, freely," I asked, "without obligation on my

part, your gift having no pertinence to what now may, or may not, be done to you?''

"Of course!" he said. "Of course!"

"I accept your gift," I said. The girl gasped at my feet. I now owned her.

"Kneel," I said to her, "to hear my will with respect to you."

Swiftly she knelt before me, trembling, straightening her body.

"Hear this, too, Flaminius," I said.

"Yes," he said, "yes!"

"She is to be delivered to my holding, the holding of Bosk of Port Kar, in Port Kar," I said.

"Yes," he said.

"And she is to be delivered in the following fashion," I said.

"Yes?" he said.

"She is to be drugged with Tassa powder," I said, "and packed in a barrel with parsit fish."

"It will be done as you wish," said Flaminius.

It was in this fashion that she had smuggled me, and several others, out of Port Kar. She would now be returned to the city in the same fashion, only as a slave.

"Do you object, Yanina?" I asked.

"No, Master," she said.

"If this is not done," I said to Flaminius, "I will not be pleased. Think, too, that someday, somewhere, we might meet again. Consider even the possibility that I, displeased, might come to seek you out."

"The matter will be attended to," said Flaminius, "I assure you, exactly according to your instructions."

"You may kiss my feet, slave," I said.

Swiftly Yanina put her head down, and did so.

I then left. "Untie me, Slave!" I heard, behind me. "The knots are too tight, Master," she wept. "I cannot undo them." "Chew through the thongs then," he said, "Hurry! Hurry!" "Yes, Master!" she wept. "Yes, Master!" I heard the movement of her chain on the tiles. Outside, in the garden, off in the distance, on one of the bridges, I saw some men approaching. They had not yet seen me. I did not even know if they would. I looked at the slender, swaying tarn wire. I took the small, flanged metal wheel, with its protruding axlelike spindle, from my pouch. I also put the thick leather gloves on my hands.

22

WHAT OCCURRED ON THE COAST OF THASSA; IT HAS BEGUN

"We were afraid!" cried Boots. "What kept you?"

"Attentions delivered upon a female slave," I said, "having primarily to do with her training."

"Of course!" said Scormus.

"Do we know her?" asked Chino.

"She was once the Lady Yanina," I said.

"Superb!" said Chino.

"She is now mine," I said.

"Excellent," said Chino.

"She is to be delivered to Port Kar," I said, "to my holding, packed in a barrel with parsit fish."

"Excellent," said Lecchio. Rowena and Telitsia clapped their hands with pleasure, delighted that the once-proud Lady Yanina now shared their condition, that of the helpless and abject slaves of strong masters. Bina, I saw, kneeling near Scormus, had eyes only for him. No longer was his use bracelet on her wrist, but his collar was now on her neck. I had little doubt that yesterday morning she would have been whipped, for having spoken without permission, as he had informed her in the hall of Belnar. This morning, however, it did not seem that she had felt a whip, other than, doubtless, the whip of the furs, at the hands of her gifted, imperious master. I had no doubt but what she had now rendered ample proof to him that she was worth far more than the golden tarn disk he had arrogantly paid for her. If she had not yet done so, I did not doubt but what he, in the manner of the Gorean master, would see to it that she soon did.

"You escaped from the city without incident?" I asked.

"Yes," said Boots, "and, later, so, too, did Andronicus, with Chino, Lecchio, and Petrucchio."

"Where is Andronicus?" I asked. "Where is Petrucchio?"

"They are at the side of the wagon, over there," said Boots. The wagons of the troupe of Boots Tarsk-Bit were drawn up on the height of a hill, amidst trees, overlooking Thassa. It was now morning. We could see Brundisium in the distance.

"They are all right, are they not?" I asked. I had not seen them. They had not come to greet me.

"Well," said Boots, evasively.

I hurried about the wagons, until I came to that place, near the edge of the trees, on a clifflike projection of the hill, rearing above Thassa, where was the wagon of Andronicus. There I saw Petrucchio, lying propped up, amidst bags and blankets. A great bandage was wrapped about his head. He looked in worse condition than he had when he had experienced the thrust of Flaminius. Andronicus was near him.

"Ho!" called Petrucchio, weakly, lifting his hand, greeting me.

"Greetings," said Andronicus.

"Greetings, fellows," I said.

"We would have joined the others, coming forth to bid you welcome," said Andronicus, "but Petrucchio is feeling a bit low today, and I am tending him."

"That is all right," I said.

"Too, we were discussing the movements of the head," said Andronicus. "I believe I may have discovered a new one. Have you ever seen this?"

"I do not think so," I said, startled, "at least not very often."

"It is, at least, one not mentioned explicitly in the texts, such as those of Alamanius, Tan Sarto and Polimachus."

"If it should be accepted as genuine, and win accreditation, being entered into the catalogs," said Petrucchio, "that would come out to one hundred and seventy-four. Although I myself am not strong on theory, I am very proud of Andronicus."

"We all are," I said.

"The theater is not a purely empirical discipline," said Andronicus. "It proceeds by theory, too."

"I am sure of it," I said. "Petrucchio, how are you?"

"Let a great pyre be built," said Petrucchio.

I looked carefully under the bandages.

"Let it contain a hundred logs!" said Petrucchio. "No, a thousand!"

"That is a very nasty bump," I said, replacing the bandages, "but it is nothing serious."

"Oh?" asked Petrucchio.

"Yes," I said.

"I will live?" inquired Petrucchio.

"Yes," I said.

"I suppose it is just as well," mused Petrucchio.

"I think so," I said.

"You must live, dear friend," averred Andronicus.

"Very well," said Petrucchio, convinced.

"Logs are very expensive," said Lecchio.

"How did Petrucchio receive this injury?" I asked. "Did he perhaps slip on the steps of your wagon?"

"No," said Andronicus. "He was struck, unexpectedly, from behind."

"And what craven sleen struck such a blow?" I asked, angrily. There was, perhaps, a matter of vengeance to be seen to.

"Well," said Andronicus, "if it must be known, it was I."

"You?" I asked.

"Yes," he said. "He was preparing to set forth for Brundisium again, once more to rescue you."

"Well struck," I commended Andronicus.

"Thank you," he said.

"How did your escape from the city proceed?" inquired Lecchio.

"Very well," I said.

"Splendid," said Lecchio.

"To be sure," I said, "I did not realize the descent on the tarn wire, with the flanged wheel, would be that swift. I struck the wall of a building with great force."

"The most difficult part of the journey, of course," said Lecchio, "would be the section where the tarn wire, from the lower roofs, stretches over to the wall, that section where you could not simply use gravity and the flanged wheel."

"Some might have found it so," I admitted.

"Fortunately," said Lecchio, "it was a matter of only a hundred feet or so."

"A mere nothing," I admitted.

"Did anyone see you?" asked Lecchio.

"I did hear a couple of fellows shouting," I admitted.

"Did you resist the temptation to do a somersault on the wire for them?" he asked.

"Yes," I said.

"It is probably just as well," he said.

"I think so," I said.

"I am pleased you did so well," he said.

"I fell off seven times," I said. "Fortunately I managed to seize the wire each time. Finally I finished the journey hand over hand."

"You are probably not yet ready to do that sort of thing professionally," he said.

"No," I said. "I do not think so." I was pleased that I had not broken my neck. The descent from the wall, once I had reached it, was simple. I had looped coiled wire about a parapet projection and, protected by the leather gloves, had descended to the ground, some sixty feet below.

"Did you hear what happened to Temenides, and his men?" asked Boots.

"No," I said.

"They were found in the city, with their throats cut," he said. "Apparently their murder was to have been blamed on us, as such a rumor seems to have been intentionally spread. But others, perhaps not privy to the plot, cleared our name, noting the papers recording our departure from the city, papers signed at an Ahn when Temenides and his men were still alive. We found this out through Andronicus. He learned it when he was coming back out of the city, with Chino and Lecchio, with Petrucchio as his supposed prisoner."

"I see," I said. I recalled I had seen Belnar give orders to a fellow upon the departure of Temenides from the great hall. It had been their misfortune, it seemed, to have displeased him. He had, too, it seemed, intended to settle the blame for the projected murder on the company of Boots Tarsk-Bit. This stratagem would permit him not only to take action against plausible suspects, given the hostility between those of Ar and Cos, this perhaps diverting attention from the true murderers, those in the pay of the ubar, but would give him a convenient pretext for ridding himself of possibly dangerous strangers, strangers who might, sooner or later, inopportunely comment on the anomaly of one from Cos, Temenides, a mere player, seated at the high table in Brundisium. Belnar, of course, had not realized that the troupe of Boots Tarsk-Bit would not return to its quarters in the palace but, instead, would immediately flee the city.

"Even though your names may be cleared," I said, "I do not think I would revisit Brundisium in the near future."

"No," said Boots, "we shall, for the time, cross it off our itinerary."

"Good," said Andronicus.

"It is their loss," said Boots.

"True," agreed Lecchio.

"I trust you are all well, and are soon to be about your business," I said.

"Yes," said Boots, "but I suspect we may soon have to find another brawny fellow, another chap of great strength and modest talent, to help us set up the platform and tents."

"I think so," I smiled.

"Perhaps I could take over the knife-throwing act," said Boots.

Rowena and Telitsia turned white.

"But who would pay to see knives thrown at a slave?" asked Chino.

"That is true," said Boots.

The slaves visibly relaxed.

"We shall miss you," said Andronicus.

"I shall miss you, too, all of you," I said.

"Doubtless we shall have to locate another player, too," said Boots.

"Yes," smiled Scormus of Ar. "I am returning to Ar."

"And doubtless a Bina, too," moaned Boots.

"Yes, Master," said Bina, kneeling beside Scormus.

"Do you think you will enjoy wearing your collar in Ar?" he asked her.

She looked up at him. "As long as you are my master," she said, "I would wear it joyfully in Torvaldsland or Schendi."

"Rowena! Telitsia!" said Boots.

The two slaves immediately knelt before us.

I regarded them, Rowena, with her long, yellow braids, and dark-haired, shapely Telitsia, once of the scribes, now merely a girl of Boots Tarsk-Bit.

"Are they not lovely?" said Boots.

"Yes," I said.

"Rowena," said Boots, "has the makings of a marvelous Golden Courtesan and Telitsia, here, I am certain, will become my finest Brigella."

"Thank you, Master," said Rowena.

"Thank you, Master," said Telitsia.

"This slave, here," said Boots, "the well-formed brunet,"

indicating Telitsia, "has begged permission to record our plays, to write them down. Is that not absurd?"

"Why would it be absurd?" I asked.

"Because they constantly change, being continually improved and refined, and because they are often being adapted to different venues and are often topical," he said. "Too, how could a mere literary image capture the essence of the living drama?"

"Too, they are not worth writing down," said Lecchio.

"I know you do not value my opinion in these matters," I said, "but I must disagree with Lecchio."

"You are more inclined to agree with me, then?" asked Boots.

"Yes," I said.

"Your opinion, then," said Boots, "is not without value."

"Even if these plays are not great dramas," I said, "of the sort of which perhaps Andronicus dreams, they are a genuine part of the vital and living theater. They are a place, whether at a crossroads or in a ubar's hall, where theater exists. In this sense they are not only a part of its tradition and history, but are, humanly, for all their vulgarity and bawdiness, rich and precious. It would be a tragedy if they were not, in one sense or another, however unworthily or inadequately, remembered."

"It is impossible that they should be lost," said Boots.

"I know of a world where they were," I said.

"At any rate," said Boots, "I did give her permission, and the materials, too, to make at least a few jottings pertinent to these matters."

"Excellent," I said.

"Do you think me weak?" asked Boots.

"No," I said. "It is a good idea." I looked to Telitsia, kneeling with Rowena before us. "Why did you want to do this?" I asked her.

"I have learned to love them," she said. "I found them precious. I did not want them to perish."

"If giving her your permission in this matter bothers you," I said, "seeming to you perhaps a bit too indulgent, there exists an obvious remedy wherewith you may assuage your qualms."

"What is that?" asked Boots, interested.

"Simply command her," I said. "As she is a slave, she must then obey promptly and perfectly, and will be subject to any disciplines which you might care to impose on her."

"A very good idea," said Boots. "Telitsia!"

"Yes, Master," she said.

"Keep some notes, or jottings, or records of some sort, now

and then, on some of our plays, or some of those of others, as you might come on them, that sort of thing," he said.

"Yes, Master. Thank you, Master," said Telitsia, once of the scribes.

I looked down at Rowena and Telitsia, and though they were slaves, they lowered their eyes, blushing at my glance. "An excellent brace of sluts," I said.

"Yes," agreed Boots, proud of his chattels.

"You are fortunate," I said. "Not only do you have two fine actresses here but two superb tent girls."

"True," said Boots. He was indeed fortunate. Both girls were so beautiful that the mere sight of them, chained by the ankle to the stake in their tents, could drive men mad with desire.

"I shall miss them, as I will all of you," I said.

"We, too, will miss you, all of us," said Chino.

"Scormus," I said.

"Yes," he said.

"I gather that Andronicus gave you the papers from Brundisium, the keys to certain ciphers," I said.

"Yes," he said.

"I hope they proved pertinent to the other papers I left with you, those originally obtained from she who was once the Lady Yanina."

"They did," he said, "as we had surmised they would." He handed me a sheaf of papers. "I have written out the decipherings for you. There was no difficulty, given the keys. I did them last night. They are all here."

I took the papers. "I am grateful," I said. To be sure, my primary motivation in entering Brundisium had been to investigate my own business, to try and discover who or what it was that had been responsible for the attack on me in Port Kar. I had learned, of course, to my surprise, that it had been neither Priest-Kings nor Kurii, but Lurius of Jad, Ubar of Cos. This information, and I did not doubt but what it was sound, I had had from Flaminius, he of Ar, though seemingly traitor to that city. "What is their purport?" I asked.

"Treason to Ar, betrayal of the alliance," he said. "Cos, abetted by Tyros, moves against Ar. Thousands of men, trained to perfection in both Cos and Tyros, embark upon vessels. In Brundisium's harbor, the joint invasion fleet is to be peacefully received. Indeed, for months Brundisium has been being secretly stocked with provisions and materials of war. It is to serve as a staging area for the subsequent penetration of the continent."

"In the light of such considerations," said Boots, "it is little wonder that those of Brundisium should seem somewhat concerned over matters of security.''

"There were fires in the city," I said. "Perhaps those stores intended to support the invasion were damaged or destroyed, this forcing a delay.''

"On the supposition that the housing of such stores was near the harbor," said Scormus, "I would regard it as unlikely. The flames, as I understand it, from Andronicus and others, were not in the harbor area.''

"That is true," I said.

"Many things now come together," said Scormus. "Even so small a thing as the presence of Ta grapes, generally associated with the terraces of Cos, at the banquet of Belnar now seems significant.''

"Most significant, perhaps," I said, "was the presence of Temenides in Brundisium, at a high table, obviously enjoying the favor of Belnar.''

"Perhaps he was a courier," speculated Boots. "Players may come and go much as they please.''

"I suspect his station was higher than that of a simple courier," said Scormus. "Such fellows, at any rate, would seldom travel with an escort of Cosian spearmen.''

"You suspect his presence there indicated some advance in this business, that perhaps some important juncture was at hand?" I asked.

"I think so," smiled Scormus.

"Ar," I said, "has the finest land forces on Gor. Cos and Tyros are mad to challenge her on the land.''

"Marlenus, Ubar of Ar," said Scormus, "is not in Ar. He is, as I understand it, in the Voltai, concerned with a punitive expedition against Treve.''

"Others, of course, could take command," I said.

"Of course," said Scormus.

"I think those of Ar have little to fear," I said.

"The war of Cos with Ar has been long," said Scormus. "Now Tyros, a traditional naval ally of Cos, is prepared to support her ambitions openly on the land. The unified forces of these two ubarates are not to be taken lightly.''

"But you have no clear idea of the numbers involved?" I asked.

"No," he said. "That is not indicated in the documents I have examined. On the other hand I conjecture they will be considerable.''

"You must take action," I said. "You must travel swiftly to

Ar, to warn them of the treachery of Brundisium, to ready them to resist the invasion."

"I think they will learn soon enough," he said.

"I do not understand," I said.

"We are too late," he said.

"What?" I asked.

"Is today not the Seventeenth of Se'Kara?" he asked.

"Yes," I said.

"Look out to sea," he said.

Rowena cried out in amazement. So, too, did others. Even Petrucchio climbed to his feet.

In the distance, at the horizon, there were sails, the sails of lateen-rigged vessels. We stood for a long time, all of us, on the summit of that hill, near its clifflike edge, the water below striking at its foot, overlooking Thassa, with Brundisium in the distance.

"There is no end of them!" said Boots.

The ships, in line after line, continued to appear over the horizon. The tiny dots of white sails, slowly, in their placid hundreds, made their way toward Brundisium.

"It has begun," said Scormus.

"Were there names in the papers?" I asked.

"Yes," he said. "Members of the high council of Brundisium, other than Belnar, are involved. His removal will not affect the business."

"Surely, too, there are contacts in Ar," I said.

"Yes," he said. "There are contacts in Ar."

"That was to have been expected," I said. "Lurius is a cautious fellow. He would not embark upon an enterprise as hazardous as this without the assurance of significant internal support."

"No," said Scormus. "And worse, it seems this bold, dark business may have actually been begun at the instigation of, and upon the invitation of, certain parties in Ar."

"There are traitors, then, in Ar," I said.

"Yes," said Scormus.

"It is the custom of Ar to deal mercilessly with traitors," I said.

"Yes," said Scormus.

"Who are these traitors?" I asked.

"On the whole it is difficult to tell," said Scormus. "Few of their names occur explicitly in the papers. On the other hand, they are apparently numerous, and some of them, I gather, are highly placed."

"Some names of traitors do occur in the documents?" I said.

"Yes," he said. "The names of two traitors occur there."

"Who are they?" I asked.

"Flaminius," he said.

"He with whom we have had dealings?" I asked.

"Yes," said Scormus.

"Yes," I said. "He is a traitor to Ar. I left him bound in Brundisium. He is doubtless free by now."

Scormus nodded.

"Who is the other one?" I asked.

"It is a woman," he said.

"That is interesting," I said.

"I do not think you would know her," he said.

"Probably not," I said.

"She has been obscure in Ar for years," he said.

"What is her name?" I asked.

"Talena," he said.

"Talena!" I said.

"Is there anything wrong?" he asked.

"No," I said.

"Did you know a Talena once?" he asked.

"Once," I said.

"It could not be she," he said.

"No," I said. "There must be a thousand Talenas in Ar."

"Probably," said Scormus. "Too, with all due respect, it is unlikely that one such as yourself, given the assumed lowliness of your background and origins, would know her."

"Oh?" I asked.

"Yes," he said, "this one once stood high in Ar. She was of high caste and noble blood. She was of gentle birth, of delicate breeding, a creature of the most refined upbringing and careful nurture, and of acknowledged and established station. She was among the loftiest of the free women of the city. On such festivals as the Planting Feast it was even she who was sometimes permitted to honor the Home Stone, sprinkling upon it the richest Ka-la-na, and the finest of Sa-Tarna grains. She was the daughter of Marlenus, ubar of Ar."

"I have heard of her," I said.

"Then she fell into disgrace, having been enslaved, thereby no longer having a Home Stone. Then, for having begged to be purchased, an act confessing the propriety of her bondage, sworn she was from her father's blood."

"I have heard something of it," I said.

"In recent years, freed, but with no Home Stone, in disgrace and seclusion, she has lived in Ar."

I nodded.

"Now, it seems," said he, "she is somehow implicated in a plot to overthrow Marlenus, that she is among the ring leaders in an insidious betrayal and projected revolt, that she is a prominent figure in a treason that could open the very gates of Ar to its enemies. It is intended, it seems, that it should then be she who sits upon the throne of Ar, attentive to the counsels of Cos and Tyros."

"The armies of Ar," I said, "will destroy the forces of Cos and Tyros."

"I do not think that is so clear," said Scormus. Again we looked out to sea. It seemed covered with ships. I had never before, anywhere, seen the marshaling of so many ships. Sails, even now, continued to appear over the horizon.

"No," I said. "The armies of Ar will destroy those of Cos and Tyros."

"Your confidence exceeds mine, particularly in the present circumstances," said Scormus.

I shrugged.

"Should that occur, however, and the traitors be found out, doubtless they would be dealt with most harshly."

I stepped away from the grassy height from which we surveyed the vast, distant fleet. I took the papers from my tunic. I went to the small fire in the camp, among the wagons. With a stick I stirred it. I threw the papers on the fire. I watched them burn.

"Did you make a copy of the papers?" I asked Scormus.

"No," he said. "But I have seen them. I am familiar with their contents. Am I now to be killed, or something?"

"No," I said. "Of course not."

"What am I to do?" he asked.

"Do whatever you think best," I said.

"Even if I had the papers," he said, "I would have no way to prove their authenticity."

I nodded, watching the last pieces of paper blacken and curl.

"Too," he said, "to whom could I, or you, report what we have found? We do not know who is privy to the plot and who is not."

"That is true," I said. With the stick I prodded the charred remains of the papers, crumbling them to black powder in the ashes.

"This is not like you," said Scormus.

"What?" I asked.

"This," he said.

"What?" I asked, angrily.

"I do not think you can so easily rid yourself of unwelcome realities, my friend," said Scormus, "whatever you might esteem them to be."

I did not respond.

"Do you think to put the torch to truth?" he asked.

I did not answer him.

"It cannot be done," he said.

"Many manage," I said. Indeed, I knew a world predicated on lies and the perversion of nature. It was called Earth.

"Perhaps," he said.

I jabbed down, angrily, at the ashes. Then I threw away the stick.

"But," he said, "I doubt that you would be very good at it."

"No," I said. "I do not think I would be very good at it."

"You cannot even walk a tightrope," observed Lecchio.

"True," I said.

"However these matters fall out," said Scormus, "they have now begun." He then walked back to the height of the clifflike side of the hill, that with the crashing waves at its foot. I joined him there, with the others, my friends, whom I must soon leave. We all looked out to sea. It was a vast fleet. The first ships had already come to the harbor of Brundisium.

"It has begun," said Scormus.

"Yes," I said. "It has begun."

DAW

Have you discovered DAW's new rising star?

SHARON GREEN

High adventure on alien worlds with women of
talent versus men of barbaric determination!

DAW

DAW Books now in select format

Hardcover:

☐ **ANGEL WITH THE SWORD**
by C.J. Cherryh
0-8099-0001-7 $15.50/$20.50 in Canada

A swashbuckling adventure tale filled with breathtaking action, romance, and mystery, by the winner of two Hugo awards.

☐ **TAILCHASER'S SONG**
by Tad Williams
0-8099-0002-5 $15.50/$20.50 in Canada

A charming feline epic, this is a magical picaresque story sure to appeal to devotees of quality fantasy.

Trade Paperback

☐ **THE SILVER METAL LOVER**
by Tanith Lee
0-8099-5000-6 $6.95/$9.25 in Canada

THE SILVER METAL LOVER is a captivating science fiction story—a uniquely poignant rite of passage. "This is quite simply the best sci-fi romance I've read in ages."—*New York Daily News.*
